THE MANDELBAUM GATE

MURIEL SPARK DBE, CLit, FRSE, FRSL was born in Edinburgh in 1918. A poet, essayist, biographer and novelist, she won much international praise, receiving the James Tait Black Memorial Prize in 1965 for *The Mandelbaum Gate*, the US Ingersoll Foundation TS Eliot Award in 1992 and the David Cohen Prize in 1997. She was twice shortlisted for the Booker Prize (for *The Public Image* in 1969 and *Loitering with Intent* in 1981) and, in 2010, was shortlisted for the 'Lost Man Booker Prize' of 1970. In 1993 Muriel Spark was made a Dame for services to literature. In 1998 she was awarded the Golden PEN Award for a 'Lifetime's Distinguished Service to Literature'. She died in Tuscany in 2006.

GABRIEL JOSIPOVICI was born in Nice, in 1940, to Jewish parents. He spent the war years with his mother living in a village in the French Alps. In the mid-1950s he and his mother moved from Egypt to England. He read English at Oxford and taught at the University of Sussex from 1963 to 1998. He has written over a dozen novels, starting in 1968 with *The Inventory*. He has also published several collections of short stories and a number of books of non-fiction, including *The World and the Book*, *Writing and the Body* and *A Life*, a memoir of his mother, the translator and poet, Sacha Rabinovitch. His plays have been widely performed on the stage and on radio and his work has been translated into the major European languages and Arabic.

Novels by Muriel Spark in Polygon

The Comforters
Robinson
Memento Mori
The Ballad of Peckham Rye
The Bachelors
The Prime of Miss Jean Brodie
The Girls of Slender Means
The Mandelbaum Gate
The Public Image
The Driver's Seat
Not to Disturb
The Hothouse by the East River
The Abbess of Crewe
The Takeover
Territorial Rights
Loitering with Intent
The Only Problem
A Far Cry from Kensington
Symposium
Reality and Dreams
Aiding and Abetting
The Finishing School

THE MANDELBAUM GATE

Muriel Spark

Introduced by Gabriel Josipovici

4172383321

This edition published in Great Britain in 2018
by Polygon, an imprint of Birlinn Ltd.

Birlinn Ltd
West Newington House
10 Newington Road
Edinburgh
EH9 1QS

www.polygonbooks.co.uk

2

ISBN 978 1 84697 432 8

The publisher gratefully acknowledges investment from Creative
Scotland towards the publication of this book.

Supported by the Muriel Spark Society

British Library Cataloguing-in-Publication Data
A catalogue record for this book is available
on request from the British Library.

Typeset by Biblichor Ltd, Edinburgh
Printed and bound by TJ International Ltd, Padstow, Cornwall

Foreword

Muriel Spark was born in Edinburgh on the first of February, 1918. She was the second child of Cissy and Bernard Camberg, an engineer from a family of Jewish and Lithuanian extraction. Her early life is recalled in loving and meticulous detail in her autobiography, *Curriculum Vitae*, published in 1992. Hers was a working-class upbringing, but while money was tight she was in no way deprived. Her mother was gregarious and extrovert, always singing songs and telling stories, and wearing the kind of clothes that made her unmissable among other, more dully dressed women in the Bruntsfield neighbourhood.

When she was five years old Spark began her education at James Gillespie's High School for Girls where she remained until she was sixteen. It was a period she remembered with great fondness. She was anointed the school's 'Poet and Dreamer' and many of her early verses appeared in its magazine. In 1929, she first encountered an inspirational teacher, a spinster called Christina Kay, who was to have a formative effect on her life. It was Miss Kay, for example, who took her and her friends – 'the crème de la crème' – on long walks through the city's Old Town, to exhibitions, concerts and poetry readings, and who insisted that she must become a writer. 'I felt I had hardly much choice in the matter,' Spark wrote later. In her sixth and most famous novel, *The Prime of Miss Jean Brodie*, the main character was modelled closely, if not actually, on Miss Kay. Like the unorthodox Miss Brodie, Miss Kay was an Italophile and a naive admirer of Mussolini, of whom she pinned a picture on a wall together with paintings by Renaissance masters.

On leaving school Spark enrolled in a course for précis-writing at Heriot-Watt College. She then found a job as secretary to the owner of a department store in Princes Street, the Scottish capital's main thoroughfare. At a dance she met Sydney Oswald Spark, a lapsed Jew, whose initials she felt in hindsight should have warned her to steer clear of him. Like her father's parents, 'SOS' had been born in Lithuania. She was nineteen, he was thirty-two. He planned to teach in Africa, and Muriel, eager to leave Edinburgh and launch herself at life, agreed to become engaged. In August 1937, she followed him to Southern Rhodesia (now Zimbabwe) and the following month they were married. Their son, Robin, was born in 1938. Soon thereafter the couple separated.

The outbreak of war the following year meant Spark could not return home as she had hoped and she had no option but to stay in Africa. In 1944, however, she obtained a divorce and returned to Britain on a troop ship. Having settled her son with her parents, she headed for London where the devastation of the Blitz was everywhere evident. She boarded at the Helena Club, the original of the May of Teck Club in *The Girls of Slender Means*, and found work in the Political Intelligence department of the Foreign Office, whose *raison d'être* was to disseminate anti-Nazi propaganda among the German population.

In the years immediately after the war she attempted to make a living as a writer. In 1947, she was appointed General Secretary of the Poetry Society and editor of its magazine, *Poetry Review*, but she fell foul of traditionalists, including Marie Stopes, a pioneer of birth control. It was a pity, Spark remarked, 'that her mother rather than she had not thought of birth control'. Her first book, *A Tribute to Wordsworth*, was co-written with her then lover, Derek Stanford, and published in 1950. A year later she won a short story competition in the *Observer* newspaper with 'The Seraph and the Zambesi'. In 1952, she published her debut collection of poetry, *The Fanfarlo and Other Verse*.

Her conversion to Catholicism in 1954 coincided with her beginning work on her first novel, *The Comforters*, which finally appeared in 1957. Praised by Graham Greene and Evelyn Waugh among others, it allowed Spark to give up part-time secretarial work and devote herself to writing. Four more novels – *Robinson*, *Memento Mori*, *The Ballad of Peckham Rye* and *The Bachelors*, and a collection of stories, *The Go-Away Bird* – followed in quick succession and enhanced her reputation for originality and wit.

It was with the publication in 1961 of *The Prime of Miss Jean Brodie*, however, that Spark became an international bestseller. It was turned into a play and a film for which Maggie Smith, who played the eponymous teacher, won the Oscar for Best Actress. Indeed, remarked Spark, so closely did Smith become associated with the part that many readers seemed to assume that she was her creator. The novel, which Spark liked to refer to as her 'milch cow', was a critical as well as a commercial success and continued to sell well throughout its author's long career. In America, it was first published in the *New Yorker*. Its editor, William Shawn, gave Spark an office in which to work. There, she wrote her next two novels, *The Girls of Slender Means* and *The Mandelbaum Gate*, which was awarded the James Tait Black Memorial Prize.

In 1967, having grown tired of the clamour and claustrophobia of life in New York, she moved to Italy and Rome.

That same year she was made an OBE. It also saw the publication of her first collected volumes of stories and poems. Novels continued to appear at regular intervals. *The Public Image* appeared in 1968 and was shortlisted for the Booker Prize. *The Driver's Seat*, which Spark believed to be her best, was published in 1970. In 1974 came *The Abbess of Crewe*, an inspired satire of the Watergate scandal, which she set in a convent.

In the mid 1970s Spark left Rome for Tuscany, settling in a rambling and venerable house deep in the countryside, owned by her friend, Penelope Jardine, an artist. Surrounded by fields of vines and olives, she was able to work without fear of interruption. *The Takeover, Territorial Rights* and *Loitering with Intent* – also shortlisted for the Booker – were among the first novels she wrote in the place that would be her final home. Among the many awards she received were the Ingersoll Foundation TS Eliot Award, the Scottish Arts Council Award for *Reality and Dreams*, the Boccaccio Prize for European Literature, the David Cohen British Literature Prize for a lifetime's achievement, and the Golden PEN Award from PEN International. In 1993, she was made a Dame.

Though in her later years she was often beset by illness, she never stopped writing. It was her calling and she pursued it with unfailing dedication. She always had a poem 'on the go' and she never wanted for ideas for novels and stories and plays. Among her later novels were *A Far Cry from Kensington, Symposium, Reality and Dreams* and *Aiding and Abetting*. Her valedictory novel was *The Finishing School*, the majority of whose characters are would-be writers, which was published in 2004. Spark died two years later at the age of eighty-eight and is buried in the walled cemetery of the village of Oliveto in the Val di Chiana. On her headstone, she is described in Italian with one simple word: *poeta*.

Introduction

Gabriel Josipovici

In a famous lecture on Yeats, T.S. Eliot, exploring the reasons why Yeats went on developing as a poet throughout his long and richly productive life, makes the following remark:

> It is difficult and unwise to generalise about ways of composition – so many men, so many ways – but it is my experience that towards middle age a man has three choices: to stop writing altogether, to repeat himself with perhaps an increasing skill of virtuosity, or by taking thought to adapt himself to middle age and find a different way of working.

Though Eliot is here talking about poets I have often thought that what he says about Yeats applies very well to Muriel Spark, and that the work of hers in which we find her 'taking thought', in Eliot's sense, is *The Mandelbaum Gate*.

It is clear that the novel was meant by Spark to be different from those she had previously written – *Memento Mori*, *The Bachelors*, *The Prime of Miss Jean Brodie* and the others that burst forth in an astonishing creative surge between 1957, when she was thirty-nine, and 1963. These were short, sharp, brilliantly observed and very, very deep, though what exactly that depth consisted in readers had trouble grasping. Clearly the author's Catholicism had something to do with it, but there was nothing here of the anguished soul-searching characteristic of the best Catholic writers of the first half of the twentieth century, Georges Bernanos in France and Graham Greene in England. *The Mandelbaum Gate*, though, was clearly going to be different. For one thing it was considerably longer than the earlier books; for another it seemed to consist of a much more traditional relation of dialogue to exposition and description than had been the case hitherto. But, most importantly, it seemed to be what so many great English novels have been through the ages, a thinly disguised autobiography, the author (here a woman in her thirties) seeking to discover her identity as she leaves her youth behind. As admirers of Spark also knew by then, her parents were Jewish on the one side and Gentile on the other, and she herself a Catholic convert; and her heroine, Barbara Vaughan, in what used to be called the Holy Land to see for herself the places from which her religion had sprung, is struggling to make sense of a similar dual inheritance and Catholic conversion.

It may also have been Spark's intention, now that she was an established writer, to give the public a big conventional novel to show them she could do other things than write short spiky works. But, being the writer she was, that was not how the book came out. As it stands it is as indelibly hers as any of the others, though something of an oddity in its length and happy embrace of such a multiplicity of genres – the crime thriller à la Hitchcock (a lady vanishes), the spy adventure à la Eric Ambler (complete with the ultimate dangerous return to safety), and of course the coming-of-age novel so beloved of English readers since Jane Austen.

Two characteristic features of Spark's fiction are central to the feel of the novel: its affinity to poetry, not only the liberal quotation of actual poetry in its pages but also the way the prose seems always to be taking off into song or dance; and the use of prolepsis, that procedure characteristic of Spark's beloved Border Ballads, whereby something that is to happen later is signalled long before it arrives, a device that would appear at first sight likely to rob the work of any forward momentum but that in fact has the opposite effect.

We are in 'the Holy Land', in that relatively brief period between the establishment of the state of Israel in 1948 and the Six-Day War of 1967 which once again completely changed the dynamics of the region, when the border between Israel and Jordan passed right through Jerusalem, and the only point of transit between the two countries, which lived in a state of more or less open antagonism, was the Old City's Mandelbaum Gate. The book opens with Freddy Hamilton, a diplomat working in the British Embassy in Israeli Jerusalem, crossing back through the gate from his weekly visit to English friends on the Jordanian side. 'Part One', we read, '1, Freddy's Walk', and we are away, experiencing an exhilarating rhythmic surge rather than processing information:

Sometimes, instead of a letter to thank his hostess, Freddy Hamilton would compose a set of formal verses – rondeaux, redoubles, villanelles, rondels or Sicilian octaves – to express his thanks neatly. It was part of his modest nature to do this. He always felt he had perhaps been boring during his stay, and it was one's duty in life to be agreeable. Not so much at the time as afterwards, he felt it keenly on his conscience that he had said no word between the soup and the fish when the bright talk began; he felt at fault in retrospect of the cocktail hours when he had contributed nothing but the smile for which he had been renowned in his pram and, in the following fifty years, elsewhere.

This is perfect. It does so much, so effortlessly. It creates Freddy Hamilton for us: his modest nature, his lack of confidence, his charm; but also the way he has settled into a comfortable life ('It was one's duty in life to be agreeable'), and the ever-so-slight smugness conveyed by that last phrase with its devastating final comma ('and, in the following fifty years, elsewhere'). All this is epitomised by Freddy's fondness for elaborate verse forms belonging to a vanished age but which, one deduces, a good public school and university had instilled into him. For the young Arab who comes to give him Arabic lessons and for whom Freddy nurtures an only half-repressed desire, this side of his nature is a source of fascination: only the English, he feels, can spend their time composing such verses for no obvious advantage to themselves but only for the pleasure of getting it right. And yet that paragraph, and especially that final phrase, signals to the reader that the author, while in deep sympathy with this aspect of his character, can see its fateful limitations. That of course is why she is writing a novel and not a rondeau or a villanelle.

This comes out into the open at the end of the first chapter, when Freddy has an awkward conversation with another guest at the hotel where he lives while working at the British Embassy in Israeli Jerusalem. This is a Miss Vaughan, a thirty-something spinster whose nervous intensity makes Freddy uneasy. She has told him she is half Jewish and is there to see the Holy Places and also to visit her lover, an English archaeologist working over in Jordan on the Dead Sea Scrolls. The man, it seems, has been married and divorced but they are waiting for news from Rome to discover if his marriage can be annulled and so make it possible for her, a Catholic, to marry him. 'Oh dear,' Freddy says. 'What does your fiancé feel about this?' 'Well, of course, he feels it's a bit unfair. He isn't a Catholic himself.' 'It does seem a bit unfair,' Freddy says. 'It seems a bit extreme, when a couple of grown-up people –'

But now he has overstepped a line.

'Do you know,' said this passionate spinster in a cold and terrifying voice, 'a passage in the Book of the Apocalypse that applies to your point of view?'

'I'm afraid the Apocalypse is beyond me,' Freddy said. 'I've never had the faintest clue what it's all about. I can cope with the Gospels, at least some parts, but –'

'It goes like this,' she said, enunciating her words slowly, almost like a chant:

I know of thy doings, and find thee neither cold nor hot; I would thou wert one or the other. Being what thou art, lukewarm, neither cold nor hot, thou wilt make me vomit thee out of my mouth.

Freddy did not reply. People should definitely not quote the Scriptures at one. It was quite absurd.

If the author has reservations about Freddy that does not mean that she sides unequivocally with Barbara at this point. But then neither does Barbara. This angry quoter of the Apocalypse is not the person she would like to be, though her ferocious insistence on telling it how she sees it is as much a part of her make-up as Freddy's reticence and his instinctive desire never to rock the boat. These two strangely matched people, both at once attractive and seemingly self-confident, yet each in his or her own way confused and insecure, are going, in the pages that follow, to undergo a series of adventures that will force them to break through the protective barriers they have erected around themselves and discover, if only half-consciously and at some cost, a richer and a fuller life.

*

When Barbara explains to an inquisitive guide on one of her first days in the region that her father was a horse-riding Englishman who broke his neck fox-hunting while her mother is a Jew and she herself a Catholic, he says: 'Then you are a whole Jew. The Jew inherits through the mother by Jewish Law.' I know that, she answers. 'But one says half-Jew to mean that one of the parents is a Gentile and the other –' 'But the Jew inherits through the mother,' the man insists. 'You are then a full Jew by Law.' 'Yes, but not according to the Gentile parent's Law.' 'What is your father's Law?' 'I'm afraid,' she says, 'he was a law unto himself.'

But the grilling has unsettled her. It has reminded her of the days of her youth when she would go from a tea of cucumber sandwiches and tennis on the lawn with her father's family to the Passover Seder with her mother's. Diaspora Jews, less earnest than their Israeli counterparts, they would make a joke of the whole thing. When Barbara is tactfully herded from the kitchen in case she uses the dish-cloth to dry the wrong plate, since meat and milk dishes are kept rigorously apart, her favourite cousin Michael puts on an exaggerated East European accent: 'Vot you expect? She is neither Yeed nor Goy ees mein cousin Barbara . . . She ees a bit milk and meat in the same dish, vot you expect?' And now, faced with the earnest guide and his insistence that she is one of them, she asks herself: Who am I? And can only come up with God's reply to Moses out of the Burning Bush: 'I am that I am.' She has come here, she realises, for many and complex motives: to visit the sacred sights; to see Harry Clegg; but also to answer the question she does not even want to contemplate and to which she has no answer: Why am I a Catholic?

In England Barbara has been a teacher in a private girls' school run by a Miss Rickwood, Ricky to her. 'Somehow, at some time, an unspoken agreement had been arrived at, to the effect that they shared the same sense of humour and disregard of men. It was, in a way, understood that when they retired . . .' But how can this understanding have come about? Barbara suddenly realises that one of her motives in coming to the Holy Land is to escape from Ricky, from all those false understandings that have been her life in the past few years. Ricky, she realises,

> was all for doing the right thing for the right reason; she was fierce-principled about motives. To Barbara, one of the first attractions of her religion's moral philosophy had been its recognition of the helpless complexity of motives that prompted an action, and its consequent emphasis on actual words, thoughts and deeds; there was seldom one motive only in the grown person; the main thing was that motives should harmonise. Ricky . . . assumed that it was both right that people should tear themselves to bits about their motive and possible for them to make up their minds what their motives were. Herein, Barbara reflected, lies the difficulty in dealing with Ricky if I should ever be drawn to have it out with her.

And now Ricky, it turns out, is in the Holy Land herself, in pursuit of Barbara, in her own mind to save her from herself, but in reality, as both the reader and Barbara realise, to reassert her hold on her. To this end she has had forged a document showing that Harry Clegg was born a Catholic and therefore cannot divorce. What she does not realise, and what Barbara, when she learns of the document, sees at once, is that it does just the reverse, for a Catholic who did not undergo a Catholic marriage is, in the eyes of the Church, not married at all, and therefore free to marry when he wishes. 'From time to time, for years afterwards,' the narrator tells us in one of those prolepses so characteristic of Spark's fiction,

> Ricky would inquire of Catholic priests, as a matter of theoretical interest, what was the position of a Catholic marriage based on evidence which both parties believed to be true, but which, in reality, was faked.
>
> They would all look puzzled, at first, and ask Ricky if she had ever heard of such a case. 'No, no,' Ricky always said. 'Only I read of it in a novel.' The priests all said in effect, 'Well, if both parties remain in ignorance and the Church is satisfied, then it's a valid marriage.'

When Ricky questions the logic of this – 'logic or no logic, some of them said, that was the case' – one replied that with God everything was possible. 'Another went into the question of the validity of the blessing Jacob received in place of Esau.' The story is well known. The now blind Isaac, sensing death approaching, wishes to bless the hairy Esau, his eldest son. But his wife Rebecca, favouring the younger brother, Jacob, dresses him in a hairy garment and conducts him to the old man, who feels him all over and concludes, even though the voice arouses his suspicions, that it is indeed Esau, and blesses him. When Esau arrives and discovers what has happened 'he cried with an exceeding bitter cry, and said unto his father, Bless me, even me also, O my father. And he said, Thy brother came with subtilty, and hath taken away thy blessing.' (Genesis 27.34-5) It may have been done 'with subtilty', but now it has happened there is nothing anyone can do about it. The reader may wonder at the unfairness of it all but that, the Bible seems to say, is how it is. God works in mysterious ways.

Not motive, then, but the act is the crucial thing. That is why pilgrimage was such a central issue at the time of the Reformation. Protestants, who saw it as, on the one hand, an excuse on the part of the pilgrim to escape his or her daily worries and have a good time on the road, and, on the other, a blatant con by the keepers of the pilgrimage sites in order to make money, were loud in their condemnation of the practice. Catholics, like their Jewish counterparts, insisted that it was not motive that was central but the act itself. And this is what lies at the heart of this strange novel about a passionate pilgrim. Barbara, like Freddy who is drawn in to share her pilgrimage adventure, may be confused and uncertain, but what they do and what they undergo in those hectic few days will stay with each of them for ever, even if many aspects of it remain obscure.

And this is what Muriel Spark herself perhaps came to understand as she wrote this novel of self-discovery: that the reason she was a novelist and not a critic or a theologian was the very reason why she had converted: because fiction is about events occurring in time and writing fiction means trusting in time and in events.

The Mandelbaum Gate, then, is Spark's way of understanding what it means to be herself. I am what I am, or, as the Hebrew has it, 'I will be that I will be'. As such it is the passageway from her instinctive early fiction to the rich and varied output of the many years to come.

CONTENTS

PART ONE

PART TWO

PART ONE

I

FREDDY'S WALK

Sometimes, instead of a letter to thank his hostess, Freddy Hamilton would compose a set of formal verses – rondeaux, redoubles, villanelles, rondels or Sicilian octaves – to express his thanks neatly. It was part of his modest nature to do this. He always felt he had perhaps been boring during his stay, and it was one's duty in life to be agreeable. Not so much at the time as afterwards, he felt it keenly on his conscience that he had said no word between the soup and the fish when the bright talk began; he felt at fault in retrospect of the cocktail hours when he had contributed nothing but the smile for which he had been renowned in his pram and, in the following fifty years, elsewhere.

'Oh of course, Freddy Hamilton. Everyone loves old Freddy my dear; Freddy's sweet.'

Freddy, of so many British consulates throughout his subdued, obedient career, would have been touched to hear it; he would have smiled. He did not really want to excite any sort of passion in his friends, or linger in their minds under some inflammable aspect. A very boring guest or a very entertaining one could provoke all sorts of undesirable feelings in people – revulsion, heart-quickenings, murderous attachments, the sort of emotions that had always led to trouble at school and university, and they led to international incidents as well.

He liked to get his verses off quickly so that there should be no apparent sign of effort on his part. As he walked through the amazing alleys of the Orthodox Quarter of Israel's Jerusalem which teemed so dangerously close to the Mandel-baum Gate, he started thinking of a triolet in his long-practised manner to catch the next day's Foreign Office bag into Jordan. Freddy had just come through the Gate. He had diplomatic immunity and so was permitted to pass through the Gate every weekend from Israel into Jordan and back again; from Jerusalem to Jerusalem. Few people passed from Israel into Jordan; there were difficulties, and for Europeans a certificate of baptism was required. Foreign diplomats were not allowed to pass by motor-car, which was understandable, as papers and bombs might be concealed in a car.

Freddy carried his weekend luggage – a zipper-bag – and took his usual route into the New City. It was the hottest day so far of 1961. He had refused the taxi-cab that waited at the Gate; he hated taking taxi-cabs anywhere in the world; he felt morally against the tips, as all his uncles before him had felt. Excepting, of course, one uncle, the one who had messed up the money in the thirties and abso-lutely ruined the family, and who had not felt strongly against giving away tips to cabbies and so on. As Freddy turned a corner he came into collision with a tiny dark-eyed boy with fluffy side-hair falling down his cheeks, too fine as yet to be formed into shining ringlets like those of his male elders among the Orthodox sect. The child's nose bumped into Freddy's knee, and Freddy took him by the hand to steady him out of his bewilderment. A bearded, befrocked old man with a very large face muttered in Hebrew to the infant, who had already regained his bearings and was busy studying Freddy from head to feet. A woman of unguessa-ble age, wearing lots of black clothes, snatched the child

4

away, and he trotted off, his legs in their long woollen stockings moving like swift shuttles to keep up with his mother, but he still craned his head round wonderingly at Freddy. The woman scolded the child meantime, evidently trying to impress on him the undesirable nature of Freddy. Freddy walked on behind the heavily garbed pair, feeling decidedly in the wrong for having touched the child's hand; they had probably taken him for a modern Jew, one of the regular Israelis of whom this sect disapproved perhaps more heavily than they did of the honest unclean foreigner. Well, thought Freddy, to continue . . .

> . . . would have preferred
> To make my grateful feelings heard,
> But every time articulate
> Scarcely a word.

It was not a triolet after all. Joanna, his hostess on the other side, had been extremely agreeable to him since his posting to Israel. He had spent three weekends in her cool villa, and she loved to have these bread-and-butter verses. There would have to be an additional stanza, perhaps two. Joanna was to visit him over here in Israel; she had not yet been to Israel. He would have to remind her about her visa, and tell her how best to make the crossing. It was not a triolet after all, but a form of rondeau. There was the business of Joanna's getting a visa, and he would meet her on this side of the Mandelbaum Gate. The intensity at the Gate was quite absurd. One could understand the border incidents where soldiers would flare up an incident suddenly and unaccountably. But there at the Gate the precautions and suspicions of the guards were quite absurd. No Israeli money allowed into Jordan, no Israeli postcards, the Jordanian police almost biologically unable to utter the word 'Israel'. The Israeli police were inordinately dramatic: 'Safe crossing,' they would say as one left the emigration hut. The Israeli porter would run and dump one's baggage half-way and run for the life of him back to his post. The Jordanian porter would wait till the path was clear; he would run the few seconds' space to pick up the bags and run for the life of him back to his post. They dramatised everything. Why did people have to go to extremes, why couldn't they be moderate? Freddy bumped into a man in European dress, rushing out of a shop as they all did. The man said something in Arabic. Freddy had thought he was a Jew. You couldn't tell the difference sometimes. Some of them had extremely dark skins, almost jetters. Why couldn't people be moderate?

It was not a triolet after all, but a sort of rondeau. Freddy turned up an alley. Another child, a girl, bumped into him in the narrow, crowded street. This time he did not put out a guiding hand, and she slipped away with the subdued expression of the children of this quarter, quite unlike the vivacious young of the regular Israelis. Freddy was rather sorry for the boys with their sausage side-curls and black knickerbocker rig-out, especially those adolescent boys who walked in a goody-goody way, by twos and threes. It must be hell for them, he thought, to be so different from the rest of the country, especially if they ever want to break away. He had felt sorry for the Arab boys on the other side – underfed, driving their mangy donkeys, thin, and in rags. He was moved to pity for all young boys, on the whole, recalling the term-times of his youth. He was convinced that the boys with ringlets were going through the same sort of hell, which was the only sort Freddy knew. The ringlets, like the Gate, were quite absurd.

6

'Quite absurd!' On the strength of this phrase he had struck up friendships all over the place. He was accustomed to exotic sights and squalid smells, narrow oriental streets, and people who went to extremes, it was all part of the Foreign Service. But outside of the Embassy, and even inside it, he never really felt at ease with chaps until sooner or later they remarked that the place was quite absurd.

> . . . feelings heard,
> But every time articulate
> > Scarcely a word.
> But you have far too long deferred
> Your visit to the Modern State,
> So choose and name the cheerful date.
> Joanna, I can hardly wait
> To meet you at the quite absurd
> > Mandelbaum Gate.

He was approaching the end of the Orthodox Jewish quarter, and had turned into a street at the end of which rattled the modern state. There, small shops burst their sides with business, large cars streaked along the highway, and everywhere the radio sets told the news in several tongues ranging from Hebrew to that of the B.B.C., or attacked the hot air with oriental jazz. Up there at the end of this orthodox street, it was said, the Orthodox Jews would gather on a Saturday morning, piously to stone the passing motor-cars, breakers of the Sabbath. And across the street, streamers stretched from building to building, bearing an injunction in Hebrew, French and English:

DAUGHTERS OF ISRAEL, OBSERVE MODESTY
IN THESE STREETS!

This, Freddy assumed to be for the benefit of any tourist-woman who might, for some mad reason, wish to walk in this Orthodox Jewish quarter wearing shorts or a low-cut sun dress; the local women themselves needed no such warning, being clad and covered, one way and another, all over.

For the time being Freddy had been placed in rooms in a Jerusalem hotel while waiting for an Embassy flat to fall vacant. He was in no great hurry for the flat, preferring hotel life where one need not mix, need not entertain one's colleagues, and could generally escape. His colleagues at this posting seemed a bit intense and know-all; they were on the young side and had not yet settled down. Freddy noticed, crossing the street, a young woman who was at present staying at his hotel, a Miss Vaughan. She was accompanied by a tall, intellectual-looking Jew. Freddy put down his bag in the hot street. He wanted to be specially civil to Miss Vaughan, having struck up her acquaintance in the cool leafy courtyard of the hotel one evening over two long drinks, and having then, on another occasion, inadvertently said the wrong thing; whereupon Miss Vaughan had felt for his embarrassment.

They crossed over to him where he waited on the kerb, and inquired if he had enjoyed his weekend. He had once before, very briefly, met her companion, a teacher of archaeology, Dr Saul Ephraim of the Hebrew University, who was acting as Miss Vaughan's guide. He had turned out to be amiable in the surprising way of the Israeli intellectuals; it took one by surprise because one did not expect a violin with its strings taut and tuned for immediate performance to be suddenly amiable. Dr Ephraim spoke a slightly American tone of English, suddenly amiable and easy as if from some resource that had been waiting under his skin for an encounter with Freddy. He wore an open-necked shirt and flannels,

8

his neck lean and long-muscled. Freddy chatted as he observed these things, telling of his weekend in Jordan: 'I've got some charming friends over there.' Ephraim would be in his young thirties. He was anxious to hear news of Jordan.

'Haven't you ever been there?' said Freddy.

'Not since the war.'

'Of course, not since the war.' To Ephraim 'the war' was the war of 1948.

'It's absurd,' said young Dr Ephraim.

An unloading of water melons began to take place close to them. Freddy had once been hit by the corner of a crate while passing an unloading operation at Covent Garden. He was nervous, and moved the couple aside along with himself.

'Both of you come and join me for a drink when you've finished,' said Freddy then, lifting up his bag.

Miss Vaughan was about to say something when an old bearded man out of the many, with small ancient eyes, approached them and spoke to Dr Ephraim in guttural Yiddish. Ephraim answered some brief thing, using his hands and shoulders to throw off the subject to the air. The old man spoke a few more words and moved away, muttering and glancing backward at Miss Vaughan.

'What did he say?' said Miss Vaughan.

'He said, "Tell your lady-friend to dress herself properly in these sacred streets as they have always done before."'

Freddy looked at Miss Vaughan to see how she was dressed. She was wearing a harmless blouse, sleeveless, and a dark skirt. He looked up at the admonishing banners and smiled his smile. He smiled again at Miss Vaughan, who stood with her sharp features and prim grey and black hair drawn back, looking less intense than Freddy feared she really was. It occurred to him that by contrast with Ephraim she would be in her late thirties. She was still questioning Dr

Ephraim about his conversation with the old man. 'And what did you say to that?'

'I said, "Well, it's a hot day." And he replied, "Well, it was a hot day two thousand years ago."'

Freddy was glad he had met the couple, for he was always lonely after his weekends on the other side. He pushed his way up the streets among the loitering mystics and beggars whom the Israelis in general abhorred, being bumped into quite often by the women who inevitably darted out of the shop doors with their purchases and their children, without looking first to right or left. He thought he might ask young Saul Ephraim to recommend him a Hebrew teacher if Miss Vaughan remembered to bring him back to the hotel for a drink. One ought to learn some modern Hebrew to get along in this country. Ephraim might take on the job himself, but Freddy, reflecting that this was highly improbable, was instantly annoyed with himself for thinking it in the first place. One did not meet many Israelis, only the officials and so on, but of course one had not much time. The weekly visits to the other side took up his free days. Dr Ephraim would be thirty-one or thirty-two. Abdul Ramdez, the life-insurance agent who kept trying, without success, to sell Freddy a policy, but who was amusing, had undertaken to give him lessons in Arabic. Ramdez would be in his middle twenties. One had to be careful about one's teachers of Hebrew and Arabic; here on the spot they were all apt to get intense. Ramdez was an Armenian Arab, or so he claimed.

A chanting of children's voices came from an upper-storey window as Freddy pushed up the street towards modernity and his hotel. This upper storey was a school; it was always in full chant when he passed, for the children of this sect learned their lessons, all subjects alike, by plaintive rote, singing them out in Hebrew. This always fascinated him, at the same time as it put him off his stroke, for usually, when he passed the spot, he was thinking of his thank-you verses. At present his mind was already on the third stanza of his current piece, so that Joanna could be suitably and gracefully reminded to get a visa and make sure that she stated she was coming on a pilgrimage to the Christian shrines.

But he could not get his rhythm right against the chanting of these children of the Orient, even after he could hear it no longer and was out among the speedy wide streets of people and motor traffic in the modern city. All the way back to his hotel, when he was really too hot to bother and his thoughts were mere heatwaves, the chant went on at the back of his head, accompanied, as always on these return journeys, by an assertive counter-chant rising spontaneously from something indomitable in Freddy; and so, pitting culture against culture, the metrical precepts of Samuel Taylor Coleridge chanted themselves lovingly round his brain:

> Trochee trips from long to short;
> From long to long in solemn sort,
> Slow Spondee stalks; strong foot! yet ill able
> Ever to come up with Dactyl trisyllable.
> Iambics march from short to long: –
> With a leap and a bound the swift Anapaests throng;
> One syllable long, with one short at each side,
> Amphibrachys hastes with a stately stride: –
> First and last being long, middle short, Amphimacer
> Strikes his thundering hoofs, like a proud high-bred racer.

Even in his bath, when he was thinking of other things, Coleridge's lines continued to churn in the background – even when they had chased away the Hebrew plain-chant; and even, although he was scarcely aware of it, when he sat out in the small green courtyard of the hotel to await Miss Vaughan and Dr Ephraim. He wanted to be specially agreeable to Miss Vaughan, having put his foot in it last week on their third or fourth meeting. Freddy hated more than anything the thought that he had hurt someone's feelings in a direct encounter. He hoped she would bring the archaeologist with the lean brown neck. The afternoon was fading, and he tapped silently with his fingers on the wicker arm of his chair and gazed up through the lofty trellis at the cooling light.

Trochee trips from long to short;

The waiter brought his drink and Freddy dwelt for a gay and not indelicate moment on the young Israeli, and he felt like Horace in the Ode, demanding simple service under his lattice vine. *Persicos odi, puer* . . .

From where he sat he saw Miss Vaughan come into the hotel entrance, alone. She moved towards the staircase but glanced towards the terrace. Freddy rose and raised an arm in a welcoming way, and she turned and joined him.

'Dr Ephraim couldn't manage as it was rather late and his family were expecting him. I ought to go and change.'

'What will you drink?' said Freddy. His first meeting with Miss Vaughan now came back to him, fused with subsequent meetings here in the green courtyard. He saw them all with that total perceptivity of his which might have made a poet of him, given the missing element. His first impression had been of a pleasant English spinster; she was a teacher of English at a girls' school; she was on a tour of the Holy Land;

Freddy had discussed with her the dear subject of formal English lyrical verse; he had, on another occasion, confided in her that he was compiling an anthology in his spare time, and had before the war published a volume of his own occasional verses. She had responded in a detached sort of way, which was what one liked. She was edgy; she wore on her engagement finger a ring of antique design embedded with a dark-blue stone; but for some reason Freddy had not felt that the ring referred to an engagement to marry anyone; such things were not unaccountable in an English spinster; it was probably somebody killed in the war.

Now, sitting with her near the same spot as when they had first spoken three weeks ago, he was filled with a sense of her dangerousness; he was obscurely afraid. He wished the young archaeologist had come with her.

But he was obliged to be particularly civil to Miss Vaughan. He fingered the wicker chair.

With a leap and a bound the swift Anapaests throng . . .

Last week he had joined her out here after dinner. The State of Israel had that day sent up its first guided rocket. He remarked that there seemed to be a lot of rejoicing going on in the streets, and one of them suggested going out later on to watch the children dancing. The children danced in the public gardens until late every night in any case. They fell to talking about politicians and the Bomb.

She had said, in a lazy casual way – for by this time they were fairly at ease with each other – 'Sometimes I think we ought to chuck out the politicians from world government and put in the Pope, the Chief Rabbi, the Archbishop of Canterbury and the Dalai Lama instead. They couldn't do worse and they might do better.'

13

Freddy had reflected on this without undue seriousness. 'There would have to be a Greek Patriarch as well,' he said, 'and then the Buddhists and the Hindus would want their say. There would be no end to it. But it's a good idea. I imagine there would be objections from the Jews to the Chief Rabbi. Most of these Jews here are unbelievers, so far as I can gather.'

'Not quite,' said Miss Vaughan. 'I think they believe in a different way from what you mean. They believe with their blood. Being a Jew isn't something they consider in their minds, weigh up, and give assent to as one does in the Western Christian tradition. Being a Jew is inherent.'

'Yes, I'm afraid so.' Freddy gave a little laugh.

As if he had not spoken at all, she continued. 'As a half-Jew myself, I think I understand how –'

'Oh, I didn't mean to say . . . I mean . . . One says things without thinking, you know.'

She said, 'You might have said worse.'

Freddy felt terrible. He groped for the idea that, being a half-Jew, she might be only half-offended. After all, one might speak in that manner of the Wogs or the Commies, and everyone knew what one meant.

He now noticed the Jewishness of her appearance, something dark and intense beyond her actual shape and colouring. Freddy felt worse. It was a diplomatic as well as a social error, here in this country. This was the first year of the Eichmann trial. Freddy felt like a wanted man who had been found hiding in a dark cupboard. He felt an urge to explain that he was not a mass-butcher and that he had never desired to become a *Sturmbannführer, Obersturmbannführer, Superobersturmbannführer*. He said, 'I like your young guide. How did you come by him?'

She said, 'He's a friend of a friend of mine, another

14

archaeologist who's working on the stuff at Qumran just now.' Plainly, she was embarrassed by his embarrassment.

Freddy clutched at the subject of the Dead Sea scrolls as at a slice of melon in the Sahara. He said, 'That must be enormously exciting. I want to visit the place myself some time soon.'

But she was occupied with her reaction to Freddy's distress. She began to speak, with furious exasperation, about the Israeli, a former Czech, who had been allotted to her as a guide to the holy places. He had been overbearing. He had been obstructive. He had taken her on a trip to Nazareth and had wanted her to whizz through the whole scene in half an hour, whereas she had insisted on spending the day there. He was a fanatical Christian-hater who had wanted to show her the cement factories and pipelines of Israel instead of the shrines, and had been reluctant to drive her to the top of Mount Tabor, the probable scene of the Transfiguration, and she had not insisted because this insufferable man . . . It emerged that she herself was a Roman Catholic.

Anxious about the extremity and urgency of her tone, Freddy looked round for the waiter. He said to her, 'Let's try the white wine.' He ordered two glasses, and called after the waiter, 'But it should be chilled.' He said to Miss Vaughan, 'They are inclined to serve it warm.'

The waiter appeared with two glasses of local white wine. In them were floating two chips of ice, rapidly melting from their original cubic form. Freddy and Miss Vaughan were silent until the waiter had gone. The ice melted entirely in the hot evening air. Freddy smiled at the two glasses on the table. Eventually, they even sipped the lukewarm mixture. 'They simply don't understand about wine at most of these hotels,' Freddy said. Well, it was a relief, at least, that they could have an English giggle about something.

Freddy now wondered if it was his long walk through the Orthodox quarter in the afternoon heat that had put him on edge. He felt decidedly afraid of Miss Vaughan. She fidgeted with the ring on her engagement finger. She looked very strained. Perhaps she, too, was feeling the heat. However, he was resolved to be agreeable in view of his blunder last week.

She said, 'Your geraniums are flourishing.'

He had given her two of his pots of geraniums before leaving for Jordan last week. They were special geraniums. He had smuggled them across from Joanna's prize collection.

He said, 'Good. I was hoping Dr Ephraim would look in. I want to consult him about a Hebrew teacher.'

'He had to return to his wife and family.'

'Oh yes, quite.'

'He might give you Hebrew lessons himself. They don't get well paid at the University here.'

'Well, I was sort of hoping that.'

She said, 'Before I go to Jordan we must arrange a meeting.'

'When are you going?' he said.

'I don't know yet.'

It was a puzzle to him that she had not already gone to Jordan. She kept saying she was 'waiting to go to Jordan'. He wondered if she waited for a visa. If they suspected her Jewish blood she would not get a visa. But, on the other hand, if she had a certificate of baptism and kept quiet it should be easy.

He saw that she was pulling at a fraying piece of wicker on the arm of her chair.

Iambics march from short to long . . .

She said, 'I'm glad to have the geraniums. I water them every morning when the post arrives. It takes my mind off things. I'm waiting for a letter to arrive before I can go off to Jordan.'

'If it's a question of a visa, perhaps I could help,' said Freddy.

'Thank you, but you can't help,' she said.

'The Christian shrines over there are far more interesting than here,' he said. 'At least, there are more of them.'

'I know,' she said, 'I hope to be able to see them soon. In fact, I'm hoping to get married quite soon to an archaeologist who's working over there. The one who's at the Dead Sea area.'

'I'm sure I could help if it's only a matter of a visa.'

'I'm waiting for news from Rome,' she said. 'He has been married and is divorced. It's a question of whether his marriage can be annulled or whether it can't be annulled. I mean annulled by the Church. If it isn't annulled by the Church then the marriage is off. There's a fifty–fifty chance.'

'Oh dear,' said Freddy. He said, 'Is it as serious as that?' She said, 'Yes.'

'Won't you be going to join him in Jordan?' Freddy said. He noticed she was pulling at the fraying wicker, and felt a panic about where this conversation might lead; he could see she was feeling strongly about something or other. He was afraid she had some tiresome deep conviction.

She said she would not go to Jordan at all if the news from Rome was against the nullity of his previous marriage. She said she would never see the man again in that case.

'Oh dear,' said Freddy. He said, 'What does your fiancé feel about this?'

'Well, of course, he feels it's a bit unfair. He isn't a Catholic himself.'

'It does seem a bit unfair,' said Freddy mildly. 'It seems a bit extreme, when a couple of grown-up people –'

'Do you know,' said this passionate spinster in a cold and terrifying voice, 'a passage in the Book of the Apocalypse that applies to your point of view?'

'I'm afraid the Apocalypse is beyond me,' Freddy said. 'I've never had the faintest clue what it's all about. I can cope with the Gospels, at least some parts, but –'

'It goes like this,' she said, enunciating her words slowly, almost like a chant:

I know of thy doings, and find thee neither cold nor hot; cold or hot, I would thou wert one or the other. Being what thou art, lukewarm, neither cold nor hot, thou wilt make me vomit thee out of my mouth.

Freddy did not reply. People should definitely not quote the Scriptures at one. It was quite absurd.

Miss Vaughan leaned back in her chair and drew her hand over her prim hair in a relaxed way. Freddy remained silent.

First and last being long, middle short, Amphimacer
Strikes his thundering hoofs, like a proud high-bred racer . . .

Then Freddy rose as one who had quietly closed a door and said, 'I must go and get off a bread-and-butter letter to my hostess before dinner.'

2

BARBARA VAUGHAN'S IDENTITY

People should definitely not quote the Scriptures at each
other, thought Barbara Vaughan, regretting her attack on
Freddy – or rather, it had been a delayed counter-attack, but
he would probably not have recognised this devious fact.

People who quoted the Scriptures in criticism of others
were terrible bores and usually they misapplied the text. One
could prove anything against anyone from the Bible. She
regretted to the smallest detail her denunciation, from
the Apocalypse, of the cool Foreign Office man. In reality she
greatly enjoyed the regretting, because it excluded from her
thoughts the other problems – the vital ones which were, for
the present, insoluble. To these her mind always came round
at length, as in a concerto when the formal recapitulation,
the real thing, wins through. But meantime she fiddled up
and down the scales with the ridiculous scene with Freddy
last night in the courtyard.

She sat on a low wall, regretting on and on and generally
gathering strength, beside the Basilica of the Transfiguration
on the summit plateau of Mount Tabor. She had hired a car
for herself that morning, for she was tired of the travel agency
guides. They had plenty of good information to offer, but
they offered it incessantly. Through the length and breadth of
the country the Israelis treated facts like antibiotic shots,

injecting them into the visitor like diligent medical officers. Well, they were proud of their country, and she had no fault to find with the facts as such. The tiring aspect of every journey she had made throughout the past three weeks was the hard work involved in separating the facts relevant to her point of view from those relevant to theirs.

The facts relevant to her point of view: Barbara Vaughan's intelligence had come to maturity in the post-graduate tradition of a great university's English department. She had then applied herself to music, but too late to meet her own exacting standards: she now no longer played the cello. By constitution of mind she was inclined to think of 'a Catholic point of view' to which not all facts were relevant, just as, in her thesis-writing days, she had selected the points of a poem which were related only to the thesis. This did not mean that she had failed to grasp the Christian religion with a total sense of its universal application, or that she was unable to recognise, in one simple process, the virtue of a poem. All it meant was that her habits of mind were inadequate to cope with the whole of her experience, and thus Barbara Vaughan was in a state of conflict, like practically everyone else, in some mode or another.

Like practically everyone else – and she was one of those afflicted by her gifts. For she was gifted with an honest, analytical intelligence, a sense of fidelity in the observing of observable things, and, at the same time, with the beautiful and dangerous gift of faith which, by definition of the Scriptures, is the sum of things hoped for and the evidence of things unseen.

'We approach Beersheba,' a guide had said on her first tour, shortly after her arrival in the country. 'Look, all this has sprung up in thirteen years.'

The guides of Israel irritated Barbara largely for the reason, not altogether obscure to her, that they were extremely virile men and yet were not the one virile man whose proximity she wanted; they were not Harry Clegg, the archaeologist at present working on the site of the Dead Sea excavations in Jordan. She was disposed to resist the guides' pronouncements from this cause alone, even if she had not the plain excuse to object continually, 'I've really only come on a pilgrimage. I really only want to see the ancient sites. I'm really not interested in Scotch-tape factories.'

'We approach Beersheba.'

Suddenly, as it seemed, from behind a few palm-trees Beersheba had appeared in a white dazzle of modern blocks reaching down to the great desert waves of the Negev. The desert lapped like a sea on the glittering strips of concrete that defined Beersheba's outlying blocks of flats.

Barbara Vaughan said, 'I'm really only interested in the Beersheba of Genesis.'

'This is the Beersheba of Genesis.'

They drove slowly through the streets. Barbara looked from the houses to the desert, and from the desert to the houses. Beersheba was the place where the patriarch Isaac, blind in his old age, mistakenly gave his blessing to Jacob, who had posed as his elder brother Esau. The old man, uneasy, felt the son's hands and arms, which were gloved in the hairy skin of a goat, and was taken in by the disguise. 'The voice is the voice of Jacob,' said the old man. He felt the arms and hands – 'but the hands –' The mighty blessing, once bestowed, was irrevocable. Smooth Jacob, not tough, hairy Esau, got the spiritual inheritance and took the place that the Lord had reserved for him among the Fathers of Israel, such being the ways of the Lord in the Middle East. Barbara reflected that God had not been to Eton. Jacob would have made a marvellous Jesuit . . . She said, 'Well, only the desert and sky look in character, but I suppose it's the authentic site. I feel sleepy.'

'This is Beersheba, the birthplace of Jacob, the Father of the Twelve Tribes of Israel. We have a new school for immigrants. To teach them trades and Hebrew. I show you.'

The modern town indeed had its own beauty. As they were driving back through the streets Barbara caught sight of a brass plate outside a dark glazed shop doorway. It read Detective Agency.

'What do they want with a detective agency in a new town?'

'Many things. The last three, four years there have been maybe some divorces. Population, thirty-two thousand. See, we have here a clinic with also an extension.'

That was how it had been since her arrival.

'I'm really interested essentially in the Holy Land.'

'This is the Holy Land.'

Saul Ephraim, of course, had been the most sympathetic. He knew Harry Clegg. One could relax with Saul. And once, when he advised her, 'Be tough with these official guides. Don't let them bully you. Tell them you only want to see places of antiquity. You can see modern housing estates and shopping centres anywhere in the world,' – for some reason she then replied, 'It's all antiquity in the long run.' The archaeologist had shrugged in his casual, Jewish way. 'In the long run!' he said. 'The modern flats won't last as long as Herod's water-pipes have lasted.'

People should definitely not quote the Scriptures at each other, thought Barbara, as she sat on the wall up there at Mount Tabor. She looked down on the green and blue of Galilee, while her mind gazed equally at the problems of years ago, of last year, last week, yesterday, tomorrow.

Saul Ephraim, her only real friend in this country, frequently brought to mind one of her cousins in their student days, when they had lingered over the supper table on long argumentative Sunday evenings at Golders Green, while the tall flowers outside the French windows seemed to grow silent and more silent. She was conscious of Saul Ephraim in this aspect as he spoke of Herod's network of sewers and water-pipes and told her how these had recently been turned to use again by the new State. He was an unbeliever, well and accurately versed in the Old and New Testaments, with a conscientious indifference to their relevance outside the field of an antiquarian's interest. This was a type of mind Barbara could understand and cope with.

On the occasion of his telling her to be tough with the guides, they had been at Jaffa, where they leaned over the sea-wall, contemplating, as they talked, the old harbour, which was too shallow to accommodate modern shipping. Some way behind them stood the reputed house of Simon the Tanner, where the apostle Peter lodged when he was fetched from Lod to come and raise Dorcas from the dead. It seemed the occupant nuns would not allow visitors on that day. Barbara again experienced a feeling that had overcome her in the recent weeks, when she had actually reached the site she was seeking: it was a feeling of abrupt indifference, as when at Nazareth she had taken great pains to find a shrine entitled the 'Mensa Christi' – reputedly a slab of rock once used by Christ as a table. She had climbed a long, hot hill from curiosity to see the object and to find out what legend attached to it. But on arriving at the small building, she had found it locked. Nearby, a gnarled old Franciscan monk, the custodian, sat dozing on a stone, the key in his hands. She did not trouble to approach him. She did not by then possess sufficient interest in the 'Mensa Christi' to do so.

So it was at the house of Simon the Tanner at Jaffa. Saul had gone round to the back door to try to gain admittance. She said, 'Don't bother. I'm not all that interested'; he gave up the attempt, with only one series of unanswered bangs on the door.

They had leaned over the sea-wall, surveying the ancient sea. Beside them was a paved courtyard leading into some low-built dark doorways. A woman from the interior screamed, then wailed, and finally emerged into the court-yard sobbing loudly. She was an Arab girl wearing a tight, short Western dress, very unkempt. She was upheld by two other women. Her dress was torn from her shoulders. She had obviously been roughly treated. She was hurried by her two women friends into another dark doorway. They were followed by two men, Arabs in European clothes. One of the men stopped to look at Barbara. He seemed to recognise her. His gaze caused her to take a special note of his face. He was blue-eyed. Where had she seen him before? Was he the guide at Joseph's Workshop at Nazareth? The woman was wailing still from within the house.

'I think one of those men is a guide,' she said to Saul when the blue-eyed Arab followed the others.

'You've got guides on the brain. No, they aren't guides,' he said.

She said, 'Oh, of course, I remember. He's the man who comes to see Mr Hamilton at the hotel – a life-insurance agent.'

'A what?' said Saul.

She then remarked, without relevance, that the Scriptures were specially important to the half-Jew turned Catholic. The Old Testament and the New, she said, were to her – as near as she could apply to her own experience the phrase of Dante's vision – 'bound by love into one volume'. Then, perceiving that Saul Ephraim was giving serious thought to what she had said, she gave a timid English laugh, and added that of course she realised one could make a fetish of the Scriptures.

She had hired a car early that morning and had driven northward through the Judean hills to Galilee. The scene with Freddy Hamilton resembled an alcoholic hangover. On the way, she began to feel a sense of her own identity, and realised that this was in fact what she had begun to lose amongst the answers she had been obliged to devise to the questions of Israelis since her arrival in the country. She recalled that day she had been driven by a guide along the road to Caesarea . . . It was eleven in the morning:

'A half-Jew?'

'Yes.'

'Which half?'

'Through my mother.'

'Then you are a whole Jew. The Jew inherits through the mother by Jewish Law.'

'I know that. But one says half-Jew to mean that one of the parents is a Gentile and the other –'

'But the Jew inherits through the mother. You are then a full Jew by the Law.'

'Yes, but not according to the Gentile parent's law.'

'What was your father's Law?'

That was a question indeed.

'I'm afraid he was a law unto himself,' Barbara had said to this questioner, a large blond Pole. He laughed at that.

She told him of her father in the wild upsurge of his middle age and downfall. 'He broke his neck while fox-hunting. The horse threw him. He landed in a ditch and died instantly.'

'My father died also in a ditch. Shot by the S.S. Why have you made yourself a Catholic to deny your Jewish blood?'

'I don't deny it. I've just been telling you about it.'

'You are brought up as a Gentile or a Jew?'

'Neither. No religion.'

'And your mother's relations and your father's relations, what religion?'

Barbara had felt displaced, she felt her personal identity beginning to escape like smoke from among her bones. 'What a lot of questions,' she said. So they drove along the road to Caesarea through the fertile plain of Sharon, cultivated to the verge of the road on each side. They had found the car to be cooler with windows shut than open to the hot breeze. But not much cooler. 'A lot of questions,' she had said, twice, with the resigned dying-fall of a victim deprived of fresh air and civil rights.

'I ask her a question, she makes a big thing of it that I am Gestapo,' said the guide to some invisible witness.

Barbara said, 'Well, it's hot.'

He said, 'I ask you, because you say you are half-Jew, you say you are a Catholic, and I ask you only what is the religion of your mother's relations and the religion of your father's relations. It is a natural discussion, if you would say to me, who are you, who is your mother, who is your father and how do you come to be an Israeli guide, and I would answer those questions. Then I should ask who are you, what is the family, your brothers and your sisters –'

Barbara thought, 'Who am I?' She felt she had known who she was till this moment. She said, 'I am who I am.' The guide spoke some short Hebrew phrase which, although she did not know the language, quite plainly signified that this didn't get them any further in the discussion. Barbara had already begun to reflect that 'I am who I am' was a bit large seeing it was the answer that Moses got from the burning bush on Mount Sinai when he asked God to describe himself. The Catechism, it was true, stated that man was made in God's image chiefly as to the soul. She decided, therefore, essentially 'I am who I am' was indeed the final definition for her. But the thesis-exponent in Barbara would not leave it at that. They entered Caesarea, home of ancient disputations, while she attempted to acquaint the guide with the Golders Green Jewishness of her mother's relations and the rural Anglicanism of her father's, the Passover gatherings on the one hand and the bell-summoned Evensongs on the other, the talkative intellectuals of the one part and the kennel-keeping blood sportsmen of the other. The Polish Israeli was bewildered. Barbara added that her parents themselves were, of course, exceptional, having broken away from their respective traditions to marry each other. And she herself was of course something else again. The guide persisted in his point: Why had she turned Catholic? If she wanted a religion she was already a Jewess through her mother. Barbara knew then that the essential thing about herself remained unspoken, uncategorised and unlocated. She was agitated, and felt a compelling need to find some definition that would accurately explain herself to this man.

He was demanding a definition. By the long habit of her life, and by temperament, she held as a vital principle that the human mind was bound in duty to continuous acts of definition. Mystery was acceptable to her, but only under the aspect of a crown of thorns. She found no rest in mysterious truths like 'I am who I am'; they were all right for deathbed definitions, when one's mental obligations were at an end. 'I am who I am', yes, ultimately, as a piece of music might be what it is; but then, one wants to analyse the thing. Meantime, she thought, the man wants to know who I am, that is, what category of person. I should explain to him the Gentile–Jewish situation in the West, and next, the independence of British education, and the peculiar independence of the Gentile Jew whose very existence occurs through a nonconforming alliance. And next, the probabilities of the Catholic claim, she thought. The fierce heat of noon penetrated her sun-glasses. She thought, later on I must make an attempt to explain: I'll explain after lunch.

But why? At Caesarea they had looked at the historic ruins and the recently excavated ramparts of Herod's city; they looked at the prehistoric Mediterranean Sea and were refreshed by it. The man was dogmatising about dates and events at Caesarea, the most important of which was, to him, the recent moment when excavations by a team of archaeologists had begun. They ate lunch at an outside table under an awning. The guide said, 'In Poland the Catholic priests used to lead the pogroms.'

'Well, they shouldn't have,' she said.

'Why are you Catholic?'

Why? Why did she trouble about these questions? The man was a hired guide. She was paying for his services. Anywhere else one would take up a properly resentful attitude. But here in Israel it was unthinkable; one paid their travel agency, they were hired, but these facts appeared irrelevant to the relationship. Here on this territory the Israeli guides were far more autonomous in their attitudes than any French citizen on home ground, or any English guide in England. The Israelis generally did not merely show one round, they guided, whether they were official guides or not. It occurred to Barbara that all in some degree rather resembled the Irish and the Welsh in their territorial consciousness, and she was reminded, too, of the games of her childhood where one's own chalked-out area, once won, contained whatever features one said it did, neither more nor less. She kept remarking to the guide that the country was beautiful, since this was easy to say, being true. It duly pleased him. He said, 'I swam for it,' and explained that he had arrived as an illegal immigrant on a ship in 1947, and had swum ashore by night.

She had returned to the hotel after the trip to Caesarea in a state of exhaustion and nervous panic that reminded her of the sensations she had experienced as a result of anaemia, for a few months, some years ago. She was now in good physical health; it was spiritual anaemia, she ruthlessly decided, that she was suffering from. Instead of saying goodbye at the door and tipping him like a tourist she acted on a desperate placatory impulse and asked him in for a drink. Then, immediately realising that she was yielding to a familiar weakness, that of humouring the constitutional tyrant, she now recalled having parked the fellow on Freddy Hamilton, who was reading a newspaper in the quiet green courtyard, and had said she would be back presently. She had taken a long time to come down from her room, and when she did she found the huge guide had begun to expand on the adventures of the past day. Courteous Mr Hamilton had seemed more than merely courteous, he was listening with deep interest. The guide was checking off the fingers of his left hand, one by one, as he said, or nearly sang, 'I gave her Abu Gosh, I gave her Ramle where is Arimathea for the Christians, I have given her Lod as you call Lydda, traditional birthplace of St George –'

'Patron Saint of England,' said pleasant Mr Hamilton.

'Correct. I gave her Haifa, I have given her Mount Carmel –'

'Ah, here's Miss Vaughan,' said Freddy Hamilton. 'Ah, Miss Vaughan, I've been hearing an account – let me . . .' He rose to help her to pull up a chair from another table. The guide continued, on his right hand, 'I gave her the grotto of the Prophet Elijah, I gave her, then, the Persian Gardens and the Temple of the Bahai Faith.'

'Ah yes, I've heard of the Bahai Faith. Very interesting. Very decent people, I hear. Founded after the last war. Money to burn.'

'In this the lady was not interested. She did not wish to visit the Bahai Temple.'

'I think we did enough for one day,' Barbara said.

'A very full day,' said Freddy.

When the Israeli had gone, Freddy said, 'Nice fellow. Seems to know his job.'

'I found him insufferably overbearing.'

'Did you? Oh well, you know, we're foreigners here now. One inclines to forget that. British to them means something different from British to us, I'm afraid.'

Saul Ephraim, to whom she had recounted that day's excursion in detail, said, 'You seem to be unlucky with our guides. Not surprising. You're British. Well, that's all right, more or less. You're a Catholic convert – O.K. But you're a half-Jew as well. The three together are a lot.'

'I should have thought being a half-Jew would be held in mitigation of the rest.'

'You ought to know better.'

She did know better. The family on her mother's side at Golders Green, with whom she spent half of the vacations of her youth, had proved as innocently obtuse about her true identity as had the family at Bells Sands, Worcestershire, with whom she spent the other half.

*

Barbara, on the summit of Mount Tabor, conscious of the Holy Land stretching to its boundaries on every side, reflected wearily upon her reflections. She thought, my mind is impatient to escape from its constitution and reach its point somewhere else. But that is in eternity at the point of transfiguration. In the meantime, what is to be borne is to be praised. In the meantime, memory circulates like the bloodstream. May mine circulate well, may it bring dead facts to life, may it bring health to whatever is to be borne.

At Bells Sands – it was the Easter vacation, just after her sixteenth birthday – her energetic tennis-playing grandmother, with hair discreetly dyed the colour of steel, sat on the arm of a chair in her white pleated dress, swinging one of her long sinewy legs, brown summery legs in good condition; the party was gathered in the dining-room after tennis; it was tea-time. Her grandmother took a tea-cup from the tray offered by the young, round-shouldered parlour maid. Barbara had been saying she must go and pack. Her cousin Arthur, then at Sandhurst, later killed in North Africa, was to drive her to the station.

'Must you go tonight, darling?' said her Vaughan grandmother. Barbara passed round the cucumber sandwiches. 'Why not go up with Arthur in the morning? Stay and be comfy.'

'No, I'm expected. It's the Passover. An important festival.'

The warmth of the spring oozed in through the French windows as if the glass were porous. The silver teapot danced with light and shade as a breeze stirred the curtains. The air was elusively threaded with the evidence of unseen hyacinths. So it must have been before she was born, when the family understood that her father was going to marry the Jewess, and there was nothing left to say.

'Well, I admire you for it,' said her grandmother.

The young men were eating the cucumber sandwiches two at a time.

'For what?'

'Your loyalty to your mother's people. But honestly, darling, it isn't necessary. No one could possibly blame you for skipping it. After all, you don't look as if you had a drop of Jewish blood. And after all you're only half. I assure you no one minds.'

'I'm awfully fond of them, you know. I don't feel the least temptation to give them up. Why on earth –?'

'Yes, I know you're fond of them, it's only natural that you should be. Only I want you to know that I admire you for being so loyal, darling. I think I'm right in saying that we all of us admire you.'

'Grandmother!' said Barbara's other cousin, Miles. 'Grandmother, shut up.'

'There's nothing to admire, no effort,' Barbara said. 'The Aaronsons don't call it loyalty when I stay here. They take it for granted.'

'Well, I should hope so, Barbara dear. This was your father's home and it's yours, too.'

Barbara perceived that she had courage, this lithe grandmother of hers. It took courage for her to speak steadily of her son, her favourite, her disappointment in life, now dead from a fall while hunting. It had been an indigenous sort of death, but the mother would have preferred him alive with his unfortunate marriage, all the same.

'Well, there's time for another set before you change and pack, Barbara,' said Uncle Eddy, gazing out at the sky as if he could tell the time by it. The lawn lay beautiful as eternity. A servant was calling in Eddy's two children from an upper window; presently their high voices came quarrelling from the shrubbery and faded round the back of the house.

There was a stir in the beech leaves like papers being gently shuffled into order. The drawing-in of an English afternoon took place, with its fugitive sorrow.

'See here, Barbara,' said her grandfather at Golders Green a few hours later, 'these are the bitter herbs which signify our affliction in Egypt . . .' He enumerated the items on the Seder table, the eggs, the cake, the paschal lamb.

She was familiar with the scene from previous Seder nights, but her grandfather, knowing she had not been formally instructed and had no Hebrew, was careful each year to explain everything. There was always a great deal she was ignorant of, which the other grandchildren, her cousins, took for granted. But she recognised the excitement of this Feast when, as a child, she and the other children had sat up late with their elders at the exotic table, every face shining with candlelight, every morsel of food giving a special sensation to her mouth, not only because it tasted different from ordinary food, but because on this night every morsel stood for something else, and was food as well. The children drank wine and deliverance with it . . . The unleavened bread, crisp *matzo* that made crumbs everywhere, was uncovered. 'This is the poor bread which our fathers ate in the land of Egypt.' Barbara had understood from her fifth year that it was not actually the same wafery substance, here on the table at Golders Green, that had been baked by the Israelites on the first Passover night, and yet, in a mysterious sense, it was: 'This is the bread which our fathers ate . . .'

'This is the night,' said her grandfather, an unageing man, to Barbara, now so conscious of having turned sixteen, 'when we give thanks to God for our ancestors' redemption. He split the sea for us and we passed over on dry land.' She listened, as if she had not heard it before, while her cousins, now grown old, between eighteen and twenty-one years of

33

age, took their places. Like herself, they had been recognisably intellectuals, with an additional bent for music, before they had turned fifteen.

The cousins, undergraduates in philosophy, law and medicine, were gathered in purposeful concentration round the Seder table, where usually, on summer evenings after supper when the table had been cleared, they leaned over the shiny wood surface far into the night, loquacious on the subjects of Nietzsche, Freud, Marx, Mussolini, Hitler, and the war impending. Now they were about to intone in due order the responses on the subject of the Exodus from Egypt into the Promised Land.

A small dark girl of eight was present, a refugee orphan from Germany who had been allotted to this family in the emergency parcelling-out of rescued children in those late nineteen-thirties. Her eyes were wonderful pebbles in the candlelight.

The young men pushed back their skull-caps, for the room was warm with mesmeric ritual as much as with actual heat.

It was only a few months ago, in the Christmas holidays, that Barbara and these alert young men, her cousins on the Jewish side, had reached the conclusion one evening that agnosticism was the only answer, their atheist mentors having erred on the dogmatic side. But here and now they were suddenly children of Israel again, Barbara always included, because, after all, blood was blood, and you inherit from your mother's side.

In former times, Barbara, being the youngest member of the Feast, yet knowing no Hebrew, had repeated after her grandfather the euphonies of the question reserved to the youngest of the company. But tonight the German child was repeating in Hebrew the question:

Why is this night different from all other nights?

It is different, Barbara had thought. The elder Aaronsons hoped she would one day marry a Jew, a doctor or a lawyer, somebody brilliant. They did not believe that her Gentile relations could be particularly well-disposed towards her. As for love, how could you expect it? The elder Aaronsons said, Barbara, bless her, she'll make a nice match in five, six years' time. They felt she would compensate for her intractable mother, who now never came to the family gatherings but only wrote letters from Paris.

Her grandfather intoned joyfully. He was in good voice. The very old Auntie Bea's rings twinkled on her moveless hand as the candles flickered in a little draught. Michael, her closest friend among the cousins, for Barbara's benefit, murmured an English rendering of the versicle liturgy to the accompaniment of his grandfather's deep patriarchal boom, and the young men's gruff responses:

> If He had brought us out of Egypt,
> and not sent judgement upon them,
> > It would suffice us.
> If He had sent judgement upon them, and
> not upon their gods,
> > It would suffice us.
> If He had sent judgement on their gods and
> not killed their first born,
> > It would suffice us.

The German child was following the Hebrew in her book with her forefinger, smiling with recognition. Barbara felt proud of the child in a Jewish way, and exchanged a glance to this effect with her young Aunt Sadie, who also glowed as Jewish women do, with approval of intelligent and happy children.

35

If He had parted the waters for us, and
not let us pass through it on dry ground,
It would suffice us.

The previous Sunday, at Bells Sands, Barbara had gone with Uncle Eddy's two children after church to roll their bright dyed Easter eggs in a dell at the end of their woods, where she and her cousin Arthur had always rolled their eggs as children. Was it only last Sunday? The scene pictured itself without warning in Barbara's mind, light-years away, and rapidly disappeared. Only last Sunday, the end of Lent 1939? She had a sense of temporal displacement. The Passover Feast was coming to an end. She heard the familiar lilt of the riddle song, 'One Kid', from the lips of her lolling cousins. They were supposed to loll. It was part of the ritual. Now, that was a thing her Vaughan grandmother, who complained of backache each Sunday after church, she being one who made a point of sitting up well, would never understand.

Afterwards in the kitchen, the small child helped with the washing-up. Nobody would let Barbara do a thing. All the women were anxious to spare her a job. It was always the same here, at Golders Green. None of her aunts, or even the old servant, would let her wash up. Now, seeing the pile of dishes, Barbara seized a clean dishtowel from a rack where it was hanging.

Her young Aunt Sadie attempted to take the cloth from her in a good-humoured way but very firmly, and vaguely Barbara was aware of a lip-silence among the women working and clattering among the plates and cutlery at the sink.

'Hee-ee, you're not kosher.' This was her youngest Aaronson cousin, Michael, standing at the doorway of the kitchen, with his owl-like face, horn-rimmed glasses, wide smile, red cheeks and Jewish nose.

His young Aunt Sadie said, 'Michael!'

Michael spread his hands and hunched his shoulders, pretending to be very foreign. 'Vot you vont in my keetch-in . . .'

Young Aunt Sadie said to Barbara, 'We use different dish-cloths for drying the plates. Milk and meat are kept separate. We don't eat both together, that you know. But we don't wash them up together, either. We keep the towels separate.'

'Vot you expect?' said Michael. 'She is neither Yeed nor Goy ees mein cousin Barbara.' He put his arm round her shoulder. 'She ees a bit milk and meat in the same dish, vot you expect?'

'Stop it, Michael. He's a clown, that boy,' said young Aunt Sadie, busy with the women. They kept pushing him toler-antly out of the way. Barbara, too, felt cheerful about his presence in the kitchen. The younger generation in this household were slightly more indulged than they were at Bells Sands, where all affection was casual, unstated, under-stood more or less. Barbara, who at Golders Green came in for a share of the unequivocal benevolence towards the young and their capers, their demands, and their wild theories, was automatically soothed by the tolerant atmosphere in the kitchen. But still, she was not permitted to stack the dishes away, lest she stack them in the wrong places.

'We've got special dishes for the Passover. Everything separate. The usual plates and things are not used during the Passover,' said young Aunt Sadie, instructively, to Barbara. Young Aunt Sadie tried to take the place of her mother, who, since her father had broken his neck in a ditch, had married again, this time to a Japanese embassy official, and lived in Paris; she was a very lost limb to the Aaronsons.

Barbara surrendered the washing-up to her relations, feeling her ignorance in these matters to be an abyss of details. She was aware, too, that she would never make an attempt to acquire the missing knowledge; there were too many other things that she had resolved to learn. She looked at Sadie and said resentfully, 'I'll never learn your ways, I'm afraid.'

'Well, you might learn some manners,' said quick-tongued Aunt Sadie.

'Sadie! Sadie! She is, bless her, a child only,' said the very old Auntie Bea.

Michael said, 'And she's been eating ham sandwiches at her tennis party this afternoon. Not kosher, that girl.'

'Cucumber sandwiches,' said Barbara.

Old Auntie Bea, who was always anxious to make the peace, and the syntax of whose utterances was the joy of the younger generation, dried her plump fingers, and nodding her head towards Barbara, said, 'Cucumbers! I have made yesterday cucumbers in pickle, twenty. Thirty-six last week in the jars I have with vinegar made, cucumbers.'

At Joppa, then, when Barbara came to be leaning over the sea-wall, she said to Saul Ephraim, who reminded her much of the Aaronson cousins of her youth, 'My Gentile relations tried too hard to forget I was a half-Jew. My Jewish relations couldn't forget I was a half-Gentile. Actually, I didn't let them forget, either way.'

'Quite right. Why should you forget what you are?' said Saul. 'You were right.'

'I know that. But one doesn't altogether know what one is. There's always more to it than Jew, Gentile, half-Jew, half-Gentile. There's the human soul, the individual. Not "Jew, Gentile" as one might say "autumn, winter". Something unique and unrepeatable.'

He smiled as if he had heard it all before.

'Then why did you choose the Gentile side in the end?'

'I didn't choose any side at any time.'

'You became a Catholic.'

'Yes, but I didn't become a Gentile. It wouldn't be possible, entirely, seeing that I'm a half-Jew by natural birth.'

'Well, but look, Christianity's a Gentile religion. It's all the same to me, but it's a question of fact.'

'Not essentially. After all, it started off as a new ordering of the Jewish religion.'

'Well, it's changed a lot since then.'

'Only accidentally. It's still a new order of an older firm.'

'Did you get your Catholic instruction from the Jesuits, by any chance?' he said.

She giggled. 'Yes, in fact I did.'

'I thought so.'

'You can discredit the Jesuits but you can't refute the truth.'

'Well, you can't expect our population to make these distinctions. Catholic is Gentile to them.'

'Perhaps I should hush it up while in Israel, that I'm a half-Jew by birth,' she said.

'You'd be wiser to hush it up when you go over to Jordan. Here, you only risk an argument, but there you might get shot.'

The wall on which she now sat on the summit of Mount Tabor was part of an ancient fortress, the foundations of which lay about five feet on the far side. Looking behind her she could see the weedy floor of this excavated plot. In the self-absorption of the hour, even this small rectangle of archaeology related itself to her life. She recalled the dig at St Albans in Hertfordshire last summer. A Roman villa was being excavated. Her cousin, Miles Vaughan, now married and living at St Albans, took an active interest in the old Roman area of the city and always entertained the archaeologists when they came in the summer to work on the ruins. Barbara was intending to spend only a week with her cousin. She prolonged her stay. She went down to the dig as a volunteer. Miles said one day, 'You're causing a scandal, Barbara – you and Harry Clegg.' He said it in an entirely jocular way, as one might say to a small boy, 'My, you're a big man!' and Barbara was shaken by this. Miles had not for a moment realised how near the truth he had struck. Neither he nor his wife, Kathy, apparently, had noticed how close her friendship with the archaeologist Harry Clegg had grown in the past three weeks. They had simply ignored the evidence. 'You're causing a scandal, Barbara – you and Harry Clegg.' Barbara was stabbed by his tone of voice. It affected her with a shock of self-recognition. She felt as if she had caught sight of a strange face in the mirror, and presently realised that the face was her own. Barbara understood then, that her self-image was at variance with the image she presented to the world. She understood that, to them, she was a settled spinster of thirty-seven, by definition a woman, but sexually-differentiated only by a narrow margin, sharp, clever, set in her ways, a definite spinster, one who had embraced the Catholic Church instead of a husband, one who had taken up religion instead of cats. It was this concept that entitled Miles to tease her. 'You're causing a scandal, Barbara . . .' But Miles, a grown man . . . he was too innocent for words. She had looked at him. Yes, he was joking. He gave her a little pat on the shoulder and went out to the car.

Barbara went and looked at herself in the mirror, full-length, in her room. Her hair was drawn back tight, her face was thin and smooth, her blouse and skirt were neat. Everything was quite neat, prim and unnoticeable. She had not guessed she looked quite like that, but now that she saw herself almost through the eyes of others, she was amazed. She wondered if she was a hypocrite; but that appearance in the glass, she thought, comes of long habit. Having restrained the expression of my feelings over the years I look as if I had none. It comes from a long habit of approaching the world with caution, this appearance of being too cautious to live a life of normal danger.

The figure in the looking-glass fascinated her. No wonder Miles did not really know her.

She had thought then, but who am I?

I am who I am.

Yes, but who am I?

Because, in fact, she was already deeply involved in a love-affair with Harry Clegg, the archaeologist. The local country people had taken note of them during the first week of their meeting. But her cousins would never do so. They would simply ignore the evidence. She looked in the mirror and understood why. And understood why she attracted the man. It was the very quality that deceived her friends. It was this deceptive, ascetic, virginal look that Harry found intriguing. It was not her mind alone, she told herself as she sized up her appearance.

All the summer weeks of their first meeting she had felt in a state of complete liberation from guilt. Moral or social censure were meaningless. The hours and days were barricaded with enchantment. She prolonged her stay on the simple excuse to Miles and Kathy that she was enjoying it. They accepted this, they were delighted. She did not mind baby-sitting in the evenings with Harry Clegg to keep her company. Harry Clegg was a scholar, of course, but not their type socially; he was a mild joke to them, a small, dark, scowling creature with too much untidy hair. A scowling creature except when he smiled. He was brilliant, the Vaughans admitted, a dedicated scholar. That he was regarded in every informed society but theirs as a distinguished man, the Vaughans did not know. They conveyed, with innocent remarks, in their diffident way, their amusement at the points where his lower-class origins were evident. Harry would never have entered Kathy's drawing-room or Miles's consciousness, nor would have wanted to do so, had he not been dabbling in the local excavations. Miles and Kathy merrily departed for dinner parties, leaving the professor baby-sitting with Barbara and presumably discussing archaeology with her for all he was worth.

But Barbara and Harry Clegg were in the spare bedroom, making love, just like the nannie and the butler in the absence of master and mistress in the old days. Sometimes one of the children would wake and call. Barbara would swear and get up. Just like the old-time nannie.

Sometimes they settled down in the rough hut on the site of the excavations, like teenagers stormed by the sensual presences of the summer night. At any other time Barbara would have thought it ludicrous. A few weeks before she would have thought it absurd. But this was no time for sophisticated thoughts. She felt herself to be in love with Harry Clegg in an entirely exclusive form as yet unrealised in human experience. It made nonsense of the rules. There were no moral laws to fit it. The form of their love seemed to her to derive from a faculty of inner knowledge which they both possessed, a passionate mutual insight so unique in her experience that she felt it to be unique in human experience. Harry Clegg – shock-haired, unhandsome – who would have guessed he would be her type? Miles referred to him as 'the red-brick genius'. But that was to reckon without Harry Clegg, who loved her. He loved her disguise as an English spinster, not merely as disguise but as part of her inexplicable identity. She was not an English spinster merely, but also a half-Jew, and was drawn to the equivalent quality in him that quite escaped both the unspoken definition 'Englishman of lower-class origin', and the spoken one, 'red-brick genius'.

It happened one day that Barbara's cousin, Michael Aaronson, came down for the weekend with his wife. He was a recognised expert in International Law, with a subsidiary interest in a firm of solicitors who had dealt with the Vaughans' family business for the past ten years, such being one of the odd and latter results of that Vaughan–Aaronson marriage which had caused so much alarm at the time. Business apart, other Vaughans and Aaronsons of their generation were now on visiting terms, this having happened gradually from some point after the war, when wedding invitations and acceptances had started to flutter between the two families; while Barbara, who was now the only visible link between them, tended to be regarded as something practically invisible by both sides. She now saw them infrequently, her life being centred in the girls' school where she taught. Michael was the only one she corresponded with, he was still her best-friend of the Aaronsons.

He was surprised to find Barbara at St Albans on a long stay. More perceptive than Miles, he noticed her absorption with Harry Clegg.

He said, when he was alone with her, 'Are you getting attached to that archaeologist? He seems keen on you.'

'Yes.'

'Good luck, then.'

Thank you, Michael.'

'He's a distinguished fellow. Looks terrible. They always attract women, somehow, when they look like that. Are you thinking of marriage? Because if you're going to get married the family won't like it.'

'Which family?'

'Oh, the Vaughans, of course. He's the wrong background.'

'The Aaronsons would have said the wrong blood.'

'Yes, the old people were upset by Spencer's marriage.' Spencer was one of the cousins, who had recently married a Gentile.

'They wouldn't worry about who I married, now,' Barbara said. 'They always knew I wasn't quite the right blood for them. Only half right. The other half was wrong.'

'Oh, well, the old people –'

The Aaronson grandparents were dead, but numerous aunts and uncles had reached their sixties and seventies since the Golders Green days before the war.

'And the Vaughans,' said Barbara cheerfully, 'always knew I hadn't quite the right background. They felt I was too fond of the Aaronsons. My environment was half wrong.'

'Then you've got something in common with Clegg,' Michael said. 'The outcast status.'

'Yes, quite, but we also have common intellectual interests. We've got a lot to talk about.' She had turned sharp and defensive, like Aunt Sadie.

'That sounds more like sense, I'll admit. You're the most sensible woman I know.'

'I'm not. He's a married man.'

'Any chance of a divorce?'

'He's got a divorce,' Barbara said.

'Oh, Christ, yes, you're a Catholic. What are you going to do?'

'I haven't begun to think.'

'Keep me informed,' Michael said, 'when you do begin to

think. Anyhow, I'm glad this has happened. I thought you'd given men up.'

'Well, evidently not.'

'I know. Silly of me.'

Down at the Fighting Cocks, the public house that stood on the verge of the Roman area of St Albans, small murmurs passed round concerning the midnight movements of a couple of the current archaeologists (for the patrons thought Barbara was one of the team). 'You're causing a scandal, Barbara – you and Harry Clegg.' Yes, but Miles and his social circle never got to hear of the small scandal at the Fighting Cocks; nobody there knew the archaeologists by name, or cared. The local people grinned as the lovers left the pub. 'Free love on the old Roman road,' commented a man, and it was left at that. Meanwhile, Barbara and Harry walked along the ramparts of Watling Street by moonlight and bedded down in the hut.

A year later, on the summit of Mount Tabor, where the warrior poet, Deborah, once mustered her troops against an enemy of the Lord named Sisera, Barbara turned and gazed out towards the Dead Sea, where her lover now was working on the site of Qumran. She recalled, the day she left St Albans, saying goodbye to Miles, Kathy, and the children. Miles took her to the station, talking of his married plans as married people do – the holiday abroad and the new garage – suspecting her of no other passion than her recent one for botany and no deeper regret than that she had given up playing the cello. She had felt then, how much more of a sexual person she was than he. She could not remember when first she had associated her Jewishness with her sexual instincts and distinguished herself from her Gentile relatives by a half-guilty feeling that she was more afflicted by sex than they were; so that, when she fell in love with Harry Clegg,

45

she felt more blessed by sex than they were, by virtue of her Jewish blood. This basic error with an elusive vapour of truth in it persisted so far as she continued to associate, without even questioning the proposition, her Jewishness with sex, and to feel that she partook of the sexual virility of the world in consequence. Miles had said, as he kissed her on the platform at St Albans, 'It's been lovely having you.'

She smiled at this in the train. She was fond of Miles and his thin, but so innocent, imagination. He would use that correct phrase, 'It's been lovely having you,' to departing visitors on platforms, without variation, till he was too infirm to see people off at all. Kathy, at the door of the house, had said the same thing. Kathy always had a full day, full of social activities and routine. It took this sort of English couple, Barbara thought, to let a love-affair ripen and come to flower under their roof without suspecting anything. They would have been horrified to know about the spare bedroom episodes. Barbara, who on later reflection was herself mildly shocked, was at this moment amused. She was in love. A trite late-flowering. A very late one. She didn't care. She would not have cared if Miles or Kathy had discovered her in the spare bed with Harry Clegg. What could they have said? 'Oh! sorry –' and withdrawn. And later: 'Look here, Barbara –' And what would they have said? That would have depended on the inspiration of the hour. She was merely amused at the notion, when it occurred to her that she had taken some sort of revenge on them, in return for the evening when she had listened to Kathy and Miles, for a few moments, gaily mimicking Harry's Coventry vowels. They were as good as foreigners, herself and Harry Clegg. And they made love like foreigners, which was all right, too.

The train carried her away to London, and all things considered, she decided she would never be able to convey to

46

Miles the exceptional event, her love, that finally justified her abuse of his hospitality. Miles would have been afraid to listen, lest it upset the brotherly arrangement he had come to with his wife.

> I know of thy doings, and find thee
> neither cold nor hot.

It was after her return, in the new term, to the school where she had been teaching for six years, that her normal process of reasoning set in, and as her love took greater hold of her, so did she take hold of it. There was a deadlock. Their love letters became a vehicle for arguments that gruelled her in the new term and infuriated her, with their revelation of something absolutely undisplaceable in her nature, her Catholic faith.

They wrote the love letters of academic intellectuals, that is to say, they were not much as love letters. Her references to their love were light and frivolous, as if it were something that didn't matter basically but was a mere luxury of civilisation. She partly believed this. His were funnily crude. On the question of what was to be done about it she was serious and practical, assembling and setting forth arguments in sober order. The nature of their love-affair underwent a change in the course of this correspondence. Barbara's letters at times resembled essays in theology. She gripped her fountain-pen with tight, tense fingers.

For in the first month of the new term, as she uneasily took up her old teaching life, she felt the relevance to the situation of her being a Catholic. As matters stood, she could not marry a divorced man and remain within the Church, unless his marriage was in fact invalidated by the Church. All this she wrote to Harry Clegg, with supporting theology, in

47

the excessively rational terms employed by people with a secret panic or religious doubt. 'The Church,' she wrote, 'is nothing if not logical. You, above all people, will understand, even if you cannot . . .'

He turned up at the school to see what the hell she was playing at. He, above all people, the third Saturday of term. She was standing at her sitting-room window using it as a looking-glass while she tied a scarf round her head. She was about to go down to the post office to send off a fat envelope, a letter to him, bulging with pregnant hopes and theological debate. She heard a scrape on the gravel as of a wild old motor-car, and saw, beyond her reflection, his quite tame Consul, a shining two-year-old, which he always drove so hard.

She ran down to meet him. She now realised quite clearly that she did not want Ricky to meet him; Ricky had become, over the past six years, her closest woman friend. Ricky was Miss Rickward, the headmistress. They had frequently been abroad together. It had even been suggested by Ricky, and vaguely assented to by Barbara, that they would share a flat together on their retirement. Ricky was forty-two, a knowledgeable spinster. Somehow, at some time, an unspoken agreement had been arrived at, to the effect that they shared the same sense of humour and disregard of men. It was, in a way, understood that when they retired . . . How? Why had all this been understood? At what point in their talkative and confidential relationship had it become a difficult thing for Barbara to speak of a prospective husband, a lover? – leave out the question of a love-affair?

She ran down to meet Harry. They stood on the gravel path and kissed each other. She got into the car and made him drive out of school bounds, miles away, into a woodland clearing in the heart of Gloucestershire.

*

From her wall on Mount Tabor, she looked over to the kingdom of Jordan, in the hazy blue direction of the Dead Sea, where Harry, in his shabby old clothes, was probably peering at, and pronouncing a fake, a square inch of papyrus placed on a table. 'They've already started to write new Dead Sea Scrolls,' he had told her in a recent letter to England. Here, of course, the only letters she got from him were notes smuggled by friends. But since that Saturday afternoon, they had stopped arguing in their letters. It was he who had recognised the fact that the arguments, however unacceptable, stood for an immovable conviction, something similar to his dedication to his field of scholarship. He would not, for the love of Barbara or anyone else, attribute a date which he believed to be false to a manuscript or object of antiquity; not to fit any theory dear to his own heart, he wouldn't. He recognised the same seam of hard rock in Barbara. He submitted to her idea of having the validity of his marriage examined by the ecclesiastical lawyers of Rome. There was a chance that the marriage could be invalidated, although it seemed to him on ludicrous grounds, by the fact that he had not, so far as he knew, been baptised. But he was obliged to prove this negative fact, and it was not so easy as it sounded. And even it was considered slim evidence towards an annulment.

Meanwhile, Barbara, searching her own motives like a murder squad, suspected that her refusal to marry him had been argued less from her fear of separation from the Church than from a fear of revealing to Ricky the existence of a man in her life. How? Why was Ricky's astonishment to be feared? Ricky's disappointment in her? It was too absurd. It was real.

Barbara dropped hints to Ricky throughout the rest of the year. 'Dr Clegg,' she said, 'a brilliant archaeologist, a friend of mine –' 'Extremely interesting,' said Ricky, 'but I wouldn't,' she said, 'let it become a burden, this letter-writing. A correspondence like this is bound to interfere with your work in term time. Is he handsome?' 'No,' said Barbara, 'not a bit.' 'Perhaps he can't find a woman,' Ricky said, with an expression of genuine academic consideration of the matter. 'Not handsome by vulgar standards,' Barbara said.

Meanwhile she had been reconciled to the Church, in a frigid sort of way, as one might acknowledge, unsmiling, the victor in battle, in whose presence one is signing a peace treaty. She was obliged to repent. What of – the love-affair? No, adultery, to be precise. Yes, but to be precise, it was impossible to distinguish the formal expression of her love from the emotion. 'Go and repent,' said the priest, worn-out with this involved honesty. 'It was a love-affair,' Barbara explained. 'Yes, well, don't pretend it was the Beatific Vision.' Barbara went so far as to repent that she could not repent of the forbidden love-making, and as is the plain expectation of all Christians she got the benefit of the doubt on the understanding that she put an end to the sex part of it.

By summer-time she was standing on Mount Tabor and looked out towards the Dead Sea where Harry Clegg was working. That morning, a letter from him had been thrust under her door, having been smuggled through the Gate in the American Embassy-bag from Amman.

Latest bulletin from the Holy Romans – they'll take at least another month to decide. But for goodness' sake, come over. You can't spend your whole summer holidays over there without seeing what's going on here, let alone seeing me. I shall not attempt any of that rotten nasty sex stuff, in fact I wouldn't touch you with a barge pole, if I had one. Hurry up, Barbara, there's some interesting stuff to see here.

She looked towards the Dead Sea and thought of his thick-featured, dark face utterly intent on the work in front of it, and forgot, in her tenderness, that she was a spinster of no fixed identity. She was aware only of the vulnerability peculiar to his detachment, and of a desire to protect him in the practical aspects of his life where he was too absorbed to protect himself. She suddenly felt to be insignificant the business of being a Gentile and a Jewess, both and neither, and that of being a wolf in spinster's clothing, and the business of the letter she would have to write to Ricky. She was thinking of the red-brick genius whose accent her cousin Miles had mimicked with such perfect exaggeration, Harry Clegg, the sweet scholar from an address, now extinguished by the war, in Coventry. He would have been, to her grandmother at Bells Sands, 'a rather common little man' for her to take up with, to her grandfather at Golders Green a non-Jewish disappointment for her to take up with. To the Jews a stumbling-block, a folly to the Greeks. But it did not matter. Even the fact that the academic world recognised his true value and standing was irrelevant. The point was, he was entirely lovable to her, this lover from last summer's Roman remains.

'Go and repent . . .'

> Goe and catch a falling starre,
> Get with child a mandrake roote.

It is impossible to repent of love. The sin of love does not exist. Over at the Dead Sea, she thought, just over there, he is ferreting about in the sand or maybe he has discovered an inkwell used by the Essene scribes, or something.

To the east, from the top of Tabor, was the valley of Jordan and the very blue waters of Galilee with the mountains of

Syria, a different blue, on the far side. On the west, far across Palestine, the Carmel range rose from the Mediterranean. There seemed no mental difficulty about the miracles, here on the spot. They seemed to be very historic and factual, considered from this standpoint. This feeling might be due to the mountain-top sensation. But was it any less valid than the sea-level sensation? Scientifically speaking?

A coach-load of organised pilgrims arrived at the Basilica. Barbara returned to her tree-shadowed wall. They were led by a Catholic priest. One of the Franciscan custodians of the shrine came out to meet them. The priest-guide assembled his flock outside the church and explained to them that this was the place where Christ was transfigured.

Only probably, said Barbara's mind; there's a rival claim for Mount Hermon, over in the distance.

In the presence of his disciples, Peter, James, and John, said the priest. His garments white and dazzling.

Wherever it did take place, she thought, I believe it did take place all right. Transfigured, and in a radiant time of metamorphosis, was seen white and dazzling, to converse with Moses and Elias.

'Do you remember what he was conversing about?' said the priest to his twenty-odd faithful.

The death he was to die.

'His forthcoming death in Jerusalem,' said the priest. 'It's described in Mark and Luke.'

He read the chapters, while the Franciscan monk waited with folded hands to escort them into the shrine.

. . . There came a cloud and overshadowed them. And they were afraid when they entered into the cloud.

And a voice came out of the cloud, saying, 'This is my beloved Son. Hear him.'

'This is also the place,' said the priest, closing his book, 'where Deborah of the Old Testament collected an army against Sisera. You get it in the Book of Judges, and her song of triumph, remember. Mount Tabor is the place mentioned. A good spot, strategically, as you can see. They all camped up here. It's only 843 feet. Looks higher from below.'

The crowd disappeared into the church. Barbara walked out of hiding and breathed the miraculous air. It was after receiving Harry's letter that she had hired the car that morning. Harry was . . . Her mind once more took refuge in the anxious memory of the scene she had made with Freddy Hamilton the previous evening. She duly felt bad about it. People should definitely not quote the Scriptures at one.

If the Ecclesiastical Courts were going to take at least another month to give their verdict on the validity of his marriage, by then she would have returned to school and started a new term. She had almost decided that morning, in the same mental gesture as she had decided to hire a car, not to return to school at all. She must write to Ricky soon. She would write to Michael first.

But why don't I go down to Jerusalem, Barbara thought, and pass through the Mandelbaum Gate? Why is it that I'm not on my way, now, from Jerusalem, across the plains of Sodom and Gomorrah to the Dead Sea? Why don't I go over and see him?

Because I'm a pilgrim to the Holy Land and one shouldn't abuse hospitality.

Because I've got to have time to think.

Because I don't really want to sleep with him in the present state of affairs.

But why don't I go?

Because it's dangerous there for someone of Jewish blood.

But no one could possibly find out.

Barbara had a separate passport issued by the Foreign Office in London, for the purpose of entering Jordan from Israel. She had the required certificate of baptism signed by a priest:

I declare that Miss Barbara Vaughan is a member of the Roman Catholic Church and has been known to me for some years.

No one could possibly guess that I'm a half-Jew.

Then why?

Because I'm a spinster that's taken a religious turn. A Gentile Jewess, neither one thing nor another, caught up in a crackpot mystique. I declare that Miss Barbara Vaughan is a member of the Roman Catholic Church and has been known to me for some years. Life is passing.

Then why do I not go down to the Dead Sea?

Because the time hasn't yet come for me to go down to the Dead Sea. When the time comes, I'll go down to the Dead Sea.

I go on, she thought, with questions and answers in the old Hebraic mode, chanting away to myself.

She thought, then, that it might be a pleasant gesture on her part to ask Freddy Hamilton, as a favour, if he would get a letter across to Harry Clegg in Jordan for her. It would save the delay of sending it by post through Cyprus. Freddy Hamilton was the sort of person who would take it as a good gesture, the asking of a favour.

I know of thy doings, and find thee
neither cold nor hot . . .

Well, it makes me hot and cold to think of what I said, she thought. People should definitely not quote the Scriptures at each other.

And she recalled, without reason, that Freddy had said to her only last week, 'Most of the Christian shrines are over in Jordan, of course. You really must go over and meet these friends of mine. They love having visitors, and there's a delightful English atmosphere.'

She smiled cheerfully and got back into her hired car.

3

A DELIGHTFUL
ENGLISH ATMOSPHERE

Freddy was over in Jordan for the weekend. He sat on a wooden bench, writing a letter, in a part of the garden that Joanna Cartwright had planted with numerous wild flowers and herbs of the Holy Land that she picked up on her rambles. Most of them were recognisable to Freddy as belonging to the same botanical tribes as the wild flowers of the English fields and hedgerows of his schooldays before everything had been changed. Indeed, some of Joanna's finds were no different at all, so far as he could see, from those pointed out to him, on walks, before he was sent to school, by that governess whose name Freddy had understandably forgotten. Joanna's flowers were not even a larger species.

Freddy's writing-pad rested on his knee. 'Dearest Ma . . .

. . . but I hope you are not serious. Surely Benny intends to remain with you at Harrogate! Dearest Ma, there must be very little for her to do. I quite fail to see how it *can* be too much for her. The hotel staff seems to do most of the *doing*, and all Benny has to do is be. I think, quite honestly, she has too little to occupy her time, and that is mainly what is making her irritable. I wish I could be more helpful, dearest Ma, but you must realise that things have changed and one has to put up with much, nowadays, that would have been unthinkable in the past. Indeed, you are fortunate in having Benny. She would not be easy – perhaps impossible – to replace!

Only a few of Joanna's wild plants were still in bloom. A young Arab boy in his teens, with skinny, deformed legs, wearing only shorts, had come out of the house with a watering-can and was drenching the precious clumps in their dark, shady corner; he had an air of special concentration, plainly having been instructed in the seriousness of the job. A few yards away, on the long green that led to the house, the lawn-spray made a whispering splash under the sun while the Arab's watering-can in Freddy's cool corner splashed intermittently. The small tickets that Joanna had stuck into the ground to mark her plants showed up in their black capital letters under the wash of water. Joanna had categorised them by their place of origin. Partly from familiar memory and partly by his immediate eyesight Freddy could read the tickets from where he sat; Gethsemane, Mount of Olives, Valley of Jehosophat, Siloam, Jericho, Bethlehem.

Last spring, when he had begun to visit the Cartwrights at weekends, these garden beds had been in full bloom. To Freddy, although he was no botanist, they had always looked very English, set here in the garden above Jerusalem; they looked decidedly different, at all events, from what they had looked all over Palestine in the prolific spring. And now, ambling about in the far associations of his thoughts, Freddy contemplated the neatly printed labels of each clump blossoming under the watering-can, and recalled another bold, amateur-handed script, poker-worked into the wood by his great-aunt herself, and how the letters had started up from her little skew-wired tickets. She had been a wild-flower gatherer who had planted a patch of her garden in clumps, labelled according to country names: Bird's-foot Trefoil, Lady's Finger, Tufted Vetch, Hair Tare, Viper's Bugloss, Forget-me-not, Ling, Small-flowered Crowfoot . . .

'I think, dearest Ma –' Freddy's fountain-pen moved like an energetic snail over the letter-pad resting on his knee. He used a broad nib that left a trail of familiar patterns, his words; it was always a matter of filling in a lot of pages for Ma, she liked him to send long letters. The pen scratched noisily against the splash of the watering-can in the hot afternoon, and Freddy functioned on with his letter, as he had done for thirty years of his natural history, a letter a week.

> . . . both try to forget the garnet brooch incident. I shall drop a note to Benny. It is true there was no reason for her to 'blow up' about it. But do remember how touchy Benny has always been. Of course, one should be careful to ascertain the *facts* before one speaks in haste, although, goodness knows, as you say, Benny has known us long enough, and really ought to exercise a little understanding, as you are good to her. At the same time, dearest Ma, don't *please* go giving away your stuff so readily. I feel Benny is quite well off without 'extras', and indeed, the garnet brooch must have become quite valuable by now. (You say it is *only* a semi-precious stone, but these semi-precious stones in old settings are become very rare.) However, I am glad that Benny is recovering her good sense and does not continue to feel aggrieved. As I say, it would be hard to replace Benny in times like these, and to be accused to her face of 'borrowing' the brooch was no doubt, to Benny, a source of . . .

Freddy looked up. I mustn't appear to carp at her, he thought. On the other hand she looked in his letters for a certain amount of response to provocation. In a manner, it kept her going, to have a sort of unreal running bicker with him, serialised into his long weekly letters and her longer weekly replies.

The Arab odd-job boy finished his watering and silently returned to the house. Like that young Hardcastle, Freddy thought. Like Hardcastle, the gardener's boy of Freddy's youth, who had moved back and forth, remotely attending to things, unloquacious, unsmiling, totally unwilling to conspire in Freddy's games. 'Still waters run deep,' Freddy's mother had said, and true enough, young Hardcastle, when he attained the age of fifteen, had disappeared from the job, from the village, from his home, last seen by the bus driver who had borne him away never to be heard of again. Many young Arab boys in Palestine reminded Freddy of Hardcastle. They slightly disturbed him. He preferred the vivacious type in the alley bazaars, arguing, cheating, flashing Arabic codewords at each other in the presence of a stranger, or shouting cheerful abuse at their fellow-youngsters who led the mangy over-laden donkeys up the narrow pathways of Jordan's Jerusalem continually.

Freddy saw the morose boy approach once more from the house. Freddy, in his shaded arbour, wished to break the silence, if only to make concrete his mournful sense of its being ultimately unbreakable. But his Arabic lessons had not progressed so far as to enable him to say, as he desired to do, 'You fellows are lucky being able to stand the sun direct on your skin in the heat of the afternoon. We English have to keep in the shade.' Freddy looked down at the letter and thought he must work round to write something on the question of the Arabic lessons he was taking from Abdul Ramdez, since his mother had replied to his first mere mention of the lessons: 'I hope you are not getting too thick with that Arab teacher. When your Uncle Hamish was stationed in Egypt, *his* Arab teacher was quite scandalous.' Yes, and so was Uncle Hamish.

The odd-job boy had moved the lawn-spray to another part of the lawn, and had returned to the house. Freddy listened for voices; Joanna had evidently not returned, for he heard none.

Usually, on his weekend visits to the Cartwrights, Freddy left his office on the Israeli side of Jerusalem early on Friday afternoon, plodding through the Mandelbaum Gate with his diplomatic pass in one hand and his zipper-bag in the other, always blinking in the glare, since he hated wearing sun-glasses, which made one look so much like a rotten gigolo or spy. He came in the heat of the afternoon so as to reach the cool bungalow sooner. Both Cartwrights were usually out till five, busy with their work. But Freddy would make himself at home. Lemon tea, then a seat in the arbour, writing letters.

'Dearest Ma . . .' Freddy stared at the bungalow to gain thought. It was a slightly crooked house. He had heard that the Arab builders simply built a house, they did not use any instruments, not even a set-square. The walls and windows were slightly crooked. But the bungalow had a decidedly English appearance, probably due to the chintz curtains flapping in the breeze, and to the garden that seemed to support it. Joanna's geraniums were marvellous, massed by the back porch. And the lawn really was green. Most of all did he feel at home with the wild-flower clumps. He had, in fact, contributed a few plant roots from the Israeli side of the border, some of which had flourished. Joanna's labels bore witness to Freddy's contributions from the Israeli side: Mount Zion, Galilee, Nazareth, Mount Tabor . . . Bulbous Buttercup, Speedwell, Yellow Cow-wheat, Hound's Tongue. Freddy supposed he was wrong, he knew little about wild flowers, really, but he had a theory that these plants that he had pulled from the soil for Joanna, and those she had gathered for herself, were not indigenous at all. Their seeds had been brought to Palestine and sown, he suspected, by a conspiracy of the English Spinster under the Mandate. A second cousin of his had done the same service for India, where she had returned after every home leave with a shoe-box full of wild flowers gone to seed. This virgin cousin had expressed the sentiment that when she scattered these flowers abroad in the fields and sidewalks of India, she was doing something to unite East and West. Her father had shouted her down, in his fierce manner, denouncing the practice. 'Never the twain shall meet –' he reminded her, as if the words were Holy Writ. The old brigadier had gone on to tell Cousin Beryl that she was only making a lot of damn difficulties for the botanists; he added – irrelevantly as it had seemed at the time – that he himself had once forbidden an Indian servant to marry a girl from Bhutan, because it would only lead to a damn muddle in the offspring. But every third summer, Cousin Beryl, dressed always in loose, white shantung garments, packed her seed box and bore it away to Lahore. So it must have been, thought Freddy, with the spinster ladies of General Allenby's time out here. He had not yet propounded his theory to Joanna. She would be sceptically interested in it. He was waiting for a moment when it was absolutely necessary for him to say something interesting.

To arrive here, a mile from the outskirts of Jerusalem on the Jordan side, Freddy had jostled his way from the guardhouse at the Mandelbaum Gate, through the Old City's network of alleys, past the Damascus Gate. It had been too hot to take a crowded bus, and not for one moment was he tempted by a taxi. Sometimes Joanna could manage to meet him with her car, but Freddy was just as well pleased when she couldn't. Past the Damascus Gate, towards the Holy Sepulchre and down to the Via Dolorosa, plodded Freddy, dodging the loaded donkeys and stick-wielding boys, who in turn were constantly dodging the vast wide motor-cars that hooted with rage and frustration down the lanes; these cars were filled with hooded Arabs of substance and their emancipated wives. Freddy and numerous tourists had to flatten themselves hastily against a wall or a tangy-breathed donkey whenever the fanfare of a motor horn heralded one of these feudal-minded carloads. At the Via Dolorosa he ran into the huge Friday pilgrimage headed by the praying Franciscans, who moved from station to station, on the route from the Pillar of the Flagellation to Calvary. Freddy, with a number of the English Colony, had followed a much larger procession than this, last Easter, along the Way of the Cross; he had found it religiously moving, but it had exhausted his capacity for any further experience of the sort.

This Friday he dodged down a side-turning into the shop of an Arab dealer called Alexandros, whom he knew, to wait there till the procession had passed. Alexandros had been conducting a business courtship with Freddy for the past five months over an icon that Freddy had his eye on. The dealer was an Orthodox-Catholic from the Lebanon. Most of the Moslem Arab shops were shut on Fridays, and Alexandros therefore did some extra trade on that day of the week. He was serving a tourist, an Englishwoman, when Freddy arrived, but he immediately sent a young assistant out to fetch Freddy some Turkish coffee. Freddy relaxed in the large cool shop and, as he waited for the deal to be done and the coffee to arrive, he thought of the hours to come, on the shady bench in Joanna's garden, getting his letter off – Yes, you are right . . . no, I think you wrong . . . anything you like, dearest Ma . . . and felt this hot effort to reach the house was worth it by virtue of the cool contrast ahead of him.

Alexandros, whose wares were superior to those of most of the other traders in the area, was attempting to persuade the customer of this fact. She seemed rather stupid and sceptical, as Alexandros implored her credence, using his arms to do so, a little more in the French merchant manner than the Arab. Freddy's feelings expanded towards the salesman and contracted against the woman. Heavy Alexandros, dark, middle-aged, went on to explain that the little wooden crib-figures, for which he was asking five pounds the set, were by no means comparable to the mass-produced figures obtainable from the surrounding shops, on all days but Fridays, for a pound the set or eighteen shillings after the argument. Freddy, newly relaxed after the glare, smells and sticky heat of his plod from the border station, was prompted by a nervous reflex to intervene in the argument, and, much as the timid spinsters of the old days, while abroad, would be moved to violence against the maltreater of the donkey, Freddy now stood up. 'Madam,' he said, to his own astonishment, 'I can vouch for the fact that those articles are what Mr Alexandros says they are, that is to say, hand-carved from pinewood. This shop, as he says, stocks only superior curios.' He sat down again. His Turkish coffee arrived and was placed before him.

The woman looked at Freddy in a reserved way; she could see that he was at home in the shop. Freddy realised she was more suspicious than ever. His irritation by her doubts of his Alexandros was increased by the fact that this fat Englishwoman was only a passing tourist and he was more or less a resident; and there had been nothing more annoying to Freddy throughout all his postings in the Foreign Service than the sight of his compatriots making mistakes while passing through.

Alexandros, delighted by Freddy's remark, was saying in a triumphant wail, 'You hear what this gentleman tells you, Madam. This gentleman is Mr Hamilton, a very high officer of the British Government. He is my customer. He comes to Alexandros regular.'

Freddy murmured, 'Perhaps the lady really wishes to think it over, Alexandros.'

The woman indicated, by picking up her gloves, that she was about to take advantage of this offer. But Alexandros spread out his hands and said, 'Madam, this crib – look at the three Kings, how beautiful, and the camels, they are alive, and Saint Joseph here. The workmanship. You have it for the sake of your family, Madam. They will say, in the next generation, "This was when the Mama went to the Holy Land! She bought this set for the Epiphany crib!"'

The woman seemed to waver at this. Then she said, 'I'll think it over and let you know in the morning.'

'It is the last. It will go by morning. When the procession is finished the people come in to Alexandros. Alexandros does not close his shop on a Friday, like the Moslems.'

'I'll ask my travel agent here. He advises me what to buy and where to go. Thank you.'

Alexandros followed her to the door. 'Who is the travel agent?'

'Ramdez. I'll ask him.'

Alexandros let her go, then. He came and sat beside Freddy. 'We can have a talk now.' He seemed to have forgotten the woman. Freddy said, 'I mustn't stop. I've got some correspondence to attend to when I get to the Cartwrights'. I expect your customer will come back for that crib-set. It's handsome.'

'Not if she follows advice from Ramdez. Travel agent, yes, he is agent for all the curio-shops, he gets his share from them all. But he is not agent for Alexandros.'

'I know Ramdez,' Freddy said. 'And I know his son Abdul over in Israel, he's teaching me Arabic.'

'The son is political for his living,' said Alexandros quietly.

'Oh, really? I thought young Abdul represented a life-insurance company.'

'Yes, like the father. The father is agent for everything.'

'Ramdez wants me to take out a policy. At least that's what they say that they're after me for.'

'Which Ramdez? The father or the son?'

'Well, both together, actually. They manage to communicate, I don't know how. Anyway, whenever I come over here, old Ramdez turns up with news of Abdul. And when I get back there, Abdul turns up with the latest information from his father. I understand they don't get on very well together.'

Alexandros laughed with Freddy. He took a bunch of keys from his pocket and opened a drawer, from which he took another key. With this he opened a glass cabinet and brought out the icon picture that Freddy admired. Alexandros smiled fondly at the flat, impassive Madonna and Child done in blue and faded gold. Neither man was quite sure of its date. They hoped it was twelfth-century. Freddy was consulting experts and generally looking into the subject in the meantime. 'It isn't normally the sort of thing I go in for,' he said, as he always did. Alexandros replied, 'It is early, not late, this icon.'

'Yes, it's early, but the tradition varies so little, it's difficult even for the experts to judge how early.'

'I see an expert soon,' said Alexandros. 'He is coming from Italy. Next month.'

'It appeals to me in any event,' said Freddy.

'It is yours. I keep it for you.' The dealer put it back in the glass case and locked the door.

'I can't afford it,' Freddy said.

'It's not a question of what you can afford. It is a question that you take home something from the Holy Land that is worth taking home.' Alexandros started packing the crib-figures into a small box padded with cotton wool. 'I am taking these to the lady at her hotel. I see her this evening.'

'Why bother to go after her, Alexandros, for goodness' sake?' Freddy said. 'It's only a fiver.' Alexandros was a sub-stantial dealer.

'I make a sale,' Alexandros said.

Freddy lifted his zipper-bag. 'I'll look in sometime tomorrow, perhaps.'

'I make a sale to the lady,' Alexandros said, and anxious to explain himself more clearly, he added, 'Why do you walk all the way from the Mandelbaum Gate to the Bungalow Cartwright? – Mr Hamilton, a Chevrolet with driver is ten shillings only for this journey.'

'I never take taxis and I never hire cars,' Freddy stated, 'not if I can help it. My father never did.'

'So I never let slip a tourist customer. So I go to the hotel after dinner and bargain with the lady and she gets the fine crib-set for four-fifteen, four-ten. It is my upbringing.'

'How do you know her hotel?' Freddy said.

Alexandros thought this question too amusing to need an answer. He said goodbye to Freddy in the French of the Lebanon, and Freddy responded, in his French of the Home Counties, to the effect that he, also, had been very greatly enchanted.

The hot walk from the Gate was well worth it, Freddy thought, if only because of the relief one felt when one

66

turned in the familiar doorway of the bungalow. On the last lap of his walk, uphill, he was tempted to start composing a set of verses to send on his return to Israel, thanking Joanna for the weekend which had not yet come to pass. A villanelle perhaps . . . It is so very different here / In modern Israel from your / Delightful English atmosphere . . . Freddy realised he was cheating. The bread–and–butter verses could not in honesty be started until he had actually set foot on the other side of the Mandelbaum Gate on Sunday afternoon. He put temptation behind him and plodded up the hill to the weekend before him.

The bungalow was set in a clump of trees not far from a steeper hill that led to a tumbledown Orthodox church and the Potter's Field, where, some way off, lived a marvellously feeble old monk, much liked by Freddy, and whose eyes alone seemed to keep his brittle limbs alive in one body, so spiritually did they burn in his skull. Freddy caught sight of the monk's blue robe moving up there among the shrubbery as the old man came out to feed his chickens; whereupon Freddy had felt at home already, and had plodded the few steps onward to the silent bungalow, the garden bench awaiting him beside Joanna's wild-flower arrangement, and the letter-pad on his knee. 'Dearest Ma . . .'

You see, dearest Ma, the trouble is . . .

The trouble, in fact, was . . . Freddy's thoughts dropped to a whisper in his brain. JERICHO, MOUNT OF OLIVES, GETHSEMANE. Hair Tare, Tufted Vetch, Hawk-bit, Corn Bluebottle. The trouble, in fact, was . . . Freddy's thoughts whispered on, refusing to be shouted down by any other voice that might arise in his brain to hush them up. The trouble was that Ma was a peculiar type of tyrant-liar whose lies could only with difficulty be denounced because of her long-sustained tyranny, and whose tyranny could hardly now be overthrown because of her long-condoned lies. It was not only these days in her old age, but by very constitution, that Ma was like this. Consequently, it had taken most of their lifetime for her four children to realise that they were part of an unspoken conspiracy to concede that Ma's falsehoods were truth. It was curious how, to this day, none of her children – although Freddy's three sisters were married women – had it in them to look any of the others in the eye and suggest that dearest Ma was not really a very nice person, let alone to aver that she had cheated them all quite openly, as if by divine right, of various inheritances, denouncing the two sons-in-law as her enemies merely on the basis of their rational questioning.

Freddy pondered his letter, with its hypocritical advice. 'At the same time, dearest Ma, don't *please* go giving away your stuff so readily . . .' It was the best Freddy could do, at this late stage in his career as Ma's son. Knowing Ma, it was doubtful whether the garnet brooch belonged to Ma in the first place. It had probably been coaxed from some other, more feeble, resident in the hotel, or even stolen from Benny, and then handed over, or handed back, at some point, to Benny. At all events, it would be a confusing affair, that being Ma's way of operating. The whole idea, anyway, was that Benny should be accused of something . . . SILOAM, JERICHO, Clary or Wild Sage. The young Arab boy had been in the garden again, and had now slipped like a lantern-slide into the house, leaving the picture as before. Ma was seventy-nine, of course, one should make allowances for that. Nonsense, Ma had always done this sort of thing. Benny would be nearly seventy, now. Poor Benny. Poor Benny, she, too, was far involved in the family secret. It was like a blood-pact. She had started to respond to Ma's moral blackmail long years ago when she was Freddy's nurse, and now Benny, a religious crackpot at the best of times, fully accepted that she was always suspect, always liable to crafty dealings, invariably in the wrong. Freddy thought, for a wistful moment, that he might in normal circumstances write to one of his elder sisters, Elsie: 'Do see what new trick Ma's up to. Apparently, she's bullying Benny about a brooch.' That is alliterative, noted Freddy, in his panic to note something. Because it was impossible to write to his sister as if circumstances were normal. She would only reply: 'Whatever do you mean by your reference to dearest Ma's new trick? Benny has been very irritable lately, I believe. She has too little to occupy her time, and dearest Ma can't be expected to . . .' They were all in it together, and it was too late. He bent over his letter, to fill in a harmless page about the housing situation in Israel.

You see, dearest Ma, the trouble is . . .

The trouble was, she should have been an actress, as she had wanted to be in her youth. She might have worked off her self-dramatising energies in that way.

The trouble is, that the Israelis have not nearly enough houses for their own people, let alone for foreigners. The days of grand mansions are over, and the Consulates and Embassies all over the world, I'm afraid, are . . .

Joanna and Matt Cartwright had arrived, their voices came from the house, mingled with other voices and many footsteps. Joanna came out, waving to Freddy. She was a vitamin capsule to Freddy, who carried small red vitamin capsules about with him to swallow after meals taken outside the British Isles. The sight of little Joanna shooting across the lawn in her red linen dress raised Freddy's spirits. Matt was still a dark shape in the shadow of the doorway, beyond the porch. He emerged, another comforting sight. Matt was a large man, without being tall; he was perpetually untidy, with a lot of grey hair. He was bringing some other people out to the garden whom Freddy did not see at first, since he had risen to greet Joanna and was kissing her. She said, 'We've brought a friend of yours in for a drink,' and she added, casting up helpless eyes and mouthing her words silently, 'and – we – had to – bring – his – awful – wife – and – daughters – as – well.' And here they were, already coming up. As Joanna turned to them brightly, Freddy recognized the elder blue-eyed Ramdez, who was accompanied by a dumpy middle-aged woman and two girls, one plump and one thin, all in European clothes. Matt Cartwright went to help with the setting out of garden chairs. A servant moved the tables to their cool corner. Freddy moved his letter-pad from the bench and the thin girl settled there beside him. Joanna was amiably introducing everybody.

Freddy, his letter-pad useless in his hand, sat suffering indistinctly. His heart, that had lifted at the sight of Joanna, had become suddenly heavy at the sight of old Ramdez thumping after her with his women. He experienced the sensation of one who has had a disturbing dream, the culmination of which was the ringing of a telephone, and wakes with relief to discover the telephone is in fact ringing beside his bed, and answers it, only to hear disturbing news. For old Ramdez, the wealthy Arab whom everyone called 'the Agent', since his business interests covered a travel agency, a life-insurance agency, a detective agency (and no doubt he was a political agent, too) – old Joe Ramdez had already impressed himself on Freddy as a terrifying liar.

*

70

Freddy had first encountered him because of the son, young Abdul, over in Israel, who came to teach him Arabic and every time remained to press him to take out a life-insurance policy. This policy, which was now some months pending, was a subject of conflict within Freddy. The Middle East Visitors' Union Life Trust was the name of the company represented by young Abdul Ramdez in Israel and by old Joe Ramdez on the Jordan side. Freddy was in very serious doubt about the standing, the existence even, of this insurance company, a policy in which, according to Abdul, would lead to the payment of five thousand pounds on Freddy's death.

'But I haven't got anyone to leave five thousand pounds to,' Freddy had said. 'I haven't got a wife.'

'You got children?'

'No.'

'You got nephews or a nice lady? You got a friend, you definitely got a friend.'

'I can't think of any relative or friend of mine,' Freddy said, 'who isn't far richer than me.'

This was precisely the truth. But he liked young Ramdez, the eager boy, and was good-humoured. This had been early in the spring, shortly after Freddy's posting to Israel.

Young Abdul said, 'You go to see my father, Joe Ramdez, when you go across to Jordan. My father's the leader of the Middle East Visitors' Union Life Trust agency in Palestine. I work for him. This is a confidence to you alone.'

'You'll get yourself into trouble,' Freddy said. Business connections between Israel and Jordan were illegal in both countries.

'I will now explain to you the endowment scheme for the Visitors' Union that will bring you a lump sum at the age of

sixty-five and you save your British income-tax with the pre-
miums that you pay each month. It is a scheme for
Englishmen. You must first join the Visitors' Union itself
which my father has formed of his own idea. You see him in
Jordan, he will explain. We work together.'

'He'll land in trouble with his government for dealing
with an Israeli Arab, even his own son. There was a case of a
melon dealer the other day –'

'My father's never in trouble with the government. He's a
friend always to the government. You see Joe Ramdez.'

Freddy had folded away his Arabic lesson-books. 'Be careful,' he said to the blue-eyed, dark young man. 'You won't be
able to carry on this insurance business for long without the
Israelis finding out.'

'There's nothing for them to find out, Mr Hamilton. I
keep all the names and records in my head. My father keeps
the documents, like what you will sign.'

This had been early in April. Presently, the name of Joe
Ramdez had cropped up in Freddy's office. He was apparently the owner of a travel and tourist agency in Jordan. 'God
knows what he's up to,' Freddy's colleague said, 'not that it
concerns us much.'

'I'll have a look at him,' Freddy said. 'One likes to know
who's who.' He filed a confidential report about the insurance business carried on between young Abdul and his
father. He reflected wearily on the difficulty of making any
real friends among the inhabitants of countries where one
was posted. He had only taken three lessons in Arabic from
young Abdul at that time. Freddy decided to discontinue the
lessons with Abdul. He made up his mind to appoint a new
teacher. A pity, because Abdul was a pleasant fellow in his
eager recklessness. Freddy had felt he could understand
Abdul. But after all one could never understand these

people. This young man was involved in too many things for Freddy's liking.

'Arabic's a terrible bore,' Freddy said to his colleague.

'Frightful. I don't see the point in learning it, really. At least, not unless one is going to stay here for ever.'

'Young Ramdez is all right,' Freddy said, 'but he seems to be involved in too many things for my liking. Life insurance. Terribly persistent about a policy. I'm getting another teacher.' As he spoke, Freddy felt greatly relieved to have arrived at this decision, he even felt a satisfactory sense of having accomplished the object of it.

And so it was not necessary, after that, actually to get rid of Abdul Ramdez by discontinuing the lessons in Arabic. And, after all, Abdul continued to call at the hotel three times a week to instruct Freddy, who had progressed sufficiently to be able to exchange formal phrases with Arab officials at official gatherings, but not as yet advanced enough to make much headway with the Arabs in the Arab quarters. Young Abdul spent one hour on each of the lessons, and lingered, usually, another hour to depict himself and his early life in romantically exaggerated scenes which delighted Freddy but did not altogether deceive him. Abdul had also boringly continued to press Freddy on the question of the insurance policy, each time exaggerating the mild interest Freddy had expressed on the previous occasion.

'As you have said you have definitely decided –'

'No, no, I haven't decided anything. I only said . . .'

It seemed that the tendency to exaggerate ran in the family. But what one could take from an attractive young fellow like Abdul in Israel was a different matter when it came to the preposterous Joe Ramdez over here in Jordan. Freddy had sat in Joanna's garden, appalled and altogether beset by an inarticulate dread while Ramdez approached, followed by his womenfolk.

'It's a question of sincerity,' Joanna said in her quick, chattery voice, as she passed the tea-cups. She was interrupting her husband to assist him in making the point of his story. Matt Cartwright, accustomed to these interruptions, went on in his slow way to describe a qualm occasioned by his having newly got false teeth. He was explaining in detail that, when a spontaneous smile occurred on his face in response to his usual feelings, something now happened in his mouth to prevent the smile taking the same form as it used to do.

'They don't fit yet,' Joanna said. 'He's got to be patient with them, till they settle down.'

Matt went on in his slow way. This story was to be their standby for some months to come. He said, 'Then, when I find myself giving a slightly different sort of smile, d'you see, so help me God, I find myself feeling a slightly different sort of emotion. I feel a bit false.'

'He feels a bit false,' Joanna chattered, 'and it makes you wonder what sincerity is. I mean to say it's a question whether the movements of one's facial muscles are adapted to one's feelings or the feelings to – Mrs Ramdez, don't you have anything in your tomato juice?'

Matt fell silent. Joe Ramdez beamed at Freddy, uninhibited by any relation between his feelings and his facial expression. The Arab family all declined alcoholic drinks. The younger daughter had a haunted look. The elder girl was, like the mother, fat and stupid-looking, but the younger daughter was like her brother Abdul, lean and blue-eyed, and she looked haunted. There is a history, Freddy thought, behind that blue-eyed young pair.

Freddy had seen the mother and girls before. They worked

74

in the travel agency. Joe Ramdez had introduced them as 'my little team'.

Joe Ramdez now said to Freddy, 'It's better to smile without the heart behind it than not to smile at all.'

'Oh, he won't agree with that – not Freddy,' said Joanna, while Freddy realised he was looking as depressed as he felt.

'Have my wild flowers been watered this afternoon?' Joanna said. 'Freddy, did you see them being watered at all?'

'I did,' Freddy said, as if it was a duty he had performed; he longed for that earlier departed hour in the afternoon before this crowd had appeared.

He said, 'I always feel this garden has such a delightful English atmosphere.'

The younger girl looked apprehensive. The father smiled with a curious histrionic glitter of the eye, by which many modern Arabs intended to express proud loathing; they had got the trick from the cinema, over the years. At any rate, Freddy realised he had said the wrong thing.

Not that Joe Ramdez really cared one way or another. Freddy was aware, however, that Joe had taken the opportunity of umbrage to put him in the wrong. Freddy said, 'I only mean, of course, that these wild flowers of Joanna's are nothing more or less than English wild flowers, planted in the countryside by silly women during the Mandate.'

'Freddy!' said Joanna.

'Early tomorrow morning,' said the wounded Arab, 'I'm taking my little team on a trip to Amman. It's our only chance before the tourist season, of really getting into our delightful Jordanian atmosphere.'

The younger girl looked desperately at Freddy. Evidently she was longing to behave in a Westernised mode to suit her clothes, and, no doubt, her feelings. There was no guessing the variety of feelings amongst the very young in these parts.

'So we must go now,' said Joe. His little team got up with him. He said to Freddy, 'By the way, I've got to send you a medical form and proposal form. A boy will bring it. I know the doctor whom you can go to. He's good for deferred endowments even when appearance is unhealthy. I had a client last week that went to Dr Russeifa with his form. Appearance was older than age given. There was impairment of sight and hearing. Pupillary and patellar reflexes were abnormal. Plenty of abdominal varicosities – well, Dr Russeifa has told me all this trouble, but he fixed the client's medical. Russeifa will make you all right. I'll make the arrangement.'

When they had gone, Joanna said to her husband, 'Did you hear what he said about Russeifa? I don't believe a word of it. Russeifa's one of the most conscientious men in the medical team.' They were both deep in local welfare work and were in a position to know what they were talking about.

'Ramdez is a liar,' Freddy said, 'the biggest I've ever met. Like an alcoholic. He lies as he breathes.'

'Well, Freddy . . .' said Joanna. She was relaxing on the bench with her drink, relieved at the departure of the Ramdez guests, and now she seemed uncertain how to chatter on, since it was unusual for Freddy to denounce anyone like this.

'They think in symbols,' Matt said.

'That's it,' said Joanna. 'It's the Arab mentality. They think in symbols. Everything stands for something else. And when they speak in symbols it sounds like lies.'

'It is lies,' said Freddy.

'Oh, Freddy, come! Why are you taking out this insurance policy with Ramdez, dear? It's asking for trouble.'

'I'm not taking out any policy,' Freddy said. 'His son, who teaches me Arabic over in Israel, has been trying to talk me into it. But I've made no definite decision.'

'You should have said definitely no,' Matt said. 'If you don't say no, they take it you mean yes. That's symbolic thought.'

'Not to me,' Freddy said.

'Is young Ramdez a nice fellow?' Joanna said.

'A remarkably pleasant young man.'

'Freddy, you mustn't let him get round you for any insurance policy out here.'

'I don't think they're really interested in insurance, anyway,' Freddy said.

'Nor do I,' said Matt.

'Nor do I,' said Joanna.

'They're interested in you, Freddy,' Matt said.

'You're a symbol, Freddy.'

'Yes, but of what?'

'Something useful in the Foreign Service –'

'God help me,' Freddy said, 'I thought that's what I really am.'

'What did you mean by saying that my wild flowers of the Holy Land are English flowers?'

Freddy felt the moment was not ripe to explain his theory to Joanna. Indeed, it might undermine her at this tired moment, which was the last thing . . . He said instead, 'Miss Vaughan, the schoolteacher lady, is very pleased with the geraniums you sent, very touched, you know. I believe she's coming over next week. As I say, she's a bit tense, but you'll do her good, Joanna dear.'

'Oh, do you know,' Joanna said. 'I was talking to Joe Ramdez about Miss Vaughan. He's promised to send one of his drivers to the Gate to pick her up. Isn't it nice of him?

Now really, you must admit that's good of him. If one of the Ramdez men is there to meet her she won't have any trouble with the officials.'

'Is he doing it for free?' Matt said.

'Oh yes, and he'll lay on a guide and everything to take her round.'

'He must have a reason,' Matt said.

'We are the reason,' Joanna said.

She was darting between her husband's chair and Freddy's seat on the bench, in her red dress, collecting their empty glasses and handing them back filled with good strong drinks. 'Joe Ramdez,' she said, 'would do anything for us.'

'You didn't,' said Matt, 'tell Ramdez that this woman had Jewish blood?'

'Of course not,' Joanna said. 'I only told him there might be trouble with her visa, seeing that it's unusual for Christian pilgrims to go to the Israel side first.'

'They mustn't know anything about her Jewish blood,' Matt said. 'She'd be in trouble. We'd all be in trouble. The government here is looking for a bit of trouble with the Jews at the moment.'

'She's only half,' Freddy said.

'Half is enough,' Matt said. 'They think in symbols over here. The Jewish half is the symbolic half.'

'Which half is the most important to her?' Joanna said.

'Don't ask me. Miss Vaughan's only a recent acquaintance, you know. Very pleasant woman, of course. And with a British passport. After all, she –'

'Most of the people arrested as Israeli spies have got British passports,' Matt said. 'She'd be taken for an Israeli spy if they knew of any Jewish blood or background and arrived here by way of Israel. Does she realise that?'

'I really don't know,' Freddy said. 'Is that true? It sounds quite absurd.'

Joanna, in her inexhaustible enthusiasm for seeing to the welfare of others, said, 'Freddy, you aren't taking Miss Vaughan's difficulty seriously enough.'

'I don't see what can be done, Joanna dear,' said Freddy, so deeply conscious of his fault that he leant forward and rested his chin on his hand to try and be serious about Miss Vaughan's difficulty. 'She's a devout R.C. and she naturally wants to visit all the shrines of the Holy Land. There's really no difficulty.'

'What about the man?' Matt said.

'Yes, what about the man?' Joanna said.

Matt said, 'I take it that's the whole point of her coming here.'

'Oh no, she wants to visit the holy places.'

'I'll take her up to the Potter's Field,' Joanna said. 'The guides won't go near the Potter's Field, they're terrified.'

'You keep away from the Potter's Field,' Matt said.

'I shouldn't go there too often, Joanna,' Freddy said. The hill road to the Potter's Field bordered on disputed territory, and wanderers in the area were likely to be shot at by the patrolmen of either country.

Matt said, 'This man that's digging at the Dead Sea – why doesn't he come up and look after her? He should go across to Israel and see her, instead of her coming here to see him.'

'The scholars aren't allowed to go back and forth. The Jordanian government won't allow it,' Freddy said. 'Of course, the Israeli scholars get to know everything in time.'

'He could leave Jordan by air and enter Israel by sea. He could easily get there if he wanted to,' Matt said.

'Well, she wants to come here for religious reasons.'

'Let her come,' Joanna said.

Then Freddy, dismayed by a disastrous thought that had occurred to him, but proud since it proved he was taking Miss Vaughan's difficulty seriously, said, 'But look, young Ramdez over in Israel probably knows about her Jewish blood.'

'Are you sure?' Joanna said.

'Well, she's been talking about it. Young Ramdez hears everything about everyone,' Freddy said. 'It's part of his business.'

'If young Ramdez knows, then old Ramdez will know,' Matt said. 'And what he knows the government gets to know. Tell her not to come.'

They moved indoors since it had fallen dark. At dinner, Joanna said to Freddy, 'You could make difficulties in Israel for young Ramdez, couldn't you, if he made difficulties for your Miss Vaughan?'

'Joanna!' said Matt.

'Well, I was only thinking in symbols. What would the Israelis do to him, Freddy, if they knew he spied for the Jordanians? Shoot him? Put him in prison?'

'Mislead him,' Freddy said.

'You could threaten him,' Joanna said.

'Joanna!' said Matt.

'I'm thinking in symbols. I'm thinking of Freddy's poor Miss Vaughan.'

'She isn't really, you know, *my* Miss Vaughan,' Freddy said. 'She's only –'

'Now Freddy, you know you're involved whether you like it or –'

'Joanna!' said Matt. 'Stop teasing Freddy.'

'A very intense person,' Freddy said.

'Who? Me or Miss –?'

'*Joanna!*'

. . . at my friends the Cartwrights'. Then after dinner this evening we had some amusement from Joanna Cartwright's puppet theatre. (Do you recall, dearest Ma, that house in Lewes we used to visit, where they had some very grand puppets? – Joanna's puppets are not quite so grand.) She is extremely agile at managing their movements. There is also an extraordinary series of gramophone records which, by clever tuning, accompany the puppets' movements perfectly. They seem to speak.

By the way, earlier in the evening we were discussing Miss Vaughan about whom I have already told you – she is staying at my hotel. She may be coming over to Jordan, but much depends on whether we can assist her to resolve some difficulties that have arisen over her entry into the country. I think this will interest you, dearest Ma, since you enquire in your letter about 'a teacher at Miss Rickward's school in Gloucestershire, very near Elsie's'. – Yes, that is Miss Vaughan! – Remember you asked me this question before. Benny will remember, I'm sure. I am glad to hear Elsie brought Miss Rickward to see you. She is decidedly the same Miss Rickward who is a close friend of Miss Vaughan out here. You were right in assuming that Miss Vaughan's fiancé is an archaeologist who is working at present in the Dead Sea area where the Scrolls were discovered. Apparently there is some hitch about the proposed marriage, since he is divorced and she is R.C. Of course, it is quite absurd, in my opinion, when a couple of grown-up people . . .

Freddy had filled most of the pages he had to fill, and it was time for bed.

At eleven o'clock on Saturday morning Freddy took Joanna and Matt to Alexandros's shop to show them the icon.

Joanna, sitting at the back of the car with quantities of shopping, waved to everyone whom she recognised, including Joe Ramdez, who stood in the street outside his business premises, wearing a red fez, talking to another Arab.

'He hasn't set off for Amman yet,' Freddy said.

'They're going to Amman in the symbolic sense,' said Matt.

'He's waiting to pounce on Miss Vaughan,' Joanna said, for the subject of Miss Vaughan and her difficulties had by now taken a fantastic turn among them, from so much talking it over. First thing in the morning Joanna had declared she had thought about Miss Vaughan far into the night. She regretted talking to Ramdez about Miss Vaughan's impending visit. But she was used to dealing with other people's predicaments, even when she had helped to induce them, and in fact could not easily adapt herself to the idea that anyone outside her immediate acquaintance had no problems to be sorted out. Her imagination clung to the intricate danger attached to Miss Vaughan's story, and she had managed, in the course of the morning, by batting the shuttlecock of Miss Vaughan's name back and forth between herself and the two men, to infect even them with a kind of irrational excitement over the ways and means by which Miss Vaughan could be trapped by her Jewish blood, could be arrested as an Israeli spy far beyond the assistance of the British Foreign Office, on her arrival in Jordan.

Freddy had begun to feel a little frightened. He certainly did not want to be involved in an international incident And for Miss Vaughan's own sake, he really must, he had decided, somehow prevent her from visiting Jordan. He had a strange difficulty now, in remembering what she looked like; he had in his mind only the outline of a frail, sharp, nervy, dark woman, fearfully indiscreet.

Matt himself said to Freddy, as they drove into the Old City, 'Can't you do something at the office to prevent her from coming over – take away her passport, or something?'

'Oh, no,' Freddy said. 'Anyway, she's nothing to do with us.' He did not like the sound of his words as they were the sort of words that always, to the outsider, suggested Pontius Pilate washing his hands of a potential source of embarrassment; none the less, Freddy felt sympathy for Pontius Pilate, a government officer, and for all those subordinates of Pilate who, like himself, no doubt, had been officially dim, dutiful, and absolutely against intervention between individuals and their doom. Freddy said, 'If she gets into trouble we can make a protest afterwards.' His reflections had been unusual in the form they had taken, and he felt they were quite absurd; it was only because Matt had now parked the car and they were emerging from it to face the narrow Via Dolorosa within sight of the Ecce Homo Arch, the place from where, by erroneous tradition, Pontius Pilate had addressed the crowd. The real Judgement Palace of Pilate had newly been excavated, and was some yards distant from the Via Dolorosa, and some feet deeper. Miss Vaughan herself, of course, was the sort of person who somehow induced one to think in terms of religion if one thought about her at all.

Most of the way to Alexandros's shop Joanna kept referring with genuine concern to Miss Vaughan's predicament, hushing her voice considerably in due acknowledgement that any mention of Jewish blood was inflammatory in these parts. The Arabs generally, when they were obliged to talk about Jews, did not permit themselves to utter the word Jew; instead, they quaintly spoke of 'ex-Jews' and of Israel as 'Israel, so-called'.

Matt said, 'It could happen by accident,' in reply to

Joanna's inquiry as to what means of execution was used against Israeli spies.

'It could happen by accident.' Freddy believed the liquidation of spies and suspects had nearly always taken place, as it were, by accident, unless there was some political reason for holding a trial. And now Freddy was grateful for the company of his friends. Joanna's serious sense of Miss Vaughan's impending danger and Matt's urgent appeals to Freddy as to what should be done gave him a sense of being with responsible people, whose safe conduct he could rely on. For it had begun to gnaw at Freddy's mind that, for all he knew, Miss Vaughan might be an Israeli spy; he knew nothing of Miss Vaughan's identity but what she had told him. Of course, he could not mention this suspicion to the Cartwrights; he would have to make official inquiries first.

At Alexandros's shop, the first person Freddy saw was Barbara Vaughan. She said, 'Oh, hallo, Mr Hamilton.' He stared at her stupidly, as if at a complete stranger. Then, just as she began to look puzzled Freddy pulled himself together and said, 'Miss Vaughan! What are you doing here?'

'I'm looking at some stuff,' she said. The crib-figures, which Alexandros had evidently failed to sell to his customer of yesterday, were spread about on the glass top of a display cabinet. Alexandros said, 'This lady likes the crib. She knows it's good. Mr Hamilton, tell your friend to take this crib and not let it go.' And he said to Barbara Vaughan, 'It is for the family – they will say in the future, "This crib was when the Mama went to the Holy Land," and that is why you should take it.'

Barbara Vaughan laughed. Joanna had murmured to Freddy, 'Is that her?' and Freddy had nodded. He introduced Miss Vaughan to the Cartwrights. She looked plumper than the image he had held in his mind, and it was part of the unexpectedness of the encounter that he noticed she spoke in a natural tone pitch and moved without furtiveness or strain.

Freddy had recovered his senses so far as to remember what he had brought the Cartwrights here for. They, in their well-mannered way, gave no indication that Miss Vaughan had been the subject of their speculations all morning and most of the night before. Everyone looked at, and admired, the icon. Barbara Vaughan gave out, as a guess, that it was done in the early sixteenth century, not earlier, because the Madonna was not done full length. She thought it unlikely that any departure from the formal Byzantine mode, such as this half-figure depiction of the Madonna, would have occurred at an earlier date.

Plainly, the jeopardised Miss Vaughan they had been discussing was a different person from the Miss Vaughan who stood, pointing out, in an ordinary English way, her judgement of the date of a painting, and who then listened with untroubled interest while Alexandros debated the question, citing a few rare icons of an earlier date that had passed through his hands.

In the end, Miss Vaughan declined the crib, but bought an antique silver fish on a chain, which she put round her neck there and then. Joanna, who had immediately adapted herself to the real Miss Vaughan, expressed admiration. Matt also added some words of approval. Alexandros explained that the fish, to which three small curious coins were attached, was of Turkish origin. 'It's a Christian symbol,' said Miss Vaughan. 'That is correct,' Alexandros said, 'and the coins are Turkish charms, attached by the Turkish convert in case Christianity should not be true. He was fully covered, as they say in regard to policies for the insurance of life.'

They left the shop in a united wavelet of amusement, and Freddy said immediately to Miss Vaughan, 'When did you come?'

'Yesterday,' she said.

'How did you come?'

'Through the Mandelbaum Gate.'

'Any difficulty? Speak low.'

'No. I've got an extra passport, you know, that doesn't show the Israeli visa. And my baptismal certificate. A guard came and met me and said, "Welcome to Jordan!"'

'Did they ask any questions? Speak low.'

'Yes, they asked where I'd come from. It was awfully funny, because they could see perfectly well where I'd come from. But as long as you don't mention Israel, it's all right. The formal answer in my case is "From England", and that's what I said. Then they asked what I'd come for. I said, a pilgrimage to the Holy Land. They had a look at my passport and said, "Enjoy your visit." That was all.'

'Well, well,' said Freddy.

'Jolly good,' said Matt.

'Where are you staying?' Joanna said. They had started winding up the narrow crowded street, Joanna walking ahead with Barbara and the two men more or less behind them.

'The guest-house at St Helena's Convent. It's quite comfortable.'

'You'll be safe there,' Joanna said.

'Oh goodness, yes. I'm the safe type.'

Joanna laughed, and Matt, who had taken both women by the arm to guide them through the crowds, laughed too. The Cartwrights responded to any excuse for laughter. Freddy felt very relieved. The whole question of Miss Vaughan was suddenly normal, as if it had never been otherwise.

They took her home to lunch, treating her as rather more than a new acquaintance, not only because she was Freddy's friend, but because one always did, in foreign parts, become friendly with one's fellow-countrymen more quickly than one did at home.

They had coffee brought out into the garden after lunch. As swiftly as water finds its own level, they had already formed a small island of mutual Englishness; their intimacy had ripened under the alien sun to the extent that the two women were addressing each other by their first names; and when Joanna said to Barbara Vaughan, 'I expect you're looking forward to seeing your fiancé again?' it was possible for Barbara to reply in a confiding manner which, at home, ought to have taken some years to mature: 'Well, d'you know, I don't at all want to see him. I've been waiting and waiting to hear about an annulment verdict from Rome – for as a Catholic I can't marry him unless his previous marriage is anulled. Then I've been in a state of conflict for weeks, whether or not to come over to Jordan and see him. One way and another, my emotions are exhausted. I simply don't feel anything for him any more. In fact, I've gone off him.'

'It's perfectly understandable in the circumstances,' Joanna said in her practised way, 'that you should go numb. But it's only temporary. Your feelings will come back.'

Freddy found himself hoping not. This Miss Vaughan who claimed so emphatically to have gone off her fiancé was decidedly more agreeable and relaxed than the febrile Miss Vaughan in love.

'He's probably the wrong chap for you,' he said in an avuncular manner which came easily to him at that moment, seeing that Miss Vaughan had just declared herself unattached.

Matt, anxious to take some sort of possession too, said, 'Get him up to Jerusalem. Bring him along here. Maybe we can sort things out.'

Barbara smiled. 'But I've gone off him,' she said. She seemed to be amused at herself in a sophisticated way, and was pretty-looking as she leaned back in the garden chair, holding her coffee cup.

'Who is the fellow, anyway?' Freddy said. He knew the man's name, Harry Clegg, and also that he was a distinguished archaeologist.

Barbara said, 'Harry Clegg's his name. He's well known in archaeology.'

'I've heard of Clegg,' Matt said.

'Yes, but who are the Cleggs?' Freddy said. 'That's all I mean.'

Joanna said, 'Freddy, if you're trying to undermine him with Barbara, she'll get her feelings back, and go and marry him tomorrow. That's what I'd do.'

Freddy said apologetically to Barbara, 'I only wondered if you knew anything much about his family.'

'Well, he doesn't seem to know much, himself, about the family,' Barbara said, 'and he doesn't care. He can't even trace his birth certificate. Really, he's a charming person; it's only that I don't feel –'

'Good God!' Freddy said. 'You should be careful who you take up with.'

An Arab servant had appeared with a fresh pot of coffee, and they kept silence until he had receded like a wave of the sea that had lapped against the garden wall. Barbara got up, meanwhile, to examine the labels on Joanna's wild flowers of the Holy Land, and to deflect attention from herself, as the social moment offered and required.

'*Cotyledon*,' Barbara murmured, examining a plant which grew about ten inches high. It was not in flower, but it had, near its base, a group of curious circular leaves, sunk in their centres, like flowers themselves. Freddy had frequently tried to place this plant from memory, for he had seen it before. It stood in the clump marked Bethlehem. 'I got it on a hillside near the Shepherds' Field,' Joanna said. 'I daresay the same plant has been growing there since the time of Christ. What's the name of it, did you say?'

'It's called pennywort, commonly. The botanical name is *Cotyledon umbilicus*. I wonder how it got to this country.'

Joanna took this in good part. 'I thought it was indigenous,' she said.

'It's possible,' said Barbara. But she did not sound convinced. She said, 'I'd have to look it up.'

'Some sort of flowers must have been blooming here at the time of Christ,' Joanna said. 'They can't all be British imports.'

'That's true.'

'I had a cousin used to take wild-flower seeds to India and scatter them there,' Freddy said.

Barbara said, 'I do that from time to time when I go abroad. To tell the truth, I smuggled a few *Anthyllis* seeds – that's Lady's Fingers – into Israel and scattered them on Mount Carmel on the sea verge. They grow well by the sea. Lovely yellow flowers. It was wildly against the regulations, but I couldn't resist it. I never can. It's a habit.'

Freddy felt happy, and was struck by the thought that Miss Vaughan was remarkably well informed. He felt it proper that she should have scattered Lady's Fingers in some corner of a foreign field.

'You could have been arrested by the Israelis,' Matt said. 'They're extremely strict about what goes into their soil.'

Barbara got ready to leave. She said she had an appointment with a guide.

'Which guide?'

'I went to a travel agent called Ramdez. They've got –'

'You mustn't use Ramdez,' Freddy said.

'Don't take on a guide,' Matt said. 'We'll take you round. Don't waste your money.'

'I've engaged one, though. This afternoon he's going to take me to see what he calls "the tomb of Solomon, son of David, the ex-Jewish king".'

Joanna said, 'Matt will go and pay him off. Stay and look at my puppets instead, then when it's cool we'll go for a drive round.'

'You see, you mustn't,' Matt said quietly, 'go round here alone. It's a question of your Jewish blood.'

'Nobody will know anything about my Jewish blood unless you talk about it.'

Freddy said, 'Actually we've discussed your position in Jordan quite a bit. Because, you see, it's more dangerous for you here than I thought it was. I intended to beg you not to come. Anyone with Jewish blood is automatically arrested as an Israeli spy.'

'My passport's all right,' Barbara said. 'I'd call for the British consul if there was any trouble.'

Their island was beginning to disintegrate. Having said his piece, Freddy felt, in reality, that Miss Vaughan was not in such danger as she had seemed to be in their imagination. Here she stood, calmly, in flesh and blood. As for her being, in fact, a spy . . .

'I think it would be a bit unfair,' Joanna said, 'to involve the British consulate in an incident of that kind.'

'Why?' said Freddy. Perhaps it was the heat, or his age – he could not fathom it afterwards, although he had no regrets – but Freddy felt much the same irate urge to declare something at this moment as he had felt the day before in the

shop when the woman customer was being tiresome with
Alexandros. 'Why, Joanna?' he said. 'Why shouldn't she
appeal to the consulate in the event of her being molested in
a foreign country?'

'It's so much a matter between Arabs and Jews,' Joanna
said. 'We can't officially take sides, can we?'

'It's a blood-feud between Semites,' Matt said, 'that's
all it is.'

Joanna said, reproachfully, as if both men were at fault,
'I'm sure this must be a very embarrassing conversation for
Barbara.'

'It doesn't seem to be about me,' Barbara said. 'You are
talking about a situation that's outside the scope of the
consulate.'

'Won't you sit down, Barbara, while we're talking?' Joanna
said. 'What I mean,' she said to Freddy, 'is that Barbara's
Jewish blood is outside official range, in a sense.'

'Jewish blood or not,' Freddy said, 'the point is, it's hers,
and it has got to be protected by her country.'

'Yes, well, to get back to the individual case,' Matt said,
'we know Ramdez. He's a snooper for his government. He
probably knows already about the Jewish part of Barbara's
origins, through his son in Israel.'

'The son is a hostage, then,' Barbara said.

'Now I think that's a bit unfair,' Matt said.

'There is too much talk,' Barbara said. 'Everything would
be easy if people didn't talk so much.'

'Why is it unfair?' Freddy said to Matt. 'I think it's a
very good point, that Ramdez can't very well move against
Miss Vaughan while his son is in Israel. Young Abdul is a
hostage.'

'Because, mad as it sounds, Jewish blood is illegal here.
I – Joanna and I – we think it's a lunatic situation. But it

seems a bit unfair of Barbara to tempt the law and risk involving a young Arab in Israel.'

'The trouble with you,' Freddy said, fully conscious and rather astonished that he was wrecking the delightful atmosphere, 'is that you blow neither hot nor cold, but lukewarm – What was that passage in the Bible, Miss Vaughan? Can you recall it? – It goes something like, you blow neither hot nor cold and I will spew thee out of my mouth. Something like that. Very apt.'

4

ABDUL'S ORANGE GROVES

'I'm a man of passions and enthusiasms, Mr Hamilton,' said young Abdul Ramdez. 'That is to say, I'm passionate in general, but I don't get worked up about any particular thing for long. In this way I avoid the great Arab mistake, as we have obsessions that leave us exhausted and incapable of action when the time for action comes. Do you know what I say to my Arab friends and also to the friends of my father when they tell me too much, do this, do that, Abdul, in the name of freedom, revenge, unity? I say, okay, okay. But do you know what I say when they ask me again, too much? Do you know what I say then to freedom and revenge, and to Nasser and to Hussein and to the national spirit? Like I've told you before, I –'

'Yes, yes,' said Hamilton, who was plainly enchanted, 'but don't say it here, Abdul. There are some terms we English don't use a great deal of.'

'In childhood I hear many terms by the English army,' Abdul said.

'Well, of course, the army.'

'Is it me teach you Arabic or you teach me English?' Abdul inquired.

Abdul took for granted the fact that he enchanted Frederick Hamilton, because he enchanted everyone, even those who were suspicious of him, except for the high-minded Israelis and Arabs who disapproved of anyone like him on principle, or the police forces of both allegiances. He observed the man who sat in the other arm-chair in this hotel sitting-room. 'Say me some poetry,' Abdul said.

Mr Hamilton sat a little more upright in his chair and recited across the space between them, lit as it was by sunlight dustily filtered through the mosquito-wire window:

> As I ride, as I ride,
> With a full heart for my guide,
> So its tide rocks my side,
> As I ride, as I ride,
> That, as I were double-eyed,
> He, in whom our Tribes confide,
> Is descried, ways untried
> As I ride, as I ride.

Abdul was amused by this. Earlier in the afternoon he had been going over with Hamilton the rudiments of Arabic versification, which, as Abdul put it, had been handed down unchanged from the eighth century: '. . . only we could begin to make changes now like we could make changes in government, and later on we could change the desert wastes and the sky even, if we could first make changes in ourselves.'

Hamilton more or less belonged, in Abdul's view, to that total category of the human race known to Abdul and his companions as the System. It included their fathers, the Pope, President Nasser, King Hussein, Mr Ben-Gurion, the Grand Mufti, the Patriarch of Jerusalem, the English Sovereign, the civil servants and upper militia throughout the world and all the other representatives of the police forces of life who, however beneficent, had absent-mindedly put his generation as a whole in difficulties. Abdul spoke often of his 'generation'. As he was a good deal older than he claimed to be, he meant by this to measure his state of mind rather than his years. He had come early to the conclusion that the easiest method of dealing with the situation, and the one that best suited his personal constitution, was to act with inscrutable folly, to mix up his elders as to his motives, to defeat and exasperate them by transparent guile and hypocrisy, to have no motives at all, but to be enchanting throughout his days. It was not a lonely course; he had many like-minded friends. It had been found and declared by an analytical witchcraftsman that Abdul's character contained intelligence among other ingredients; he knew largely what he was doing. He had reflected upon himself as an Arab, and decided upon a course. His friend, Frederick Hamilton, who sat with Abdul in the sitting-room of his hotel in Israel, was part of the System. Nevertheless, Abdul liked him, as he was easy to manage and did not make demands for his full money's worth of Arabic lessons, but rather seemed pleased to sit and talk in English to Abdul, at his appointed hours, for himself alone. In a way, it seemed to Abdul, Hamilton was not aware that he was part of the System.

'Say that poem again.'

As I ride, as I ride –

'It is a fine poem, Mr Hamilton,' Abdul said when Hamilton had finished.

'It isn't considered to be so. But it's interesting because there are forty lines with the same rhyme. It's by Browning, a famous Victorian poet.'

95

'I have seen "The Barretts of Wimpole Street" about Robert Browning. It was popular with the Arabs as we have many stories in Arabic like that, where the father forbids the marriage to the daughter and the lovers escape.'

Mr Hamilton looked at his Arab grammar and said, 'I suppose we should get on with our work.'

Abdul did not see any need to reply for a moment or two. He was smelling the room and Mr Hamilton. There were Miss Vaughan's geraniums, now, in addition to those which Hamilton had always had. Abdul could never smell anything from Hamilton himself, which was just as typical of the man as certain odours were typical of other people. Abdul's father had always deplored his son's highly developed sense of smell from his youth up. Joe Ramdez had considered it to be an atavistic trait in Abdul, and thought it was uncivilised of him to cultivate this habit of smelling people in rooms. Abdul claimed that he could 'smell an enemy', but his father discovered that Abdul's enemies were not his enemies, and denied Abdul's claim to any smelling talent in this direction.

'You could try the next exercises on page fifty-three,' Abdul said to scentless Mr Hamilton. But he smelt again, and suddenly, holding up his index finger, said, 'Oh!'

'What's the matter?' said the Englishman, looking up from page fifty-three.

'I smell your new suit, the fabric.'

'No, it's an old suit.' Mr Hamilton opened the jacket and squinted inside the inside pocket. '1934,' he said. 'It's marked 1934, so that means I've had it for twenty-seven years. It's older than you, Abdul.'

'It smells,' Abdul said, groping for the association of the smell, not remotely reflecting that he was, in fact, older than the suit.

'I've had it in moth-balls during the summer. I've just got it out as the nights seem to be getting chilly.'

'I like moth-ball scent,' Abdul said. 'When I served at the altar in Cairo, the Coptic priests smelled of moth-balls as they kept moth-balls among their fine resplendent vestments.'

'I thought you belonged to the Armenian Church.'

'No, the Coptic Church.' Abdul did not see any need to explain why, a few weeks ago, he had given Hamilton a long account of how he had broken with the Moslem faith to run away with an Armenian girl, to further the wooing of whom he had adopted Armenian Christianity. He did not see any need to refrain from so enjoyably muddling up his friend and he continued to talk of the Coptic Church in Egypt: 'You see, my father sent me to school in Cairo when he saw that I was too far advanced for any of the schools in Palestine. Many of my friends were sent to school in Beirut but I was sent to Cairo, where I was baptised a Christian in the Coptic Church.'

'What I am not sure about –' said Mr Hamilton. He was flicking through the notebook on which he had been writing his Arabic exercises for four months since April last.

It occurred to Abdul that Hamilton was not well. He had already perceived this when he had come into the room, but had immediately veiled the idea from his thoughts, since Hamilton had behaved normally, had said, 'Well, Abdul, how are you?', had got up, smiled in his usual way and sat down, partly distrustful, as usual, and partly enchanted. In the meantime Abdul had sat down, too, and then started to talk about himself, so that the sense of Mr Hamilton's being not well had passed from him. Abdul noticed now that the man's hair was not combed well, as it usually was. Otherwise, he looked the same.

'What I'm uncertain about,' said Hamilton, flicking through his notebook, 'is whether I'm getting anywhere. It took me a month to learn the Arabic characters. By the end of May I could read and write "The house is small", "The king is angry with the doctor" and "Is the bride ready? No!"'

Abdul laughed and Hamilton smiled eagerly, as if surprised at the success of what he had said.

' "News about the experiments reached the upright princes yesterday",' said Hamilton, reading aloud from the textbook. 'That was last month. Since then I've done "Mohammed (may God pray for him!) was a good man", "Your speech was delightful but you did not mention the blood which flowed in the Arabs' battles" and so on.' Abdul laughed again, which Hamilton seemed to appreciate. 'But I never have occasion to use phrases like that,' said Hamilton, putting on a sad air; 'I ought to learn some vocabulary and understand what the Arabs around me are saying, and talk to them, perhaps.'

Abdul said, 'The Arabic for the street you learn later, Mr Hamilton. I'm laughing at these exercises as you read them in English, as you make them sound like poetry that means much. Read some more.'

Hamilton said, 'What does it mean, that phrase "May God pray for him!"? Do the Moslems ask God to pray? Who does God pray to?'

'It's only a saying,' Abdul said, 'of the elderly people. They say "May God pray for him and save him!" all day, as they speak of their dead relations all the day long.'

He was watching the Englishman to see how unwell he was, and in what precise way he was afflicted. Hamilton read another exercise: ' "The students of Damascus University have arrived in Cairo for an important meeting with their Egyptian brethren." Of course,' he said, 'it isn't true to say

I've made no progress, but I can't say that I'm learning enough to mix with ordinary Arabs. I don't want to master the language like a scholar, I only want to be able to make myself understood while I'm out here, during the next few years. Now I managed to pick up enough Hungarian to get along with when I was posted to Hungary, and I did that by means of conversational lessons rather than schoolroom stuff, and I'm wondering if our best plan isn't to adopt that method, and –'

'You wish to spy among the Arabs of Israel to report their pro-Israel activities in Jordan,' stated Abdul, 'or else you report them to the Israelis for anti–Israel talk.'

Hamilton said, 'Good gracious me!'

Abdul said, 'I don't think you are a spy.'

'I should hope not,' the man replied.

'Then you shouldn't entertain suspicions of me.'

'Why, Abdul! Why, of course I simply never –'

'I'm difficult for you to understand,' Abdul said. 'And we should be turning to page fifty-four.'

Hamilton translated, 'Despite what the unbelievers say, the righteous are under the protection of Allah.'

'It's boring,' Abdul said. 'We should make our own exercises, and you could talk better with the Arabs in the street.'

'Entirely what I've been thinking,' said Hamilton. He looked so unwell that Abdul wanted to give him some kindness or make him laugh as one would do a sick child.

'Let us try, for the next lesson, before we come on to particles and conjunctions, some exercises with new words in them. Bad words.'

This sort of suggestion usually cheered Hamilton up although he always refused to let Abdul go further than that. Once, Hamilton had said, 'Where did you learn English?'

'Some from my father, some from my mother, but most from a beautiful English schoolmistress that I had when I was fifteen. Her father was a colonel in the British Army.'

Mr Hamilton had said, 'Did she plant English wild-flower seeds in the countryside, by any chance?'

'I don't know,' Abdul said. 'But I planted Arab wild-flower seeds in her. She was my first woman.'

Hamilton had said, 'Now, now, now,' but nebulously smiling meanwhile, as if at some reflection of his own which Abdul could not share. Hamilton had then seemed to realise with sudden alarm that Abdul's words had been uttered in the presence of the geraniums, for he looked at them in a guilty way and said, 'I ought not really to permit such things to be said about an English girl.' But Hamilton was not making any big issue out of it and seemed to be cheered up, on the whole.

'Bad words,' Abdul now said. Hamilton smiled faintly. Plainly, he was not well. Abdul was neither glad nor sorry, partly because he had become unaccustomed to having any emotions during the hours of daylight. For that, he needed his company of friends at Acre, and some dancing with a little howling maybe, with the long chants going on in the background.

In the meantime he said with a giggle, 'Bad words next week. You could throw away your grammar book if it bores you.'

'I don't want bad words,' said Hamilton, looking round the room in a disorganised way. 'What I must do, obviously, is master a larger vocabulary.'

'True,' said Abdul. 'Take a set of conversational sentences, then, like for instance, "I am an honest man, but you are a deceiver." "Why do you call me a deceiver?" "Because you have promised me to take out a life-insurance policy through my father's agency, and you have said to your English friends in Jordan that you do not intend to do so." "How do you know of this?" "Because the servants of your English friends are spies for my father." Of course,' Abdul said, 'this group of sentences would be better expressed in conversational Arabic, but you might as well try to put them together in the formal style.'

Hamilton said, 'I have not promised to take out any life-insurance policy.' But his voice was tired.

'My father,' said Abdul, 'sends messages to me at risk to his life to persevere with you about the policy. So I fulfil a pious duty to my father, and finish. I do not care personally about insurance policies, they're crazy things.'

Hamilton's head rested on the back of his chair, since he was slumped low in it this afternoon, not, as usual, sitting alertly. He let his head rest back, as if about to close his eyes which, however, remained half-open, focused on Abdul between their lids.

Abdul sat in silence, experiencing the torpor and boredom of afternoon life, much as he had very often done in the presence of his elders during his childhood. It seemed reasonable, after a while, to suppose that Mr Hamilton had fallen into a kind of doze, for although his eyes were not entirely closed, his breathing became more rhythmical and loud, as one in sleep. Abdul's eyes slid to the round table beside him, where Hamilton had been writing letters. Two were sealed in envelopes, ready stamped for posting, they lay one on top of another at an angle, the top envelope concealing the address on the lower. The top envelope was addressed to Professor M.S. Dexter, All Souls College, Oxford, England. Beside these sealed envelopes lay some pages of unfinished letters which Abdul had already noticed in a contributory way to his sense of Hamilton's being out of sorts; usually Hamilton was a man who finished doing one thing before starting another.

The man was now nearly asleep. Abdul sat in a deliberate, breath-held stillness, looking at his Englishman. He found himself wondering if Hamilton was going to die, tomorrow or next week, or now, his soul wafting away from him, preserved in a faint moth-ball atmosphere. Abdul turned his head silently so that he could read, by squinting obliquely, the nearest of the three unfinished pages on the table, evidently a continuation on the back of the first sheet.

have just written to a friend at All Souls, a Fellow, to tell him I've discovered a rhyme for 'Capricorn'. My friend, Sam Dexter, probably knows more about rhyme than anyone in the country, although of course, his subject's Old French. Goodness knows what he'll think of this rhyme for 'Capricorn' – I saw it in an American picture magazine, in an advertisement for a breakfast food called 'Apricorn'. (I understand Apricorn is, as its name implies, a kind of packed cereal food flavoured, by some process, with apricot essence.) Whether Dexter will allow 'Apricorn' as a word at all, I very much doubt.

But you see, dearest Joanna, I must keep my mind occupied with something. To be suddenly confronted with a doctor's order of two weeks' rest is not, in itself, conducive to peace of mind. As you say, I could have gone to Greece. But I am unused to moving about without previous plans. I could think of nothing to do on the spur of the moment but wait here. Besides, there is always a chance that if any news of Miss Vaughan should reach us I may be of some assistance. Until the mystery of her disappearance has been cleared up, one is bound to experience some anxiety, merely from having recently been acquainted with her, however little actual connection one has had with the person. The newspapers seem to have dropped it in the last few days, I expect by special compliance with the investigating authorities and our Embassy in Amman – I have had no further trouble from the reporters, as I trust you have not. I expect at least some news will emerge before long. One must hope for the best but it is impossible not to fear the worst.

I have been making every attempt to regain my powers of concentration even to the extent of attempting (in vain, alas!) a verse or two in *terza rima* to say some pleasant things to you, dearest Joanna, who have been so good since my stupid collapse. To lose one's entire memory, even for a couple of days, is disconcerting to reflect upon *afterwards*. One's confidence is greatly undermined. I still have no recollections of how those two days passed. I am advised against mental effort for the time being but of course, it is impossible to resist attempting to solve the mystery. I must have slept – I must have shaved, and so on. When I got to the hotel I felt tired and hot as usual after my walk from the Mandelbaum Gate on Sunday afternoons. But it was Tuesday, and they had been looking for me. I am convinced that I had an attack of sunstroke and it must have affected my memory. But where did I sleep? Where is Barbara Vaughan? Please, by the way, thank Matt for his note. But I do not think I would wish to consult the psychiatrist although I am sure, as Matt says, he is brilliant. Psychiatry is too abstract for me to take up at my age, I'm afraid. When I go to a doctor I like to come away with a bottle of medicine or some pills, or a prescription to be made up. However, the suggestion has

The letter had been left off half-way down the second page. Abdul looked over to Hamilton, who had now fully closed his eyes in sleep. He began to read again, carefully, the first part of the letter only – 'Apricorn' . . . 'Capricorn' . . . He dwelt on the glamour of the name 'All Souls' which he knew to be that of an Oxford college. For he was less interested in the rest of the letter and the evident personal crisis that had occurred to Hamilton than he was fascinated by the entire vision of that state of heart in which one wrote to a Fellow of All Souls about a rhyme for Capricorn. It could not result in any large benefit to Hamilton or his friends, nor could this piece of information damage Hamilton's enemies. It was disinterested and therefore beautiful, even if it was useless to the immediate world. And this was something Abdul could never make his middle-class Arab acquaintance understand – how it was possible to do things for their own sake, not only possible but sometimes necessary for the affirmation of one's personal identity. The ideal reposed in their religion, but somewhere in the long trail of Islam, the knack of disinterestedness had been lost, and with it a large portion of the joy of life. His father would never accept that Hamilton's activities were as meaningless as they looked. What is his motive? Is it political? Why does he write those verses to send to the Cartwright house? Are they in code? Why does he spend so much time in Jordan? Have you found out why he is learning Arabic? Have you read any of his private correspondence? Has he agreed to take out a policy yet, will he come to see me and complete the form? Why does he want to know street Arabic? Why does he stay on at a hotel, this Hamilton? This Hamilton, why does he walk everywhere instead of taking a taxi? There must be a reason, everything means something. Is it political? Does he practise a vice? But me, Abdul thought – if my father, cousins, uncles, had any knowledge about me, it would be the same thing. Have you joined the nationalists then? Are you in with the Sufis? Have you turned in with the Jews, after all, like the Sheik of the Negev? What do you do at Acre? What have you done, did you do, are doing, might, will do at Acre with those youths of mixed blood, mixed sexes, those young Jewesses, those Arabs, those Jews, those Arab girls, those Yemenites, Syrians, those Israelites, Samaritans, those boys, girls, boys . . . Are you a nationalist?

'Nationalist of what, Father? What territory, what people?'

'I don't understand you. Don't forget you're an Arab. Are you a monarchist?'

'Which monarch do you refer to, Father?'

Such conversations were few, for Abdul's meetings with Joe Ramdez, on the other side of the Gate, were arranged with dangerous difficulty. Abdul felt now, as he frequently did, a sense of being mentally closer to Hamilton than to his own father. Even so, that was not saying much, for Abdul's affinities with his own generation, and within that category, with the secret mixed-blood conclaves at Acre, placed on him and his companions the necessity of a double life; the gulf that separated him both from Hamilton and his father was wide; it was deeper and darker than had usually existed between generations. Perhaps not since the times of the Prophet . . .

Hamilton was stirring in his chair.

'Are you asleep, Mr Hamilton?' Abdul said softly.

Hamilton settled his head back again and breathed deeply.

'Are you awake, Mr Hamilton?' Abdul said.

The brief twilight had fallen and was fading into night. Abdul felt tenderly towards Hamilton. He squinted to see if he could read the other unfinished scrap of a letter that was lying on the table, but it was too far away. He reached out his arm and picked it up.

. . . is not, dearest Ma, and cannot possibly be, the person whom you went to hear playing the piano (or the violin – in your next paragraph you refer to 'this famous German who played the violin' but first you have mentioned *piano*) at Auntie Bella's before the Great War. The Eichmann who is on trial here in Jerusalem is an inferior sort of person with no connections whatsoever. I believe his antecedents are quite obscure. I do not think he plays the piano or the violin. You must be thinking of some other German. The Germans are a musical nation, of course, and so it is conceivable that this fellow used to play the fiddle, as indeed used Nero, you remember.

Hamilton stirred, with opening eyes. 'Poems,' he mused. 'Poems.'

Abdul, the letter still in his hand, said, 'Speak more of those lines, Mr Hamilton, the rider's song. "As I ride, as I ride."'

'You know, Abdul,' said Hamilton, who had now fully woken up, 'it is wrong to read other people's letters.' But he did not seem much concerned on this point, and while Abdul returned the sheet of paper to the table, Hamilton recited, keeping time with his right hand:

> Could I loose what Fate has tied,
> Ere I pried, she should hide
> (As I ride, as I ride)
> All that's meant me – satisfied
> When the Prophet and the Bride
> Stops veins I'd have subside
> As I ride, as I ride!

'I don't know in my head what it means,' Abdul said, 'but it means something in the blood-veins.'

'Yes, a little something. You know, Abdul, I think I've had a touch of sunstroke. But I must pull myself together. I have been advised to rest. But I begin to think I would be better advised to occupy my mind with something difficult. I want to take Hebrew lessons. Do you know Dr Saul Ephraim of the Hebrew University? He was a friend of poor Miss Vaughan – have I told you that Miss Vaughan has disappeared, over in Jordan? We are very anxious about her. Well, I must get in touch with Ephraim. Do you know him?'

'I know his youngest brother better. I know him well, Mendel Ephraim. The brother Saul has no dealings with him, though. He's out of the family.'

'Really? What does he do?'

'He's a smuggler. This is a secret that I am passing on to you for your spy records. He smuggles leather goods, shoes and so on, across the border by night. I trust you with a secret, Mr Hamilton. I am in smuggling with him also.'

'Oh, Abdul, I don't know where I stand with you. Now, before you go, there is something I very much want to ask you. It's important and serious, Abdul, and I want a serious answer if you can give it.'

'Why didn't you ask before?' Abdul said.

'Because it's important, you see, and I don't want you to treat my question frivolously. I want to impress on you the seriousness –'

'You are asking me what has happened to Miss Vaughan?'

'Yes. Do you know?'

'No, but I'll find out.'

At Acre, the stronghold of the Crusaders on the Mediterranean, west of Galilee, the fortifications stand in golden ruins, piled on the foundations of earlier ruins. It seemed to Abdul Ramdez that the laborious construction of ruins had been the principal means by which the forebears of the whole human race, stretching back into history, had passed the time of day. Arabs lived in the shelter of the eighteenth-century ruined fortresses, and even now in the years of the establishment of Israel, burning with its mixture of religion, hygiene and applied sociology, the poor Arabs still hung out their washing on the battlements, so that it fluttered all along the antique sea-front, innocent of the offence it was committing in the eyes of the seekers of beautiful sights and spiritual sensations, who had come all the way from the twentieth century, due west of Acre. Indeed, the washing draped out on the historic walls was a sign of progress, enlightenment, and industry, as it had been from time immemorial; it betokened a settlement and a society with a sense of tomorrow, even if it was only tomorrow's clean shirt, as against the shifty tent-dwelling communities of the wilderness; and however murky the cave-like homes along the shore, and however indolent the occupants, they were one up on the Bedouin, at least in their own eyes if not in the sight of the tourist cameras which photographed the Bedouin shepherds continually but deplored the hung-out washing at Acre.

Acre had many years ago become the spiritual home of Abdul Ramdez, although he nominally resided in Jerusalem. His real age was thirty-four. He had found, by experience, that nobody questioned that he was twenty-five when he gave this age as his; he was youthful-looking and had cultivated and kept in good repair the mannerisms of his youth; and Abdul had found, too, that most people took a man, in all respects, for what he said he was.

It will have been seen that it would be a waste of time to rely on any statement about himself and his life spoken from the lips of Abdul Ramdez. The facts are as follows. He was born in 1927 at the small and ancient town of Madaba in the Transjordan, east of the Dead Sea. He had three sisters, four

half-sisters, and one brother. At that time the family consisted of his father, an unmarried uncle, Joe Ramdez's first wife,
who acted as general manager of domestic life, a second wife
(Abdul's mother), who looked after all the younger children
regardless of whether she or the other wife had borne them;
then, also, Abdul's elder brother and five of the seven
Ramdez girls, who were still children, the other two being
married. In addition, there lived in the house a female constitutional victim, heavily garbed in black, of indefinite age
and origin, who did the bulk of the housework from early
morning till late at night. At Abdul's birth in 1927 there were
fourteen persons in the household.

It was a middle-class urban family such as the British
Mandatory officials liked to deal with, since they understood
them better than the more tribal and nomadic Arabs, on the
one hand, and the elusive rich ruling families with sons at
English schools, on the other.

In the year of Abdul's birth, when the Transjordan became
an independent state, the entire family, accompanied by, and,
as it were, borne on the back of, the veiled servant woman,
moved across the Jordan River into Palestine, where the
British Mandate remained in force. The reason for this move
was that Joe Ramdez, until then a schoolteacher, had found
the British Army and civil service officials to be both agreeable and profitable. He had taught them Arabic, had taken
them to see the sights they ought to see and kept them away
from a few things they ought not to see, and obligingly
upheld their axiom that the Arabs think in symbols, this
being a more workable view for them to hold than that they
did not think at all. So he followed the Administration to
Jerusalem, where Abdul grew up in the new small suburban
house, following the servant woman everywhere every day
from the opening to the closing of his eyes, until he was eight

years old. She was called Kyra and, unlike the other women of the household, had never brought herself to any point of emancipation. She wore her black veil to the market, with her basket in one hand and Abdul's hand in the other.

Joe Ramdez prospered and formed his travel agency, employing a few Arabs from Nazareth as guides to Christian pilgrims throughout Palestine. Abdul remembered a few of the British men, and sometimes their wives, driving up to the door for their Arabic lessons on occasions when his father did not go to them. Quickly, the women and girls of the Ramdez establishment would scuttle out of the way, leaving the main room, where they had been lying full length on settees, to loll somewhere else or to make tea. A continual lolling of lazy women about the house, perpetual sunlight and heat, and red plush upholstery, formed the distorted impressions that Abdul retained from his childhood, although in reality the women of the Ramdez house were moderately active and did all that was necessary to the general comfort, and the winters were cold, and actually only one room had been furnished with red plush upholstery. It was true that the other rooms were full of untidy beds and were hung with female clothing all over the walls and that the women did not have much chance to participate in the visits of the Europeans. Abdul's younger sister, blue-eyed like himself, was exceptional among the females, in that she felt it keenly when she was hushed out of the way with the other girls while Abdul was proudly introduced to the strangers.

The red plush had covered the long settles; these lined three of the walls of the square room that led straight in from the road. Here the visitors were received and here Abdul sat noiseless, in a trance of red plush, while the English got their Arabic lessons from his father. The walls bore three enlarged photographs, one of General Gordon, one of Abdul's grand-father on his mother's side – a Syrian of mixed Arab and Norman stock, the progenitor of the blue-eyed children – and one of a crowded pilgrimage to Mecca, moving up to the Great Mosque. After the lessons the Ramdez women would slink in with cups of mint tea and swiftly merge back into the gloom of elsewhere.

That was life in the old days. At the age of eight Abdul went to school in Jerusalem. His father prospered. Presently, the house had two refrigerators. The first and elder wife, whose children by Joe Ramdez were now married, returned, perhaps by inducement from Joe, to Jericho whence she came; whereupon Abdul's mother started calling herself Mme Ramdez, and, with clothes more modern than ever before, assisted in the travel business, walking forth from the front door daily.

Abdul went to the University of Cairo at the age of six-teen. There he belonged first to one, and then to another, cell of Arab politics. With eighty-odd of his fellow students he one day marched behind a banner marked 'We Want Freedom', past the British Headquarters, was fired upon, and escaped with a fright only, three of his fellow-students being slightly wounded. This was in 1944. The demonstra-tion, Abdul learned later that day, was against King Farouk, although some of the participants claimed it had been against the British. Abdul had thought it was probably against the proprietor of Shepheard's Hotel, who had been attempting to ban the students of late; but he did not worry very much. It made him feel good to belong to an Arab movement. He liked to feel that it was something to be an Arab, although he disliked the Lebanese and wished all the Arabs were Palestinian or Transjordanian and less alien in their ways. Abdul's teacher in history, a Syrian, was pro-Hitler. Another of the teachers, an English communist, was the guiding spirit of another student faction. The cells split open from time to time, forming themselves anew, after some shouting, fighting, and expulsions of students, into regional structures, so that the Lebanese, the Egyptians, the Tunisians, Arabians and Syrians were plotters in separate fields of political allegiance. Every man among the Arab students proclaimed himself a nationalist, this word being their only common denominator. 'Islam', another word of rousing properties, was at first rousing only to the Moslem believers. The atheists among the students were at that time greater in number than at any time before or since; agnosticism, or any form of recognised doubt, was unknown to all but Abdul, who presently discovered it by chance. In the meantime he had joined practically every movement in the university, demonstrating with them sometimes but meeting in secret as often as possible for seditious discussions, since he liked them, they roused him up.

When he had turned seventeen he took on the teaching of Arabic to an Englishwoman who was an officer in the Women's Auxiliary. She lived at the big hotel, where Abdul called three times a week. She was twenty-seven years old. She had the use of a friend's empty flat where, after a few weeks, she slept with Abdul. It was as near a love-affair on both sides as could be. On her side, it was a desperate reaction to grief; her husband had not long since been killed in battle. On his side, it was an impact with self-knowledge in many forms. He had already had sexual relations with young Arab girls in Cairo. But even physically he realised himself more acutely as a man with this Western woman, discerning at the same time, by a process of reflection acquired from her, that he had hitherto regarded all Westerners, both male and female, as a masculine type of race.

Every time he slept with this girl he found himself with a problem which for want of a more precise definition, he termed 'spiritual'; he was afraid of her. When he spent days and nights at the flat without sexual relations with her, as he frequently did, he found himself with a physical problem; for he wanted very much the physical contact with this bold foreigner. That she herself was taking some sort of risk in carrying on this relationship did not occur to him, until she was suddenly unavailable, detained and being questioned pending a court-martial; Abdul lay low. He started attending to his studies, he did not go near the flat or any busy part of Cairo. He remained in the college precincts, attending lectures and reading his books from early morning to early evening, when he went to bed and lay listening for the footsteps of the police. Within three weeks he heard that the English girl had been recalled to headquarters in Britain pending her release from the forces, on the recommendation of one of those psychiatrists whose main job in war-time was to smooth over such events as this, and Abdul realised, with relief, that her lover's identity was unknown.

Meanwhile, Abdul had acquired from the woman something ineradicable, and which was so much part of her nature that she had been herself totally unaware of it: self-humour. It was a form of endowment at the same time that it was a form of corruption. It undid him as a middle-class Arab enemy-hater with a career in the army or a position in business.

'I am an Arab nationalist,' he had announced to her. 'I despise the British.'

'Nationalist of what nation?' she had said, quite innocently. 'What place, what territory?' He made these responses his own and used them for years afterwards.

'Islam is united.' But he knew it was not.

This was not the only innocent remark the girl had made which affected him. From the histrionic or dramatic point of view he was henceforth a spoiled Arab. He could not take any propaganda seriously. And she had unwittingly instilled scepticism into him, had taught him to be a doubter and, at the same time, a faint-hearted hater. He was by no means the only Arab of his generation to react in this way to the fervour of the resistance movements at Cairo while the big war was going on outside. Many were influenced by the Lebanese who mostly considered themselves to be a different cultivation altogether from the rest of Middle Eastern humanity. Many joined the Allied forces.

Abdul, then, joined all the student factions, merrily uncommitted at heart and, in the same spirit, out of the sheer desire for discovery and scope, would have joined the British Army had they accepted him. He was found to have tuberculosis, was sent back to Palestine and, within a few weeks, to a sanatorium in Lebanon. There, his sister Suzi, the blue-eyed one, came to visit him at various intervals, sometimes accompanied by Mme Ramdez and sometimes by black-veiled Kyra, smelling like her usual self with the addition of eau-de-cologne which she had applied to her forehead in consideration of foreign travel.

It was at this time that the secret affinity ripened between Abdul and Suzi. She was then fifteen, Abdul nineteen. He talked of new ways of life and outlook, undreamt of even by their modernised parents. His imagination went wild in most particulars, but Abdul conveyed to her, as only tubercular patients can, the excitement of what was in his mind. He said that the modernisation of Joe Ramdez was simply a new form of the old exploiting mentality. In this way Suzi discovered the future as an idea, and together the brother and sister merged in a pact of personal anarchism; they started to fool everyone; they conformed to outward demands and resisted in spirit, the Arabic mysticism in their nature easily adapting itself to this course. Suzi, on one of her visits with Kyra, had a love-affair with a French officer and managed to convince her suspicious chaperone, and later her mother, that she was merely cultivating his acquaintance in her role as a spy. To be a spy of some sort was the respectable thing for any literate Arab, even if it only involved spying on each other. To spy on a Westerner was a matter of special commendation. The girl noticeably handed a note to Abdul in his hospital bed, every time she visited him. These were really love-notes from herself to Abdul; and they were partly sincere, for the temperamental sympathy between the brother and sister was not unlike an erotic passion, so new to their Palestinian lives was their liberation of spirit; Abdul's attitude to her as a woman was not to be found in any other Arab of her acquaintance, and only superficially in the French officer, who very soon left with his regiment for other parts. Abdul treated her as a girlfriend, and she was bold and merry with him; it delighted him, even more than had his encounter with the Englishwoman in Egypt.

He read her notes, when they began to reach him by messenger three or four times a day, with enormous secret amusement, returning similar messages even before old Kyra's eyes. He explained to all Arab personnel at the hospital who might be concerned that these notes were in aid of 'the Arab struggle'. This was highly acceptable, and nobody inquired what sort of struggle to what precise end.

After the end of the war, Abdul, partially cured in both lungs, returned to Palestine where the huge Jewish immigration had turned the old Arab hostility to the Jews into hysterical hatred. The British military were active everywhere, unable to cope with the illegal immigrant shiploads that managed to come ashore, week by week, in spite of the vigilant army and air force in Palestine and their ships off the coast. The British were hated by the Arabs for not killing all the Jews.

Joe Ramdez had opened at Haifa a small branch of his travel agency which was one of the main British sources of secret intelligence concerning the illegal immigrant ships. Abdul was now placed in charge of this establishment, where he gaily accepted payment by both British and Jewish agencies in the matter of illegal immigrants. One way and another he had a bright time of it, distrusted on all sides, yet frequently confided in on the mere hypnotic strength of his attractive personality, and was eventually retained by various intelligence agencies more from fear of what he could divulge than from his usefulness as a spy. Joe Ramdez took his son's duplicity for granted, the only difference between the two processes of thought, father's and son's, was that, whereas Abdul knew and joyfully recognised his double-dealings for what they were, the father took a double course of life to be a single, natural line of human proceeding and would have been wild with anger if anyone had openly called a lie of his a lie, or suggested some moral defection on his part; and he expected the same treatment from everyone outside his own family. But when a British officer said to Abdul, leaning over the desk at the travel bureau in Haifa, 'Ramdez, what a frightful, bloody young liar you are!' Abdul replied, 'I know,' with his quick, young smile. In any case, he was not quite twenty-one at the time, which alone was very disarming. Abdul adored life, the Mediterranean waters, the sun, and his sister Suzi.

Bullets were flying from all quarters. Abdul closed down the agency in Haifa. He took off his smart-cut suit of clothes and put on a white shirt and khaki shorts. Bullets from the small black window apertures of the Arab quarters sang about his ears; the bullets pelted down from the mountains of Carmel. Abdul did not return to his lodgings. He waited in an upper store-room of the travel agency until this local rising had been put down, then he emerged one night, thin from lack of food, and closed the doors of the travel agency at Haifa for ever. He got to friends at Acre, where he obtained a birth certificate dated 1931, which made him a plausible sixteen years of age. There, too, on the strength of some knowledge of the Catholic religion that he had picked up while in hospital in Lebanon, he persuaded a simple and ancient Franciscan monk to baptise him before witnesses and sign a baptismal certificate. Abdul did all these things without any distinct notion of their subsequent usefulness, but merely on the prompting of an instinct for self-preservation. By no means did he wish to fight in an Arabs' war with the Jews or anyone else. A careful copy of the baptismal certificate was made for him by his friends, with the substitution of Suzi's name, and this copy was conveyed in secret to his sister in Jerusalem. Certificates of baptism were useful for crossing borders in this pilgrim territory, they were useful for many things. He began to love Acre, with its band of friends and its crowds of poor.

Presently he set off for Nazareth where Christian Arabs were mostly congregated. He begged lifts all the way from the British military, explaining that he desired to get to the hospital at Nazareth as he had been spitting blood and was afraid of being sniped at by the Jews. How old was he? Sixteen. He had, in fact, developed a short, recurrent cough. The British soldiers searched him for bombs, found five pounds in his pocket, his birth certificate and baptismal certificate; that was all. He had not changed his name. Abdul

Ramdez, a fairly common name, was as good as any. He coughed frequently. 'Hop in,' said the Englishmen. On the second lift that he got in a military jeep, which took him all the way to Nazareth, he found himself coughing less controllably than before, and towards evening he did indeed spit up blood.

At the tubercular sanatorium in Nazareth, after he perceived how the war was going, he took lessons in modern Hebrew. He now had assurances that his lung disease, in spite of long neglect, could be quite cured. He got modern Hebrew lessons from a Baptist missionary woman who visited the hospital, and explained to the suspicious Arab patients that a knowledge of Hebrew would enable him to continue his profession of spying on the Jews when he should be discharged. Once or twice his textbooks were destroyed in hostile rage by one or another Arab, but on the whole he managed to convince almost everyone of his nationalistic loyalty, by almost daily renewals of vows of hatred against the Jews. He felt no hatred on so large a scale, since all his energies went into his will to live well in the world, to get the best he could out of Palestine and to be free to say any frivolous thing that came into his head regardless of the impression it might make. At night, when he lay among the row of sleepers, he felt the security and comfort of being together with his own people. By day, he surged with individuality again.

The state of Israel was three years old and was warily at peace, separated by an armistice line from Jordan, when Abdul left the sanatorium. Jerusalem was now divided; his father's home and business establishment were in the Jordanian sector. Infrequent messages, mostly verbal, had passed between Abdul and his family while he was in hospital, carried in secret by various individuals – a foreigner, a Red Cross officer, an Arab spy, a Church of Scotland minister.

Abdul was aware that none of the family except Suzi had any conception of his mind and how deeply bored he was by the mentality that now presented to every Arab in Palestine the blood-duty of becoming a professional victim. Abdul saw years of futile service ahead in this uninteresting cause. He knew of the homeless Palestinian refugees massed along the frontier, and he discerned then what a foreigner could not so accurately foresee, that there was a living to be made out of the world by preserving a refugee problem. Abdul guessed, and was presently proved right, that his father, for one, was doing his big bit on the refugee question and would in time make a fortune out of it. Joe Ramdez was in fact already active in newly established agencies for negotiating contracts with merchants for supplies bought by foreign relief funds.

Just before he had left hospital, Abdul had got a brief note in Suzi's handwriting. 'How are Abdul's orange groves thriving?' He puzzled for a few moments, then smiled. The displaced poor were already being urged to recall the extent of the lands and possessions from which they had fled before the Israelis' onslaught. More and more, the bewildered homeless souls, in thousands and tens of thousands, agreed and then convinced themselves, and were to hold for long years to come, that they had, every man of them, been driven from vast holdings in their bit of Palestine, from green hilly pastures and so many acres of lush orange groves as would have covered Arabia.

Abdul had earned some money by teaching the children while in the sanatorium. On his discharge he bought a car on the instalment plan and drove to Acre, passing through the green hills and battered villages of Judea. He said to himself, at times when he sped past some fruitful plantation, 'There go Abdul's orange groves.' He was bored far beyond the point of fury with his elders, he was bored with the fervent industrious Jews bursting with their new patriotism. It had been necessary for him, a Palestinian Arab, to obtain a permit before he could leave Nazareth. He was an inferior citizen still; the Jews had only replaced the British. The officious Israeli policeman who issued the permit, a man younger than himself, made Abdul feel sick. He was beyond fury. He laughed. The Israeli guard called a fellow-officer to his side and then asked Abdul what there was to laugh at. Abdul explained that he was newly out of hospital and it was a nice day. He was allowed to go. He did not want to grow older than he was then, in 1950. At that time he was twenty-three.

At Acre the people he had known were gone, but as happens, the place itself, by some invisible influence or tradition, had drawn the same sort of people, the young or the young at heart who belonged to nothing but themselves, for whose temperament no scope existed in any society open to them, and who by day enacted the requirements of their society. These were lapsed Jews, lapsed Arabs, lapsed citizens, runaway Englishmen, dancing prostitutes, international messes, failed painters, intellectuals, homosexuals. Some were silent, some voluble. Some were mentally ill, or would become so.

But others were not. Others were not, and never would become so; and would have been the flower and pride of the Middle East, given the sun and air of the mind not yet to be available. They met in a cellar at Acre, lined with wooden benches, lit with oil lamps and cleared for dancing. Abdul would have preferred the beaches or the cafés, and the open sky, but at least in the cellar an Arab could laugh at the Arabs or mimic the solemn Israeli guard without being knifed or shot. Three knifings were to occur within this little community over the next ten years, but they were not political; they were to do with sex or drugs, and in two cases the wounds were slight; in the third the body was successfully disposed of from a fishing-boat.

Nothing much had changed by 1961, the year of the Eichmann trial, when Abdul Ramdez drove to Acre, the golden city of the Crusaders on the Mediterranean. At Christian festivals, Easter and Christmas, he was able to pass over to Jordan openly with mass pilgrimages to visit the Christian shrines, on the strength of his baptismal certificate, acquired with that good foresight before the war with Israel. Suzi, with the certificate he had obtained for her, got past the officials to meet him at the churches. She was still unmarried at thirty-one. She was unhappy, and only Abdul knew it. Sometimes he crossed the border illegally, but he did not always see Suzi on these occasions. He had contrived to meet his father several times since the partition of Palestine. 'Are you a nationalist? . . . A Nasserite? . . . What party? . . .' But messages between Joe Ramdez and Abdul passed frequently. They were comparatively easy to smuggle back and forth across the border.

Nothing much had changed at Acre over the years except the place of rendezvous and Abdul's real age. He was now thirty-four, but he kept himself lean, was strict with himself and looked no more than the age he had decided on. He did not trouble about the future. Twenty-five. Foreigners like Hamilton were puzzled at times by Abdul's maturity of knowledge.

'But surely, Abdul, you must have been a young infant at that time. How could you remember King Farouk before he grew fat?'

Abdul piled lies upon truth, without attempting to convince. He felt he was making an almost poetic effort. He derived huge pleasure from mixing everyone up so much that they saw through it in the end.

'Sometimes, Abdul, I wonder if you're just treating me to a big leg-pull.'

Hamilton had said this one day. Abdul thought it intelligent of him. He said, 'Well, what have I got to lose, Mr Hamilton? You know that all the Arabs in Palestine are dispossessed. There's nothing to lose, now that Abdul has lost his orange groves.'

'Did you possess orange groves?'

'Vast groves.'

'I don't believe it. Come, Abdul!'

'I am an Arab,' said Abdul, looking fierce, 'and you may not accuse me of a lie. Anyway, I have lost a good travel agency business in Haifa. The Jews have got it.'

Hamilton had laughed and regarded him fondly.

Abdul drove to Acre on the following Sunday and thought for a while of the Hamilton he had seen a few days before, unwell, bewildered. Someone at Acre would know, or find out, what had happened to the Englishman over in Jordan and what had happened with Miss Vaughan. It would be a pity if Hamilton started to make trouble, and stopped being friendly.

The new meeting-place at Acre was more spacious and comfortable than any previous one. New young people came in from time to time.

The building stood in the great muddle of the poor Arab quarter. It was equipped as a laundry, and in the daytime the lower ground floor functioned as a cheap washing establishment where, in one room, an unpunctual and inefficient supply of warm water was available, with wash tubs and soap, at a cheap rate, to the poor women who had to do their washing themselves, and who were slightly advanced beyond the river-washing set.

The club-rooms could not really be called club-rooms, since the traditions and organisation of any sort of club-life did not belong to them. These meeting-rooms were in the cellars and on the floor above the laundry. Windows from all sides kept watch on any possible police approach from the sea or from the street. Some of the upper rooms were always hung with washing, hauled high on pulleys, which, at night when the lights were on, could be glimpsed above the half-curtains from the alleys outside.

Two Pakistanis, students from the Hebrew University of Jerusalem, came to open the door for Abdul. They were temporary caretakers, since the laundryman who looked after the house at Acre was away to the north on business.

Abdul had two rooms of his own on the upper floor, but everyone else used them. The rooms had some rush matting on the floors and brightly-covered low divans, with a bare wood table in each, and, in one room, a wireless set. He went there sometimes to sleep, and read, or talk. He went to talk about nothing or everything, and, quite often, about business.

Soon Abdul and his friends would move their premises. It had always been like this, and there could be no question of their applying for a night-club licence to make their meeting-ground legitimate so far as that would have gone; the part of their activities which was illegal could have been protected by a night-club pretence, but the Israeli police surveillance would have been intolerable. The law could not altogether prevent, but it could harass, those few young Jews and Jewesses who came to the house at Acre because there was no other place acceptable to the reality of their feelings in the world around them. The group was seldom more than twenty-five in number at any one time.

'What have you been doing?' Abdul said in English, as the students knew no Arabic or Hebrew.

One of the Pakistanis, a very small man, replied, 'Considering the lilies.' This was a well-worn remark in that house, but it was new to the Pakistanis, who did not know its origin and merely liked it.

An Arab girl in khaki shorts and shirt brought in some coffee. She spoke to Abdul in English seeing that the Pakistanis were present: 'Mendel came back safe. Hassan is returned. Mendel saw your sister.'

Abdul put down his coffee, he hugged and kissed her for all this news.

The taller Pakistani said, 'Your sister Suzi has been very involved. She sent a message, she is very involved.'

'Very involved,' said the girl. 'Mendel will tell you, he's coming soon, he's on his way.'

'What is she involved about?'

'The tourist agency. Very interesting.'

'She must be up to something,' Abdul said, and went to the window to smell Acre. Night had fallen and he heard the splash of oars.

It was ten at night, in the cellar of the laundry at Acre. Here the Crusader foundations could be seen, quite clearly, rising unevenly up to two feet above the flagged floor, until the Crusader stones met the stones that had been set upon them, probably by the next conquerors – the Turks, perhaps.

The light from the oil lamps was thinly misted from their smoke. About a dozen people, young, not of local origin, were gathered, or were drifting in and out of this room. It would have been impossible to tell from their appearance only which of these young men and women were Jews and which were Arabs. The difference was discernible in their accent of speech, although colloquial Arabic was mostly spoken. The two students from Pakistan and a handsome large-limbed Western girl with a mass of long brown hair, who was the daughter of a Church of Scotland clergyman resident at Tel Aviv, were the only non-Semites. The rest were Arabs and Jews, most of whom were maturely sixteen years of age and upward to the reaches of their late twenties or early thirties. Abdul, if anyone had considered it worth finding out, was the eldest. They were dressed in jeans, dresses or shorts, and corporately they had the coffee-bar look of the young, everywhere.

A girl was plucking the strings of a guitar, making soft aimless Arabic music with few notes. Nobody was dancing at the moment. Abdul had fetched a tin of beer from a scarred, lop-sided oil refrigerator which stood in the passage outside, from which anyone who wanted beer took it, depositing the money in the ice-tray. Abdul sat drinking alone, watching the door until Mendel Ephraim appeared.

Mendel Ephraim was one of his closest friends. He was the youngest brother of that Saul Ephraim, the teacher of archaeology at the Hebrew University, who knew Barbara Vaughan and had sometimes acted as her guide in Israel. Ephraim resembled his brother in his taut sinewy look, but he had a slight shoulder-blade stoop; he looked like an intellectual eagle. He was twenty-six. The family had given him up because of his failure as a son, a Jew and an Israeli; they held him in suspicion, but did not know what to suspect him of. He had a job in a tobacconist kiosk at the foot of Mount Zion. Mendel's failure to respond to the State of Israel was their greatest puzzle and embarrassment. Many of the Ephraim family were unbelievers, and it would not have mattered if he had refused only the religion; but many non-religious Israelis were accustomed to speak in historical terms of Israel's destiny; the Old Testament was to them a sacred book because it was the history of the Jews rather than a spiritual record; and it was quite common for those who did not accept any religious or divine element in life to maintain that the Messianic prophecies had in fact been fulfilled in the establishment of the State of Israel. 'The country, Israel, is the Messiah,' they said frequently. Young Mendel Ephraim was as indifferent to this social mystique as he was to religion. He had worked on a border *kibbutz* and been caught, nearly shot, while attempting to cross into no-man's-land, heaving a spare-part of a tractor, which he explained was urgently needed by the Arab farmer on the other side. He had been closely interrogated about these communications with the farmer which had led up to the jaunt, but all he would admit was, 'I could see he was in trouble with his tractor. You could see. Anyone could see.'

The family had given him up. It was known he was friendly with Abdul Ramdez the Arab, and he had to spend a lot of time shaking off the private detectives and secret-service agents who followed him from time to time. He was never certain whether these spies were employed by his family or by the state. He did not care. He shook them off when he travelled out of town, being well acquainted with the terrain of the countryside and its devious hill routes, and having accustomed himself to cave life. He was not entirely alone among his generation in his truculence; there were other Jews like him scattered about.

Abdul, however, seemed to him even more akin in mentality, being far more humorous than most, and more articulate. Besides, he was in a way of business with Abdul. Whether Arab or Jew, it was part of life for Semites who, like themselves, were of long merchant origin to be occupied in some business.

*

Mendel had got himself a tin of beer. He came and sat down at Abdul's shadowy table. They kept silence for a few moments. Then Abdul said, in Arabic, 'You're back safe.'

'I've got news for you.'

'Yes, later. You're back safe, that comes first. Hassan's safe, too.'

The courteous contours of the old language half-imposed themselves on these preludes to their conversation, sentence by sentence, as if tradition itself were fumbling its way among the aberrant communications of the two men. Mendel said, 'I have news for you about your sister. The business can wait.'

'The business can wait, but tell me immediately how much danger there was, this trip. Did you have difficulties?'

'Only when your sister Suzi recognised me. I thought she would call out when she saw me at the Holy Sepulchre this morning.'

'You didn't go to the city in broad daylight? Mendel, you're mad. What did you do that for?'

'Well, I was dressed-up the Arab part.'

'Somebody might have spoken to you. The voice, Mendel. It's dangerous. Anyone can tell by the intonation that you're no Arab.'

Mendel spoke in a harsh whisper. 'If I had been forced to speak, I would have had laryngitis. Lost my voice. It was exciting, though. I'll never forget it.'

Abdul said, 'There is a reason that you found Suzi.'

'Yes, I'll tell you the news. Just before dawn I got to the Potter's Field, and we were wrapping up the sacks in the cave, ready to return. I saw Suzi coming out of a car. She went into that old house just past the church.'

Abdul laughed. 'Suzi must be up to some game.'

Mendel said, with a sardonic Jewish spread of his hands, 'Helping her father in the travel business, like a good girl. Like you help him with the insurance.'

Abdul said, 'Get on with the story. Was it connected with Miss Vaughan? The police are looking for her all over Jordan. There's a big fuss.'

'Yes, well I questioned the old monk, but you know, he doesn't answer, he just gives you a blessing, Father, Son, Holy Ghost. So I keep a look-out. After all, finding her up there in the Potter's Field, I thought she might be in some trouble. She wouldn't be the only one in trouble that you find up there. In the middle of the morning she comes out with two tourists. One is a man. The other is veiled and dressed like an old Arab woman, like your servant.'

'Kyra,' said Abdul.

'I look and I think it is Kyra. It looks like Kyra. But no, it is an English tourist woman called Barbara Vaughan who wants to pray at the Christian shrines. I am to find this out later. But when I see Suzi and I see Kyra at the Potter's Field, I see them drive off with the man, down to the city – so I walk to the city and I find the car at the Holy Sepulchre. By this time it's eleven in the morning, you know, so I have to look like a Christian Arab, genuflecting and kneeling wherever they go. I'm just behind them. I end up at the Catholic Mass at the place of the crucifixion of Jesus, or maybe the place of one of the thieves, better still, for my part. There are a lot of people, tourists and some Arab women. I move in and stand next to Suzi, and she sees me, and she looks startled. It is at this point I feel afraid, since an Arab woman looks hard at me as if I'm up to no good with a woman, as if I'm trying to make friends with Suzi at the church service. But Suzi pulled herself together and looked away, and the suspicious woman began to pray, and the service went on. Then, when the Orthodox service began at the next altar, and the chanting began, I was able to whisper to Suzi. Guess what I said?'

'Shalom,' said Abdul, putting on the Hebrew inflection.

Mendel said, 'I said, "I've got laryngitis, Suzi, you understand, so I can only whisper. What's going on with you?" Then she told me about the tourist who's going all over Jordan with her, disguised as the old servant. Suzi told me this, but understood she had to fit in her talk with the chanting of the Orthodox people standing beside us. So she chanted, they chanted, we all chanted. But they were very close by, these chanters, and she's a clever woman, your sister Suzi. The tourist is a half-Jew. No wonder she looked like old Kyra clutching the edge of her veil and very weak on her feet. It appears the police might be looking for her and she thought, maybe, I must be the police. It's a bewildering place, the Holy Sepulchre. Suzi said to tell you she's all right and she'll be seeing you soon.'

Abdul said, 'I've been to the Holy Sepulchre. I was there once.'

Mendel said, 'The tourist is returning to Israel.'

'How?'

'Somehow. She's called Barbara.'

'I hope Suzi won't attempt to cross over.'

'She said she's all right and she'll be seeing you soon. Leave her alone. She needs a bit of pleasure. A little bit of danger, a bit of pleasure, what's the difference?'

'When did you get back?' Abdul said.

'This evening. I walked back up to the Field as if I owned the place, and all the orange groves beyond it as well. Very slowly, striding like an Arab. I'll show you –'

Mendel got up and walked with a leisurely swing of the arms, like an Arab. Abdul laughed and so did some others who had been dancing on a flagged space on the other side of the room.

Mendel sat down. 'I lie up in the caves until sunset begins. I look for Hassan and he comes. He's a bit hungry. So am I.

The bones, you know all those bones, are hard to lie on. Anyway we haul off at sunset and get across. No incident. We've got five gross of sandals, some dozens I think, leather purses, also a few more things.'

Abdul took from his pocket a rubber stamp, breathed deeply on it and brought it down sharply on the scrubbed wood table before him. It left a clear blue mark: MADE IN ISRAEL. Then they both laughed very loud together for a long time, as if they were boys in their teens like many in the room, instead of men of twenty-six and thirty-four.

Mendel went upstairs to sleep on one of Abdul's divans. Abdul went to start rubber-stamping the soles of smuggled sandals. These goods had been hauled up to the Potter's Field, day by day, on mules, and dumped at the back of the bone-littered caves that surrounded the field. It was their third successful haul. Abdul had gone on one of these trips and next time it would be his turn again. These goods sold in Israel for a huge profit, and even so, Abdul reflected, they sold cheap in the shops, and it was a public service. After a while Abdul, too, lay down and slept. The noise from the cellar was like a faint rhythmic lullaby, for the doors of the meeting-place had been made nearly sound-proof.

About midnight the men stirred. Abdul rose and heated up some spicy lamb stew on an oil stove. He took some to Mendel. They ate without speaking, sitting side by side on the divan. Then they washed at the tap outside the rooms and descended once more to the party. The outlaws were in full swing.

Abdul said to Mendel, in English, 'Do you know, I've discovered a new rhyme for "Capricorn".'

Mendel replied, 'Abou Ben Adhem (may his tribe increase!).'

'Well, you're crazy,' Abdul said, 'but it's a good life. You may have one of my orange groves when I get them back, you may have two.'

A young Jewess came to join them, playing with her guitar meantime. She was playing a popular jazz tune from Jordan to which accompaniment a slim Arab girl was doing a mimic version of an obscene dance performance that was current in the nightclubs of Amman. The tune was called 'I Love Hussein', which was sung with variations by the guitar player. The dancer wore only a filmy scarf wound round her body in a comic fashion that seemed to all, in the excitement and heat of the night, far more funny than it was. Then Mendel danced with a girl while Abdul squatted on the floor beside the guitar player.

Drugs of various kinds, kef, marijuana, and various experimental mixtures were now being passed round. Some of the younger people started howling and dancing convulsively before the excitants had time to take effect. They were stopped by the more practised smokers and drug-eaters, and told to wait till their reactions were involuntary, at which time the significance of their experience would be more completely revealed. Besides, too much noise might invite a police raid. In the deep hours, Mendel and Abdul, narcotically exalted, began to chant their Song of Freedom which never failed to hypnotise the audience by its depth of meaning, although the words of the song varied every time, being a spontaneous composition. But the notes of their chant were familiar, they were those of the mosques, the synagogues, and the churches of the Coptic, Syrian and Greek rites; the same set of notes would break into the air of Acre, presently, at three in the morning, when the muezzin would rise to call from the minaret nearby, and the same arrangement of notes could be heard from the windows of Rabbinical and Moslem schools all over Israel.

The two men chanted, sitting cross-legged with their audience encircling them, in the heat of the party-cellar until one after another became drowsy and either curled to sleep on the spot or stretched and departed into the sharp dark air of early morning. The cellar was aired merely by vents in the upper walls, and by cracks in the ceiling which let in some small whispers of the fresh night from the open windows above. The young Jewess strummed on the guitar, her cheeks bright with the heat and her black curly hair falling over them. Abdul and Mendel, fiery-eyed with a sense of portentous utterance, their voices merging each with the other as one verse ended and the next began, in true style, chanted on to the end and beyond the end, when, with full and satisfied hearts, followed by the few who remained wakeful enough, they fell upstairs to sleep. And even as they climbed, they chanted in colloquial Arabic jargon mixed often with Hebrew:

'My father goes blah O blah O blah for the love of Allah,' chanted Abdul.

'My father goes chime chime chime O mine, hard luck, chime,' sang Mendel.

'My mother goes quack all day, she goes quack, clack-clack.'

'My sister goes tittle-ittle ittle tittle-ill-tee tee goes my sister.'

'Eichmann went to battle and killed the children of Israel.'

'Mohammed put all the children of Israel to death also, for the love of Allah. There was blood.'

'The children of Israel have dispossessed the holy ones of Mohammed. They are refugees. They weep.'

'It was a long time ago, my friend. Even yesterday was before our time, it's dead too.'

'The past has got nothing to do with you, my friend, and nothing to do with me. It's all dead history.'

'Behold what Deborah did to the children of the Canaanites. She slaughtered them with her army.'

'Look what the wealthy shepherd did to the *kibbutzim* in 1946. He shot and killed, the wealthy Sheik and his men. Blah, chime, amen.'

'Look what the Stern Gang did at Dir Yassan, they massacred the lot. Blood, blood.'

'My father, blah, blah. Long live Ben Gurion! Long live Nasser! Long live Islam! Long live all fat men! Israel! My mother goes quack-quack all day.'

'Recall Judith the beautiful, who killed the captain asleep. My son, my son. Tittle-tee.'

'It's all a long time ago. Great is the God of Israel! Mighty is Allah! We dance and sing and make love with each other, it is better than all that religion and hatred all the day long.'

'The Arabs have been neglected by history.'

'The Jews have been rejected by history. Write it down. You might forget it.'

'We want Freedom.'

'Self-government is better than good government. Write that down too.'

'Hussein went to school in Harrow which is in England.'

'Everything is different now. Please all come to the party. My mother makes a party for the girls to do the Twist.'

'Yes, everything is changed. I speak French and English. We all make love together.'

'Come and live in Abdul's orange groves, and pick as many oranges as you like all the afternoon.'

'Come along to Abdul's orange groves.'

5

THE VIA DOLOROSA

On Saturday the 12th of August 1961 when Barbara Vaughan had last been seen, Freddy had accompanied her from the Cartwrights' front door to Matt's car outside in the roadway. Freddy remembered the afternoon that Barbara had spent with them, he remembered it vividly. Matt was going to drive Barbara back to the convent. Joanna had come out to the car, with a parcel in her arms, and had bundled into the back; she wanted to be dropped somewhere. Freddy had waved them goodbye. He had returned to the house. It was empty.

This was the last thing he remembered until he was walking along his usual route from the Mandelbaum Gate to his hotel on the following Tuesday, which was the 15th of August. Only he had thought it was Sunday the 13th of August. Tuesday at four o'clock instead of Sunday at four o'clock, his usual time for returning to Israel after staying with the Cartwrights in Jordan. Freddy went over and over the facts in his mind. He had come out to wave goodbye . . . he was bareheaded under the hot sun . . . he had returned to the house . . . it was Saturday the 12th of August . . . the house was empty . . . then Freddy was following his usual route to the hotel . . . he was tired and hot. He had gone to bed. The manager had come up to his room and inquired if Freddy was all right . . . the ambassadors had been looking for him.

'Which ambassadors,' said Freddy from his sleepy pillow, 'what do you mean?' It turned out that he meant Freddy's colleagues from the legation. It had turned out that this day was not Sunday the 13th but Tuesday the 15th.

'A touch of the sun,' Freddy said.

Amnesia, was the doctor's conclusion. Some mental disturbance.

Nonsense, I'm suffering from sunstroke.

Had he been drugged by the Arabs? Had he been robbed? There was no evidence of either. In any case, Freddy said, I would be sure to remember if I'd been drugged or robbed.

It was very confusing. Begin again. The manager appeared. 'Are you all right, Mr Hamilton?'

Freddy said he was, and closed his eyes.

The manager said that the ambassadors had been on the telephone two or three times.

Freddy opened his eyes. 'Ambassadors?'

It appeared that the manager was referring to Freddy's colleagues at the Legation.

'The ambassadors . . . Are you all right . . . the Legation.'

'What do they want?' Freddy said, lifting his head off the pillow.

'They want to know where you are. All day yesterday, and all this morning, you didn't come. They say your friends where you stay in the Jordan Embassy don't know where you have gone since Saturday. They look also for Miss Vaughan, who was a guest in this hotel, and went to Jordan.'

'I don't stay with anyone in any embassy,' Freddy said. 'The Jordanian Embassy is in Amman. I stay with friends in Jerusalem who are part of a welfare relief mission. Everyone knows them.'

The manager said, 'Now I phone your office and tell them you are safe. Do you like some tea, coffee?'

'There won't be anyone there,' Freddy said. To the Israelis Sunday was a week-day; they always forgot that the Legation offices closed on Sundays.

Freddy said, 'It's Sunday. There's no one there.'

'Sunday?' said the manager.

Freddy leaned up on his elbow.

'What day of the week is it?' he said.

'Today is Tuesday the 15th of August. They look for you in the office two days. Where you have been is not my business, Mr Hamilton, all right? As I say to him, we can put you through to his room. He says, I been put through to his room but there's no answer from his room. Then another gentleman calls me to speak –'

'It can't be Tuesday. It's Sunday. I always come back on Sunday evening,' Freddy said, and lay back among the pillows. The manager departed. Freddy decided to compose a very special set of bread-and-butter verses for Joanna, to compensate for his boorishness. There had been a slight fuss about Barbara Vaughan in the garden. You blow neither hot nor cold. He decided to have a rest first, and get up for dinner, by which time he would have accumulated some executive energy to apply to the verses.

His younger colleague, Rupert Gardnor, anxiously disposed to laugh it all off as a lark, arrived that evening with Dr Jarvis. Freddy sat up, fresh from sleep, and began again. From what Gardnor told him, it appeared today was Tuesday indeed. Freddy believed Gardnor. 'I must have lost my memory,' Freddy said. 'I couldn't tell you where I've been. Hand me my wallet, like a good chap. I hope I haven't been robbed.'

They decided Freddy had not been robbed. He said, 'I must have had a touch of sunstroke.' Gardnor said, 'I'll wait downstairs.' It was uncertain whether he meant he would wait to see Jarvis or Freddy. Jarvis gave no response; he was busy with Freddy.

Jarvis said he would look back tomorrow and make a more thorough examination; the pulse was a bit unsteady; the temperature was normal.

'I'll be at the office tomorrow,' Freddy said.

'On no account.'

Freddy didn't like to think of them discussing him down there. He got up and dressed quickly.

He expected to find Gardnor still in conference with Jarvis when he came down. Instead he found Gardnor drinking in the courtyard.

'The vet gone?' Gardnor said.

'Yes, he's coming back tomorrow. But I'll be in the office tomorrow.'

'I'd follow his advice,' Gardnor said. 'You might have a relapse.'

How does he know what his advice was? Freddy thought. He said, 'It must have been sunstroke.' He ordered a drink and tried to be fair to Gardnor.

They dined together. Gardnor said, after dinner they must find some quiet spot where he could tell Freddy the latest. 'The latest is rather amusing.' By the latest he meant some secret matter in the office.

Freddy expressed himself keen to hear the latest. He said he didn't feel very hungry. 'And the point is,' Freddy said, 'where did I stay? I must have slept. I must have shaved.'

'Well, you didn't sleep and shave on this side of Mandelbaum,' Gardnor said. 'It must have been on that side. We've checked at the Gate, and you came through at 5.18 p.m. today.'

'It passes my understanding,' Freddy said.

'Could you have been drugged? How do you feel?'

'A bit upset,' Freddy said, 'but I haven't been drugged. Jarvis had a look at my eyes with his torch and said, "Well, at least you haven't been drugged" – I suppose he'd know.'

'Oh, yes.'

'Sunstroke,' Freddy said, and accompanied his friend to a quiet corner of the public lounge where Gardnor, in a quiet but gleeful voice, described the latest. This was an involved story about an Israeli counter-intelligence ruse. Freddy felt very drowsy and wished Gardnor would go home.

'The Israelis,' Gardnor breezed on, 'are anxious about an intelligence leakage that they've traced to Beersheba . . .' Freddy felt his eyelids droop, and propped them open as it were with invisible matchsticks. Gardnor's story was connected with the water-pipe-line project, planned by Israel to stretch from Galilee to the Negev, and, branching beneath the desert scrub, to blossom there. This plan had already aroused wild hostility from the Arab States, as much by its symbolism as by its practical advantage to their enemy, Israel. The Arab Press and radio presented the plan as one designed mainly to deprive their people of their own rivers and so kill them off. It was no secret either, in this year of the Eichmann trial, that the pipes were already being laid. In the Israeli press the exact diameter of these huge water-pipes, 108 inches, had been published, but many Arab agencies, prompted both by the accepted rules of propaganda and by genuine suspicion, had reported these monstrous sucklings of Arab life-blood to be the largest known, although, they said, the exact dimensions were as yet withheld by the Israelis.

Gardnor now described to Freddy how the Israeli Intelligence, keen to track down the spy who they knew was operating from Beersheba, had arranged to spill from a rail truck two sections of the metal pipes. For several weeks they had lain by the side of the track gleaming in the sun for all to see who passed on the parallel motor road, and then were explained by government press officers as having fallen accidentally from one of the goods wagons which bore these pipe sections regularly to their destination. The pieces of pipe-line were even pointed out to tourists by the guides, to show off the great engineering plan by which the wilderness of the Negev would open like the rose in a few years' time. Those pipes over there, the guides would say as they drove slowly past the spot – our water-pipes, to bring water from the north to cultivate the desert; they are 108 inches in diameter; look at them!

Gardnor said to Freddy, who sat round-eyed with the effort to keep awake, '. . . and in fact, I happened to see them myself when I was down there last Sunday week, and I thought at the time that they looked rather big, you know. Of course, one can't actually judge these measurements if one isn't an expert, and, of course, I only saw them from the road, which was about two hundred yards from the place where the pipes were lying. But anyhow, it *did* cross my mind at the time that those sections of the pipe-line *did* look a bit bigger than I'd expected, from the official description. And of course 108 inches in diameter is a lot, anyway. Well, anyway, what the Israelis had done –'

Oh go home, Freddy thought, sitting with his eyes forced wide. He began to close in on his ordeal, and to consider his own dumb sufferings, a course of mind which Freddy normally abhorred. Gardnor's hushed confidence continued to scorch Freddy's eardrums, and he sat and put up with it, not caring whether he followed the story or not.

'. . . The Israelis, you see, were after the spy chap operating in the area. And what the Israelis had done,' Gardnor assured Freddy, 'was to build a special couple of pipe-line sections far bigger than those they're actually going to use, and to plant them beside the track. Great huge fellows they were – as I say, I saw them myself and they looked enormous, as I say. And of course, they kept a watch on the spot. Well, last Sunday night –'

'Last Sunday, the thirteenth?' Freddy said. His eyes moved to Rupert Gardnor's face, which had faintly checked its expression at this interruption. Freddy's mind was fixed on last Sunday and its adjacent days as on an aching tooth and its touchy neighbours. Freddy said again, 'Last Sunday, Rupert, did you say?'

But Gardnor was mercilessly intent on cheering up a colleague in his misfortunes. 'Last Sunday,' Gardnor said more clearly, moving closer in the evident assumption that Freddy had not heard his lowered tone. 'Yes, last Sunday night, apparently. Well, they kept a watch . . .' Freddy was touched and soothed by the man's polite implication that there was nothing really the matter with him, and that nothing really had happened. The man was behaving exactly as he himself would have done, of course; that was to say, one would naturally take the line that a few days' lapse of memory suffered by a chap in one's own department was different from what it would be if it happened to anyone else. He allowed his eyes to relax from their propped-open fixedness.

'. . . kept a watch on those pipe sections. Eventually, after a couple of weeks – as I say, last Sunday night – they spotted a man hanging round the place. He got over to the rail track and started measuring the diameter of the pipes. Well, you see, these were the specially planted ones, not the real ones, which are *in fact* 108 inches in diameter. These were much bigger. And as expected the Arabs got the information within the course of the night. It was also received by an Israeli agent over in Jordan, who signalled back the news over no-man's-land at dawn. The size of the fake pipes was, I think, something like 195 inches, but that isn't the point. The point is, the Israelis have got their spy over here – the man who was measuring it. He's an Israeli employed by a quite innocent detective agency in Beersheba – and the Arab Intelligence, of course, are now in a stew as to whether the diameter of the fake pipes, I think 195 inches, really is the size, or whether the official size –'

'The size of those fake water-pipes,' Freddy said suddenly, for no reason that he himself could think of at present, 'is 185 inches, not 195. The size is 185 inches, that I know.'

Gardnor's immediate reply was a long silence, which was the first of the silences in conversation that Freddy was to encounter, and which now woke Freddy out of his half-doze. Then Gardnor said, 'How do you know?'

'What?' said Freddy.

'Oh, nothing,' Gardnor said. 'Only the information didn't reach Jordan until Sunday night, and there was nothing about it in our office until after they'd arrested their spy. We got a memo, Monday morning, from the Israeli Intelligence, and I suppose the Americans are in the know as well, in case we took the ruse seriously and started making inquiries and representations and so on. But you weren't there in the office, Monday morning. That's why I'm wondering how you know anything about the affair.'

'I don't know anything about it. At least, only what you've told me,' Freddy said, in distress. 'But you're right . . . my dear Rupert, I honestly don't know where I've been since last Saturday afternoon. It will come back. A touch of sunstroke –'

Gardnor smiled in an embarrassed way and said, 'Oh yes, I know, but you do seem to have heard something about the fake water-pipes, and you seem to be informed about the exact size. And all this stuff, you see, came to us as Top Secret, of course.'

'I've heard of Topper Secrets,' Freddy said.

'That's true. It isn't so very significant. But one won-ders . . . it's rather as if you'd picked it up somewhere, and one wonders . . . well, Freddy, do you mind if I mention this at the office? I mean, if I don't, it wouldn't be quite the thing, you see, Freddy. What would you do?'

'I'd put in a report,' Freddy said. 'You'll have to do so.'

'I know.'

Freddy said, 'I think if I could get some sleep it would all come back.' Gardnor was really in rather a hurry to observe his duty.

'Of course,' Gardnor said, sitting upright now, very tense and anxious, 'it would be better if you put in a statement your-self. I prefer it, quite honestly. Could you write it tonight?'

'No,' Freddy said. 'It's your job, if you feel it's so terribly pressing. You know you'd be questioned, anyway.'

'Well, I'll say it's done with your approval, and I'll send you a copy. Do you mind if I have another drink? Makes you feel like the bloody Gestapo when you've got to do a thing like this and report an ordinary conversation with one of your own chaps.'

Freddy said, 'Oh, come!' He sat back with closed eyes while Gardnor ordered his drink, and shook his head when Gardnor asked him if he wanted one.

When Gardnor's whisky arrived with a tinkle of glasses and loose change Freddy opened his eyes again. Gardnor said, 'There's another point, Freddy, that may have escaped you. It isn't so much a question of what you've heard in the missing days, as a question of what you might have said, presuming you've been in the way of hearing things of a security nature.'

'The point hasn't escaped me,' Freddy said.

Gardnor's face, which was normally placid and healthy from a recent sun-tan, looked pasty, as if he had eaten something that disagreed with him.

'I'm sure I said nothing out of place,' Freddy said. 'Sure of it.'

'So am I.'

'But I agree, that's a question that is bound to arise. Well, it'll all come back, anyway. A good night's sleep –'

Gardnor now took the hint, swallowed down his drink and left.

Freddy, on that first night of his return from oblivion, pondered for some hours, lying awake in his exhaustion. He had a sense of having exerted himself a great deal, of having been to a number of different places. But what had he done and where? His memory gave no answer. Freddy gave up for the night; he let his mind murmur ironically to itself the boast: 'I can call spirits from the vasty deep,' and he fell asleep, turning his mind's tongue on Hotspur's reply: 'But will they come when you do call for them?'

'I am told very privately,' Freddy said, 'that she is hiding somewhere in Jordan, and is safe so far. Where exactly she is, or whether she will remain safe is another question, I don't know. My informant could say nothing about that. I intend to mention nothing to the authorities until she's out of the country, and I know of course, Joanna, that you won't either.'

'We won't breathe a word,' said Matt. 'Who told you she's still in the country?'

'I'm not in a position to say who my informant is.'

Abdul Ramdez had in fact come to Freddy at the hotel, the day after his visit to Acre, to give him the information that Freddy had asked for. 'She's still in Jordan, she's in hiding. She's safe so far. But you will not inform the authorities, Mr Hamilton, or she will no longer be safe, and moreover, someone very close to me will be in danger also. I can say no more.'

'You can trust me, Abdul,' Freddy said. 'If there's something I can do to help her, anything that you may hear of, let me know. When will she be leaving Jordan? How will she manage it unobserved?'

'I think soon. She will get away. I don't know how it is to be arranged. I tell you all that I am able, as you are so anxious.'

'I won't forget this kindness, Abdul.'

Freddy said to Joanna, once more, 'Not a word. It might lead to bloodshed.'

'Oh, Freddy, I wish you wouldn't keep talking about bloodshed.'

'It's a dangerous part of the world,' Freddy said. 'So I beg you, not a word to a soul.'

'Of course not. They would only start searching –'

'Now, Joanna, don't blame yourself,' said her husband. 'You were perfectly all right to her.'

'It was I who was at fault,' said Freddy. 'It was –'

'Now, Freddy, we've had all that. Do put your feet up and rest. It's you we're worried about.'

'It was the beginning of my sunstroke,' Freddy said.

'You've got to rest. Sit on the sofa, Freddy. That chair's uncomfortable.'

'I can't rest,' Freddy said.

He called the partial collapse from which he was still suffering his 'sunstroke' for want of any better explanation of its cause. Dr Jarvis, on his second visit to Freddy at the hotel, had thought it was probably an attack of 'coast memory', which he said was a type of amnesia that affected white men in the tropics, especially Africa.

'That would be caused by sunstroke,' Freddy had said.

It was difficult to know the point at which one was justified in being affronted by a doctor's remark. This particular quack, Freddy considered, had gone a bit far when he had replied, in an off-hand sort of way, that he believed this type of amnesia was sometimes hysteric in origin but that of course he did not know what type of amnesia it was – he wasn't a specialist in that subject.

'Well,' Freddy had said, aloofly, 'I hope – I *hope* – that it isn't hysteric in origin.'

'Hysteria in the medical sense doesn't mean, necessarily, a wild outbreak of emotion, screaming and so on,' the doctor said. 'It's a term we use.'

'Oh, I know all that,' said Freddy.

This doctor said, 'We may use the word "hysteric" to describe any symptom – it may only be a headache or a stomach disorder, caused by some form of mental disturbance.'

'Yes, but I've got no mental disturbance,' Freddy said firmly. 'So if you are thinking of recommending me to see a psychiatrist, my answer is no. Not while I've got my wits about me, and remain officially sane, do I consult any psychiatrist.'

'Your sanity isn't in question,' the doctor said, as one appealing to reason. Freddy felt deeply resentful of this doctor, who was an English Jew, now an Israeli practising in Jerusalem. His name was Jarvis. Many Foreign Service personnel, including the British, used him for their regular doctor. He had already attended Freddy, some months ago, when Freddy had arrived in the country with an arm swollen and inflamed from a new vaccination. Dr Jarvis had seemed a very agreeable and efficient fellow at that time, but now Freddy found himself in unaccustomed distress; he felt a choking resentment and could hardly recognise himself in the sensation. Why, he thought, is this Jew called Jarvis? It's an old English name, how does he come by Jarvis? His father must have been Jarvinsky or something; I should just like to ask him which of the Jarvises he is, which of the two branches, the Kent Jarvises or the others in Wales. I should just like to see how he'd answer that question. Jarvis, indeed, with his talk of mental disturbances. But Freddy, in his distress, was still graced with those habits of good behaviour which restrain wild-running excesses of thought; he was endowed also with that gift which some men keep furtively out of sight like a family skeleton, an inward court of appeal with powers to reverse all varieties of mental verdicts. And in the space of time that it took Dr Jarvis to sit down at the table in Freddy's hotel sitting-room and write out a prescription, Freddy reflected, I suppose the man is performing his job according to his lights.

Bewildered as Freddy was, and gripped intermittently by waves of panic about his forgotten days, he said, 'My father had a favourite joke about psychiatrists. He used to say, "Anyone who consults a psychiatrist wants his head examined."'

Dr Jarvis smiled as one who tries to do so. 'Look,' he said. 'I haven't said a word to you about a psychiatrist. In fact, I haven't got a great deal of time for them, myself. They all hold different theories. There's hardly two who would treat a patient in the same way. You don't know where you are with them. They're a lot of bloody robbers as well. I've known people, sick people, remain in the hands of psychiatrists, two sessions a week, for twenty years, and nothing to show for it.'

'You don't say so!' Freddy said, cheering up a little.

Twenty years . . . A few days' temporary absence of mind due to sunstroke was really nothing to worry about.

'All I was going to suggest,' said Jarvis, 'was that we get a diagnosis, as far as that's possible, to see what caused your loss of memory and perhaps prevent it happening again.'

'What sort of diagnosis? Who from?' Freddy said. 'I don't want to be unreasonable, but these mental specialists – as you say yourself, they aren't agreed, they've got no proof, no unassailable theory. Whereas if you settle for sunstroke, well, that's an old-established thing, and you know where you are.'

'Let's make it sunstroke,' said Jarvis.

'Oh, all right, I'm willing to be diagnosed,' Freddy said. 'I'll go as far as that. But I won't necessarily accept their diagnosis, or act on it, or answer their probing questions. Probing questions are plain bad manners to me, and that's the long and the short of it.'

'Oh, well, bad manners, good manners – they don't exist in the Unconscious.'

'I don't believe there's such a thing as the Unconscious,' Freddy said. 'How could there be a certainty about something unconscious? If something is unconscious then it's unknown. So the Unconscious is only a hypothesis at the best.'

'Hypnosis is sometimes employed in cases of amnesia,' said the doctor, his face abstracted from Freddy's protests, 'to establish association with whatever has caused it. There's also a recent drug that releases memory, but I'd have to look into it.'

'I would never agree to be hypnotised. Out of the question. No one should submit their mind to another mind:

> He that complies against his will
> Is of his own opinion still.

147

– that's *my* motto. I won't be brain-washed, thank you.'

Jarvis was unmoved. 'I don't advise further consultation at the moment. Seeing how you feel about it, there wouldn't be any point. It would only tend to make you feel worse. I'm going to insist that you take some leave. Get these pills: three a day, half an hour before meals.'

'Are these the memory drugs?' Freddy inquired, scrutinising the prescription.

'No, that isn't the drug I referred to. Those are just old-fashioned sedatives.'

'I feel perfectly all right, actually,' Freddy said. 'Perfectly normal.'

He felt terrible, actually, and when the doctor had left, he sat with his head in his hands, while currents of horror, unidentifiable, unknown to experience, charged through his mind and body continually. Mind or body, it was impossible to distinguish one from the other, they were both and neither. The telephone rang. It was Gardnor, wanting to come round for a little chat, as he put it. Freddy said he would see him at five-thirty. He shivered although the day was warm. He poured lots of water on his neglected geraniums. He shivered again. Then he got his winter suit out of his cabin-trunk where it hung among the moth-balls. If he still shivered by evening, Freddy decided, he would then put it on. What day of the week was it? Time was apt to become confusing.

Before lunch that day, some letters were brought up to him. One from Ma, one from his sister Elsie and one from Joanna. Freddy decided to spend the afternoon writing letters. He took his letters down to lunch with him, but read only Joanna's:

Thank God you've been found, Freddy dear, we were off our heads with anxiety. And whatever *can* you have done with

Barbara Vaughan? – Of course, it's only a coincidence, your disappearing together, but really, Freddy, we did seriously wonder if you'd eloped with her!! I'm in constant touch with the people at your end, in case there's anything I can do at *this* end. Rupert Gardnor tells us you're in good hands. Follow the doctor's advice, won't you, Freddy dear, and . . .

Freddy decided to start a set of verses in *terza rima* for Joanna. He did, in fact, start them on the way upstairs after lunch, but then he fell asleep. When he woke it was half past three. He wondered what had happened to Miss Vaughan, then lost the thought. He checked the calendar – Wednesday, the 16th of August. It would not do to go wrong again. He opened Ma's letter.

He could not make head nor tail of most of it. She kept referring to her 'last letter' in which she had apparently described some dreadful threat of Benny's following some new dreadful upset about the old garnet brooch. It was plain, Freddy thought, that she had forgotten to post, or perhaps had not even written, this last letter. At all events, Freddy did not know what she was talking about, and could only guess that the two old women were being tiresome as usual. He decided to ignore the bit about Benny, her threats, and the garnet brooch, and reply only to Ma's query about Eichmann, who she fancied was a famous pianist she had met in the old days.

His sister's letter was a brief intimation that her friend, Miss Rickward, was to arrive in Jordan next weekend and that she believed Freddy knew a Barbara Vaughan, who taught at Miss Rickward's school. 'Between ourselves,' Elsie had written, 'it was a shock for Miss Rickward to learn that Barbara Vaughan was engaged. Poor Miss Rickward is making a trip out there to see what Miss Vaughan is up to and so on, and any assistance you can give . . .'

Freddy put them aside. He would answer all the letters tomorrow. Perhaps in the morning. Abdul was coming tomorrow. Freddy fell asleep again till Gardnor arrived at five-thirty.

By the end of that week Freddy realised that he was more than ordinarily a subject of concern at the Legation. Gardnor came on four successive evenings, and on Friday took Freddy to his flat for dinner. Freddy was touched beyond the ordinary. There was a look of private strain about Gardnor that Freddy had not noticed before.

It appeared that Gardnor's report had set off an agitation in the office. Freddy was not quite clear what it was about, but it seemed that most of them felt he should be in hospital, receiving treatment for his lost memory.

'It will come back in its own time,' Freddy said.

Rupert Gardnor was now very much on Freddy's side. He was extremely anxious to impress on Freddy that any form of treatment, especially hypnosis, would constitute, in his view, a weak course of action.

On Friday they sat drinking in the leafy courtyard of Freddy's hotel.

'I feel,' Freddy said, 'that if I concentrate on other things, the memory will return in due time.' And he thought desperately of some other thing to talk about to Gardnor, there and then. He could only think of a successful bet he had once laid with his fellow officers at sea during the war, already having tried it successfully in a forfeit game with his nephews and nieces at a Christmas gathering. 'I bet you a round of drinks,' Freddy now said, 'that you can't spell desiccated.'

Gardnor took him on, and spelt it 'd-e-s-s-i-c-a-t-e-d'.

'Wrong,' said Freddy.

Gardnor tried again, for another round, spelling it 'd-e-s-i-c-a-t-e-d'.

'There are two c's,' said Freddy.

'Well, I never knew that before.'

'No one does,' Freddy said.

'You could make a living out of it.'

'So I shall, if I lose my job.'

'Well, I hope it won't come to that.' Gardnor spoke with such a trace of seriousness that Freddy looked to see what expression he wore. But he seemed cheerful enough.

'We've got a new man coming from London next week,' Gardnor said. 'I've no idea who he is.'

'Really? What's his job?'

'I don't know. I only heard about him late this afternoon. But I suppose he's from "Q".' 'Q' was the Foreign Office Internal Security department. Gardnor spoke softly. Two or three other tables on the terrace were occupied.

'Why d'you suppose that? Has anything new been going on?'

Gardnor looked round casually and beckoned to a waiter who was hovering in the vine-framed doorway that led from the terrace to the hall. He ordered some drinks to be served indoors. When they had moved indoors and got their whiskies-and-soda in a quiet corner of the big room, Gardnor said, 'There's been a leakage about the agreement with Kuwait. The Jews don't think it comes from any of their men, they think it's us.'

'Well, that's the Embassy's affair,' Freddy said. 'It's nothing to do with us here in Jerusalem. Whitehall should send its snooper to Tel Aviv, that's where he should go.'

'Oh, we can't pretend to know nothing of Kuwait,' Gardnor said.

'No, that's true. Well, we'll discuss it another time.'

'Everyone feels you should have treatment, Freddy. But I disagree – I mean, for your own sake. You look jolly fit to me.'

'When Barbara Vaughan turns up, if she does turn up safely, she may throw some light on the mystery. I don't know, of course; but she did disappear from the convent on the same day that I disappeared from myself, so to speak.'

'We're more or less certain she's gone away. Her boy-friend left Jordan about that time. They've gone off together.'

'I hope so,' Freddy said.

The following week Joanna met him at the Jordan end of the Gate and drove him to the house. She said, 'I've made inquiries of anyone who might have recognised you on those days last weekend, Freddy, but no one saw a sign of you. I've asked Ramdez, I've asked Alexandros and all the shops, even the barber. No one saw you at all. Of course, they always deny everything, on principle. Where can you have been?'

'I must go over everything carefully from the beginning. Perhaps here in Jordan it will come back to me.'

It was now ten days since Barbara Vaughan's disappearance. She had not been seen since she left the Cartwrights' house on that Saturday afternoon of her visit, when Freddy had unaccountably turned on the Cartwrights: 'The whole trouble with you is, you blow neither hot nor cold . . .' Of course, the row had blown over. The Cartwrights had apologised effusively for their tactlessness and for blowing neither hot nor cold. 'Yes, it *is* true, Matt,' Joanna had said to her husband. 'There are some things too serious . . . poor Freddy is right. Poor Barbara . . .' All that fuss had blown over. Barbara had returned to the convent-hostel where she was staying; at least she had been driven to the door by Matt and Joanna; at least that was what Joanna and Matt said. Freddy found himself in an uncomfortable state of suspecting absolutely everybody's testimony and this, in turn, made him feel guilty. But he was certain, now, where at first he had only begun to notice, that small silences occurred in the course of conversations with visitors and friends from the Legation. They were keeping something back from him, he was sure. When at last he had agreed to come across to Jordan to stay for a while with the Cartwrights, there again he noticed the hesitation, the silences.

'Has Barbara Vaughan been found?'

'No, Freddy, you know we'd tell you if she had. Personally, I think she's left the country.'

'If you hear that she's been found, be sure to tell me. I was privately informed that she is safe so far. I can't tell you more than that, and I can only tell you that much in confidence. But if you should hear that she is dead, killed, by whatever means, be sure to tell me.'

A little silence. Then, 'Freddy, dear, you're being morbid.'

'I know, Joanna, but one must face the –'

'Freddy, you know that Clegg had gone on leave just before she disappeared. It's only reasonable to suppose they've eloped.'

'I don't believe it, Matt.'

'But he went away, just as she did, without telling anyone where he was going. She must have got out of the country somehow. There's a Dutch line from Amman. Goodness, it would be easy. She was just another tourist with a passport; how could they remember her face? It's such an ordinary face.'

'Well, Joanna, there's no record of the name Vaughan on any of the airlines. I don't –'

'Oh, it's easy to move about and pass these border posts, Freddy. A little money goes a long way out here. Everyone's bribable.'

'Well, I'm not convinced, that's all. She had changed towards Clegg, you remember.'

'Well, she must have changed back again.'

Freddy said, 'If one wasn't involved, it would be awfully funny. In fact, it is funny. The woman disappears, then it turns out that Clegg has disappeared; and at the same time I disappeared for a few days. It'll make a jolly good story one day if Barbara Vaughan gets out of it alive.'

The small particle of silence flickered in the air between Freddy and the Cartwrights again. Then Joanna said, gaily, 'It will all blow over, Freddy.'

'Time for drinks,' said Matt. 'What will you drink, Freddy?'

'Promise me one thing, Joanna,' Freddy said.

'What?'

'That you'll be careful when you go clambering about the hills up here looking for wild flowers. That short-cut to the Potter's Field, you know it's dangerous. It borders on Israel. In fact, it's disputable whose territory it is.'

'Oh, Freddy, I've done it dozens of times. Why do you say this?'

'I've got a premonition of bloodshed,' Freddy said. 'Which isn't like me at all. But somebody – I can't help feeling – is in danger of bloodshed.' He was thinking, wildly, as he had done all week, it might be Abdul on his smuggling trip, if he's to be believed . . . It might be Barbara . . . Joanna, gathering wild flowers . . . Somebody I know.

'Freddy, that's an odd thing for you to say,' said Matt, suspiciously.

'He's not in the brightest of spirits, dear,' Joanna said, angry at her husband's tone.

'Not in character,' Matt said. 'Freddy, tell us honestly. Have you really lost your memory? Is it true? Or is it a matter of expediency? I think you'll be frank with us.'

'We're on your side, either way,' Joanna said.

'Then is that what the Foreign Office suspects?' Freddy said. 'Is that what they're thinking?'

'In fact, I did hear a rumour that they're anxious about something,' Matt said. 'Something in the security line.'

'I lost my memory all right,' Freddy said. 'I haven't a clue what happened to me. Matt, you old humbug, what a question to ask me.'

Joanna hugged Freddy. 'We're on your side, anyway,' she said. 'You should let the doctors question you and try to bring back the events. They do it by a process of association.'

'I can wait a while,' Freddy said. 'What actually happened is bound to come back.'

What actually happened to Freddy between the late Saturday afternoon when he lost his memory in Jordan and the early Tuesday afternoon when he regained it in Israel was to come back to him a little later – the outlines of his movements forcing themselves back to him, at first, in a series of meaningless threads. The details followed gradually, throughout the days and into the years ahead and occurred, then, in those fragments, more or less distorted, which are the normal formations and decor of human memory.

The little heated fuss in the garden had blown over. That was definitely one of the things he remembered on his return to Israel. 'The trouble with you,' Freddy had heard himself tell his friends, 'is you blow neither hot nor cold.' Blow cold, blow hot, it had all blown over. Matt drove Barbara back to the convent, and Joanna, cheerfully breezing-down the recently inflamed atmosphere, left the house with them, a bulky parcel of groceries in her arms. She was holding it like a baby. The parcel was not tied with string; it was loosely bundled together in brown paper; one could see portions of a sugar-package, a bag of flour, and a tin of something sticking out of the upper end of the bundle, like an infant's head. Joanna had said that, while the car was out, it would be a chance to take that stuff to someone or other, one of her poor Arab families. Freddy had seen many such bundles of groceries being borne out of houses, at home and abroad, by many such busy Englishwomen, killers of two birds to the stone, all through his life. At home, the Welfare State had done nothing to change their habits. The scene was all the more typical in that Matt had already gone out to the car, thrusting past her, without any attempt to relieve his wife of the bundle; there was no hint of expectation on her part that he should do so. Freddy's aunts and sisters, all their school friends and the wives of Freddy's school friends had been forever dashing out of the house to get a place in the car, with breathless parcels of groceries entwined in their arms, while the husbands pushed past them to the driver's seat.

This had been the last scene to impress itself on Freddy's mind before he mislaid the records. He was on the road, his head bare under the hot sun. He waved goodbye as the car drove off, with Barbara beside Matt in the front and Joanna in the back.

After that his actions and thoughts were as follows: He returned to the house and felt it to be suddenly empty. He thought he had better go up and rest. As he went towards the staircase he passed the letter tray. Two letters had arrived for him by air mail from England. This was not unusual. Quite often his mail, having arrived at his office in Israel after he had left on Friday afternoon, would be put in the diplomatic bag and sent through the Gate to the Consulate in Jordan; one of the consuls would then have it sent over to the Cartwrights where they knew Freddy was staying. And so it was quite to be expected that Freddy should find a letter or two lying on the tray addressed to him, at any odd hour of the weekend.

He took the two letters upstairs, glancing at the envelopes. He saw that one came from his mother and the other from Benny, and when he reached his room he was tempted to put them away out of sight, unopened. This feeling, too, was usual, his habitual reaction to letters from Harrogate where his mother and Benny resided at great expense, mistress and servant grown old together and living on that vital substance of mutual reproaches and complaints against the hotel, which formed the main themes of his mother's letters to Freddy. Benny's less-frequent letters were equally tedious; her religious feeling, so jolly in the hymn-singing nursery days, had become a mania and a great bore to Freddy: 'Mr Freddy, the Lord knows and only He knows what it is to live with her. I have tried to bring home the Word of Jesus to her heart, but the Devil and his Minions have got her in their bloody claws. Mr Desmond gave a sermon last week that was your living Mother to a T. I have spoken to the girls, Mr Freddy, but it is up to you –'

The 'girls' were Freddy's elder sisters. They were quite capable of solving any of their mother's problems, and took some trouble to do so. But Freddy was aware that his mother did not want a solution to her problems, she wanted a solver of problems, and no one would suffice but Freddy himself. Benny was to some extent a participant in the unspoken plot to get unattached Freddy to resign his job and come and live with them. It was an old story to Freddy, who had no intention of laying himself, a human sacrifice, on the altar at Harrogate. In the course of the years he had sometimes become alarmed at Benny's religiosity. Her letters bore more and more graphic references to the Devil and his sulphurous regions, and more and more exhortations to Freddy himself to come home from his heathen posts to Christian Harrogate, and serve Christ rather than the Foreign Secretary. And Freddy had duly sent off his weekly letters to his mother, and to Benny from time to time, adapting their tone according to his judgement. It was largely a matter of keeping them quiet.

Freddy, then, looked at these two letters and felt, as he commonly did, that he wanted to shove them out of sight. But as usual he decided to open them and answer them right away so that the job would not be hanging over him. He was annoyed with his mother for having written a second letter in one week, without waiting for a reply to the first; he was afraid she was getting very forgetful.

Freddy sighed. He hung his coat on a chair and sat down in his shirt sleeves, feeling cooler and more as one getting down to business. He put on his reading-glasses. Benny first: he smoothed the thin sheets and began reading. The old story, only worse. He skimmed over it.

Dear Mr Freddy, the time has come at last to tell you my Temptations are getting beyond human endurance . . . Yesterday your Mother said . . . and on Tuesday, do you know what she did when I went over to the chest of drawers? She . . . Your mother is . . . I hear those Voices again in my dreams and in the early morning . . . Blood . . . Mr Freddy and those temptations come back to me that I told you of last month . . . You had better come, Mr Freddy . . . Mr Desmond says to pray . . . I dare not tell him all my mind as he is so good . . . but I have prayed . . . I started to speak of my fears to your sister Elsie. But you know how bossy she is, she would have me in a Home, so I shut up after that. Your Mother goads me on, she is a true friend of the Devil . . . She . . . She . . . She . . . I am afraid . . . afraid . . . There will be Bloodshed come out of it . . .

Really, Benny is letting her imagination run wild, Freddy thought. As if the heat and humidity of Jerusalem isn't enough to try one's reason, without those letters . . . Elsie is probably quite right to suggest Benny's going into a home, but that would leave Ma without a companion. Let them both go into a home, Benny and Ma, too. Ma, of course, Freddy thought, is behind all this religious excess of Benny's. She would goad anyone to strangle her or slit her throat, and in a way one quite sees how poor Benny feels. Freddy, looking up from Benny's letter to reach out for the other one, caught a glimpse of himself, smiling, in the little looking-glass on the dressing table. The smile disappeared. He opened his mother's letter.

I fear that Benny is . . . isn't quite . . . Benny, I'm afraid, is definitely . . . She has, of course, pilfered my garnet brooch again. Three pounds were missing from my purse and nobody but Benny had access; literally nobody. Elsie is, I'm afraid, most unsympathetic. She has a heart of iron although I write of my own daughter. I see no alternative for you but to come . . . Benny . . . Benny . . .

Freddy took his letter-pad and wrote:

DEAR BENNY,

I have your letter and am sorry to hear you are feeling unwell just now. I hope Mr Desmond has advised you to see the doctor. You should tell Mr Desmond all your troubles, you know, Benny, and if he is a good man, as I know he is, he will understand. These Ministers of Religion know that very good Christians have troubled minds from time to time.

You must bear with my mother. She is getting old, you know, like all of us.

I am extremely occupied just now on some important Government business, but as soon as I can get leave I shall come to join you for a few weeks at Harrogate, and we shall have a merry time.

You know how much we all appreciate you. You must look upon me, and upon my sisters, as your friends. We depend upon you. Don't let us down after all these years.

Your devoted,

Freddy

He wrote to his mother's doctor:

Dear Dr Arlington,

I understand – by the tone of letters received from my mother and our old servant Miss Bennett – that the latter is in a somewhat troubled frame of mind. I shall be grateful if you will have a look into her general health the next time you call in to see my mother. I'm afraid these old people are apt to let their imaginations run away with them.

You know my sisters' addresses of course, in case anything serious should be found wrong with Miss Bennett. But unless she is suffering from a serious ailment, I, for one, would prefer to keep her as active as possible. The idea of going into a 'home' seems to upset her; and as, of course, she has been with our family since her girlhood, I would like her to end her days in the comfort provided by the hotel, and with the feeling of being useful to us, as indeed she is.

Yours sincerely,

Frederick Hamilton

Next, he wrote to his mother:

. . . be patient, dearest Ma. You know that Benny will give

you back the brooch eventually. Are you quite *sure* you did not make Benny a present of this brooch? You are always so marvellous. Remember, only a few weeks ago, there was a question of the garnet brooch. I do not recall how it was resolved (if indeed you informed me) but you see, Ma, Benny is . . . You are, of *course*, Ma dearest, the *only* one who . . .

Freddy put these letters in envelopes, one by one, and addressed and stamped them. He then put them in his pocket. He went out for a walk intending to post them.

It was nearly half past five, and a great sunset had begun to blaze across the hills of Jerusalem, darkening the valley of Gehenna that ran beneath him to join the valley of Jehosophat in the east. Freddy crossed the sandy motor track which led to the Cartwrights' front door and picked his way to the footpath, the short-cut from the city, up which he had trudged on all his visits. He stood there, on the stony path on a ridge of the Hill of Evil Counsel which rose behind him to its summit at Haceldama, the Potter's Field, bought, by repute, with the unwanted blood-money of Judas and serving, throughout subsequent generations, both the dead and the living, as a graveyard for itinerant paupers and a hide-out for smugglers. The all-over properties and associations of this spot were hallowed by a small, musty Greek Orthodox shrine and that ancient, frail monk who was sublimely unaware of anything in the world around him except his hen-coop and God; within the latter category were included all of the human race who crossed his territory on their sightseeing tours or smuggling business, for he seemed to look right through them into God, and treated all accordingly with mesmerised awe, having very few words actually to say to them. Freddy had always found this old monk extremely satisfying company. One could talk to him without the effort of conversation; the monk would express all that was necessary in the pose of his shrivelled body under its loose blue robe, and in the light of his dark eyes, enormous in their deep bony sockets. Freddy had once said, looking round him, 'This is called the Hill of Evil Counsel but it should be called the Hill of Good Counsel.' Not that the monk had ever given him any counsel, but that was how Freddy felt about the man's responsive silence. The time Freddy had stood in the doorway of the dark Orthodox chapel and, regarding the heavy-laden altar and the exotic clusters of coloured lamps hung round it, said, 'It's not really my cup of tea, you know,' the old man had conveyed his complete endorsement of that idea by some emanative gesture that Freddy could not locate in any particular movement the monk had made. Freddy, in this first hour of his absence, turned and looked up towards the field; he could see from where he stood on the footpath a projecting angle of the monk's quarters, and caught a glimpse of the blue cassock as it seemed to potter about the yard, bearing the old man's spiritual bones and con-stitution inside it. He is rounding up his hens for the night, thought Freddy, and at that moment the thought also went through his head that, if necessary, he could spend the night up there. He was quite sure the monk would give him a bed and would not mind being woken up at however late an hour, since everyone was the sweet Lord to him.

It did not occur to Freddy that there was something irra-tional in this notion. But as if he recalled a decision already reached by a form of reasoning, he returned to the Cartwrights' house and packed his clothes into his zipper-bag. Next he took his writing-pad to write a note of excuse to Joanna. None of the house servants was evident, but they were probably hanging around, and would witness his two departures from the house, one without his bag and the other with it. He took a little thought, then wrote:

JOANNA DEAR,

I've decided to return earlier than expected to attend to some private business that's cropped up. I'll write next week. Forgive haste. Bless you, Joanna dear.

FREDDY

That would not mystify. Joanna must have seen his letters on the tray before she left. He put his writing-pad into the zipper-bag and zipped it up, leaving out the letters he had received from his mother and Benny, now replaced in their envelopes. These he put in his pocket, stuffing them in with a rustle of air-mail paper, beside the three unposted letters he had written.

Freddy went to the lavatory, not from need, but in case there should be a long journey ahead of him without access to a lavatory. Then he took up his zipper-bag and went down, leaving his note to Joanna on the letter tray. As he walked out of the door he could still hear the gurgle of the lavatory drain behind him; it was a newly installed system, but even so, Joanna had been complaining that it was too noisy and not really very reliable; one had to yank the chain in a certain way or it wouldn't work; one had to acquire the knack.

He crossed the motor road and saw below, where the evening had deepened, the lights of a car; it was most probably the Cartwrights', since the road only existed to serve a few residents in the area. They were returning and he would be gone. He picked his way cautiously over a few feet of scrub-land to the rocky footpath which branched away from the main road, winding down the Hill of Evil Counsel. The sunset was at its climax, touching the spires and hills of Jerusalem so that they seemed to rise from vague darkness; in the east the Mount of Olives with its three summits, the Hill of Offence, the Hill of Olivet, and the Hill known as the

Viri Galilaei; to the west, Mount Gareb; and in the north, the Scopus range. Freddy went down as it were to meet them, for in the illusory light the mountains had seemed to mingle with the domes and minarets of Old Jerusalem. He suddenly knew what he was looking for, he knew his first task, but he began to puzzle about where he could find it without going too far, or encountering any difficulty, or having to go to an hotel and waste money on a drink. Then an idea occurred to him: Alexandros. Freddy experienced a great sense of relief that puzzled and amused him; he entered the windy streets of the Old City feeling very young and happy – more wide-awake than he had felt for years. The letters were in his pocket, those to his mother, Benny, and his mother's doctor, together with those from his mother and Benny. To dispose of them quickly was his first object.

It was twenty minutes to seven when he reached Alexandros. Most curio shops in the area were still open, but Alexandros seemed to have shut early. A light was on in the shop window and at the back of the premises. Freddy peered inside the doorway and knocked. No one seemed to be in the shop. He rattled the letter box. A few passing tourists stared at him and at the shop, and loitered, as if wondering what sort of bargain this man was after, and whether they themselves were missing something. A voice from above his head called something in Arabic. Freddy stepped back on to the street and looked up.

'My friend!' said Alexandros.

'Am I disturbing you?' Freddy said.

'I come.'

As he let Freddy in, a middle-aged European couple with an Arab guide tried to follow. Alexandros spoke to the guide in Arabic, the drift of which Freddy was able to understand. As Alexandros was apparently about to refuse these late customers, Freddy said, 'I would like to speak to you privately, Alexandros. Attend to them first.' Freddy retreated towards the dark far end of the shop, as one not wishing to be observed.

The man and woman, conversing with each other in German, pressed into the shop, sensing resistance.

'I will deal with them quickly,' Alexandros murmured. 'They are not a serious type of customer, but perhaps they buy.'

'May I use your lavatory?' Freddy said.

'Of course.' Alexandros then spoke to the guide, instructing him in Arabic to wait with his tourists inside the shop and see that they did not touch anything. He led the way to the small closet behind the shop and Freddy followed.

'It is the Western style as you see,' Alexandros said, and Freddy realised that this was indeed an unusual feature for an Arab establishment, where one would normally expect the system of sanitation set into the floor. 'The last tenant of the shop was a Jew,' said Alexandros with his French-Arab gesture of the hands and shoulders that so much conveyed his impartiality to the humours and chances of war, fate and life.

Freddy tore up first the letters from his mother and Benny. Down they went. He waited for the cistern to refill, rightly judging it to be a slow one. He did not want to block up Alexandros's lavatory, or force the cistern to work by repeatedly yanking the chain. While he waited, he realised that the contents of the three sealed envelopes he had in his hand would probably not go down so easily as had the air-mail paper from Harrogate that he had just got rid of, since his own writing-paper was heavier stuff. So he took out his cigarette lighter and, thankful to find it was in working condition, burned up the three letters he had written that afternoon, holding them over the lavatory pan, and dropping in the charred remains one by one, first Benny's, then the doctor's and lastly Ma's. He pulled the chain. Down they went. But not quite. A few charred fragments – those last corners of paper that he had held between finger and thumb – remained floating. Freddy waited for a further four minutes until the gurgle faded to a whisper, pulled sharply and hoped. His total effort was doomed to success. The last of the Harrogate relics disappeared. He emerged from the tiny cabinet to find Alexandros hovering anxiously outside the door.

'Are you all right, Mr Hamilton?'

'Perfectly all right,' Freddy said. 'I was just disposing of some tiresome correspondence.' As he followed Alexandros into the front shop, settling on a sofa in the large space reserved for special customers, Freddy assured his host that he had been careful as regards the drains.

'Mr Hamilton,' said Alexandros, 'you're a wise man. If a correspondence is tiresome, what can a man do? He tries his best, he tries to say one thing, he tries to say another thing. Then after a few months, a year, two years, if there is no satisfaction, then pouff? – he should put the entire affair down the drain. Finish.'

Freddy said, 'It lasted longer than two years. It has gone on all my life. Family trouble.'

'Oh well, your family; I thought it might be a lady. In the case of the family, Mr Hamilton, a man must do the same as with a woman. If they make troubles without end, troubles all the time, there is a point where a man must put the business down the drain. Let the family go their way. Finish. I see you have delayed long enough.'

'I should have done it years ago,' Freddy said. He could feel Alexandros looking at him with approving wonder, and realised that some new thing about his appearance was conveying an unaccustomed liberated impression. 'Do you know,' Freddy said, 'I feel quite young, Alexandros.'

'You're not an old man. Myself, I tell you in confidence, I don't live in an old man's way. I'm fifty-seven.'

'I'm fifty-five.'

'Middle age,' said Alexandros, sinking into a chair opposite Freddy. 'If a man has lived older than his years till middle age, then he should start to live younger.'

'One can make a fool of oneself,' Freddy said. This apparently touched a talking-point in Alexandros. He stood up and said, 'One may do this, always. Agreed. But this depends also on the company. In the consideration of this or that company – this person, that person – one is foolish, one is wise. I also make a fool of myself in the consideration of my wife that I have left my business at Beirut in the hands of my second son, to come here among the Moslems. My wife is a good woman and a fine Mama of the family. But she does not trust my second son's wife, a woman who is a Catholic also like ourselves. My wife is telling me I am a fool to leave the business in Beirut where this wife of my son can make changes. My wife is also against the Moslem religion. Here in Jerusalem she won't speak to our neighbours, she weeps that in Beirut we have all Christian neighbours. So, to my wife I look like a fool. But to my sons I am not foolish. They say, the Papa goes to Jerusalem, he makes a specialised business of fine goods, he sends his first son to the university and his second son he permits to have a life for himself in Lebanon. Another thing, Mr Hamilton – myself, also, I like the Moslem religion all right. I am an Arab. The Christian religion agrees with the religion of Islam in many particulars. But women do not know of this.' He sat down.

Freddy said, 'I often think all religions have something in common when you take away the damn nonsense. How do you feel about the Jews? I've got a special reason for asking you, Alexandros.'

'The Jews,' said Alexandros, in the quieter tone of voice demanded by the subject, 'are good for trade. There is no business here in Jordan since the Jews have departed. The prices are too low. They understand the markets and the variety of quality merchandise for the visitors of one quality or another quality. The country is poor because the Jewish economy is absent. You must not say Alexandros told you this. Not to anyone, please.'

'As persons? How do you feel about the Jews individually? I want to ask your advice about a friend who's got Jewish blood. I've got to attend to it right away, in fact.'

Alexandros spread his hands and cast up his eyes. 'I have known good and bad. People – they are people.' He looked then at Freddy's zipper-bag and said, 'But you do not intend to return to Israel tonight? The Gate is closed. It's too late.'

'I know,' Freddy said.

Alexandros waved a hand towards the curtain which hung across the narrow staircase. 'You must dine with me, please. I then drive you back to the Cartwright house in my car.'

'I won't be returning to the Cartwrights'. My friends think I've gone. But to tell you the truth, Alexandros, I mean to stay in Jordan until I've helped a friend of mine out of difficulty. In fact, now that I've got rid of those tiresome letters I've got an overwhelming desire to do so.'

Alexandros folded his arms.

'I suppose,' said Freddy, 'you think I've gone off my head. And if so, I can only –'

'Mr Hamilton! I am far from thinking such a thing. To my mind you are an extra sane man. Is it a man or a lady, this Jew?'

'A young woman of my acquaintance,' Freddy said. 'That lady who bought the silver fish from you. She –'

'Zobeida! . . .' Alexandros was over by the staircase, pulling the curtain aside, linking himself still to Freddy's presence by an arm outstretched in his direction – 'Zobeida! Make a place at my table for a guest. Lela! Tell Zobeida I have a friend –'

'Look,' Freddy said. 'I don't want it known that I'm still in Jordan. I don't want the Cartwrights to hear. I have a reason.'

'Then nobody shall hear,' said Alexandros, and disappeared upstairs.

Saturday night to Tuesday afternoon: the events were to come back to Freddy in the course of time; first, like an electric shock of fatal voltage, but not fatal, and so, after that, like a cloud of unknowing, heavy with the molecules of accumulated impressions and finally when he had come to consider the whole mosaic of evidence, when he had gathered the many-coloured fragments of what actually happened, and had put the missing parts in place, then he came to discern, too late for action but more and more clearly as the years sifted past, that he had been neither a monster nor a fool, but had behaved rather well, and at least with style and courage. Looking back at the experience in later years Freddy was amazed. It had seemed to transfigure his life, without any disastrous change in the appearance of things; pleasantly and essentially he came to feel it had made a free man of him where before he had been the subdued, obedient servant of a mere disorderly sensation, that of impersonal guilt. And whether this feeling of Freddy's subsequent years was justified or not, it did him good to harbour it.

Now, on the first evening of those missing days, Freddy began to see himself, as he sat at Alexandros's table, in a physical way under such an aspect as he had seen himself in his Cambridge days when he had been a boxing half-blue. It may have been that Alexandros was now regarding him with the special interest called for by the occasion; Freddy was not sure of this, for Alexandros was offering his special reserves of hospitality, as he would his rare pieces, which were generally kept from display in the shop. However that may have been, Freddy felt, as the conversation proceeded, a sense of his appearance which he had not thought about for years; and although his thoughts and speech were given to the eager matter of discussion, a left-hand accompaniment, as it might be played on the piano, went on in his brain concerning his own physical presence; 'well preserved', thought Freddy, would describe the effect, and certainly I'm in good shape due to walking and exercise; hair turning grey, but plenty of it; five foot ten, no stoop; rather short neck. It's a pleasing appearance – how astonishing – but that's merely a fact I simply haven't thought of since I left Cambridge – or, at least since . . .

Alexandros had sent the women of the household away before Freddy joined him upstairs. It was a charming room, containing a few very good objects that apparently Alexandros could not bear to part with; there was no suggestion of an antique dealer's residence, it was that of an uncomplicated, tasteful Arab, and it might have been a room in the house of any Western man of Freddy's past acquaintance who had a leaning towards Oriental rarities if he cared to have rarities at all. The ceiling was low and white, as were the walls. The floor was newly laid with plain polished wood, partly covered by two modern and remarkably handsome Persian rugs. On one wall was hung a carpet of great age and mellowness, the most beautiful Freddy had seen. Its colours glowed forth throughout the evening in a process of slow revelation. A pair of mosaic jars that Freddy could not closely examine, forming table-lamps, were placed at either end of the room, and glimmered quietly in pale blue, green, and russet under the shaded lights. Freddy also noticed a Dutch landscape painting on the more shadowed of the walls, and on the largest wall, a dazzling Russian icon in a large, wrought-silver frame. The rest of the room was furnished casually – a good, small table, a dining-table covered in a white lace-edged cloth and laid for the meal in shiny silver and china which was discernibly Mme Alexandros's best, some rush-seated chairs and a narrow soft couch with damask-covered cushions. It had seemed to Freddy, as he entered this room, that his perceptions must have been getting terribly dull over the years, and now that they had begun to return, he was more enthusiastic than ever about the rightness of his tearing up the letters and disposing of them down the lavatory.

He said to Alexandros, 'I hope Mme Alexandros is not put out by our dining alone.'

Alexandros said. 'Another time, you will meet my wife here in my home. There are many days before us. I told her it is a matter of my business. As you don't wish to be seen, Mr Hamilton, it is important that I serve the dinner to you myself.'

It was a dish of rice, chicken, and olives. Alexandros had fetched it and had again disappeared, returning with an unlabelled bottle. 'Wine from Palestine,' he said. 'It comes from over the border, but not through the Mandelbaum Gate.' Freddy recalled an Embassy row in Jordan because one of the consuls had brought over a bottle of Israeli wine, with the label on it, which his servant had reported to the authorities.

They ate, and Freddy felt Alexandros's eyes upon him and experienced that sense of his own physical qualities, and the qualities of the room, and, most of all, the carpet glowing on the far wall. And he, in turn, perceived large Alexandros in his physical presence, sitting opposite him, fleshy, brown-skinned, thick-jowled with curly black hair, Semitic nose, and vital dark eyes. But the heavy man, by a spread of the fingers or a gesture of neck and shoulders, gave out a weightless courtesy. Freddy felt he could lift Alexandros on one finger, and was perfectly at ease with his own self-awareness harmonised at the back of his mind with the immediate subject of their conversation, Barbara Vaughan's predicament.

'She's nothing to me,' Freddy said, 'in the usual sense. And I'm nothing to her. She's engaged to an archaeologist who's working on the Dead Sea material. She says she's gone off him, but –'

'Off him? That is to mean she's changed her mind and doesn't love him now?'

'That's what she said. But I rather doubt that she means it. The point is, whether she's in danger, roaming about Jordan. A half-Jew . . . I think she is in danger.'

'You have had sleep with her? Excuse me that I ask out of curiosity. One desires to understand all sides of a business.'

Freddy thought this intelligent of Alexandros. 'As a matter of fact,' he said, 'I haven't slept with her. I don't know if she's the sort of woman that one would want to sleep with. I'm afraid I hadn't thought of it.'

Alexandros raised his brows, gave a shrug that might have signified anything, and, in the same gesture, put a large portion of his dinner into his mouth.

'Too nervy,' Freddy said. 'It would be a lot of hard work to sleep with a woman like that, I should imagine.'

'I imagine very different,' Alexandros said. 'It is of course one of the things of interest that one asks oneself in secret thought when a lady comes to the shop to buy – how is she like in the bed? – and I have thought this morning when she came to the shop, that she is a sexual woman.'

'Would you say so?' Freddy realised, with envy, that Alexandros never permitted himself a moment's boredom.

'To the finger-tips.'

'How astonishing.'

Alexandros nodded slowly. He was evidently delighted to be established as the expert that he was.

The evening warmed around them. 'She's in danger if it is known that she is a Jew by blood,' Alexandros said.

'Even though a Christian?'

'She has been first to Israel, so she would be thought a spy.'

'I'm not sure how seriously my friends, the Cartwrights, realise it. I'm afraid we discussed the question rather a lot –'

'Yes, I know,' said Alexandros. 'The servants of the Cartwrights have reported. My shop boy has told me already this evening that we have a Jewish tourist in Jerusalem, and she was the one who bought the silver fish from our shop. One cannot help this news spreading. They fear Israeli spies.'

'She's a half-Jew.'

'This makes more suspicion. You should know this, as you are in a foreign service.'

'Indeed, I understand.'

Alexandros said, 'Perhaps you must see the British consul and arrange for her to leave the country. Keep her in the convent for the meantime. It is a pity, but –'

'A pity!' Freddy said. 'It's a damn disgrace that a girl can't go on a pilgrimage of the Holy Land, a Christian convert visiting the shrines, without fear of arrest.'

Alexandros radiated response. 'You are right! Perhaps you let her take the risk. Perhaps the danger is not so much. The government spies will follow her but perhaps they will hesitate to make an arrest.'

'Ramdez is her travel agent,' Freddy said. 'I can't think what possessed her to go to Ramdez. Obnoxious fellow.'

'If Ramdez is the agent, then she could meet danger from private retribution. Ramdez is dangerous.'

'Private retribution?'

'An accident may befall her on her travels. Between the police posts are many miles of desert. She may suffer an accident. This, too, you know of.'

'I do understand,' Freddy said, struck now by his recollection of political deaths by accident. He jumped to his feet. 'Alexandros, we must do something.'

'Be seated, Mr Hamilton.' Alexandros, in his usual manner, prolonged the last syllable to synchronise with the action that accompanied it. His gesture now was to place his two large hands on Freddy's shoulders and press him back into his chair. He then left the room, but without seeming to withdraw any of his presence, for Freddy could hear his footsteps, heavy with long-accepted proprietorship, beating towards the back of the house, and from there, his voice domestically urging his requirements in Arabic, above a kitchen clatter.

Freddy had an urge to make himself useful by piling the used plates together. It was a habit he had acquired since the war when visiting servantless friends. But he forbore. Alexandros would prefer to do everything himself. He was a marvellous host.

Alexandros could be heard on his return, treading more quietly in caution of the stuff he was carrying, which nevertheless rattled a little as he entered. It was a dish of fruit, coffee and a decanter of brandy with cups and glasses. 'I make a good waiter at the table,' roared Alexandros, setting down the tray with the last word, 'tabe-oool'. And when he had shut the door he sat, clasped his hands as if congratulating himself and said, 'My wife and her servant are thinking I am making big business with a representative from a great museum, as I have told the household. I have said the negotiations are very secret as you are in rivalry from another collector who follows you to gain knowledge of your expert discoveries. We have many such dealings here in Jerusalem. There was much secret business with great collectors and great museums and their spies, and also with many governments when we came first to Jerusalem, as those were the years of the discovery of the Dead Sea scrolls. There were many fragments in many hands. As also with other items of antiquity in Jerusalem. So Alexandros can make a story to silence his household of this meeting tonight, and Alexandros is a good waiter at the table.' He unclasped his hands and poured coffee, pushing the used plates and cutlery out of the way. 'And we make a plan for Barbara.'

'Alexandros, you're a good fellow.'

'I'm not too old to enjoy this rescue of a woman,' said Alexandros.

'Neither am I, come to think of it. I'm prepared for anything. But I don't want to involve you in any danger, Alexandros.'

'Danger is pleasure. What else is pleasure when a man has been married to one wife thirty-two years? You are married with a wife in England?'

'No. Few people know it but I was married once.'

'She has died?'

'No. It was when I was very young. The marriage didn't last a year. She turned out to be no good. Incurably no good. What we call a bad lot.'

'It was bad luck.'

'Oh, I've forgotten about the whole thing. It was a misfortune that can happen to a family like any other misfortune.'

'I had a cousin who was like this. In Beirut. She was with many men of different nationalities. I don't know if she's dead, living. We refused her in the end from the family. What could we do? We gave her money, but this failed. Nothing sufficed. She is perhaps in prison. Have you divorced this wife?'

'Oh, yes, and made a settlement on condition of her not marrying again.'

'This is honourable.'

'It's like buying a horse. If it turns out to be a bad horse, one should keep it off the market in case some other chap should get hold of it.'

'Exactly. I do not disagree.'

'Not everyone,' Freddy said, 'would agree with us. In Europe, these days, it's considered unfair to stipulate a condition that might deter anyone from marrying again. But in my view I did the only possible thing. It's a question of one's point of view. It was the only conceivable thing to do. Anyway, it was a long time ago. Nobody mentions the affair in our family, except my old mother from time to time, when she wants to be tiresome. It was a long time ago. My goodness, it must be getting late!'

'Only eleven o'clock,' Alexandros said. 'There are ahead all the hours of the night. And we have only to plan everything.'

They had not drunk a great deal; it was more the stimulus of their evening, wrenched as it was from the line of habit, that gave them heart to leave the house together at half past two in the morning, burning with an imperative sense of duty towards Barbara Vaughan. Freddy's had been the idea of getting her up in Arab disguise, while Alexandros, his hand clapped suddenly to his brow to hold intact the brimming tide of inspiration, had contributed the Ramdez daughter as her best possible escort.

'Which daughter?' Freddy had said. 'Aren't there two?'

'The unnatural one,' Alexandros said.

'With the blue eyes, like young Abdul?'

'That's the woman. She is not so bad. It's only that she should have been a man. There was a mistake in the making of her. She holds opinions different from her parents. So here they say she's the unnatural one.' Alexandros sprang to his feet. 'We go,' he said. 'It's a matter that can permit only of arrangements in the dark of the night.'

He advised Freddy to keep well into the shadow of the houses, but himself walked with a sort of arm-swinging march in the middle of the street where the moonlight lay. He seemed to be exercising some of Freddy's new resources of freedom as well as his own natural supply. Freddy kept pace with him from the shadows, not for one wild moment doubting the success of their plan, conceived as it had been in an hour of genius and of brotherhood; all was perfectly feasible, or as good as done, and he walked in that dispensation of mind in which impossible works are in fact accomplished and mountains are moved.

They turned into the Via Dolorosa, and there Alexandros strode on in the light of lamps and moon like the Archangel Michael leading his legions to storm the gates of Hell which should not prevail against them, as was written. Freddy moved in to keep pace beside him in the narrow street. They now walked shoulder to shoulder.

They came at last to the convent where Barbara Vaughan was staying. It looked very much closed for the night.

'I speak personally to the janitor,' said Alexandros, moving into the lamplight to verify the amount of paper money that he had produced from his pocket to harmonise with his intention.

'This is on me,' Freddy said, getting out his wallet.

'The janitor is inexpensive. Keep your money to speak to the officers behind the desks if inquiries should arise concerning Barbara in the course of the holy pilgrimage.'

Freddy waited. The night now began to give out the chanting of the minarets, from Israel across the border to the west of the convent, then nearer, to the north, from the direction of the Holy Sepulchre. It was three o'clock. The chanting voices echoed each other from height to height like the mating cries of sublime eagles. This waiting for the return of Alexandros in the morning hours of Jerusalem was one of the things Freddy was to remember most vividly later on, when he did at last remember the nights and days of his fugue. From the east, beyond the Wailing Wall, a white-clad figure raised his arms in the moonlight and now began his call to prayer, and soon, from far in the south, then in the south-east, and from everywhere, the cry was raised.

6

JERUSALEM, MY HAPPY HOME

'Who's there?'

The voice answered, very close to her but on the other side of the door, with hushed urgency, 'Freddy Hamilton. Don't make a noise. Let me in.'

It impinged on Barbara that this was highly improbable, that she was in a convent bedroom, and that there was no lock to the door. She hesitated in a woken daze long enough for the voice to announce itself again. This time it said, 'Is that Barbara Vaughan?'

'Yes.'

'Well, it's only me. Please open the door and I'll explain.'

This sounded authentic. She slid one arm into her dressing-gown and was about to open the door when the handle turned and Freddy's face appeared.

He said quickly, 'Don't make a noise. This is a convent, you know.'

She said, while sticking her other arm into the sleeve, 'What's the matter?'

He came in then, and silently closed the door behind him. He said, 'Forgive me for intruding like this. An emergency. I've come to get you out. You're in danger, but I've got everything planned and you'll be quite safe with me.'

She was still unclear about the reality of Freddy in the room. She had set the front of her hair in two rollers, which she now removed and put into the pocket of her dressing-gown as she said, 'It's terribly late. This is a convent, you know. What's happened?' But now she giggled, partly with relief that the quiet, repetitive tap-tap at the door which had eventually wakened her was only Freddy's.

Freddy said, 'I'm afraid it's all very informal. But I just want you to pack your things and come with me. There's a car coming round to pick us up and we're going up to the Potter's Field to spend the night. Everything is planned, so don't worry. Just pack quickly and quietly, and come with me.'

She felt a returning wave of the fear she had gone to sleep with. 'Am I to come like this?' she said, plucking at her dressing-gown.

'There's nobody about outside. You won't be seen. There's only me and Alexandros from the curiosity shop, a man I could trust with my life. Alexandros will drive us to the Potter's Field. Hurry, Barbara. In an emergency, one can't be Victorian about things, you know.'

She started to pack her bags and laughed softly to herself again, for Freddy's word 'Victorian' brought comfortably to mind a private family joke – how one of the deep-voiced Vaughan aunts had declared when her son had been igno-miniously expelled from school, 'I refuse to be Victorian about it. Of course, the boy is a little *oriental* in his ways, I'm afraid, but then his father is a little oriental and so was his grandfather. And in point of fact, no one in the family, right back to William the Conqueror, has ever been Victorian about it.' Barbara said to Freddy, 'How did you get in? Have I got to bring everything? I haven't paid for the room. It's ten past three.'

Freddy said, absent-mindedly, while looking round, 'This is no time to be Victorian . . . Is there anything I can do? Don't forget your sponge-bag.'

She packed on. 'If any of the nuns . . .'

Freddy fastened the locks of her suitcase while she put the final objects in her small case. She told herself that Freddy Hamilton was behaving unexpectedly and that it was an odd situation. Meanwhile she looked at the bed. 'I'd better –'

'Oh, leave the bed. Hurry.'

She fumbled with her hair, feeling it strange to be going out with her hair straggling loose, and wearing her slippers and dressing-gown as if being taken suddenly to hospital or prison. But it never occurred to her to object to this departure.

Freddy looked out of the window, peering sideways towards the front of the convent. 'It's there,' he said. 'Good old Alexandros. He's waiting with his car.' He lifted the suit-case and said, 'I'll go first. You follow when I get down the first flight. Not a sound, remember. This is a convent.'

She pulled the bed straight as he spoke, and tucked in the loose blanket to give it a made look. She put three pounds on the dressing-table. 'It's too much,' Freddy said. 'Three would be exorbitant.' She took one back. 'Quite enough,' he said. 'The Catholics are rolling in money.' It was as if he had said 'the foreigners' in one of those private exchanges between Britons.

He lifted the case, whispered, 'We're off!' and opened the door. He whispered again, 'Not a whisper,' and stopped to listen lest anyone in the house had been aroused. The oldest nun, a scholarly antiquarian who was reputed to know more about Jersualem, more of its unrecorded secrets, than anyone else, was snoring at the top of the house; she had told Barbara that she had been given a room at the top of the house because she snored, and had mentioned the fact quite casually, in the course of remarking on the difficulty to old bones of climbing the stairs; the ordinary social vanities did not enter the lives of these nuns.

Freddy, with the suitcase, had reached the landing below; he had one more flight to descend. Barbara followed, gripping her hand-luggage and, quite unnecessarily, the edges of her Liberty dressing-gown which were already held in place by its tie. Freddy was now on his way down the last flight of stairs, to the ground floor. She found herself palpitating with the thought of being discovered leaving this place in her night-clothes with a man and her luggage; the other residents were five middle-aged pious Catholic women from Stuttgart, and the nuns were nuns, and moreover had particularly fussed over Barbara as being Englishly cool, spinster-like and, as she supposed, a bit more nun-like than the five loquacious matrons from Stuttgart. This breathless fear of Barbara's as she began to follow Freddy down the stairs then bore upon her common sense as being so excessive as to weigh the balance of probability in favour of its being groundless; the nuns, she reflected, were hard workers and hard sleepers, while the Stuttgart pilgrims no doubt slept so very much like logs. By the time she had turned the bend on the staircase towards the lower landing she had become confident of an easy exit, and crept down the remaining steps in synchronised time to the snores of the attic nun. She paused on the landing and looked along the corridor to where the Mother Superior, a woman of about Barbara's age, had her quarters.

From the floor above, where she had come from, a noise of running water and padding footsteps came in muffled spasms between the overwhelming attic snores; this was probably caused by one of the German women moving around in the night, having awakened either by habit or by the sound of Barbara's packing and departure. A tinted glass window above the staircase she had just come down let in the moonlight, but the next flight down to the front hall was in blackness by contrast to that dusky amber windowlight above. Barbara lingered on this landing, between the half-light and the pure dark, as if waiting for something. Along the corridor, where the Mother Superior slept, nothing stirred. Barbara did not know why it should. Almost disappointed, she moved to follow Freddy cautiously down the very dark staircase.

Freddy, half-way, came to a curve in the stairs and bumped the suitcase loudly into the wall. Barbara halted on the third step and whispered down to him, 'Are you all right?' He did not reply, but she could hear him continue to pick his step by muted step. She glanced behind and upward, and could not place her sense of something unaccomplished in the silence. The front door was unlocked and Freddy now held it open so that the moonlight flooded her last footsteps from the sleeping convent. They had got away.

Immediately on passing into the night air she realised that she had almost hoped to be caught, it would have been a relief and a kind of triumph and justification. For there had been a decided element of false assumption in her reception at the convent the previous day, after they had inquired politely, and estimated her type. Of course she was an English Catholic convert. She was indeed the quiet type. But there was a lot more than met the eye, at least she hoped so. She had thought, as the Mother Superior made her benign speech of welcome, and the old novice-mistress hovered with an admiring smile, if only they knew. And she was inwardly exasperated, as she had been with her cousins last summer, when she had carried on a love-affair with Harry Clegg, there in the house, and they, in their smug insolence, had failed to discover it. And why? She thought now, with the old exasperation, what right have they to take me at my face value? Every spinster should be assumed guilty before she is proved innocent, it is only common civility. People, she thought, believe what they want to believe; anything rather than shake up their ideas. And if a nun had in fact put in an appearance on the landing when Freddy had bumped her suitcase at the bend of the stairs – a startled nun switching on all the lights, the Mother Superior perhaps – what would she have said?

Freddy was opening the door of a large car, at the wheel of which sat a man whom she recognised as the Arab shopkeeper from whom she had bought the ornamental fish that morning. Freddy had pushed her suitcase in the back of the car, and turning to her he said, 'Hurry!' She had never seen Freddy Hamilton looking so happy. She had not thought he had it in him.

And what would she have said if one of the nuns had caught them, if one of them came to the door even now that she was getting into the car, lifting the Liberty dressing-gown as if it were a long evening dress and she departing from a late night party? 'My dear good woman, things are not what they seem, as you in the religious life ought to know. Foolish virgin, hasn't experience taught you to expect the unexpected?'

She said to Freddy, 'What on earth would we have said if we'd been caught?'

Freddy said, 'If they're decent women, as I'm sure they are, you could have explained about your Jewish side.'

The faint sound of the bolt being slid into place behind the heavy studded convent door reached them through the car windows. Whoever had let Freddy in was locking up again.

She said, 'They're decent women but I don't think I would have got much sympathy as a Jew, even if they'd believed the story. It would have embarrassed them, in this environment.'

'What d'you think, Alexandros?' Freddy said as the car started. He was in the front while Barbara sat behind with her suitcase. She looked back. Not so much as one belated inquiring light had gone on in any of the windows.

Alexandros said, 'Madam, they would think something else to see you come with a man and your baggage. Maybe they shall say in the morning that you are a wolf in the raiment of a sheep.'

'So I am,' Barbara said.

'What a jolly good idea this is,' Freddy said, and they all laughed at each other's words with an overflow of relief, success, and the moonlit morning air; meanwhile, the car wound and swirled unhindered to the south, across Jerusalem, in the direction of the Potter's Field.

Ten days before she had left Israel Barbara had received two unexpected letters from England and failed to receive an expected letter from Harry Clegg in Jordan, smuggled to her in the American bag from Amman. When returning to her room she always looked for the envelope lying on the carpet by the door. The absence of any word from Harry Clegg had made the presence of the two English envelopes, which arrived together on the same morning, rather irritating. One was from Ricky, her old friend, the head of the school where she taught. The other was from her cousin, Michael Aaronson.

She first opened Miss Rickward's letter. In a way she had been missing Ricky, whose faults were many but amorphous, and whose virtues were well defined, among them being an exceptional capacity for retaining knowledge, shrewd intelligence of a scholarly order, and a scrupulous, almost obsessive literal honesty; all of which virtues, apparently in the nature of things, precluded humour. Ricky was a good talker, in that she could converse seriously for hours on a subject, the absence of any wit in her talk having the compensatory value of keeping the main topic in line, without any of the far-flung diversions that humour leads to. Ricky could discourse for hours on the history and development of the existentialist philosophy. It had been pleasant for Barbara, it had given her a remote sense that she was doing something in life, if only mentally, to sit and listen, with an occasional comment, while Ricky expounded the doctrine that existence precedes essence.

But could Ricky apply this notion to the world she existed in? To Barbara? Herself? Barbara had looked round the room of her hotel in Israel that morning, and was irritated by the unmade bed. She decided to take her letters downstairs and read them in the courtyard; then forgetting her decision, sat on. Ricky could discuss the psychological and biological differentiations of the male in all their subtleties past and present. She could speculate on their future. But did she recognise an attraction between a man and a woman before her eyes? When one of the girls at her school, a large-built matron of fifteen, was found to be pregnant by the local cinema owner, Ricky said, 'The poor child was only proving the theory of reproduction for herself. She's a natural empiricist, an intelligent child,' and might have written as much, as solemnly, in a letter to the parents of a girl who had burnt her fingers on a hot test-tube.

Barbara had glanced at the crack beneath the door, not quite aware of what she was still hoping for; the stir and thrust of a white envelope from Jordan.

Ricky once had an admirer, the shy widowed father of one of the girls. He had sent her the enviable present of a bunch of roses, fourteen, each one of a different species. 'I wonder,' Ricky said, 'where he got the impression that I'm a student of horticulture. Someone must have given him that impression, Barbara.'

But there was no end to Ricky and the various ways in which Barbara genuinely missed her. Barbara was, moreover, aware of various ways in which Ricky resembled Harry. The main difference was that Harry was a man. The next difference was his actual achievement in life, which was already recognised everywhere; whereas Ricky, of South African origin, having come to England on a scholarship, had gone far, but achieved little. Both, however, had done what they had done through their own efforts without family advantages. And Harry seemed to resemble Ricky in appearance, more in Barbara's memory than in the presence of either. Barbara had never seen them together, and she partly knew that the resemblance she discerned was, after all, a matter of the lights and shadows cast on their features by some lonely lamplight of affection within herself.

Ricky was a keen promoter of Scripture-reading at school; she was herself a lapsed Congregationalist with a puritanical bias. Once, after last summer's holidays when Barbara had fallen in love with Harry Clegg, Ricky was setting the senior girls an essay on the subject of the Second Coming to be illustrated by scriptural texts; she demonstrated this procedure by quoting a passage on the return of Christ to judge the world: 'Then shall two be in the field; the one shall be taken and the other left. Two women shall be grinding at the mill; the one shall be taken and the other left. Watch therefore . . .' Barbara, standing by, listened distantly to Ricky's moral implications, but heard closely the literal ones. It's certainly a point, thought Barbara, that two engaged in a common pursuit do not consequently share personal identity, and absurd though it is to affirm this evident fact, Ricky feels towards me as if the opposite were true. Sooner or later she'll have to find out that my destiny is different from hers.

She had opened Ricky's letter first. The one from her cousin Michael was not likely to be a personal stimulus one way or the other. The letter from Harry was what she had wanted, and with that instinct for any sensational distraction, any quarrel, any irritant, of one who has endured a near-miss, she opened Ricky's letter first. Disappointingly at first, and then astoundingly, it read:

MY DEAR BARBARA,

Thank you for your two postcards which both arrived last week, on Tuesday and Friday, respectively. I am pleased to hear you are having a not uncomfortable trip. The experience should be a profitable one – in the spirit if not in the letter!

I hope the food (if I am not treading on holy ground by mentioning that mundane but essential factor) is not unwholesome. How well I remember those weeks following your return from Spain . . . 'Nuff said!

You will be surprised to learn that I have been through a very strange experience during the past fortnight. It is an experience that can only be described as a troubled if not a shattering one. Indeed, I was undecided, or, as one might say, torn in mind, with regard to the advisability or otherwise of mentioning the matter to you. Suffice it to say that my nights, for the past week, have been both anguished and sleepless. Yesterday I arrived at the decision to inform you of my distress, giving you the full account of its cause, and . . .

Bewildered, amazed at the emotion and mounting tone, Barbara sent her eyes flowing down and across the next few pages in frantic grasp of their gist. Ricky had learnt of her engagement to Harry Clegg, that was all. Elsie Connington, a mother of one of the pupils who had become more closely connected with Ricky than with herself, and whom Barbara now recalled having once met, had entertained Ricky for the weekend, in the course of which they had visited Elsie's mother at Harrogate, a Mrs Hamilton. Elsie was Freddy Hamilton's sister, it appeared . . . Freddy had written to his mother that he had made the acquaintance of a Miss Vaughan, who hoped, the Catholic Church permitting, to marry a Harry Clegg, an archaeologist. And the old woman had passed this on to Ricky. So it appeared, and so it was. Barbara felt furious, first with Freddy for his gossip. She wondered why he had failed to tell her that his niece was at her school: then, realising he was probably unaware of this fact, she turned on herself for confiding so much in Freddy. At last, she read through the letter again, and began to feel a wholesale sense of nausea:

Words cannot express my astonishment, my dear Barbara, let alone my horror. I said that I, as your most intimate friend, must emphatically deny any such idea on your part. I said that your acquaintanceship with Mr Clegg had been brief, casual and quite innocent of any romantic nonsense, since you were, to my certain knowledge, not in a remote degree inclined towards matrimony. It would be disastrous if you made a mess of your life.

It was naturally disconcerting to me to be informed by a third party that Clegg was in your part of the world. The fact that you had spoken of him to Mr Hamilton would appear to me, pending further evidence, to indicate . . .

Barbara said aloud, '*Pending further evidence* – Oh, my God! Oh, Jesus Christ!' What has it come to, she thought, between Ricky and me? Ricky's letters were usually written with difficulty, woodenly. But this uncharacteristic outpouring, this confession, almost – what had it come to? It's like a letter, she thought, from an insufferable man to his unfaithful mistress, or a wife to a wandering husband, or a possessive mother to a teenage daughter, or a neurotic Mother Superior to a nun with a craving to get out. Who am I to Ricky and who is she to me? She's only a friend. I've taken no vows.

Barbara let up the Venetian blinds of her room, hot as the Israeli morning already was. She sat down and brought Ricky's image to mind, her dark, short-cut, curly hair, the plump, apple-coloured tomboy face. Small and sturdy, Ricky took shape before her, wearing her tweed skirt and wool jumper with flat brogues in winter, a cotton dress and sandals in summer; dark hairs showed through her stockings on school days and, on summer holidays, shaggily coated her bare legs. On many summer evenings before school broke up, Barbara had sat on the small veranda outside Ricky's sitting-room, drinking after-dinner coffee, listening to the gramophone record in the background, her eyes fixed absently on Ricky's dark hairy legs. Barbara was aware of them now, as she recalled her own fascinated stare, as she thought, how has an ordinary friendship between two women reached this point? How? Ricky must be a latent Lesbian; and I? I'm in her clutches, but she's in mine. Yes, why, Barbara thought, haven't I told her about Harry? Why? Or why haven't I written as I intended to do, why not? It was only right if she was my closest friend, as I thought she was. It is only natural that Ricky should expect me to confide what's going on.

Only the night before, Barbara had returned to the excessively difficult attempt which had hung over the past three weeks, to write an honest letter to Ricky. Again, it had been unsuccessful. Barbara could see, from where she sat, on the writing-table close by, abandoned sheet after sheet of paper, not yet torn up and tidied away for the morning, where she had left them on the frustrated night before:

DEAR RICKY,
I have been meaning to tell you –

DEAR RICKY,
I know you will be surprised, but I feel I must –

MY DEAR RICKY,
I have been touring strenuously so haven't had time to write properly. But now I want to write a decent letter and tell you, first of all –

VERY DEAR RICKY,
You will be happy to know I am hoping to marry Harry Clegg – the archaeologist whom I met last summer. We are very much in love. Much depends on the decision of the Church as to the annulment of his previous marriage, bu –

DEAR RICKY,
The heat, combined with strenuous –

I didn't tell her, Barbara thought, because I intended to write. And I haven't written because I was afraid, and that's the truth. It's as if I were married to Ricky, only worse.

She thought, it's the male element in Ricky that has attracted me. Then she imagined herself in bed with Ricky, in physical contact, shuddered a lot, and thought, I must get married, I really must. This is no good. She recalled the freedom of last summer, and longed for her humorous lover.

At all events, she thought, I must leave the school. Ricky has become over-familiar and I must leave the school. Immediately; not even a term's notice; I must write and do that. This decision brought her immense relief. Barbara could not understand why she had not thought of anything so simple before. She had small private means and was not pressed to find another job immediately.

She sat up to the table and wrote:

DEAR RICKY,

There are many things I cannot explain at the moment, but I shall do so in time. I do beg you to have patience with me, both for failing to discuss my plans with you and for now reaching a decision I feel must pain and know must inconvenience you.

I can't return to school, and regret very much that I can't give you a term's notice. I can only hope you will be able to replace me at this short notice, and it won't upset your trip to Brittany. Please, dear Ricky, go to Brittany for my sake, or I shall feel bad about it.

My plans for the future are so far unsettled, but I truly can't return to school.

I'll let you know later about collecting my things, and will ring you myself, as soon as I get back to England. I'm going to Jordan next week to visit the shrines – can't say how long I'll stay there.

Don't worry about this, will you? I assure you there's nothing to worry about.

Love,

BARBARA

She saw, without stopping to bother about it, that her hand-writing was slightly larger and heavier than usual. She sealed and stamped the letter, took it down to the letter-box, thrust it through the slit, went and had a look out of doors at the shining street and returned to her room, where she pulled down the cool blinds and slumped, heavy with relief and the recent weight of what she had been carrying. She felt very much one of the Vaughans at that moment. Whatever the points of inward debate or the pinchings of self-accusation, none of the family would have hesitated to act otherwise; intrusive people must be put down, and that was the long and the short of it. She now remembered saying to Harry, when they had discussed their marriage:

'I don't know how I shall break it to Miss Rickward.'

'How do you mean?'

How did she mean? It was only possible to answer, 'Well, she'll miss me. We've become very attached after six years, and she doesn't think of me as marrying.'

'Oh, bugger *her*,' said Harry.

Recalling this, Barbara laughed to herself and opened the letter from her favourite cousin, Michael Aaronson. She had not expected to hear from him as they did not correspond regularly, but she reflected that Michael always seemed to turn up, by mail, or in person, at a welcome time. And his news was, in fact, an announcement of his arrival in Israel the next day. He had been 'sent or called, depending on how you look at it' to 'confer or be conferred with' on the Eichmann trial.

Michael was diffident about his career. He had taken his degree in international law before the war, and had been called in for the Nuremberg Trials. He had since been occupied in practice as a solicitor, but Barbara perceived his pleasure at being once more involved in an expert's field. He expected to be in Jerusalem for two weeks. He would be fairly occupied, but 'Be sure to be there,' he wrote.

She realised how lonely she must have been, and felt so good about the prospect of seeing Michael that the thought of Ricky's lonely distress came back guiltily upon her, but even so she did not regret her letter. She went out for a walk, called in at the travel agent and rearranged her dates; today was a Monday, and she had planned to cross into Jordan on the Wednesday of that week. It was necessary to give advance notice to the travel people, since they were obliged to make advance arrangements for a crossing of the Mandelbaum Gate, and only certain days were available to individual travellers. She obtained a permit for Friday of the following week, which would probably precede Michael's departure, but she was unwilling to linger in the country much longer.

For it had become imperative for her to continue the pilgrimage. She sat in a café, trifling with her coffee spoon. The relief of leaving her job and learning of Michael's arrival enabled her to summon peacefully to her attention the image of Ricky, still mutedly importuning. Ricky would, of course, ascribe hypocrisy to her motives in coming to the Holy Land 'on a pilgrimage'. Barbara was content to be thought deceitful, hypocritical. It consoled her guilt towards Ricky. And yet her own ruthlessness and swift action continued to surprise and please her. She thought, I'm satisfied with that letter. But Ricky's a kind woman, she'll be hit by my leaving her. In a sense Ricky gave me a home.

She sagged with relief. It felt marvellous to be homeless. Ricky would think of the motives that had drawn her here to the Holy Land. A religious pilgrimage! A lover. A man. Barbara was already a Catholic when she had met Ricky; they had carefully avoided religious discussions; and only once or twice had she discerned Ricky's irritation with some observance of her religion, and felt irritation when Ricky let fall a remark about some Catholic dogma which revealed not only her disapproval, but a muddled notion of what the dogma was. Ricky was all for doing the right thing for the right reason; she was fierce-principled about motives. To Barbara, one of the first attractions of her religion's moral philosophy had been its recognition of the helpless complexity of motives that prompted an action, and its consequent emphasis on actual words, thoughts and deeds; there was seldom one motive only in the grown person; the main thing was that motives should harmonise. Ricky did not understand harmony as an ideal in this sense. She assumed that it was both right that people should tear themselves to bits about their motives and possible for them to make up their minds what their motives were. Herein, Barbara reflected, lies the difficulty in dealing with Ricky if I should ever be drawn to have it out with her. For she has settled with herself that her motives are sound, and she opposes my marriage in good conscience.

She decided, in any case, never to have it out with Ricky. Having it out with people was not in her nature, all the Vaughan in her upbringing went against it. She longed for Harry, the only man she had known who conducted his courtship with few words and without any demands for heart-sought declarations and the wear and tear of mutual disclosures from the interior.

She thought of Ricky, sitting in her room on a winter evening, leaning back, relaxing among the effervescence of school life, the rumble of books and papers, with her legs dark-shadowed under her stockings. Ricky's own books, clean and bright, lined the walls to the ceiling. Ricky had no doubt read most of them, closed them, and put them away, unchanged by them as they were by the passage of the years.

Titles that she had not been conscious of taking special note of appeared before Barbara's inward eye: *The World of Zen, Antic Hay, The Notebooks of Sigmund Freud, A Skeleton Key to Finnegans Wake, Neurosis and Human Growth, Thus Spake* . . . One way and another, she felt she knew Ricky through and through, and firmly closed her mind to its whispering intelligence that Ricky, having now, in that letter, surprised her, might do so again. Coleridge's *Table Talk,* Aristotle's *Poetics* . . . Oh well, thought Barbara, paying her bill. And, feeling specially strong, healthy and Vaughan-like she returned to her hotel to see if any word had come from Harry Clegg. At the front door she met Freddy Hamilton emerging with a zipper-bag in his hand and a suitcase at his feet. A Legation car drew up.

'I'm just off to Tel Aviv; got a job to do there,' he said. 'Hot, isn't it? I'll be glad to be back with my friends in Jordan, weekend after next. It's cooler there. When are you going over?'

She was involuntarily reserved. 'Next week, probably. It depends.' But she told him of her cousin's promised arrival the next day. 'Something to do with the Eichmann trial.'

This seemed to remind Freddy Hamilton of something. He said, 'I'm not sure that it's safe for you to go over, really. Let me make some serious inquiries first. I'm sure they don't welcome Jews or part-Jews, especially coming by way of Israel. At the worst you'd probably be deported. Probably – but one never knows – they get hot-headed. Is your fiancé meeting you in Jerusalem?'

'I don't know. I don't think so.'

'It might be better if he could. Those Dead Sea scholars might get better protection for you than the British Government could. That's what things have come to. How well you're looking! The climate must suit you.'

Thereupon she forgave him for gossiping about her to his mother. All the same, she would be careful what she told him in the future, now that Ricky had met the old lady. And so, on that Saturday of the following week, when she next saw Freddy with his friends, unexpectedly, in the curiosity shop in Jordan, she decided to answer, if he should inquire about her fiancé, 'I've gone off him.' That would put an end to the gossip. It was not Freddy Hamilton's business, certainly not his mother's, nor Ricky's. 'I've gone off him' – light and airy. She decided to stick to that, and they could think as they pleased.

The best piece of furniture in the room was the camp-bed, and Barbara lay upon it, awake, gazing straight through the small window at the night sky, which, by contact with her emotional eyesight, was elated with stars and lyrical energy.

The camp-bed was so new that the old monk's domestic man, himself an ancient, but sturdier, benignity, had to untie the cords and wrappings, fresh from the shop. The servant's few teeth caught the light from the paraffin lamp as he gloated over his treasure of a camp-bed: 'One of our ladies, not rich, has given this to keep open the door for strangers. Here the officers are afraid to come at darkness. God is good.' He muttered on, while they set up the bed, stiff at the joints as it was with newness. Through the thin walls Freddy could be heard moving about and creaking his bed as he sat, presumably taking off his shoes since a shoe-like thud on the floor, dropping dead-weight with tiredness, was followed presently by another. Alexandros's car started up below; he was to send early tomorrow a young woman, Suzi Ramdez, who was accustomed to taking English visitors around the country, and who could be trusted.

Now Barbara lay awake, marvelling at her escape from the convent. She was also extremely intrigued by the change that had come over Freddy Hamilton, and by the fact that he had engineered the escape at all. She thought, it's like the enactment of a reluctant nun's dream, and she laughed softly in the darkness, thinking of the absurdity of the phrase 'escape from the convent' that had kept recurring in their conversation in the car, on the way to the Potter's Field, and which didn't really apply to her, a free, travelling Englishwoman, at all.

But it had been an escape of a kind, as witness to which she could cite her present sense of release. She was sure there was a certain amount of physical risk in her venture into Jordan. But try as she might, she did not care. And the urgent sense of apprehension she should be feeling, all facts considered, was lacking, try as she might to reason with herself. If she should be arrested openly there would be some sort of fuss, if she were to come to some secret harm, well that was that. The reality of the hour was her escape from the convent, and there was no room for any sense of a more immediate danger in the face of the familiar and positive dangers of heart and mind that were, in any case, likely to arise anywhere one went, across all borders and through all gates.

She thought, it was really very funny, that escape from the convent. It would make a good story to tell her cousins on the Vaughan side when they asked her about her visit to the Middle East. And the Vaughan side of herself lay on the camp-bed considering the funny aspect of the affair, since this was what they liked best to do; whenever the Vaughans were thrown, provided they managed to pick themselves up, they usually ended by making a good story of it.

For the first time since her arrival in the Middle East she felt all of a piece; Gentile and Jewess, Vaughan and Aaronson;

she had caught some of Freddy's madness, having recognised by his manner in the car, as they careered across Jerusalem, that he had regained some lost or forgotten element in his nature and was now, at last, for some reason, flowering in the full irrational norm of the stock she also derived from: unselfquestioning hierarchists, anarchistic imperialists, blood-sporting zoophiles, sceptical believers – the whole paradoxical lark that had secured, among their bones, the sane life for the dead generations of British Islanders. She had caught a bit of Freddy's madness and for the first time in this Holy Land, felt all of a piece, a Gentile Jewess, a private-judging Catholic, a shy adventuress.

'This is more fun,' Freddy had said in the car, 'than I've had for years.'

'It is for me fun that I have sent to Suzi Ramdez a secret message in the middle of the night, to her bed where she sleeps. A very fine woman, Suzi Ramdez. Her father would come to me with a knife –'

'Is there any danger of his finding out?' Freddy said.

'Plenty danger. But Joe Ramdez does not kill. If he comes to me tonight, tomorrow, with the knife, still he does not strike. Alexandros has plenty friends, and those friends are enemies of Ramdez.'

'You never have a dull moment out here,' Freddy said, meanwhile grinning at Barbara, who sat in the back with her suitcases and savoured Freddy's phrase 'out here'. Every place east of Europe or west of the Atlantic Ocean was more or less one of the colonies to Freddy.

'We did that escape from the convent beautifully,' Freddy said. 'Great fun. We did it a treat. Every stair was creaky –'

'Every stair,' Barbara said. 'I nearly died.'

'I expect I'd have been lynched by the nuns if I'd been caught. Have they ever had a man in the convent before?'

'Not in the sleeping quarters. Maybe, of course, the doctor.'

'The doctor,' said Alexandros, 'is not a man. The doctor is permitted in the harem after sunset even. "Many doctors come by night to the rich man's harem": Arab proverb by author Alexandros.'

Freddy went on elaborating his version of the escape from the convent, and Barbara added her bits, slumped in her dressing-gown among the suitcases, building up, for Alexandros, the breathless suspense of the descent down the convent staircase. 'I nearly *died*!' It was not any escape from any real convent, it was an unidentified confinement of the soul she had escaped from; she knew it already and was able to indulge in her slight feeling of disappointment that they had not been caught. It was fun to get away but it would also have been fun to get caught and to have had to explain something, and for Freddy to have explained. It would have made a funny story to tell Harry later on.

She could not understand how Freddy, in the course of the few hours since she had last seen him in the Cartwrights' garden, had so come to lose his unbecoming and boring balance, his tepid correctness. He was not at this moment so terribly drunk, and had certainly gathered enough wits to plan the night's escapade and the elaborate course of the bright pilgrimage to come, the details of which he was now explaining with enthusiastic precision. He had thought of everything. 'You, as Suzi's servant, will have to be deaf and dumb, because, of course, you can't speak Arabic. I'll come as far as Jericho with you, then leave you with Suzi, as I ought to be back at the office Tuesday at the latest . . . Suzi Ramdez apparently is experienced in Catholic pilgrimages . . . Marvellous plan, don't you think?'

Barbara reclined, happily making her responses in the dialect of their tribe: 'Absolutely brilliant . . . terrific idea, Freddy . . . Yes, honestly, I'm thrilled . . .'

'Well, of course, Alexandros thought of it first.'

'No, pardon me, you had the first word.' Alexandros rushed his car into gear as they turned up the Hill of Evil Counsel.

'We both cast the first stone,' Freddy garbled lyrically, and went on to tell Barbara how he'd got some boring letters from home and written some boring replies but had put them all down Alexandros's lavatory.

'What a brilliant idea,' Barbara said, and half-wished she had thought of doing the same with Ricky's letter and her reply to it. Ricky must have received her letter early last week. Barbara had not expected to hear from Ricky, for her plan at the time of writing had been to leave Israel within the next few days. Fortunately, now, it would be ages before she knew, if she ever did know, how badly Ricky had taken it. Barbara had not supplied an address in Jordan. 'Marvellous idea,' Barbara said. 'I had a ridiculous letter from England to answer last week, but I answered it. I should have put it all down the loo, reply and all, that's what I should have done.'

'One always should,' Freddy advised her, as from long experience. 'Any correspondence that's bloody boring, just pull the chain on it. That's my motto.'

With only a small delay after their first battering onslaught at the door, they were handed over by Alexandros to the ancient monk, who peered and smiled behind his lamp, and handed them over to his ancient friend who had turned up, crumpled from sleep in his blue robe. They were then taken over a stony path through the yard to another, more ramshackle house. There Alexandros left them, embracing Freddy on both cheeks, while Freddy, first remarking cheerfully, 'like a couple of French generals', responded.

It was going on towards four in the morning when she was left alone in the little attic room to which she had been taken. It contained a large, sagging horse-hair arm-chair with the stuffing emerging from both arms, two sacks which served for floor mats, a marble-topped table on which stood a basin and a ewer filled with dusty water, a wooden box on which stood a pair of field-glasses in good and shiny condition, a new cake of carbolic soap, a dented celluloid miniature of the Taj Mahal, an English novel, dated 1910, entitled *Diamond Cut Diamond*, a tin of lighter fuel, a broken pottery beaker, a small rough towel marked 'Hotel Dixie', and a pair of elephant-figure book-ends. Another large wooden box, marked 'Fragile', was open and contained, at the bottom, about six pairs of unused sandals; there was a large wicker hamper with the lid half-gaping to reveal a top layer of gold-embroidered ecclesiastical vestments, and the room also contained an icon hung on a nail in the wall, a tarnished silver altar-lamp, a pair of primitive mill-stones such as the country women still used for grinding corn, and, on the flat top of this hand-mill, a well-worn pack of playing cards and a packet of drinking straws. Barbara, her luggage, the new camp-bed and a grey army blanket had now joined the company. She, having taken some note of all this, had turned out the lamp, and now lay in her dressing-gown, with the blanket folded at her feet in view of the warmth of the air that coursed in towards her from the stairs, and was moved to praise the sweet Lord's ingenuity, marvelling at her escape from the convent and at Freddy's unexpectedness. Later, when she discovered that Freddy had obliterated these days from his memory, what shocked her most of all was that so much of that carefree and full-hearted Freddy had turned sour with guilt. She herself then reminded him of this or that delightful incident, piecing the days together for him, fragment by fragment. But they were, to him, stolen days, and not for many years could he come to think of them with total pleasure.

But even now, before the pilgrimage had begun, Barbara discerned some temporary quality in Freddy's mood. Not knowing the cause, she formed the theory then, as she lay contemplating the early morning sky above the Potter's Field, that Freddy was given to fluxes of temperament, and, like a man who knows he has played the fool while drunk, might presently regret or might laugh unhappily about all this wild commitment of his. Not that Freddy's new spontaneity and forthcoming spirits resembled a fearful mania. He was decidedly at ease.

A change began to come over him, she thought, in the Cartwrights' garden, when everyone was arguing so absurdly about the rights and wrongs of my Jewish blood: 'Jewish blood or not,' had said Freddy, 'the point is, it's hers . . . And the trouble with you,' Freddy had said, 'is that you blow neither hot nor cold, you are lukewarm – how does it go, Miss Vaughan? – lukewarm, and I'll vomit thee out of my mouth.' It would make a splendid story to tell her Vaughan cousins. Freddy must meet the Vaughans; his next home leave, she would get her cousin Miles Vaughan to ask Freddy to dinner. Very likely she would be married by then. Very likely. The Vaughans would accept Harry Clegg without a murmur once she was married to him, and they had seen the funny side of everything.

The expected letter from Harry had not arrived, but a note from his friend at the American Embassy in Amman had been enclosed in the envelope, smuggled in by the American bag, which had appeared under the door last Wednesday morning. This friend, whom she had never met, was obviously well informed about their situation; he wrote informally but cautiously, and she understood that she must read between the lines:

DEAR BARBARA,

Harry asked me to let you know he has left for Rome to see some members of the Congregation of the Rota about some ancient documents. He'll write you from there some time next week. He'll be staying at the Hotel Regina Carlton.

He doesn't feel, by the way, that you'd be vitally interested in the excavations at Qumran at the moment, and he isn't there to show you around. I've been to that area myself, of course, but, not being an archaeologist, I get more fun out of the many books that have been written about the findings of the scrolls and the excavated Essene community offices. There's some talk of a documentary film of it though. Some of the unit (though not the producer, of course . . .) who are working in the Transjordan at the moment, on the Lawrence of Arabia movie, toured the site and think there's good material for a documentary.

Well, Harry looked fine and sends his love. But you'll be seeing him yourself quite soon, I hope.

Sincerely yours,

MARTIN J. FONTEYN

From this, she gathered that Harry had gone to be interviewed about his plea for annulment at the Congregation of the Rota in Rome, where all the documents had been sent. And also that he did not want her to go to Jordan, not only because he was no longer there but also because he now thought it unsafe. The whole rigmarole about the film unit visiting Qumran was plainly an occasion for citing the case of the producer, a Jew who was prominently reported to have been conceded permission to work on Jordanian location only on the strength of the film's economic benefit to the country, but was obliged, so people said, to sleep on a yacht each night, three miles away from Arab soil. Barbara rightly deduced that what Mr Fonteyn was trying to convey was that Harry now considered it risky for her to travel into Jordan on account of her Jewish blood.

She had almost decided then not to go on with the pilgrimage but to remain in Israel until at least she heard from Harry in Rome. Her cousin Michael was due to arrive in Israel that afternoon, nine days before the small hours of this Sunday morning, when the stars were flickering out in the early light while the many-shaped furnishings round the camp-bed on which she lay gradually cropped up again, pale blue, and while from all quarters live sounds of cockcrow had come to pass, and of monastery cats supremely celebrating.

Michael had arrived in Israel in the late afternoon of that Wednesday, his welcome, full-faced bespectacled self. He was immediately immersed in his legal business, and would not be free until dinner. Barbara filled in the hours by driving round Jerusalem, as she had so often done in the past weeks. She now went everywhere without a guide in a hired car, and had revisited most of the ancient sites up and down the small narrow country where layers of Rome and Byzantium reclined a few feet beneath the soil. She was brown from the sun of Tiberias on the shores of Galilee and the sea-walk at Acre. She had sat in the cool shade of the ruined synagogue at Capharnaum and waded among the pebbles. Most of all she had sat in the cool churches of Israel, where sometimes a priest, one of the Franciscan custodians of the Catholic shrines in the Holy Land, would come and sit beside her and talk about the only sphere he knew, the Christian Incarnation whose physical centre, for the time being, was that particular spot. Nazareth: this is where it really began, the mission of Jesus to the world. Cana: this is where Jesus turned the water into wine for the wedding, his first miracle, and everything begins with that. Capharnaum: all the important teaching and miracles of Jesus took place here, in the synagogue and round about; it was here St Matthew worked in the customs house, a publican, and was called to follow Jesus; Peter and Andrew came from Capharnaum; here in the synagogue that must have been here before these ruins were built, Jesus gave the New Testament, here in the synagogue, pledging himself to be the Bread of Life to the people of the world, and that was the new Covenant; and he walked on the water at Capharnaum, stilled the storm, raised Jairus's daughter from the dead, and the centurion's steward, Peter's mother-in-law, the man with the withered hand, the man possessed by an unclean spirit . . . Barbara looked out beyond the ruins to where the antique sea sparkled, and fully assented that here precisely at Capharnaum, as at Nazareth, as at Cana, the spiritual liberation of the human race had begun. And here at Capharnaum, said the Franciscan friar . . . the man sick of the palsy, and numerous other sick and possessed . . . just behind the sea-road, the Sermon of the Beatitudes . . . the multiplication of the loaves and fishes; all at Capharnaum; and here is a curious thing that you find in the Gospels of Matthew and Luke: Jesus said of it, 'Thou, Capharnaum, which art exalted unto heaven, thou shalt be thrust down to hell.' A little way up, at Bethsaida, was where James and John lived, and Peter, Philip and Andrew were born. Mary Magdalen came from Magdala, along the lake.

At the place of Mary Magdalen Barbara had found locked gates and a high wire-net fence; peering through she saw a black car with the white diplomatic number plate. This site was in the hands of the Russian Orthodox; at that time the Russians in Israel were particularly suspicious and it was quite common for the Russian-held shrines to be closed to the public. Barbara waited a while in the sun to see if there was any sign of life in the small conventual house. Not a curtain stirred. Here, too, at this birthplace of doubtful authenticity there had undoubtedly been a beginning. She had driven along the coast to Tiberias and had gone for a swim in Galilee, and afterwards eaten one of its fish, sitting in her bathing-dress at a shoreside café; there she was joined by a young woman, also wearing a swimming-suit, whom she had known casually years before in London, and had met again briefly a few days ago in Jerusalem, Ruth Gardnor, now the wife of someone in the British Foreign Service; she was spending a few days at Tiberias. Barbara sat and talked to her about their only mutual acquaintance in this country, Freddy Hamilton, and after they had agreed several times that he was sweet, and Ruth Gardnor had sighed, said 'Poor Freddy!' and explained that the man had been crushed, ruined, by a dominant mother, they parted with amiable insignificant promises to meet again soon.

In the last few days before Michael's arrival Barbara had concentrated her driving in the area round Jerusalem, partly to have access to her hotel while awaiting the smuggled news from Harry Clegg, and partly because she was anxious to get away across the border into new territory, the other part of the Holy Land, and enjoyed gazing over to Bethlehem or to the Mount of Olives, and, on a clear day, the domes and walls and rooftops of Old Jerusalem. She would stop the car at various points, day after day, as she discovered the best angles for sighting her target.

> Jerusalem, my happy home,
> When shall I come to thee?

The lines sped to mind, and simultaneously seeing in her mind's eye the medieval text to which she was accustomed and, with her outward eye, an actual Gethsemane passively laid out on the Mount of Olives across the border, she sensed their figurative meaning piled upon the literal – 'O my sweete home, Hierusalem' – and yearned for that magnetic field, Jerusalem, Old and New in one.

> When shall I look into thy face,
> Thy joys when shall I see?

Saul Ephraim, finding her hired car parked one day near the Hebrew University, drew up his own battered vehicle beside it and sounded his horn till she appeared from among the thick-leaved bushes where she had been standing, some yards off the road, to get a better view. Saul said, 'If you stand there long enough you'll get shot. It's practically on the border.'

'Has anyone been shot standing there?'

'Maybe not exactly on that spot, but shooting incidents occur from time to time. Someone gets shot, then we retaliate, and someone else gets shot, maybe two, three. Keep away from the border.'

She had asked Saul Ephraim to look in after dinner on the night of Michael's arrival, hoping to arrange a small guided tour of the countryside during Michael's visit. Her memory now played on Michael's arrival as she lay on the camp-bed, yielding her present excitement to a passive in-gathering of past facts as did the stars their bright pointedness to the first blue light of dawn.

'I've given up my job.'

Michael said, 'Tired of it?'

She had explained or tried to explain the very involved and subtle affair of Ricky, and how it had crept on her, become intolerable, Ricky's personality . . . Ricky's incredible letter finally . . . finally . . . She gestured the inarticulate end of her sentences – 'It's difficult, Michael, to explain; Ricky's been a good friend, but it's just –'

Michael took the words out of her hands.

'She was too possessive,' he said, as if there were no subtle, unique, inexplicable quality about the relationship. And of course, when he said it, she knew this was the ultimate definition and felt relieved. Michael resembled Harry in his habit of making obvious rational comments about difficulties he did not feel were worth the trouble of analysing. Harry, who would give years to a problem of archaeology, would dismiss most personal complications with a brief, banal, but altogether reassuring phrase or two; Barbara never failed to feel consoled by his common sense, so very like Michael's now, when she was beset by some interior burden that didn't really matter: 'She was too possessive.' Barbara laughed.

'Well, I've left the job. I'm not even giving a term's notice; just not going back.'

'Are you still thinking of getting married?'

'I hope . . . the Church . . . this annulment . . . the documents . . . Harry's in Rome . . . the . . .' The jagged edges of the celluloid Taj Mahal, seen from the side, took shape in the pale first light over the Potter's Field and looked like the half-profile of a face she had never seen before; all around her, conical, circular and angular bulges began to appear; she distinguished the field-glasses that she had seen by the light of the paraffin lamp an hour ago. It would soon be bright morning. Michael had said, 'You really must stop messing the poor fellow about, you know, Barbara. If you want to marry him, marry him. He's free and you're free to be married according to the laws of the land.'

'You know that to me marriage is a sacrament. If I marry outside the Church I'll have to remain outside the Church. That's going to be difficult for me. Year after year – it will be difficult.'

'Yes but what else are you going to do?'

'He's gone to Rome . . . annulment . . . questions . . . his marriage; it's just possible that it could be found invalid . . . his wife's married again, she's quite cooperative about everything. It's a legal question, you know, like any other legal question.' Michael quite saw that. He was never obtuse about the legal formations of the Catholic Church.

Someone shuffled in the house below, and she knew it was five in the morning. She was to be ready by ten. Suzi Ramdez would arrive at ten. Barbara thought she might sleep now, but it didn't matter if she missed a night's sleep, it was worth it. She had taken her last look at Jerusalem from the other side of the Mandelbaum Gate that afternoon of Michael's arrival when, before returning to the hotel to meet him, she had gone to the top of Mount Zion where David's Tomb was preserved, and had seen, in the Abbey of the Dormition, the reputed room of the Last Supper and the crypt where by tradition the Blessed Virgin lay before her death or, as some said, her falling asleep before her assumption into heaven, whatever that taking up might be, to wherever heaven was. It was from this site of the Dormition in Israel that Barbara had seen Old Jerusalem, distant yet not far, where she now lay waiting in the early morning for her new guide on the pilgrimage.

'I wouldn't go to Jordan if I were you,' Michael said. 'All things considered, I wouldn't go.' Saul Ephraim had joined them with his Israel-born wife, who spoke only Hebrew. Saul said, 'They're bound to know by now that you've got Jewish relations. The Arabs have their messengers, you know.' He looked round, and Barbara caught sight of an Arab porter, far away in the entrance hall. Their own party was now sitting in the open, under the leafy trellis, and one could see through to the adjoining room, and through again to the hall. The Arab porter was talking to someone, a familiar outline; it was Freddy Hamilton's Arabic teacher, the blue-eyed young man called Abdul. Saul said, 'They could make a lot of trouble for you. There is a definite danger from police officials, they are armed, they act in hot blood and explain afterwards. People who come here do not realise that. Particularly, you have come from England first to Israel, then you go to Jordan. The normal route is from Jordan to Israel. They suspect Israeli spies. Why didn't you go to Jordan first?'

'Oh, personal reasons, you know.'

It was through Harry Clegg that she had come to know Saul Ephraim, his former colleague. Saul looked at his wife and said something evidently witty in Hebrew, for she laughed. Saul explained, 'I'm telling her that your fiancé's over in Jordan, and that's why you came here first.'

Michael had turned thoughtful since Saul had urged the probable danger of her appearance in Jordan, and lawyer that he was, he protested. 'But look here, you know, there *are* internal laws and international laws. Even if Barbara was a full Jew she couldn't be touched if she possessed a British passport. It's the Israelis they're against, it's a political matter, not a religious or racial one. The Arab States don't recognise Israel, they claim that the Jews in Israel are usurpers of their territory. The worst that could happen to Barbara, by law, is deportation as a spy, and only then on the combined evidence of her Jewish blood and her entrance into the country via Israel – that might create reasonable grounds for suspicion. But otherwise she couldn't be touched. Not legally.'

'Not legally,' said Saul, spreading his fingers in irony; he explained the argument to his wife, who replied vivaciously. 'She says,' said Saul, 'that they carried off a couple of men from the *kibbutz* she worked on before we were married. They raided and captured the men. One was a Britisher. They didn't do it legally, of course.'

There was talk, talk, talk. It became an academic subject, absorbing them for over an hour. Barbara said, 'It's difficult to separate the apocryphal from the true in this part of the world. It always has been.'

'Anyway, all things considered, don't go,' Michael said.

'And you say Harry's in Rome. So what's the point?' said Saul.

'Yes, what's the point? But I'm on a pilgrimage. The other Christian shrines are over there –' On, on, on. 'But we have Nazareth. We have a Christian shrine up on Mount Zion,' Saul said, and repeated this to his wife, who showed interest. Barbara said, 'It's the crypt of the Dormition,' and explained to Michael the legend of the Virgin's Falling Asleep. 'Some say she actually died, some say she only fell asleep. The Church has left it open. I was up there today, in fact . . .' She had been to pray at the crypt of the Falling Asleep. The noises of the first light over the Potter's Field had halted now, pausing for the authentic dawn. The shuffling in the house had stopped. The recumbent statue of the Virgin at the crypt was an unusual representation. The two suitcases, one small, one large, stood beside a much larger, open box with her clothes spilling out of them; then she perceived they were not her clothes, but those vestments bulging from the hamper that she had noted by the light of the oil lamp.

Saul had said, 'For a stage of the pilgrimage you might go to the Eichmann trial.'

'I haven't been,' she said.

'I know. That's what I'm saying.'

'I don't see that she wants to go there,' Michael said. 'I think the whole thing's a mistake, myself.'

They turned out for a walk in the teeming streets that were only now cooling down, and Saul argued fiercely about the necessity of the Eichmann trial. Michael said, in the end, that since it was on, Barbara should go, should come with him for an hour or two tomorrow.

'Why?'

'Why? Because it's got to do with you.'

'And a subject for a Christian pilgrim,' Saul said.

She had thought of the trial as something apart from her purpose; it was political and temporary. In the same way she had placed the *kibbutzim* of the country in the category of sociology, and had resisted attempts to be shown over one of them. She had seen over a model *kibbutz* in Surrey.

She said, 'Look, I've got a tidy mind. Everything's a subject for a Christian pilgrimage if you widen the scope enough. I only want to cover a specific ground without unnecessary diversions. I can follow the Eichmann trial in the papers.'

Sharp-witted Saul said, 'You can follow the history of the Jews in the Bible without visiting the historical spots. This trial is part of the history of the Jews'; and Michael was saying, 'You should come.'

'I don't want any advice. Thanks all the same.'

'Quite right,' said Michael. 'Only take my advice about not going into Jordan. You might cause us a lot of worry.'

'All right.'

But in the end she did the opposite on both counts. 'All right.' She heard her own voice again in that dawn and retrospect at the Potter's Field, in that attic where to the left of her camp-bed she now noticed, at eye-level, a shining rifle laid parallel to herself; it rested on a dark, oblong object; it had a small clump of dry furze, broom or withered flowers protruding from the barrel; she had not seen this thing in her first survey of the room by lamplight in the earlier darkness, and was most of all mystified by the fuzzy plant stuck into the gun's gleaming barrel. She shifted her head slightly and saw two unequal slivers of light along the recognisable arms of the horse-hair arm-chair from which the stuffing escaped at the ends, no rifle at all, no clump of shrivelled flowers, only the two arms of the old chair at the perspective of eye-level, one protruding slightly about and to the left of the other, and both catching the morning light to resemble the barrel and butt of a gun. 'All right,' she had said to Michael and Saul, conceding their point that she might cause her friends a lot of worry by going into Jordan from Israel, however lawfully. She recalled, now, her sense of uneasy reprieve. She planned in her mind to return to England with Michael in two days' time. Tomorrow, she had thought, while he's at the Eichmann trial or conferring with the lawyers, I can go and pray at Nazareth, at Capharnaum, Galilee, or perhaps only to Mount Zion again, the Tomb of David and the place of the Dormition of Our Lady. But next day she went to the Eichmann trial instead; the next day for no reason at all, for some reason she could not remember, it was something Michael said abstractedly at breakfast when he was in a hurry and ready for the day's business, it was some clear thing she would never now remember, probably some word of Michael's, innocently reinforcing some decision she had already made, overnight, in sleep.

Lying on the camp-bed she wondered whether to try to sleep or whether she had better make an effort to stay awake.

She was too interested to sleep. Michael got her a public ticket for the trial, a ticket for visitors or maybe the Press; her handbag was searched and her person examined for the bulges of a possible revolver, camera, or tape-recorder by a policewoman in a small sentry box. She was allowed to pass through to the gallery, to the Press seats as it might be; and there she had listened by ear-phone to the translations of Eichmann's defence, as in a familiar, recurrent but always incomprehensible dream. The prisoner in his bullet-proof glass enclosure was already an implanted image in the public mind; he had been photographed and filmed from every angle, as had the three judges, the defending and prosecuting counsel, and the public. Saul Ephraim had said, 'It isn't the most interesting part of the trial,' meaning that the impassioned evidence from survivors of the death-camps was over; after that, it had been generally agreed that court proceedings had entered a boring phase; Eichmann was being examined day by day by his own counsel, in a long-drawn routine, document by patient document. Many journalists had gone home. Barbara was not prepared to be taken by the certainty, immediately irresistible, that this dull phase was in reality the desperate heart of the trial. Minute by minute throughout the hours the prisoner discoursed on the massacre without mentioning the word, covering all aspects of every question addressed to him with the meticulous undiscriminating reflex of a computing machine. Barbara turned the switch of her ear-phones to other simultaneous translations – French, Italian, then back to English. What was he talking about? The effect was the same in any language, and the terrible paradox remained, and the actual discourse was a dead mechanical tick, while its subject, the massacre, was living. She thought, it all feels like a familiar dream, and presently located the sensation as one that the anti-novelists induce. Or it is like, she thought, one of the new irrational films which people can't understand the point of, but continue to see; one can neither cope with them nor leave them alone. At school she usually took the novels and plays of the new French writers with the sixth form. She thought, repetition, boredom, despair, going nowhere for nothing, all of which conditions are enclosed in a tight, unbreakable statement of the times at hand. She had changed her mind, without awareness, at that moment, of any disruption in the logic of personal decisions, but merely allowing herself to recognise, in passing, that she would inevitably complete her pilgrimage to the Holy Land in Jordan. This mental fact was the only one that seemed able to throw light on the ritualistic lines which the man in the glass box was repeating, or to give meaning to her mesmerised presence on the scene.

Bureau IV–B–4. Four–B–four

I was not in charge of the operation itself, only with transportation . . .

Müller needed Himmler's consent.

I was not in a position to make any suggestions, only to obey orders.

And technical transport problems.

Strictly with time-tables and technical transport problems.

I was concerned strictly with time-tables and technical transport problems.

Bureau IV–B–4. Four–B–four–IV–B–4.

High on the tribunal platform the three judges sat attentive to what was said, their faces distinct from each other, but each bearing the recognisable scars of the Western intellectual. The large black-robed counsel for the defence stood facing them, every now and then raising both arms as if bestowing a benediction upon the signs and tokens of his proper business in life, those carefully numbered documents on a lectern before him, but in reality simply jerking his arms free of the overlapping sleeves of his gown. Women reporters in casual dress and sandals, some of advanced age, came and went, the new-comers halting with their identification cards before the armed guards at each doorway. The Israeli citizens were mostly men, shirt-sleeved, arms folded. Sometimes derision, short and spontaneous, pelted forth from the public seats, intruding upon one of Eichmann's monologues. The presiding judge would then look alertly across the hall – but the people were already silent and the lips in the glass-bound dock continued to move.

This had been a stage in the trial where individual and small groups of victims were being dealt with, in one sense easier to grasp than the hundreds of thousands of dead that had so far formed the daily theme of the trial, and in the same sense, more horrifying. A little later, in the recess, she heard a man say, 'Thirty children yesterday, today a Mr Wilner.'

The counsel for the defence consulted his document and drew his client's attention to specific names, Misters this and that and their sons, locked in reality. And his client, a character from the pages of a long *anti-roman*, went on repeating his lines which were punctuated only by the refrain, *Bureau IV–B–4*. Barbara felt she was caught in a conspiracy to prevent her brain from functioning.

At first glance the impression is created that in fact from the order of the documents as they are clipped together here, *Bureau IV–B–4* . . .

The man was plainly not testifying for himself, but for his prewritten destiny. He was not answering for himself or his own life at all, but for an imperative deity named Bureau IV–B–4, of whom he was the High Priest.

A searchlight from the city of Jerusalem in Israel, 1961: the voice of the presiding judge was uttering a question:

> You mean, that the remark that the man is dead, in spite of all the tonics administered to the man, was also part of the information received by you from the General Government?

The witness, having sprung to attention, gave formal ear to this speech from an alien cult concerning a man being dead. He then sat down and patiently expounded, once more, the complex theology in which not his own actions, nor even Hitler's, were the theme of his defence, but the honour of the Supreme Being, the system, and its least tributary, Bureau IV–B–4.

> According to office routine, a question was addressed by Bureau IV–B–4 to the Government General area and after a reply was received from there. After a reply was received. Reply was received. Here, Bureau IV–B–4 of Head Office of Reich Security. Here IV–B–4 for the first time enters the correspondence after the matter was channelled through the department, and it informs the Foreign Ministry, referring to that letter of the Foreign Ministry from the 16th of June 1942, that the above-mentioned Jew of Argentinian nationality died on the 12th of April of that year in spite of aid and all the matters listed there. Listed there. All the matters.

> And here is once again one of these cases where Bureau IV–B–4 only served as a kind of through station, transit station.

This must have been written in the report received from the Government General area, because. Because otherwise . . .

Presently, a slight hesitation occurred in the court proceedings, a pause. The counsel for the defence looked courteously towards the tribunal, as if waiting for one of the judges to say something, while they, in turn, were under the impression that he was about to speak. The presiding judge then leaned forward and accompanied a sign for the lawyer to proceed with a brief remark in German. 'What are we waiting for?' duly said the English translator's voice in the ear-phones.

– What are we waiting for?
– We're waiting for Godot.

The lawyer proceeded: 'I come now to the matter of the Jewess Cozzi –'

It was a highly religious trial.

To get through by telephone that night to Harry Clegg's hotel in Rome, she had kept Michael waiting for three-quarters of an hour; they were to go out to dine at a restaurant. When she had finally made her telephone call she found him sitting in the courtyard with Saul Ephraim, a white-haired wiry woman who turned out to be a reporter from an Israeli newspaper, and a young rabbi who was learned in the archaeology of the Dead Sea, and who had met Harry Clegg several times. When he had introduced Barbara, Michael said to her, 'You won't be going to Jordan?'

'Yes, of course, it's all settled.'

'What did *he* think of the idea?'

'Well, he knows I want to go, and he *sees* the point.'

The lady-reporter, whom Saul had brought to interview Michael, said she did not see the point, that a Jew should go to an enemy country in a time of war, 'And we have war conditions right now.' She had come to Palestine in 1936, she said, and did not know of any time when there was not a state of war with the Arabs. The young rabbi said he understood she was a Catholic with a British passport; there would be no difficulty for her in Jordan. Saul and Michael had obviously spoken generally about her position, while she had been upstairs getting through to Harry in Rome. The young rabbi said, if she was going on a pilgrimage, she was going on a pilgrimage.

Which was exactly what she had said to Harry a few moments before when eventually she had got through to the Regina Carlton Hotel in Rome and he had been brought to the telephone. He said he was in the middle of dining with a priest.

'What priest?'

'How do I know what priest? They all look the same.'

She did not pursue the question, but inquired how things were going.

He said, 'Fine. But I don't think you'll get your divorce.'

She said, 'I'm not trying to get a divorce, I'm not even married. It's you who are divorced and you are trying to get the Church to recognise it by annulling the marriage, Harry dear.'

'Yes, that's what I mean. It's you that wants it, that's what I mean.'

She said, 'I'm going to marry you anyway.'

He said, 'I know.'

She said, 'How do you know?'

He said, 'Well, I just haven't any doubt about it. It's all on the cards.'

She started to laugh, but stopped as soon as possible because of the expense by long-distance telephone. It was so much part of his charm that he was very innocent of chivalrous attitudes, and also, she thought it funny that he had reached this conclusion by ordinary deduction while she, delicate probing instrument that she was, had taken a year to settle on the fact that she would marry him anyway. She said, 'The only point at issue is whether we can get married by the Church or not, that's to say, whether I'm going to have peace of mind for the rest of my life or not.'

He said, 'I know. That's what I'm here for. I went along at nine this morning and I've got another appointment for tomorrow.'

'Along where?'

'To see the officials, they're all high-up priests, at the Congregation of the Rota. It's all supposed to be secret, I had to give a promise of secrecy about the proceedings. But they were very civil. "If you please, Signor", and "Yes, Signor". They asked a lot of questions. I was there for four hours, then a break, then two hours, and I've got to go tomorrow.'

'I think you're a hero.'

'Oh, it's all right. This priest I'm dining with says there isn't a hope. He's got nothing to do with it, of course, only he's a Belgian staying at this hotel, and I've been telling him the case. He says there's always a long delay unless the divorced party was a Catholic married in another Church. That's the only occasion when it's easy.'

She said, 'I know.'

He said, 'Did you get a message from me through Fonteyn at the American Embassy in Amman?'

She said, 'Yes, but I'm going on to Jordan next week. I'm going to finish the pilgrimage.'

He said, 'I don't think you should. Something might blow up and you might find yourself in trouble.'

She said, 'Not with a British passport'; and she said, 'I went to the Eichmann trial today. Michael's here, and –'

He said, 'Michael who?'

She said, 'My cousin Michael. He's here as a consultant on the Eichmann trial. It made me feel rather sick. It's more appalling than you'd think from the papers.'

'It makes everyone sick. Why don't you go home to England?'

'I've given up my job. I'll tell you about it when I see you, maybe in Jordan.'

'I'll be here for two or three weeks. I've got some manuscript business to see to besides this game at the Rota.'

'Well, I'm going to Jordan, anyway. I feel a terrible need to do something positive, and if I'm going on a pilgrimage, I'm going on a pilgrimage, that's all.'

'I understand,' he said, 'only take care of yourself, dear girl.'

'I'll write to you tonight,' she said.

Saul Ephraim's friend, the young rabbi, said, 'If she's going on a pilgrimage, she's going on a pilgrimage,' and shrugged, smiling. She smiled back. The woman reporter's hand rested on a notebook that lay on the broad wicker arm of her chair. She said to Michael, 'Will you see something of our country? Israel is for a Jew also the Holy Land, not only for your Catholic cousin.'

It passed through Barbara's mind that this woman might put something about herself in the report she was going to write about Michael. She did not want to be reported in the Israeli newspaper as Aaronson's convert cousin who was about to continue her pilgrimage in Jordan, but she was too much afraid of the woman's irony to mention this thought, and felt certain that any plea for discretion would be distorted to mean that she was denying her Jewish relations. Instead, she asked the rabbi about his work in archaeology, and they talked of Harry, and the rabbi said he had got much private information from Harry about the latest discoveries at Qumran; all the men on the spot, he said, were against the conditions of keeping the Jewish scholars out of it, but they were forced to comply.

The woman reporter departed and they went to eat. Barbara walked along with Saul Ephraim, and said, 'I hope that reporter won't mention me in connection with Michael. There's no point in drawing attention to oneself.'

'Why should she mention you?' Saul said. 'Your cousin is the one she's interested in, he's the legal expert, and they make something of his visit in the paper in connection with the trial. But who are you, Miss Vaughan?'

Barbara was silent. She had always found Saul Ephraim to be friendly and confiding, but there was now a touch of quick-fire resentment in his tone and words. She could not find the cause of it, and in the newly bright morning at the Potter's Field, remembering what Saul had said, she rested in that question, as she knew one must from time to time.

She was getting hungry as the noises of the morning clattered in the house below; she could hear evidence of the chickens being fed in the old monk's house at the other end of the yard. She remembered the names of the various sorts of food on the menu the last night she had spent in Israel with Michael and Saul Ephraim. Since her arrival in Jordan less than two days ago she had eaten very little, largely because of the heat and the exhaustion of the preceding days. Her only square meal had been lunch on Saturday at the Cartwrights', those desperately well-meaning friends of Freddy Hamilton. She felt very hungry and wondered if they would be offered anything to eat before departing from this hideout. Philaphel, Chamous, Eggplant in Sesame-seed, Sanich, Kebab, Pila, Tchina: the names had been spelt in Roman characters beside the Hebrew on the menu of the last meal she had eaten in Israel, with Saul Ephraim and Michael. Michael was to leave the next day, by night flight. She left before him; he had accompanied her, with Saul, as far as the Israeli customs shed at the Mandelbaum Gate. Saul said to her, 'Touch the Wailing Wall on my behalf, and pray. When we have cause for grief, all the old people among us, and many of the young, grieve still more that we are separated from our Wall of Lamentation.' She had been to touch the Wailing Wall on Saturday morning, alone. The nuns in the convent had been surprised when she asked to be directed there; they had said that the guides were not often requested to take pilgrims to this spot, but it was a holy place of the Jews and very ancient, and they would send a guide with her who would show her the Wall and the Temple area as well. Barbara declined a guide, and she said she would see everything properly next week. She had walked round the Old City, alone, marking her route by a tourist map she had obtained from a travel agent, Ramdez, recommended by various Catholic organisations in England as well as by the convent nuns here, as specialising in the provision of guides who understood the Christian shrines. A woman at the Ramdez office had given her the map, and she had wandered round alone, planning a more detailed tour of the city; she had touched the Wailing Wall for Saul Ephraim and prayed, but unobtrusively, since she was watched by numerous loafing Arabs, in various stages of undernourishment and deformity, who slowly sidled up, apparently to befriend her; she had been at first astonished that their attitude was not at all hostile, considering their plight; then she had felt very nervous. So she had wandered up the Via Dolorosa until she had come to Alexandros's shop, and there had been found by Freddy, in the process of buying a silver fish on a chain . . . by Freddy and the Cartwrights, and had been taken home by them, and entertained, and finally been involved in that absurd discussion in the garden. The change in Freddy, she thought, occurred there in the garden, where that clump of wild flowers, carefully tended wild flowers, frequently watered wild flowers . . . she couldn't remember what they had been exactly but she had recognised them at the time; silvery dimpled leaves, *Umbilicus rupestris*, Navelwort; spiky pink flowers, *Epilobium angustifolium* of the Willow-herb family . . . Freddy said, 'Jewish blood or Gentile blood, the point is it's hers.' That was unexpected. Barbara had thought she had recognised his type, and knew him through and through; but no. And the Cartwrights, who had known him far longer, were decidedly taken aback. 'Your trouble,' Freddy had said to them, 'is this. You blow neither cold nor hot. How does it go, Miss Vaughan? – Neither hot nor cold. You're lukewarm. Lukewarm, and I will vomit thee out of my mouth.' It had been an embarrass-ing moment, exhilarating moment, an interesting . . . Barbara closed her eyes against the glare of the risen sun beating its rays through the window. I'd better get up now and see what's going on, she thought. Freddy's trouble was obvious-ly his overbearing mother. It was truly exhilarating to think of his tearing up all those letters and putting them down Alexandros's lavatory, it made one's pulse beat cheers for Freddy. His mother, like Ricky. Only Ricky had not got away with much from her; not for long, Ricky hadn't. Freddy had been weak for too long. 'Crushed,' Ruth Gardnor had said, crossing her long brown legs under the open beach-robe at Tiberias on the shores of Galilee. 'Poor Freddy has let himself be crushed by her.' She might, herself, have been crushed by Ricky, if she had not had so much of her stubborn, hard-riding father in her. Ricky was altogether too masculine and too feminine; both and neither. Poor Ricky would have had her letter by now. Barbara opened her eyes and moved to rise from the camp-bed . . .

She woke, blinking in the sunlight, upon the opening of the attic door and moved to rise from the bed. A young woman, a blue-eyed, brown-skinned Israeli, came in. No, a blue-eyed Arab woman, dressed in a blue shirt and dark skirt, like a lithe Israeli. She was carrying, over her arms, some cloth that looked like the black-out curtains of wartime England. 'What's the time?' Barbara said, feeling down into the pocket of her dressing-gown for her watch, and realising, then, that the young woman was Suzi Ramdez.

Suzi dumped the black stuff and sat down on the horsehair arm-chair. 'Ten minutes past ten o'clock. We arrive at the Holy Sepulchre at eleven for the Mass. That's first stop. Have you slept good? It's a beautiful day, Barbara. I call you Kyra for the rest of the trip. Kyra is my servant. I have sent her to far away on request from Alexandros. In Jerusalem everyone knows Kyra, but we will not remain long in Jerusalem. I do this by arrangement with Alexandros because I am the secret lover of Alexandros. Alexandros is beautiful. My father would kill me to know what we do, but Alexandros would prevent him. Do you bring news of my brother Abdul? You must wear these black clothes. I laugh to think of this, like playing children again. You are my Arab servantwoman and you must be deaf and dumb so you do not understand Arabic when addressed to you by Arabs. Kyra is not deaf and dumb, but I say to any friend that speaks to you, stand back, she has a sick throat and chest. I shall be always by your side. Alexandros has given all this instruction, to be at your side.

So don't speak. What is the news from my brother? Are you the lover of Freddy? He is quite a great beauty, a real man. I read many English books, German and Italian also, poetry particular in original language. Alexandros has told my mother I am the most intelligent woman in the kingdom of Jordan; he does not say to my mother the best lover, believe me. I am too proud to marry a man of fine family but no education. Freddy has said to tell you we are under starter's orders: what is starter's orders?'

'A horse-racing term,' Barbara said. 'He means –'

'Yes, true, I guess the meaning, we better hurry up.'

'I'm only half-awake,' said Barbara, getting off the bed and tentatively picking at the black garments she was to wear. 'But I'll thank you properly when I wake up properly.'

'You are to be a deaf-mute anyway,' Suzi said. 'So we talk only in private, in the car, where your lips are hid by the thick veil. You must be like a servant to me always, you keep by me like you are humble. I hope your God Jesus is going to be sincerely grateful for all this business you make for him. We pack your silken dressing-gown in the bag and you put all of your clothes off first. It is right to be an Arab woman from the body outwards. This next to your skin is from Kyra's box, almost new from the shop but these two garments, the robe and the veil, are dusty like for Kyra. Myself, I would not wear those black, old-fashioned clothes if I had a million pounds for it, but you are a woman of great principle and determination like Alexandros has informed me at our meeting in the night.'

Barbara dressed in the black garments, which were bulky but not as heavy as they seemed. 'How can I see through the black veil?' she said.

'In the light, the veil will be no more difficult than sun-glasses, you will discover.'

'I ought to have practised the part.' The robe was shorter than that worn by most Arab women of the old order. 'Is it too short?'

'It is like a poor woman's dress that has been given for alms by another lady. It's all right.'

'I caught a glimpse of your brother the other day, but I didn't see him to speak to,' Barbara said, feeling that this was the first piece of information due.

'That is a pity.'

'I didn't know I was going to see you.'

'Abdul must have been doubtful of you for a friend, or else he would have sent a message. He's my favourite man like Alexandros. Now you come and eat some breakfast. Do you drink coffee or tea? There is tea but it is not like English tea. Come, follow.'

There was no time to think; it was a lovely feeling, and Barbara was still sleepy. It was good to be in other people's hands, responsible only for a plausible wearing of the servant's clothes and the representation of a deaf-mute Arab woman. There was no time, as she dressed up and listened to Suzi's talk, to reflect on what was happening; her thoughts merely fluttered, like a moth approaching and retreating from a bright light. She dipped her face-cloth below the surface of the dusty film on the water in the jug and wiped it over her face, saying, 'Where can I wash?' while Suzi said, 'There's a water-tap downstairs, but you get a big wash tonight, it's not so necessary for you to be washed just now.' And indeed, it mattered so little that Barbara laughed with Suzi, put on the veil, then lifted it so that she could see better to pack the dressing-gown in her suitcase.

'Give me the passport and the money. The luggage and belongings we leave here; they are safe,' Suzi said. 'Freddy is ready. Come, follow.' Suzi arranged the veil over Barbara's eyes once more.

She was afraid to descend the dark wooden staircase with this veil covering her face, and she lifted it again as she followed Suzi downstairs. Freddy was there, drinking coffee at a table in a large whitewashed room. Before he could see her she covered her face again, to make an effect. Freddy looked up. 'Is she coming?' he said. Suzi's laughter rippled; it was the laugh of a cultivated woman. Barbara thought then, it's going to be all right, and astonished herself by her confidence in this unknown Arab girl; and it seemed the tone and quality of Suzi's laughter was the reason.

Freddy said, 'Oh, of course, there you are, it's you, Barbara.' She threw back the veil and said, 'Does it work?' He said, 'You look absolutely splendid. I wish Alexandros could see you.' He said something about her being hot in all that stuff. Suzi began explaining that it was quite light in weight, and moreover very well designed for hot weather as the folds could billow and catch the breeze: 'The Arab women of this old type are no fools.'

Barbara was looking at the food on the table – bread, watermelon, olives and cream cheese. She took coffee and said, 'Can we get some food after Mass?' and explained that she intended to take Holy Communion and was obliged to abstain from solid food for three hours beforehand. Suzi began cheerfully to issue voluble caution not to reveal her eyes while taking Communion, 'But lift the veil so – I am accustomed to taking Catholics to the Holy Sepulchre, but for you it will be necessary to take the Holy Wafer with the eyes covered, as this is necessary for you, to make sure you are not seen by others. The priest will –' Barbara meanwhile was assailed by a consideration from the distant reality of her private life; she thought, if I do intend to marry him, whether the Church allows it or not, does the intention alone constitute a mortal sin? She thought, then, if there's a doubt in one's mind, then it's all right. Rather wearily she felt her old identity returning in spite of this new disguise and the elation of the fantastic moment she had plunged into. It's too much for me, she thought, all this bothering myself and questioning all the time; I've had enough of it.

She said, 'Oh, I won't risk it.'

Suzi said, 'You are very wise. It's best that you should not move from the crowd to the Communion rail, but you will stay by my side and nobody will notice you if you keep quiet and humble. If anyone who knows Kyra well shall approach us in Jerusalem, maybe I shall say you are Aliyah, the niece of my servant Kyra. I shall say something, believe me. You say nothing.'

'I thought she was to *be* Kyra,' Freddy said. He was reading a local English-language newspaper, which was several days old, just as if he were breakfasting late at home with this morning's Sunday paper.

Suzi cut a slice of the crumbly bread and passed it carefully to Barbara. 'There's no need to fast then,' said Suzi. Barbara ate her breakfast with a sense of reprieve which seemed to extend over the three of them, and over the white-washed room with its plain wood furnishings and the surprising telephone hung on the wall. Suzi's dark, thin face had a touch in it of Western anxiety, the mark of the emancipated; Freddy's face, too, gave the map of his life. But for the moment, they were both relaxed; she thought, there's something in this undertaking that lifts a burden of nerves from us all; by every reasoning the physical experiment alone should be nerve-wracking to contemplate, but it isn't. Suzi said, 'Finish up your coffee.' Barbara did this, glancing at that page of Freddy's paper which was turned towards her. 'Eichmann's

Quality Truthfulness' stated these local headlines, 'Marilyn Monroe Gall-bladder Operation'. Barbara said, 'I think it's going to be fun.' Freddy did not reply for a moment, busily finishing what he was reading on his side of the paper. 'Hero's Welcome to Major Gagarin in London', stated Barbara's side. Freddy cast down the paper and jumped to his feet, taking a deep, contented breath as if the air were full of blessings. 'Yes, hurry up, girls. We start in five minutes. Under starter's orders! Get ready. The car's outside.'

Barbara said to Suzi, 'Might this lead you into trouble?'

Suzi laughed. 'Everything I do might lead me into trouble. One day I shall run away. Now there is no danger for me except that my father, Joe Ramdez, shall suspect that I play a trick. If we fall in with the police we say you are an eccentric English lady, as they understand this. Or I say something to the police and to some I can give money. You say to them you are English if the police arrest you, and that you always wear the national costume of the countries you visit. I do not think this will happen with the police, as I am never stopped at the police posts with my tourists, and Freddy looks like my tourist.'

'It's good of you,' Barbara said, and followed her to the car.

'That is not all the opinions of me,' said Suzi as she went ahead. 'But you speak like Kyra.'

It was a large blue American car of the type generally provided for hire by the travel agencies. 'You get in the back,' Suzi said to Barbara, adding, as Barbara gathered up the folds of her clothes to do so, 'Never mind that you have difficulty to get in and out of the car as this looks O.K. for an Arab village woman.'

Freddy started up the car, and looked round the empty yard. 'Shouldn't we say goodbye?'

'They are all gone farther down the hill to the monastery to be busy with the Masses in the church,' Suzi said. 'And we are sightseers and tourists now, so we don't say goodbye.'

'We're off!' Freddy said. 'The pilgrimage is begun. First stop, the Holy Sepulchre.'

Suzi said, 'Now I tell you the places of interest that we see. We leave Haceldama and we approach the ancient Jerusalem. Over there is Mount Scopus and we come to the valley of Jehosophat, which is the scene of the Last Judgement. I have read your Bible and Christian books besides the Koran, and the Bible also is a great book.'

'But rather obscure,' Freddy said. He added, 'mystifying', in case Suzi had not caught his meaning.

She said, 'That is not so much a fault when you can read two or three times, and you can find different opinions as to meaning. Incidentally, over there, as we turn, is Israel, where you came from; the people here do not use this name for that territory, you must not speak this name, it's better to avoid. Is it true that the Jews have imprisoned Martin Buber in the Hebrew University, and will not permit anyone to go visit with him because he speaks in favour of the Arabs?'

PART TWO

7

THE PASSIONATE PILGRIMS

Freddy Hamilton, Barbara Vaughan, Suzi Ramdez – each, in later years, when they looked back on that time, remembered one particular event before all others. It was different in each case. Alexandros, too, had his special recollection that was to gleam suddenly. Michael Aaronson remembered only the worry and waiting, as he sat in his office looking out over London Wall, when it was certain that Barbara had disappeared.

'What I remember most vividly of all,' Barbara told her cousins later on, '– and I'll never forget it – was when I went into the wrong room at the house at Jericho and found Ricky in bed with Joe Ramdez. I nearly died.' For Freddy it did not come easy to talk of those days, lost in comedy and found again in tragedy: as if switching the dial of the wireless from confused station to station, he would rapidly send the pointer of his mind through a range of recollections until he came upon the clear moment of waiting outside the convent where Barbara was lodging, while Alexandros bargained with the porter for the unlocking of the door. But he would not speak of it. Instead, he would dwell on another more concrete moment – and by that time it was common knowledge that he had stood in the hot sandy courtyard of the house at Jericho and recognised, before he himself could be observed,

Gardnor's wife walking towards a palm-tree, and casually extracting a small folded paper from a deep slit in the ragged bark. 'It simply came to me immediately there and then,' Freddy said to a small group of colleagues, one Saturday afternoon two years later, when they had returned to the house where they were guests, after watching village cricket. 'It just came to me that this was Nasser's Post Office, as we called it. We'd been looking for the spot high and low since the leaks began some months before. When I saw Gardnor's wife I simply knew it. And then I went and got the damned sunstroke and forgot it for two or three weeks. However, it all came back. Just in time for us to get Gardnor. Unforgettable. Gardnor's wife, at Nasser's Post Office, getting her orders and passing on our stuff.' Freddy took his fountain-pen from his inside pocket, and from his outside pocket he brought the cricket score-card, on the back of which he drew for his friends a diagram of Nasser's Post Office – the road, the house, and the palm-tree, marking with a cross the spot where he had first stood and then crouched, concealing himself behind his car, while Mrs Gardnor went to the tree and collected the message from the tufted bark. 'Of course,' he said, 'I put in some more investigation on the spot. And I proved right. I wasn't mistaken. Unconsciously, I must already have suspected Gardnor. We all did, as it turned out. But as he himself admitted in court, he knew we couldn't act without real proof . . . It was only a stroke of chance . . . quite absurd . . .'

But to take the events as they happened, so far as is human: Freddy went first, an unobtrusive foreign visitor among a crowd in the forecourt of the Church of the Holy Sepulchre, and was followed by Suzi and Barbara, unnoticeable among another crowd, on that first Sunday morning of the pilgrimage. Some of the people had come for sightseeing purposes;

these blocked the way until they had done gazing at the many-shaped structure, clicking cameras, craning up to the domes and terraced rooftops that expressed the divine ideas of those zealots and their conquerors who made them, and staring also at the heavy wooden props and scaffolding which modern times had contributed to the edifice in order to prop it up. When the people at last surged into the huge, cool, and altogether sepulchral interior, they separated into several groups, each clustering round its own guide or pastor for further directions. Freddy, who had been to the church before, began to make his way to the flight of stairs leading to the Choir of the Greeks at Golgotha, where the Anglicans and Catholics worshipped at their respective Orthodox and Latin altars. As he broke away from the crowds, Freddy failed to notice a procession moving towards him from the chapel which stood over the Holy Sepulchre itself, in the centre of the huge rotunda where the crowds were gathered. The people had made a pathway for the procession, which comprised a Coptic priest followed by his incense-swinging acolytes, newly emerged from a Mass. Freddy, vaguely assuming this procession to be only one of the little bands of variously garbed visitors among the others congregated in the area, sacrilegiously barged into one of the acolytes, and extricated himself with an apology which was not understood, so that he was abused by the thin, pale acolyte with something between a hiss and a spit.

From their part of the hall Suzi and Barbara could see the encounter. Barbara said, 'Oh, goodness,' and was immediately seized by Suzi, who gripped her arm to remind her to be deaf and dumb. An English female voice not far from Barbara said, 'Oh, look at that terrible man –' obviously referring to Freddy. Barbara had turned to look in the direction of the voice, and then, when she quickly realised she was not supposed to have heard it, she fixed her veiled eyes, very unhearingly, very unspeakingly, in front of her. But the voice had been disquieting; for a moment Barbara had thought she recognised it.

Presently, they were up in the Greek Choir where two Masses, one Orthodox, one Latin, were in progress, assisted by two congregations haphazardly thronged, kneeling or standing on the bare pavements before each altar, only a few feet from each other. The Greek Orthodox service at the main altar of Calvary that stood above a round earth-hole, the traditional site of the Cross, was mainly attended by an English mass-pilgrimage numbering about sixty and an American group of about twenty-five, mostly women with a few ageing men, and several clergymen, who were evidently leading the pilgrimages. Among them were also some individual pilgrims of unguessable nationalities and numerous local Arab worshippers, the fruits of the missions to Palestine from generation to generation. Only two Arab women over in the Greek congregation were veiled and dressed as Barbara was, but she was thankful even for them, for in fact at the Roman Catholic altar where she now stood with Suzi she was the only veiled woman.

And in fact, the three Franciscans who stood aside throughout the Mass, custodians of their altar, sent each other a communal glance at the sight of Barbara. The glance was a familiar question: when would these Arab convert-women throw off their old traditions and understand that Catholic Arabs were not obliged to cover their faces but only their heads? – they were as bad, in their way, as the young tourist girls who came, not only to visit the holy places, but to the Mass, without any covering on their heads at all, and with dresses without sleeves.

But the venerable brothers had more than Barbara to bother them that day. It was a memorable Sunday that lasted them all their old age, one of the worst of the increasingly bad memorable Sundays when the modern foreign priests, chiefly English and American, came to the Holy Sepulchre with their pilgrimages to say a Mass at the Altar of the Nailing of the Cross. That would have been very good, but instead of saying their Mass and going away, these upstart clergy very often insisted on giving a sermon. Sermons were not encouraged, as the demand on the use of the famous altar by visitant priests and their pilgrims was heavy on Sunday mornings, and even a short sermon held up the next Mass on the list.

But it was not so much the fact of the sermon on this particular Sunday, but its substance that made the occasion a prototype, for the three honest custodians on duty, of things to be deplored during times of recreation; and thus it contributed to bind together their staunch years to come.

The visiting priest of that hour was an Englishman in his middle thirties. He was one of the priests accompanying a pilgrimage of about forty English Catholics; they now mingled with the local congregation and with the other foreign pilgrims among whom was a close-knit body of Japanese nuns. As the nuns somewhat established the variegated quality of the scene, Suzi had worked Barbara through the crowd to a point near them, whose long black robes provided a protective colouring for her outfit. The eyes of the Franciscans had automatically moved to the young priest on the altar, and they kept a special watch on the assisting acolyte, a local Arab boy; for it was their duty, to which they devoted extreme diligence, to see that the ritual was correctly observed at this Altar of the Nailing of the Cross. At the other altar in the chapel the Greek rite proceeded under the equally jealous eyes of its custodians, and the chanting murmur of the Orthodox responses droned busily about the ears of the

Latin persuasion, so that the blessed mutter of the Roman Mass could scarcely be heard by the faithful; the Franciscans were accustomed to this and were aware that nothing could be done about it. It was true that from time to time feelings came to a boil, and a quarrel would take place between the subordinate brothers of either communion, not to mention the words that had been known to arise when the Copts, Syrians, or even the Gregorian Armenians overstepped the mark on the sacred site of the death, burial, and resurrection of the Saviour. Doctrinal arguments, these simple servants of the Orders left to their superiors; but the question of who had the privilege of sweeping whose paving stone was their province; not many years since, it had come to a fist-fight at Bethlehem on a Feast of the Nativity because a young novice brother of the Orthodox had presumed to clean a certain painted-glass window, this task being properly within the province of a newly arrived Franciscan brother, who, simple peasant boy as he was, nevertheless perceived that the prestige of the One True Church was upon his shoulders, and started a fight.

Sometimes there had been errors of protocol on the Franciscan side, as they humbly conceded amongst themselves. Not long ago, when the Archbishop of Canterbury visited the Holy Land, a few good Franciscans, carried away by the event, had kissed his ring on his arrival at the great Sepulchre. On being told later by their superior that they ought not to have done so, their spokesman offered the reason: 'We thought it might move Her Majesty to do something for us.' It was indeed difficult to realise that the British Mandate was at an end.

The English priest at present saying Mass on the altar had nearly reached the moment for his sermon; he had no right to give a sermon, no matter how many English pilgrims he had brought, when time was pressing for the next Mass on the list. As if to aid and abet him, the Orthodox Mass had only a few seconds before come to a quiet end. He had not even asked permission; had merely said as he brushed from the vestry, 'I'm going to say a few words to the pilgrims, very few.' The friars' eyes were upon him as he concluded the Ordinary of the Mass and turned to the congregation.

'I will say a few words,' he said, 'on the text of St Paul's Epistle to the Hebrews, chapter 13, verse 14: "We have an everlasting city, but not here; our goal is the city that is one day to be."

'In the Name of the Father, the Son, and the Holy Ghost. Most of us have come a long way to Jerusalem. It has been the instinct of Christians since the time of the Early Church to see Jerusalem before they died. Jerusalem was a place of pilgrimage for the Jews, centuries before the time of Christ. The act of pilgrimage is an instinct of mankind. It is an act of devotion which, like a work of art, is meaning enough in itself. The questions, "What useful purpose does a pilgrimage serve? What good does it do?" are by the way. People put themselves out to visit places sacred to their religion, or the graves of poets and statesmen, or of their ancestors, or the house they themselves were born in. Why? Because that is what people do.

'We usually expect to receive for our trouble the experience of a strong emotion. We expect to be moved, when we reach our destination, by awe or nostalgia; or we hope for a shade of sadness or in some way to be spiritually exalted. But so far as feelings are concerned, our feelings when we get to the place are usually a matter of good or bad fortune, as the case may be. A lot may depend on the weather. And this is more particularly the case where a pilgrimage of religion is concerned. A religious pilgrimage has always been associated with difficulty, danger, heat and bother and general human wear and tear. We who have come by air from the West have so far had an easier journey than the devout Moslems do, who surge in their thousands to Mecca by cheap transport, any transport, to pray at the shrine of Mohammed. We have it easier than Mary and Joseph did when they came up to Jerusalem for the feast and, in the course of all the jostle and bother and commerce of the pilgrimage, lost their child and only missed him when they were on the way home, so that they had to trail all the way back, a day's journey. I say that we –'

The friars had already summed up their man and they conveyed their verdict to each other by the flicker of a glance. One of the new upstarts; comparing the Moslems to good Catholics in the same breath . . . So far, so bad. They discerned that worse was to come.

'We had a streamlined journey to Jerusalem,' went on this firebrand. 'But we have come in the hottest and least comfortable season because it's the only time we could manage to come at all. Otherwise, quite rightly, we would have chosen to come in the spring or autumn. However, we know that Our Lord Jesus Christ was here in the summer time, when life was less comfortable than it is today, when the smells were smellier and the sick and the poor were more numerous and less hopeful of cure. Don't let yourselves be bothered by the commercialism that goes on around the sacred places. There was commercialism in the courts of the Temple in the time of Christ. Don't be put off because the shrines that commemorate what was once the simple life of Jesus are overwhelmed with glittering ornaments, silver lamps, jewelled inlays and the like. They are nothing like the Temple was that Our Lord frequented himself, healing the ordinary sick among all the grandeur. And we have come to be reminded of Our Lord. It does not count what feelings are, if our feelings can be conditioned by the weather or the artistic tastes of the people around us. A good disposition is more precious to God than fine feelings. In Jerusalem, our Blessed Lord suffered, died, and rose again to life. It is enough that we are here.

'So it seems to me that you shouldn't expect to feel exalted by awe and reverence on days like, for instance, today, among the crowds in the narrow streets and the temperature rising. In the next few weeks don't wear yourselves out rushing round the shrines just for the sake of having said a "Hail Mary" and touched every altar with your rosary, like a child who invents for himself a sense of impending doom unless he steps over every crack in the pavement. There is no need to visit every shrine in the place. There are far too many shrines. Some of them are sheer fake, others are doubtful. That's not to say that the important sites that mark the life of Jesus, such as the spot we stand on at this moment, are not sacred places. They have been sanctified by centuries of the great Dead who have come –'

The three friars gazed at the priest as with one gaze. They had known it. The incipient *défroqué* was undermining the Holy Land, and as he went on to enumerate for practical purposes the shrines which his pilgrimage might well skip and the dubiety of their origins, their thoughts went to their brethren, the custodians of the Holy Land to whom these places were their whole heart and life; tears came to the eyes of the eldest friar as he thought of the venerable Franciscan, well past ninety, who kept the house where Our Lady was conceived by St Joachim and St Anne, and who had wanted nothing for himself all his life but to show it to the pilgrims and pray with them as they came, and collect alms for the poor of the place, and die there on that spot. Now this enemy of the Faith on the altar was openly preaching what other young foreign priests had only so far hinted. Moreover, he was saying more than a few words, he was preaching at length, and he should not be preaching at all. The youngest friar, a lay-brother, murmured fiercely that he would tell this priest after the Mass that he had transgressed by setting back the time of the next Mass. Already a fresh batch of pilgrims was waiting at the entrance. But the aged friar made a gesture of restraint towards the young brother. The other friar, also an old man, then whispered his support of the young brother, but he too was silenced by the elder one: 'Observe meekness,' he said softly, 'it is our calling. Moreover –' He paused to give full ear to the voice from the altar, to hear what next outrage was being uttered. When he had heard enough he continued, 'Let us not provoke this man lest the bishop should say to us, "You have knelt to kiss the ring of the Schismatic of Canterbury, but one of our own good Fathers you have treated with reproof."' At this they folded their hands and waited to hear what the Judas and intellectual standing at the Altar of the Nailing of the Cross would say next.

He was saying, 'It is not absolutely certain, for instance, that the Holy Sepulchre stands on the site of Golgotha. There are strong arguments of archaeology in favour of this place where we stand being the place of the Crucifixion, and for a Catholic these arguments are strengthened above all by the fact that this place was traditionally revered as Golgotha before the Emperor Constantine, in the fourth century, built the original church on this site. Archaeology is continually enriching our knowledge of the holy places. Where doubts of historic authenticity exist, they are as thrilling in their potentialities for quest and discovery as a certainty would be. The weight of probability leads most of the experts to believe that this is the site of Calvary. But other learned people have argued against it. Whether true or not, our religion does not depend on it. We know for a certainty that Our Lord was crucified, that he died and was buried, and rose again from the dead, at a place outside the walls of Jerusalem; if not at the spot where we stand, then at some other spot nearby. If you are looking for physical exactitude in Jerusalem it is a good quest, but it belongs to archaeology, not faith. In the time of Christ the people built up the tombs of the Prophets, as he reminded them with a bit of irony. I am sure some were authentic, some doubtful. Jerusalem has been in many hands. Then, as now, soldiers patrolled the Holy Land. Jerusalem has been destroyed, rebuilt, fought over, conquered, and now is divided again. The historical evidence of our faith is scattered about under the ground; nothing is neat. And what would be the point of our professing faith if it were? There's no need for faith if everything is plain to the eye. We cannot know anything perfectly, because we ourselves are not perfect. When we have come to perfection in time, then faith, like time, will be done away. "We have an everlasting city," St Paul has said, "but not here; our goal is the city that is one day to be." For there is a supernatural process going on under the surface and within the substance of all things. In the Jerusalem of history we see the type and shadow of that Jerusalem of Heaven that St John of Patmos tells of in the Apocalypse. "I, John," he says, "saw in my vision that holy city which is the new Jerusalem, being sent down by God from Heaven, like a bride who has adorned herself to meet her husband." This is the spiritual city that is involved eternally with the historical one. It is the city of David, the city of God's people in exile: "If I forget thee, O Jerusalem, let my tongue cleave to the roof of my mouth; if I prefer not Jerusalem above my chief joy." It is the city of Jesus, not only of his death, but of his rising again alive. It is the New Jerusalem which we seek with our faith, and which is the goal of our pilgrimage to this old Jerusalem of history. "What is faith?" said St Paul. "It is that which gives substance to our hopes, which convinces us of things we cannot see."'

The priest glanced at his watch and the friars at each other. He made a slight gesture of pulling himself off a subject that was leading far, and said, 'I don't mean you to be afraid of saying your prayers at the wrong shrine. It's always the right place if you pray there.

'We know the creed of our faith and what we believe. Outside of that it is better to know what is doubtful than to place faith in uncertainties. Doubt is the prerogative of the believer; the unbeliever cannot know doubt. And in what is doubtful we should doubt well. But in whatever touches the human spirit, it is better to believe everything than nothing. Have faith. In the Name of the Father, the Son, and the Holy Ghost. *Amen*.'

They felt he had done his worst. The friars stood moveless, watching him return to the altar and begin the second part of the Mass.

'*Credo in unum Deum, Patrem omnipotentem, factorem coeli et terrae, visibilium omnium, et invisibilium –*'

Suddenly he had broken off and had turned once again to the people. This alone was irregular . . . But he was about to speak, with an advisory finger pointed . . . 'I forgot to mention the Milk Grotto, near Bethlehem. Don't go near the Milk Grotto. It's a pure fake. They claim there's a legend that milk from Mary's breast fell in this grotto where for some reason she happened to be nursing the infant Jesus, in consequence of which the walls of the grotto turned white. They make up packets of white stuff from the walls for pilgrims to take away. The stuff is supposed to be a comfort to nursing mothers or some such hocus-pocus. Keep away from the Milk Grotto, it's only a chalk cave.'

The communist agent returned to the altar and began again. '*Credo in unum Deum . . .*'

When the Mass was ended and he moved from the altar towards the friars, the youngest again made a move as if to say a few wild words. But both elders restrained him; and when the Englishman brushed past them, muttering the prayers appointed to be said after Mass, the friars stood mute, with downcast eyes, content to wait for their justification in Heaven, which, being all Italian territory, would be so ordered that foreign firebrands like this one would be kept firmly in their place.

Freddy already thought highly of Suzi, who had told him what a lovely smile he had. This was something he vaguely recalled having heard before at an earlier time of his life; it was a pleasant reminder – '. . . Freddy's attractive smile', or '. . . your nice smile, Freddy' – something like that. Suzi was very outspoken but that was the Ramdez touch; Abdul was the same. By the time he came to stand outside the Holy Sepulchre after the service, waiting for the girls to emerge, he had forgotten Suzi's compliment about his smile but only thought highly of Suzi. The girls had gone to look round the Holy Sepulchre and visit the other shrines. Suzi had told him to wait for them outside, had pushed confidently through the crowd, followed mutely by Barbara. Things seemed to be going well. Freddy had thought the sermon rather long but quite practical in its way. He had been to a Roman Catholic Mass once or twice before, for funeral services, and considered there was too much of it. He was not, anyway, a very religious man. He entertained a patriotic belief in God, but since his youth he had been to church about as seldom as he had been to Buckingham Palace. However, he disapproved of letting young chaps into the Foreign Service who openly professed to have no religion at all. A security risk, Freddy felt decidedly. He looked up at the scaffold props of the Holy Sepulchre and wondered if Joanna and Matt would hear of his lingering presence in Jordan. He didn't really care one way or another; and when his mind turned on those tedious letters from Ma and Benny, his anxious replies, and the all-responsible letter to the doctor which had gone swirling down the lavatory at Alexandros's place, he felt respectably at one with the world. Things were going well. It was like being at the races when one had started off with a pound each way and the horse had come in, perhaps second, at a good price; then, if one did quite nicely in the second race, even at a modest price, one knew one's luck was in for the day.

One's luck was in at last, and the enterprise of Barbara Vaughan's pilgrimage had got off on a good start. He thought highly of Suzi Ramdez. Somewhere along the road to Bethlehem, their next goal, a pink gin before lunch would be a good idea.

Barbara, meanwhile, existed in numb misery. The clothes she was draped in, although they were loose, seemed to form a kind of oven for her burning body. The crowds pressed as if deliberately all round her, pushing crude faces close to her veil. Her eyes prickled and she felt their roots were red hot. Everything in her life was remotely in the past. Harry Clegg was a few feet of overexposed film. Nothing worse, she thought, can happen; it was the only thing she could think, but if she had tried she could not have placed what exactly that happening was, than which nothing could be worse. At a point during the sermon, she had wanted to say something to Suzi like 'I want to go out and be sick', but being in any case uncertain whether she actually wanted to be sick or not, she had remembered she was a mute. From the sermon she had got the erroneous impression of a sanctimonious voice pounding upon her physical distress. Now she followed Suzi, who was treating the crowds like those waves of the Red Sea between which the Israelites passed dryshod; the people made way for Suzi, but on Barbara they pressed with enlarged noses and twisted mouths on the other side of her veil. She was beyond feeling ill, it was merely that nothing worse could happen.

She stood beside Suzi before a stone slab and wanted only to lie on it full length, without the black shrouds she was wearing; she yearned for its coolness and for a long sleep, a sleep of death. Through her fever she heard the voice of an English-speaking Arab guide addressing the group which Suzi had joined. He was saying that this was the Holy Sepulchre itself, the tomb that had belonged to Joseph of Arimathea, where Christ was laid on that first Good Friday when his body was taken down from the cross. The body of Christ was embalmed with spices and herbs and wrapped in a linen shroud as the cool night was falling. Suzi took Barbara's arm to draw her closer to the front of the group where the guide was pointing to this and that memorial of the burial of Christ. Barbara's head was drumming; her ears had begun to ache. She held back and clung only to the one thought that nothing worse could now happen.

They were going down some cool dark steps. The guide had gone ahead and waited below for another group of people to move away before he collected his brood about him. The brood was talking softly, menacing Barbara. She heard that this was St Helena's Chapel, where the true Cross had been found in the fourth century. Barbara wanted to return to the slab and lie on its cool surface; an image of Tess of the d'Urbervilles in the last scene at Stonehenge passed her mind and was gone indiscernibly, so that she did not know what caused her to start and give a little shudder, as if touched by a bat that had somehow got into the crypt. She had stopped on the dark stairway, and the people behind her wanted to pass down. Suzi reached up and took her arm. Nothing worse can happen now. A woman who did not seem to belong either to the group that was about to leave the chapel or to the approaching group was standing apart looking round her, sturdily clutching with one thumb the shoulder strap of her sling-bag; in the other hand she held a slip of paper about which she evidently wished to consult someone. Barbara and Suzi had reached the ground of the crypt. The woman approached their guide, but he had turned to consult with the departing guide about some guide-business. The lone woman then approached a man among the crowd that Barbara and Suzi had joined. She was within breathing distance of Barbara's veil. She was Ricky. She was Miss Rickward. She said to the man, offering the slip of paper, 'Excuse me, but can you read Arabic?' The man said, no, he was afraid he couldn't, but perhaps the guide . . . He looked round for their guide, who was nowhere visible at that moment. 'You see,' Ricky was saying, 'it's an address that I've been directed to. I'm looking for a friend.' The man then caught sight of Barbara at the same time as Ricky did, and he started to say, 'There's an Arab woman there, she'd be able to –' Ricky approached Barbara with her piece of paper: 'Excuse me, but can you tell me –'

Suzi's arm shot forth like the arm of one holding back yet another Red Sea. 'My poor servant is dumb,' declared Suzi. 'Very dumb, also holy. Praise be to Allah! She can utter no word, neither falsehood nor blasphemy. Do not approach my holy mute, I command you, but stand at a distance, and if there's anything you want, ask *me*.'

'Oh, I beg your pardon,' Ricky said, stepping backward, as did the other people in their near vicinity. Suzi was reading the words on the piece of paper. She read out, 'The Crusaders' Inn. Ask for Jaber Khalil, from Amin Mahgoub, St Helena's Convent.' Suzi explained how to get to the Crusaders' Inn while Barbara looked at Ricky through her veil without feeling a thing, since nothing worse could happen than had already happened behind her throbbing head. She heard Suzi tell Ricky to ask for the proprietor, Mr Khalil, while Ricky informed her gratefully that she had got the address from the doorman at St Helena's Convent; she had not been allowed to enter the doors of the convent as an outbreak of an infectious disease had occurred there that morning. 'And,' said Ricky, 'I'm trying to catch up with an English friend. I thought she might have come here for a church service.'

'Good luck, then,' Suzi said, shaking off the intruder as firmly as if she had not been in total ignorance of any connection between Ricky and Barbara. Suzi moved with the group towards the Altar of the Finding of the Cross, where the guide was now standing ready for them. Holding fast to Barbara, she thrust far into the stifling crowd, who now made a little space for this woman of Jerusalem and her picturesque servant.

'She has seen all the Holy Sepulchre,' Suzi said, when they found Freddy in the courtyard. 'But Barbara must come again on the return journey.'

'I'm ill,' Barbara said. 'My throat's closing up. I've got a fever.'

Suzi said, looking straight ahead, 'Don't speak. Say nothing. Even now, you might be noticed. Wait till we get to the car. You must keep it up.'

'It must be those clothes,' Freddy said. 'She'll be all right when we're on the road to Bethlehem. I think if we can get a drink somewhere before lunch it would be a good idea. Let's get moving.'

But there was no mistaking the fact, when they got a look at Barbara's unveiled face on the way to Bethlehem – the hectic flush and the dead-white ring round her mouth – that she was ill beyond what could be accounted for by the heat and the clothes she was wearing. They turned back to Jerusalem and once more Freddy banged on Alexandros's shop door, while Suzi stood on the pavement supporting Barbara, looking up at Alexandros's face in the window.

'The lady wishes to contribute to your Arab Refugee Fund,' Freddy said, falling back on his past experience of Hong Kong and so forth. He said, 'The lady wishes to remain anonymous.' He handed over ten English five-pound notes out of Barbara's newly-acquired supply. 'And is honoured by your acceptance of this donation for so great a cause.'

Dr Russeifa stuffed his payment into the inside pocket of his coat, thanking both Freddy and the lady on the refugees' behalf. Freddy, careful to mind his manners, then asked the doctor to state his fee for his professional services. 'No fee,' said Dr Russeifa, 'I am perfectly honoured to be of assistance to the unfortunate lady. This outbreak of scarlet fever has of course made her a victim, and is without doubt the fault of our enemy, so-called Israel, who sends such germ-warfare to our country daily.'

The disease had not spread far; Freddy's information was that there was one case, a Swedish pilgrim, in the convent where Barbara had stayed. Barbara was now lying on a sofa in a small room in Alexandros's living-quarters.

At first she had said she didn't care what happened. She had murmured that nothing worse could happen, and closed her eyes. After taking two aspirins and a glass of water, she opened them. She had partially recovered her senses and had become talkative by fits and starts. She had insisted on writing out a large cheque on her English bank which Alexandros said he could cash.

A doctor, Freddy had insisted. He said it was probably some local bug she had caught, a temporary thing, but still one must have a doctor.

Alexandros knew of three English doctors in Jerusalem. Freddy had met one of them at the Cartwrights'. He hesitated. Alexandros said, 'Would these English doctors make an official report of it?'

'Yes, I'm afraid they would have to. Especially if she's got something infectious. They'd have to put her in hospital of course, and, of course, inform the British Consulate and the Jordanian authorities.'

'Suzi!' called Alexandros, and went to fetch her before she answered his call. She had been with Mme Alexandros explaining things in such a way that the woman could not possibly understand yet could not decently admit to being puzzled. Alexandros had brought Suzi into the little room, conferring with her in Arabic. He then threw wide his arms and announced, 'We have Russeifa. Dr Russeifa is the doctor for the Joe Ramdez Insurance Company. You give him quite a little cash and he will attend to Barbara very quiet.'

'A mild case of the scarlet fever,' Dr Russeifa said. 'The temperature is not too high, one hundred degrees is nothing.'

'Well, really,' Freddy had said, 'ought you not to report all cases of the disease?'

'I shall report the case. You must assure me she will be kept in isolation two weeks. The treatment is simple. Only tell me she will be kept in isolation and looked after in bed. Then I report that the case is all right and has left the country. I give all the instructions necessary to the young woman Ramdez, who will, in turn, give them –' Alexandros's hand was in the doctor's and they were suddenly exchanging profuse smiling words in Arabic while the doctor was being propelled by Alexandros to the door. Alexandros escorted Russeifa heavily downstairs, he could be heard decisively locking the shop door and marching up again. He rubbed his hands together once and said, 'Now we know what to do. Goodbye to Dr Russeifa.'

Barbara, on the sofa, said, 'There's a woman in Jerusalem who's chasing me. The headmistress –'

'Just lie quiet, my dear,' Freddy said, thinking her delirious.

'We leave for Jericho as soon as we are ready,' Suzi said.

'Jericho?' Freddy said. Everything had been out of his hands since Suzi and Alexandros had conferred together.

'My father's first wife lives there,' Suzi said. 'She is in seclusion, and if we pay her a little she will keep Barbara, as she has kept other friends so often.'

'Do you know,' Freddy said. 'I think Barbara ought to go to hospital.'

Alexandros went to a table beside the sofa on which lay a heavily gilt leather-bound book. 'The Koran,' he remarked, as he took from between its pages a folded half-sheet of newspaper. He said, 'I received the newspaper of Israel early today. I get it on all Sundays and burn when it is read. But this piece I have kept.' He handed it to Freddy, who saw the photograph of a bespectacled man under a heading: 'London Consultant for Eichmann Trial'. Under the photograph was the title 'Mr Michael Aaronson'. And beneath that again he read, while Suzi came and looked at it too:

254

Mr Michael Aaronson of London, an international law expert who took part in the Nuremberg Trials, has been in Israel on a short visit for consultation on the Eichmann trial. Mr Aaronson, who declined to reveal the precise legal points of the discussions with the authorities, said he was greatly impressed by the conduct of the trial from the point of view of International Law. He said he was not in agreement with that section of the British press which continues to question the right of Israel to hold such a trial on her own territory.

Mr Aaronson, who is in general law practice in London, also said that what little he had seen of the country had proved a strong incentive to return at leisure, which he hopes to do one day with his wife and three children.

While in Jerusalem, Mr Aaronson was able to spend some time with his cousin, Miss Barbara Vaughan, who has been spending a vacation in Israel. Miss Vaughan, who teaches school in England, is a Roman Catholic convert. She claims that her new religion is not in conflict with her Jewish blood and background, and is enthusiastic about Israel and the Israelis. Miss Vaughan left on Friday for a tour of Jordan.

'Does this paper get round, here?' Freddy said.

'It comes to the authorities, of course, and you may be sure the Army Intelligence,' Alexandros said. 'By now they are on the watch for her. You know, this rumour will reach the people that there is a Jew from Israel in Jordan, and there could be a hue and cry among the people. The government has made the people think in a certain way of a Jew, and so whatever is the law for a British subject is neither here nor there when they have to contend with their own people's voices. Many Arabs here have voices that they will use to their own advantage. So now you take her away to Jericho where she can remain till she is able to leave the country.'

Alexandros sat down, so dejected that Suzi said, 'I would come over to console you in my arms, Alexandros, but I might carry to you the scarlet fever.'

Alexandros got up and went to the silver-framed icon in the wall, from behind which he produced a bulky envelope. He then unscrewed the base of the mosaic lampstand, from which he took a small cardboard box. 'I give you the rest of the money,' he said.

'Are you sure you can cash a large English cheque?'

'Oh yes, I can cash through London. It is illegal.'

Alexandros opened the envelope and brought out a batch of English five-pound notes, which he counted. Then he opened the small box and extracted four fifty-dollar notes. Suzi said, 'What a lot of money, but Barbara says she couldn't care less. I hold her travellers' cheques also.'

'If it comes to the point where she does need money, then money will be the answer,' Freddy observed. 'Travellers' cheques are less useful in certain cases.'

Alexandros thought this funny, and began to throw off the weight of the affair. He said, 'She may yet finish the pilgrimage. What is two, three weeks in bed? Then,' he said, his voice rising in a chant of triumph and hope, 'the police are no longer looking for her, and we see she will go to Bethlehem, she will go to see the Shepherd's Field and the Milk Grotto perhaps; she will go to the Mount of Olives, the Garden of Gethsemane, and the Basilica of the Agony; she will visit the palace of the High Priest Caiaphas and the church of St Peter in Gallicantu, also Absalom's Pillar, also the Tombs of Zacharias and James, along the Kidron Valley and the Valley of Jehosophat, by the Tombs of Kings, and she will go to Bethany and the Tomb of Lazarus.' Now Alexandros was standing large, seeming to occupy most of the room, like an Arab lord of ancient times calling over the sites of past victories, or a prophet the titles of the Lord's decreed grounds of abode: 'She will see the house of Martha and Mary, also Jericho and the River Jordan at the spot where Christ was baptised by John the Baptist, the dove descending; and the Dead Sea and the Wilderness of Temptation.'

Suzi Ramdez always said that the main thing about herself was that she was ambitious. Her strength lay in her vagueness about the limitations of her life; and her weakness derived from its actual limitations which she stood ready to demolish at any time. Beyond any rational expectation she enjoyed the respect of her father, Joe Ramdez. His character twisted around him, spreading and clinging like a vine, while hers was a solitary palm-tree outlined sharp against the sky. Her acceptance of him was total. She knew he was in business for political purposes, that he was in political things to enable him to score off personal vendettas; she knew he was also in business for business purposes, and was a political informer for the Jordanian Secret Service, that he passed intelligence to the United Arab Republic concerning the Jordanian Government; and that these activities were all balanced to a fine point which so depended on instinct that he could no more have put them down on paper than he could actually see his own face. They all revolved around blackmail of sorts, the arranging for forged visas and other papers, and, when dealing with foreigners, a plausible technique of feigned misunderstandings. Suzi did not think of her father as a crook or a traitor, but she knew that he was. He thought of himself as a patriot, an Arab, and overwhelmingly as a man who, in all his actions, did justice to himself. In a world of officials and businessmen who continually and piously did themselves justice he was at home. His indulgence towards Suzi was a secret weakness. He put her in charge of the travel agency over the heads of her mother and her elder sister Lia, who was married to a poor hotel clerk. Suzi was the manager of the Joe Ramdez Company, travel agents. Joe had put her at the top because she never asked the sort of questions that betrayed civic fear, as did his wife. He tolerated her out-spoken ways because she took the place of his son Abdul, and he felt he might eventually lean on her, as on a son, in his old age. When she had refused to marry any of the men he had procured for her, he had not insisted. When she had turned twenty-eight he had given up urging her to marry. She was now thirty-three. Privately, she bossed her mother and sister as if she were a man, but with everyone else Suzi was at pains to be accommodating. When she went out with the family she was the most demure of them all, so that it was difficult for their friends to place an actual finger on Suzi's difference from other daughters. Alexandros told her he knew of a rich Lebanese, a widower, who would want her for a wife even though she was not a virgin. She said, 'I don't need to marry an old widower. I could marry a young man, and if he was looking for a virgin, that's all right, because Abdul has told me of a clever surgeon in Cairo who could stitch me up. But I don't want to marry a man who wants a virgin; maybe I'll go to Tangiers and marry a European or an American who looks for a woman, not a virgin.' Alexandros had been her lover for more than four years. She made him laugh and feel strong like no other woman. He respected the women of Islam generally, and Christian Arab women, like his wife, were good women. But they did not have the power of pro-voking laughter as Suzi did; and they made a man feel strong only because they were weak, not because they were free. The nearest thing to Suzi he had ever seen had been a lovely Indian princess who had done business with him in Beirut. She had been educated abroad, was freely-spoken, and had made her husband laugh as he stood, in turbaned elegance, watching business being done.

Suzi had told her father that morning that she was taking Freddy on a sightseeing tour. She did not mention Barbara, having been warned by Alexandros not to mention Barbara. Joe Ramdez had been excited to hear of Freddy's tour of the countryside. He told Suzi to remember Freddy's position, by which he meant her to see what she could get out of him by way of information. 'Naturally I am keeping his position in mind. Otherwise, why do you think I am doing this job myself rather than give him a hired guide?' He was proud of Suzi. He said, 'No matter if it does not appear to be secret, or if it is not secret, any information is valuable.' It was difficult for the government officials, all of whom were spies of some sort, to know what was secret or not, in any case. They would frequently be dazzled by a report already available in publications which had not reached them, or which lay forgotten in their files. He said to Suzi, 'Don't be too friendly with him. Remember you are an Arab. He will communicate more if you make him feel an intruder in our land; that's always the way of the British.' When she left the house he said, 'Take a proposal form for the life insurance.' She said she already had a proposal form, and bounced off.

The life-insurance agency served many purposes, as did the travel agency. Mainly, it gave basic information about visiting and resident foreigners, from which could be traced, through the Ramdez network of Arabs who had fled for politics or crime to other parts of the world, even more personal and professional information. Information was always good. It could be turned into money more often than not. Every government bureau throughout the world prized information; however irrelevant it might seem today, it might be relevant one day. To know of a Foreign Service man's private habits, for instance, his friends, his parents and his blood-pressure, could be very rewarding, very useful.

Suzi had driven off to the Potter's Field in independent spirits. She was the manager and fairly rich. She had met Alexandros in the night, which was good. She liked to do something for Alexandros. She remembered meeting Mr Hamilton and Miss Vaughan before, on the day the family had visited the Cartwrights. They had drunk fruit juice in the garden. Mr Hamilton was called Freddy and had a lovely smile.

Barbara said from the back of the car, 'If you're going to catch it, I'll feel awful.' At present she felt less awful than she had felt earlier in the day. Suzi at the wheel was making a cheerful tumble of talk. She said, 'It will be the blame of your religious high principles.'

'I'll try to live them down.'

'I think I've already had the scarlet fever. I know I had a rash and was to be kept in bed with aspirins one time when I was seven. Latifa, my father's first wife, will know.'

Freddy said, 'I haven't had it.'

'Oh dear!' Barbara said.

'But I don't feel I'm going to catch it, somehow or other,' he said.

'It would be the penultimate straw,' Suzi said. 'The worst straw would be for Barbara to be captured.' She had made Barbara curl up with her head down when she passed the first sentry post on the road to Jericho. Her conversation was like the turning wheels of a fast car. Freddy began to sing 'The Eton Boating Song' in a tuneful, unpractised voice.

'What is this?' Suzi said.

'"The Eton Boating Song".'

'You went to Eton when a little boy?'

'No, Lancing. But I sang in the choir.' Freddy looked round at Barbara and inquired with only his facial expression how she was getting on. Barbara raised her veil and winked back. Freddy sat up straight again and was silent for a while, staring at the desert hills. Then he said, 'The last time I sang it was in my cabin with a few fellow officers one night outside Montevideo harbour. We sang other songs as well, my dear. We were celebrating the scuttling of the *Graf Spee* on 18 December 1939.' This had to be explained in detail to Suzi, who was, Barbara thought, as splendid a listener as Freddy was a waffler. She was feverishly delighted with them. 'We refer to it as the Battle of the River Plate,' Freddy was saying, 'but there was very little battle, really. We just made it too hot for her, so she couldn't stay in and she couldn't come out.' Suzi said, 'Who was she?' 'The *Admiral Graf Spee*, my dear,' Freddy said.

And it was plain to Barbara that he hadn't lost his carefree mood on account of her scarlet fever. She felt weak and hot, but was no longer in misery. She kept realising, with a shudder of gladness, the fact that she had a real sickness; it was a respite from responsibility for herself, and that felt good.

'We come to another police post,' Suzi said. Barbara curled up, with her head down, an old sleeping bundle.

'Now look up,' said Suzi at last, 'they are all gone by. I raise my brown arm and wave at these police. We are coming now to the terrible plains, the pressure is terrible, they are the lowest spot on earth, thirteen hundred feet below sea level where were the wicked cities of Sodom and Gomorrah which God destroyed.'

Within a few minutes they were in the desert plains. For some reason never explained, in the middle of the wilderness by the roadside, an advertisement board was set up, stating 'Boutay for Pianos' and nothing else. 'Whether or not this is the plain of Sodom and Gomorrah,' Freddy said, 'by God, it feels like it. Are you all right, Barbara?'

'I feel drowsy and heavy. I may expire,' she murmured. She closed her eyes and felt she could just about cope.

'We stop to get a drink at the Dead Sea Hotel,' Suzi said. 'We shall buy drinks and take them to the car.'

Freddy was rustling something, the road-map, muttering something. Barbara opened her eyes. Freddy said, 'We don't need to go all this way to Jericho. The road –'

'A police truck is coming. Keep down, Barbara,' she said, and when the rattle of the motor had passed into the distance behind them, Suzi said, 'I need to be seen on this route with my tourist in case they check up already for Barbara. We need to drink something from the Dead Sea Hotel, but we buy it quick.'

Freddy said to Barbara, 'Did Alexandros show you that piece in the Israeli newspaper?'

'No. I don't think so. What piece?'

'About your meeting your cousin in Israel; and it published the fact that you were coming to Jordan.'

'I knew it,' said Barbara. 'I just knew that would happen. A frightfully resentful woman came to interview my cousin Michael, and I got mixed up with her. What did she say?'

'This piece said you were a Jewish convert Catholic very keen on Israel – something like that; anyhow, enough to set off an alarm over here. I thought it was as well to tell you, so you'll know where you stand just now. But don't worry. I'll get something else put in the Israeli paper tomorrow when I get back – something about you deciding not to go to Jordan after all, but spending the rest of your time in Israel instead. We'll have to cook up some story to hang it on, but don't worry. I know the editor of one of the papers. A very decent old chap, we're on good terms with them at the office. I'll see to it the moment I get back. I'll be there before the next bag goes. Don't worry.'

Barbara was outside the context of worry. She sighed and said, 'Freddy, dear, you're sweet.' Whereupon he beamed round at her.

'You have such trouble for your religion,' Suzi said, 'but you were clever to become a Catholic rather than remain a Jew, as the Jews get in trouble from the Christians as well as the Arabs. It is no life to be a Jew. I would do like you if I was to be in your place.'

'Oh, but she believes in it,' Freddy said. 'It's a matter of conviction, isn't it, Barbara?'

'I suppose it is,' she said, 'but at the moment I don't feel conviction about anything.' The air was breathless.

'Oh, at the moment, naturally – That's one of the things the sermon was about, you remember. He said, "Don't trust your feelings," or "Don't judge by your feelings when you're out here in this heat" – something like that – remember?'

'No, I don't remember a thing.'

'Did you convert to be a Catholic on account of a feeling?' Suzi said.

'No, I took a long time to make up my mind.'

'You did right and clever. I would do the same if –'

'Her religion's sincere, I'm sure,' Freddy said.

'I do not say insincere. I say she did right and she did clever. I am most sincere, believing myself in religion, but I also do correctly and a clever thing to remain a Moslem in any country where Moslem is O.K.'

Freddy began, 'But look –'

'Leave us alone, Freddy,' Barbara said.

'It's too bad that you have to suffer for your pilgrimage,' Suzi rattled on. 'The Moslems, too, suffer for pilgrimages maybe and maybe not, some have a jolly good time on these journeys. But you believe, that I know, you have Jesus to be God and he was crucified and suffered for your sins; isn't it so?'

'That's right.'

'Well, you say he took your sins upon him. The Christians say he took all this blame and suffered for it in their place. So if you have these misfortunes now, it is not your blame at all. You have no sins whatsoever to suffer for, as your God Jesus has taken these sins. Therefore all your suffering and inconvenience of scarlet fever is God's blame.'

Her logical premise at an end, she said, 'Keep down, we come to the Dead Sea Hotel.' Barbara glimpsed through her veil and the quivering heat of the air the great expanse of the steel-blue salt lake and a lonely structure, the hotel, and saw before she curled up a white-shirted young man on a veranda, idly peeling the paint off green wooden supports. The car slowed down but did not stop. It cruised along while Suzi said, 'I take my tourist for a view of the Dead Sea only, as there is a Secret Service boy on the veranda at a table and there must be men inside. Look only at the spots across the lake that I am pointing to, Freddy. Keep down, Barbara. We see what we see.' In a few minutes the car had begun to put on speed and soon Suzi said, 'You can sit up again now. I shall tell you if any car follows or passes.'

Barbara longed for a drink. Freddy said, 'I'm thirsty – I don't know about you girls. It was madness of me not to bring something.'

'It's God's blame, as I said. But never mind; we go to Jericho very quick,' Suzi said. 'In Jericho is the most ravishing beautiful water. I will get you to Jericho as I have promised Alexandros.'

Freddy started to sing again. It was one of the things that puzzled him most, and shocked him, when these incidents came back to mind after his lapse of memory, that he sang quite a lot on the way to Jericho. He was to remember it clearly with a sense of special irresponsibility: 'But why was I singing?'

The house at Jericho was some distance from the town. Nobody came out to welcome them, as if, Freddy thought, by special arrangement, or by habitual practice. Suzi hurried Barbara indoors and disappeared at the back of the house. Freddy followed with his zipper-bag and stood waiting in the large room into which the front door opened. The floor was tiled with a chipped but attractive bird design, which suggested that the clay-like fabric of the house had been set on ancient foundations. A round dining-table stood in the middle of the floor, surrounded by chairs. Freddy presently pulled one chair out and sat down with his zipper-bag on the floor beside him, gazing out of the open door into the sandy forecourt where a palm-tree, Suzi's car, and a primitive well were the only visible objects.

There were three other doors in this room, one in each wall, leading, as Freddy correctly assumed, to three different wings of the house. The old foundations had probably been laid in the form of a cross by some Crusader mission or a later Christian community, and the house was no doubt built on the site of a church or a chapel within a larger place of worship. The door through which Suzi had hustled Barbara was the one opposite the front entrance. A small sound of voices came from this direction, as if they were quite a long way off, behind another closed door. Freddy was extremely thirsty. It occurred to him that Suzi might have intended him to follow her into the part of the house where she had taken Barbara, so he took his bag and went over to the door. It had been locked from the inside. He tried the two side doors, but these, too, were locked. From each door there came a sound of quiet, distant voices, too far away from him to distinguish whether the speakers were men or women. He put down his bag and went out into the forecourt to see if it gave access to the back of the house.

It was then that he saw Ruth Gardnor. Long-legged in blue slacks and a white blouse, she walked out of an alley that lay between a high, ragged wooden fence and the side of the house, in the breathless gold afternoon, and, like a fashion model, without looking one way or the other, made straight towards the palm-tree. Freddy was near Suzi's car. He did not think of concealing himself until he had seen her take from the tufted bark of the tree a brown envelope and slip it into the pocket of her slacks. Then he crouched, while she returned across the forecourt, pacing steadily as she always did. Gardnor's wife. Her hand left her pocket and swung empty with her moving arm as she walked. She did not trouble to look round her, and Freddy was again struck by the impression that this was a performance of pre-arrangement and habit, in the same way that he had felt the absence of anyone about the house to welcome them when Suzi's car had drawn up outside.

He got back into the room, sat down and waited; meanwhile he thought over the amazing notion that had entered his mind. This is Nasser's Post Office, he thought, and Gardnor is the man we're looking for. Gardnor is our man. The more he thought of it the less amazing it appeared; in fact, everything pointed to Gardnor. Intelligence was not Freddy's present job, but he was informed enough about what was going on in the office in Israel to know of the recent intelligence leaks, and, although no theory had been formed as yet, questions had been more or less asking themselves, and had not been answered. And where was Nasser's Post

Office? This is it, Freddy thought. And Gardnor is our man. Yes, thought Freddy, but one doesn't reach conclusions this way. Let's start again; start from nothing: I know nothing but what I've seen. I shall simply have to see more, and get some definite idea what's going on. If this is Nasser's Post Office then our people in the field ought to have got it first shot, they really ought.

He had been half-conscious of the well in the forecourt as if it was nudging him. Soon he was fully conscious of his great thirst. His thirst asserted itself. The door through which Suzi had disappeared was now opened as quietly as if it had never been locked. Suzi looked in: 'Oh there you are! Where have you been hiding? Barbara is in bed now and going to sleep. She has had mint tea. Come to my sitting-room and my wash-place. Do you like mint tea?' Freddy followed her into a long passage with skylight windows. There were doors on each side of the passage. He started to say that he hadn't been hiding, but Suzi continued: 'We better discuss the plans for the future two weeks, because I am absolutely at sea what to do for the best, except I know that in the case of very bad fortune for Barbara the British Embassy in Amman must help her, but thus she gets no more pilgrimage in Jordan; or else my friends, one or two, can help, but thus she has to give great lots of money. So it is best that we have good fortune . . .' She opened a door into a sitting-room furnished in Western cretonne comfort, and ended her speech '. . . like I have pledged to Alexandros. So we plan for good fortune.'

Freddy put down his bag and smiled at her. 'Show me this wash-place of yours, there's a good girl.' She had looked at him when they got into the room, with her very deep-blue eyes set in her brown face, looking extraordinarily like Abdul. When he came back she was pouring out tea, and he kissed her. He thought, this is quite absurd; he had intended to lead the conversation somewhere in the direction of Ruth Gardnor, and her presence in the house. Suzi said, 'You have a lovely kiss as well as smile.' He thought, then, that his kissing her was not incompatible with investigation into Ruth Gardnor and what went on in this house; on the contrary. And he thought, I might even have planned it but I didn't, it's quite absurd. He kissed her again.

Later on that evening she said to Barbara, 'Freddy likes me, and I think it is because he likes Abdul. Never mind why, it's fine.'

It occurred to Freddy that he was a different sort of man from most men in all important respects. He did not mean morally, but essentially. He was astonished that he had never realised this before, and wondered if other men felt the same. He was increasingly at ease with Suzi without being aware that this was mainly due to relief at finding her part of the house well appointed, in Western style. The day had been a strain. He drank his tea, took more, kissed Suzi again, and, as she nuzzled up to him, he told himself that of course he would not think of using her as a mere means to some external purpose. He said, 'This is a large house. Very fine.'

'It's an old Crusader church in the foundation.'

'I thought it must be, from its shape. Who lives here besides your stepmother?' He suddenly did not want to let her know that he had seen Ruth Gardnor, now that things had become personal.

'Friends, contacts, clients of my father,' she said, 'also employees for his night-clubs, also at times, sub-agents for travel, insurance, et cetera, et cetera. Are you married to a wife?'

'No,' Freddy said.

'Have you been married?'

On imperceptible second thoughts Freddy said he hadn't.

'I thought at first, you must be the lover of Barbara. But when I see you together I know you are not lovers, I mean bed-lovers.'

'We're getting into deep waters,' Freddy said, reclining among the chintzes.

'I can swim,' she said.

'I dare say.' She was beside him on a large flowered and frilled divan which was presumably her bed, but he was only partly aware of the girl's outline since he was looking particularly at her blue eyes and their setting between her brow and cheek-bone. He said, 'Abdul's giving me lessons in Arabic, you know.'

She laughed, short, clear, with a touch of general mockery. She was very like Abdul. 'I can give you lessons in Arabic,' she said.

'I dare say.'

She said, 'Speak in Arabic what Abdul has taught you.'

He repeated, in slow formal syllables, one of the exercises from the Arabic grammar, 'The affairs of our nation became secure after the murder of the author of that harmful book.'

'Abdul is wasting your time. You do not need to speak these words except in Egypt and Syria. Here we have not murdered the authors of books, I don't think. We don't have authors of books much, though. Poets, a few. Sometimes the assistant in the store can be a poet. The Prophet Mohammed was not favourable of poetry. I think he was in the wrong for that, but I can't say anything against the Prophet out loud, naturally. The Arabs love poetry, and they ignore that the Prophet was against it. When I say this, that, this, that, against the Prophet and the religion, the people say it's the reason no one has married me. Also because I have lovers;

they don't know this exactly, but they know enough, and they say, "No one will marry Suzi Ramdez. Why buy a goat when you can get two pennies' worth of milk."'

'I shouldn't worry about *them*,' Freddy said. 'You should have your poetry and your boy-friends.'

'They are lovers, not boys.'

'I write poetry,' Freddy said.

'Make me a poem.'

'All right. When I go away I'll write a poem to say thank you.'

'Maybe you wait and see how much you want to say thanks to me. What is your job for the British Government besides poetry?'

'Oh, it's nothing much,' Freddy said.

'You handle all the intelligence and the top secrets of these treaties with the Arab countries? Do you get wind of all the intrigues between Syria, Lebanon, Egypt, Kuwait and so forth?'

Freddy marvelled at this direct interrogation. 'No, I'm not much more than a sort of filing-clerk, actually.'

'Filing-clerk is best job for getting the secrets. When we seek for spies in our government we look first for the filing-clerk. They know all.'

'Well, I don't know all. None of us knows all, in fact. We're a jolly incompetent bunch. Always getting caught on the hop. It's well known.'

'But what is not well known is the top secrets.'

He was not sure how naïve she was. She was remarkably like Abdul. He said, 'Where is Barbara's room?'

'In this wing of the house. Two doors to the left. Now I'm going to look at her. If she sleeps, that's good. By tomorrow there is no more infection, but she just stays in bed.'

'I'd be *most* interested to see over the house before I leave.'

'Oh, no. The other parts are not mine. It's forbidden to enter. Latifa, my father's first wife, is very old-fashioned.'

She left the room and must have been away about half an hour, for Freddy dozed off for a while, and she was still absent when he woke. He had at first intended to spend the night in Jordan, crossing through the Gate on Monday morning. But now, since he had seen Ruth Gardnor, he was determined to wait an extra day, if necessary to find what she was doing here and see if his suspicion about the place had grounds. He could put up at a hotel in Jericho, no doubt. He wondered if Suzi knew of Mrs Gardnor's presence in the house, and if Suzi herself intended to remain with Barbara in this house during her two weeks' incarceration.

Among all the factors that filled Freddy with an exaggerated sense of his irresponsibility, when he came to remember these forgotten days, was his treatment of Barbara. He was amazed, when it all came back to him. That he could have contrived the scheme at all, dressing her up like that, and so exposing her to far more suspicion, had she been caught, than if she had been going round undisguised – permitting her to travel with scarlet fever – allowing it to go probably unreported – then leaving her in the hands of total strangers in Jordan, with a promise, never fulfilled, to arrange for an announcement in the Israeli papers that she was still in Israel – and then, the subsequent upset, with Barbara's relations pressing for news, and the embassies and Arab authorities all at odds . . . When he tried to convey this to Barbara later on, she replied, genuinely surprised, 'Irresponsible? No, you were splendid, Freddy. You were never responsible for me; I'm responsible for myself. I knew what I was doing. I'm grown-up.'

In Suzi's sitting-room he had faith in his plan, he was beyond questioning the success of Barbara's pilgrimage.

One who can move mountains does not stop to doubt the success of Barbara's pilgrimage, and the scarlet fever was to him only a slight set-back which, by happy chance, had led him to Nasser's Post Office here. Suzi had not yet returned; he withdrew again into a half-doze and was once more on that afternoon's journey from Jerusalem, through the steep craggy wilderness of Judaea and the oppressive plains, to the heavy Dead Sea with its saline content bearing no breath of life.

He was still in his second doze when Suzi returned. She sat and watched him, amused and quiet, as later her brother Abdul would watch him, that day in the following week when he would call at Freddy's hotel in Israel to give him his Arabic lessons, smell the moth-balls of Freddy's winter suit, and wait, idly reading Freddy's letters, till Freddy should wake from his tired sleep.

Suzi watched him and decided to put him up overnight and take him back to Jerusalem the next morning. She had spoken to Barbara, who was now cool and lucid. Barbara was very happy about her scarlet fever since it would keep her out of the way of her English enemy, Ricky. Suzi had very quickly understood, when Barbara told her about the headmistress of the school who was pursuing her out of love and hatred, and who would like to stop Barbara's marriage to her lover, Harry. It seemed perfectly understandable to Suzi, and she had only interrupted Barbara's explanation to say, 'We have also these things of oppression among our Arab women,' and, 'I wouldn't have thought that the English have also these affairs where the woman pursues the woman to stop the business of lovers, and makes hell.'

'Oh, you'd be surprised,' Barbara had said. 'And what's more . . .' And when Barbara next explained that the headmistress was that very one who had tried to speak to her at the Holy Sepulchre, they had both laughed with very much hysteria; Suzi had fallen limp upon Barbara in her laughter, and Barbara had said, 'Don't. You'll catch my scarlet fever.'

'I've had it already. My stepmother just told me.'

Then they started all over again until the laughing was spent out and Barbara closed her eyes with a weak, final, convulsive gasp.

Presently Suzi had said, 'Freddy will put that piece in the newspaper of the Jews, and then I shall see that it is made known to this English mistress. If she goes round asking, "Where is my friend?" and, "Has Miss Vaughan been here?" – this will be easy to get done. Soon she gets the reply that you never came.'

'I'd rather be taken into custody by the Jordanian police,' Barbara said, 'than be caught by her.'

'This I can well understand. The police want always the body but not the soul.'

'Not in every country.'

'No. This is an Arab virtue. The Arabs don't intend to interfere with a person's soul except when women are jealous, or a father is furious, and then they're crazy of course.'

'The Western people do it all the time. They do it more and more.'

'There's an Englishwoman staying in this house. She'll be here for ten days or so; very kind. So when I must go tomorrow to Jerusalem, she'll take care of you. I have to come back here, Wednesday, and I can come again at the weekend.'

'You're taking a lot of trouble . . .'

'I do this anyway. I come here very frequent. Alexandros has asked me to take care of you. So I do a couple of extra journeys maybe back and forth, for Alexandros and for you, until you're well.'

'Who's the Englishwoman?'

'Very nice girl; very kind. She can be trusted; she won't ask questions if you do not ask questions of her.'

'What's she doing here?'

'You should not ask this question; then she won't say of you, "What does she do here?"'

'Where's Freddy?' said Barbara.

'In my sitting-room. Perhaps I keep him here for tonight and take him back tomorrow morning. Do you think he'll propose to sleep with me?'

'Six to one against,' Barbara said.

Freddy opened his eyes, and saw Suzi lolling on the divan, watching him. He said, 'Oh, hallo, what's going on?'

'Barbara is much better. Like Dr Russeifa prescribed, it is a mild attack.'

'You mean, as he diagnosed.'

'Yes.'

'What he prescribed was the treatment.'

'She'll be through with the treatment tomorrow. Afterwards, it's only stay in bed.'

'Was I asleep?' said Freddy.

'Yes, I was watching you.'

'What were you thinking?'

'I was thinking that life is love.'

'Very profound. And love is life.'

'Very true and very apt,' she said.

Their dinner was conducted in intimate style, a candlelight affair. Freddy found himself envying Alexandros, the usual guest of honour who, Suzi told him, stopped here frequently on his way to Madaba where he purchased coins and other antiquities from a coin-dealer there. The coin-dealer, she explained, employed a team of small boys over a large area round Jericho, where excavators were busy; and these boys were permitted by the diggers to pick up a few small oddments, such as coins, and even when they were not permitted to do so, the boys got a lot of findings. These were turned over to the central dealer at Madaba, an Orthodox priest, who often came by quite rare things that way. Alexandros was one of his best customers, Suzi said, and this made for many trips, many occasions to stop the night at Jericho, where she herself was obliged to come also to the house on business.

Freddy envied rich-voiced Alexandros in this room. He reflected that life was love, and that he had been living all his life in a half-dream, as if he had been a somnambulist or an amnesiac. One had rehearsed the motions, not minding what they were all about. Clough, dead and famously lamented a hundred years ago, had located the virus:

> One has bowed and talked, till
> little by little,
> All the natural heat has escaped of the
> chivalrous spirit.

Only one small skip of flame, Freddy thought, and I see by its light all the other ashes cooling off in the fireplace.

'Don't be sad,' Suzi said. 'I wish Abdul was here. What are you miserable for, Freddy? You sit and look down through the meat on your plate, right through the plate, and through the tablecloth . . .'

It was lamb on a skewer. The tablecloth had a lace edge. 'I'm not miserable, my dear,' Freddy said, with a smile.

'Nor happy neither.'

Neither hot nor cold. 'Make me happy, then,' he said. 'You're the hostess.'

She plunged into the job. 'You have a lovely smile. Abdul should be here. I'm sad for Abdul that he's nothing and I have all the position with my father. He could be here, we could have got papers for him, but he won't be the son of his father and be in his influence. When we were children Abdul used to discover finds in the ruins when the archaeologists came to dig at Jericho and Jerash and Madaba. My father was not rich, only a teacher, at that time when we were little. But Abdul didn't give his little things of the ruins to his father to sell to the dealer and help for his education. Some, Abdul gave to me, and others he gave away to the most wealthy of the foreign tourists who came to the place. They said, "What a sweet little boy!" and Abdul would laugh so much at that. Because he would take no money for his presents. Sometimes I see them try to give it back and I hear them say to him, "Sorry – no baksheesh," and he would run away leaving them with the ancient coins, ornaments, whatever, in their hands. He plays tricks today, the same. My older sister, who is helping now in our travel bureau, says Abdul has a mad devil inside him. But my father's first wife, Latifa, who lives in this house, always took Abdul's part. She said he was a good child to give presents to the rich visitors as that's what our Arab tent-men did in the old days. She said a speech to Abdul's defence: Everyone gives to the poor; they try to save their souls by it. But if a poor man gives to the rich, his soul is already with God, and the souls of the rich are mysteriously moved and relieved of a burden.'

Freddy gave himself up to the pleasure of talking about Abdul, as far as he could. He felt it was just bad luck that he could not derive the total experience of Suzi that was available to him, so like she was to Abdul and so vivid. He thought it was just bad luck that this one excitement should be surrounded and vitiated by another: the question of Gardnor's wife. And although he told himself, there at Suzi's table, that his duty in life came first, pleasure second, and that he would not wish it any other way, and that he would keep his wits about him, in reality there was not much to choose between the excitement of possibly exposing Gardnor and the excitement of Suzi's potentialities; and as the evening proceeded these combined possibilities were highly erotic in their effect. Gardnor, he thought, is our wanted man. Gardnor, in his glittering confidence, a dispenser of sympathy and understanding to absolutely everyone; Gardnor, living it high with an attitude to debt that belongs to the eighteenth century; Gardnor in that very smart and expensive workman's cottage in Chelsea, with a Bonnard lit up over the mantelpiece and a Picasso in the lavatory; Gardnor and his wife and other superior women; Gardnor, Freddy thought, is our man. Gardnor, Freddy reflected, has too frequently made a point of his atheism; if a man can't hold religious convictions, well he can't, but it's a private and secret thing, and if a man can't keep his own top secrets how can he be expected to keep his country's? The unmarried fellows, Gardnor had said, half-jokingly in Freddy's presence, are our big security risk. And he had given Freddy an emancipated smile, then glanced at his wife before glancing at the clock; the Gardnors, in London, always had to go on somewhere else. Gardnor, Freddy thought, is the man we've been looking for; and this is Nasser's Post Office. The pieces fitted together as he watched Suzi's blue eyes and brown hands; and the disquietude that came over him at Gardnor's subsequent trial, the pity for Gardnor which he expressed when sentence had been passed and it was all over, were perfectly sincere since he could not help recalling with shame the sensual joy that had gone into the discovery. He told Suzi she was the most extraordinary woman he had ever met, and told himself it was just his hard luck that he could not be wholeheartedly her man, but needs must probe for Ruth Gardnor. He said, 'Who else is in this house at the moment besides Latifa and ourselves?'

'Perhaps a tourist or a paying guest. Nobody permanent but Latifa and the servants. A few girls perhaps; my father brings them to train for the night-club, they come from Aden, Tangiers, sometimes Europe. This is a big secret I'm telling you, about these girls. Can you keep a secret?'

'Of course.'

'Can you keep secrets if it would help your country to know them?'

'Those sort of secrets never come my way,' Freddy said. It was just hard luck finding himself on duty like this. He added, 'But I would always keep a beautiful woman's secrets.'

She said, 'I wouldn't trust you if I had any secrets.'

He said, 'Abdul trusts me. I know about his trips across the border. You see, Abdul trusts me more than you do.'

She said, 'What a stupid boy he is to trust you, and you've done nothing for him, not even have you given him your life insurance. You know, Freddy, I like your lovely smile. When Abdul was in hospital in the Lebanon, I visited that place to see him and I met with a French officer . . .'

Suzi's clock struck midnight. So ended Sunday the 13th of August. She showed him to a small room largely filled with a broad divan bed and hung with fine rugs; Freddy sensed the hand and style of Alexandros. Suzi, in her speech-making way, made the following announcement: 'I have to go and attend to duties and many other dutiful affairs, including Barbara and her great safety in this house. Then, one hour's time or more, I wait a message from Alexandros as we don't talk this business by telephone which is unsafe from the government eavesdroppers and press officers. So we do all business by night messengers, and all this business takes maybe two hours. Now you sleep. Maybe I wake you up later on to say goodnight.'

She left abruptly with a business-like something on her mind. Freddy was suddenly and blindly enraged. Wild-bloodedly he was convinced he had been deliberately tricked by her; and that she had known far more about him than he had himself; and that she had realised, where he had not, the lack of hope and fun in his life up to this evening, and had held out hope and snatched it away. Freddy cursed her in his mind for the miserable unspeakable Arab girl that she was. Then he sat on his bed for about ten minutes, and started to reflect that she probably couldn't help going about her business, and that she probably could not guess how fugitive his sexual feelings were and how hopeless, to him, was a lingering lapse of two hours between the idea and the execution. He thought, I'll be damned if I'll sleep with her now. And this way of putting it consoled him. He decided to find out, if he could, what Suzi was up to, and out of his mind faded the cloudy drama that must have begun to form earlier in the evening: the notion that he would gain her confidence, through making love to her, on the question of Ruth Gardnor's presence in the house.

He opened his door into stillness. Very soon he heard some movements from a far wing of the building; whether these sounds were voices he could not tell. He decided to go out for a walk in the night air, and well-mannered emotions returned to his heart.

He went out for a normal walk in the night air. Three weeks later, when his lost memory crushed back upon him, the most elusive part of all was that night and the two days that followed.

'Take it easy, Freddy.'

'Gardnor's wife was in that house.'

'Yes, we've got all that, Freddy. We've got Gardnor, too.'

'You've got Gardnor?' Freddy said to his questioner; but he had already been told this several times.

'Yes, thanks to you, Freddy, we've picked up the lot.'

'It was Nasser's Post Office,' Freddy said. 'I knew it the moment I saw . . . You're sure of the place? I could draw a sketch.'

'Yes, we got it this morning, half an hour after you told me. Take it easy, Freddy. You ought to be in bed, you know.'

'I knew there was going to be bloodshed,' Freddy said. 'I've had a feeling of bloodshed ever since I lost my memory. But I thought it would be here, out here in Palestine. I didn't think it was going to happen in Harrogate.'

'Freddy, you *must* rest.'

'If I'd posted the letters I wrote,' Freddy said, quite lucidly, 'this wouldn't have happened. But I didn't post the letters. I put them down the lavatory.'

'There's absolutely nothing you can do about it, Freddy. Believe me, absolutely nothing you could have done.'

'I'll have to get back to England and see about Benny. If she's tried for murder –'

'She going to be found unfit to plead. They'll put her away somewhere safe. Now, Freddy, the point is that you've got to take it easy. Don't try to think about everything, and when anything occurs to you, jot it down. The whole business will come back to you eventually. No hurry. We want you to get a rest.'

'You've got Gardnor?'

'Yes, we've got Gardnor. They're getting a statement.'

'One thing you can do,' Freddy said. 'You can get me a booking on a plane tomorrow –'

'Not tomorrow, Freddy. Honestly, doctor's orders. In a few days . . . Joanna and Matt can take care of you, and anything you want, we're here, you know.'

'Poor Gardnor,' Freddy said. 'I'm sorry for Gardnor, you know.'

'Well, we all feel that, Freddy. But he hadn't any pity for you, remember.'

'He tried to pin it on me,' Freddy said.

'Oh yes, but we had our own ideas about that. You know what we knew.'

'I wish I could remember exactly what happened after I went out for a walk after dinner that night.'

'It'll come back, Freddy. You've done enough talking for today. Very useful talking, believe me.'

Freddy looked at the two telegrams on the table and at the three memorandum papers which placed the long-distance calls on record. Had they been lying there since early morning? 'I knew there would be bloodshed,' he said, 'but I thought it would be here in this dangerous place, not Harrogate.' The telegrams, and the records of long-distance calls between Jerusalem and Harrogate had, he was sure, been on the table since early morning. Joanna had not moved them. The doctor had left. Freddy had refused to go to bed. He sat with the others to eat lunch on the veranda, while the chap from Whitehall kept jumping up to answer the telephone.

The doctor had said he would return later. 'I don't need him,' Freddy said.

'Eat something, Freddy,' Joanna was crying very desperately, unable to stop. She wasn't wearing her red dress today.

'Freddy, eat something. Oh, there's the telephone . . .'
The chap from the office went to answer it.

'Didn't I say there would be bloodshed?' Freddy said.

'Yes, Freddy, you have been saying so. Don't talk of it any more.'

Freddy said, 'I once heard a story of a man who went on a holiday and forgot that he'd left his dog chained up. When he'd been away a fortnight he remembered the dog and was afraid to go back in case of what he'd find. If I hadn't destroyed those letters –'

'Here's Matt,' said Joanna. 'Matt, come and sit by Freddy and don't let him talk too much.'

'What did that damned doctor give me?'

'A sedative – nothing – something like aspirin.'

'Did my mother linger? She must have lain a long time before –'

'No, it was instantaneous, Freddy.'

'How do you know? That's what they always say.'

'It's absolutely plain,' Matt said in a firm voice, 'that death was instantaneous.'

Freddy's colleague returned.

'I didn't think it would be Harrogate.'

'Everyone from the office sends no end of good wishes and we all want you to rest, Freddy.'

'You've got Gardnor?'

'Yes, we've got Gardnor.'

Miss Rickward, when it thankfully dawned on her that the travel agency in Jerusalem to which she had been recommended would be open on Sunday like other Arab places of business, had walked into the Ramdez place and found the proprietor, Joe Ramdez, alone and in charge.

Joe Ramdez was at that moment totalling up last

quarter's sum of insults and injuries received from his enemies, and it so happened that the balance outweighed the
injuries and other deeds of justice inflicted. This sometimes
occurred within one quarter's accounting, but never before
to so large an extent that the balance could not foreseeably
right itself in Joe's favour within a short time. But at this
moment of a Sunday in the summer of 1961, Joe sat with his
elbows resting on his desk and his head on his hands,
attempting to assemble into a process of thought the cracking explosions of anger that were going off in his
brain-particles; this was difficult, because the only thought
that could possibly emerge from his calculations was that he
was losing ground on all sides; business, government, home,
he was losing. It was then that a tourist, whom he did not
immediately consider to be a woman of moral force, great
courage, beautiful strength, substantial means and stout
sympathy, entered the door; he was to perceive Miss
Rickward in this light within a short time. Meanwhile he
looked up and saw only a tourist, and did not know what to
do with his exasperation since the tourist trade was a mere
apparatus for his affairs, and being a genius within the limits
of his environment, Joe Ramdez held the superficial in con-
tempt. He inwardly placed on his wife and Suzi the
respective curses of husband and father for not being on
duty, and the curses of a brother-Arab on his three worst
enemies, Sadok Abboud, Abdullah el Sabah and Ismah-
Azhari, for putting him into a mood of anger and grief; then
he turned his attention to boring Miss Rickward.

She made herself interesting before long. A Miss Vaughan,
she said. She had come to look for a Miss Vaughan. The convent was closed to visitors on account of an epidemic, and the
address she had been directed to was not really suitable; it
did not look clean. 'I must find somewhere to stay,' Miss

Rickward informed Joe Ramdez, 'and I must find Barbara Vaughan.'

That morning when Joe had received from his government contact that information was required concerning a British Jewess, under the name of Barbara Vaughan, who had arrived in Jordan from Israel last Friday, he had questioned his family as to whether they knew of her. His wife had no recollection of the name. Suzi, in a hurry to leave on some profitable trip with a British Embassy man, a friend of Alexandros, treated the question with impatience. 'How should she come to our agency if she's an Israeli spy?' Joe Ramdez was intimidated by his daughter's vigorous reactions to most of his suggestions, and had inquired only in a casual manner if she had come across a Miss Vaughan. He had found no record of her name when he looked for it on his arrival at the office; this, of course, meant very little, since the putting down of anything in black and white, except when absolutely necessary, was discouraged by Joe.

Before leaving the house he had called his wife a dumb animal, whereupon she had lit a cigarette and blown smoke contemptuously across the tea-cups. He had come to a point where he longed for a new wife and regretted having committed himself so far to modern progress. He repeated to himself, while opening up the office:

Let him who believes in God and in the supreme Day harm his neighbour; let him treat women well. She was made from Adam's rib; and it is the upper part of the rib that is the most curved. If you try to straighten it you will break it, and if you let it alone, it will stay bent. Let man therefore treat women well.

Joe's father had been adept in applying these words to every situation that concerned a woman, and Joe was now thinking of them with a stress on the curved rib: his second wife was a bent creature in her heart, and would never be straight. He was in a mood to place his curse upon the emancipation from the old tradition and, in general, the course he had permitted his family life to take with the result that now he had only old enemies and no old comforts.

Then had walked in that sturdy portion of English rib, Miss Rickward, presenting him with her exceedingly interesting inquiry for the whereabouts of Miss Vaughan.

'Be seated, Madam,' said Joe, 'and I shall send for coffee.' Immediately a rustle in the back quarters preceded a young boy who passed through the front office and out of the door as silent as a beam of light. By the time he returned, Joe had gone a long way to measuring Miss Rickward's substance, and with the experience he had long acquired of the Englishwoman on her travels, calculated that her cheap, shapeless, pink-and-red cotton dress, broad brown sandals, large old dark-brown leather shoulder bag, unvarnished fingernails, short dark curly hair, weather-pink face, a touch of lipstick, eyes the colour, near-grey, of Western spiritual compromise, and her yellowish, much-filled teeth, added up to a woman of some authority and wealth.

Sipping the thick coffee, she let fall the words 'Oh, how distressed I am!' and also a tear. Joe Ramdez was moved, he was delighted to find that she was as vulnerable about her friend as any high-class Arab woman would be about her most important friend or enemy in the harem. Joe was delighted to find Miss Rickward was vulnerable at all. Moreover, she did not look like a ferret, as so many Englishwomen did. She said, 'I mustn't trouble you with my personal difficulties. But I would so much appreciate any help you can give me in tracing this lady.'

'You have my help,' Joe said. 'We'll get her.'

Ricky said, 'She can't be far off. Possibly she has gone to the Dead Sea, and if so, I must follow her there. She has got herself entangled with a man who is one of the Dead Sea Scrolls team, and she threatens to marry him. Only Miss Vaughan doesn't know, as I know, the type of person he is, the type of background and so on. I've found out a lot about his personal history –'

'Those scholars at the Dead Sea are a gang of ruffians,' Joe said, thinking of the one he had fallen foul of over a deal, the first year that the scrolls were discovered and the forgeries began.

'You're extremely sympathetic,' Miss Rickward said. Her voice was still shaky with distress. 'You Arabs are gifted with sympathy and a sense of brotherhood. I've read quite a lot about Islam.'

Joe said, 'I work for the renewal of the people's hopes and the completion of their happiness.'

'I admire Islam,' she said. 'Barbara Vaughan is a Catholic. Catholicism, I'm sorry, I can't admire.'

Joe Ramdez laid his large hand on hers and inquired closely about Barbara Vaughan.

After she had taken Freddy to his room and left him there Suzi went on a tour of the house. She was sorry to have to leave Freddy to cool off just when he had warmed up, but there were certain duties to be performed before she could settle down for the night with the easy mind she needed for that purpose.

First, she went to Barbara's room and opened the door to hear if the patient was sleeping. Barbara stirred, 'Suzi?'

'All right? Don't wake up if you're all right.'

Barbara put on the bed-light and leaned up on her elbow. 'What's the time?' Her face was still flushed.

'Do you want water?'

'Yes, a good idea.' Barbara poured a glass of water from the jug at her side.

Suzi came in and closed the door.

'How do you feel?'

Barbara was taking her own temperature. Eventually she said, 'A hundred. That's not bad.'

'A mild attack,' Suzi said, sitting on the edge of her bed. 'Speak quiet. I wish you could have been well enough to sleep with Freddy.'

'I don't want to sleep with Freddy.'

'Don't you think Freddy's attractive?'

'Yes, more than he was when I met him in Israel. There's a curious change come over Freddy.'

'You wouldn't sleep with him?'

'No, I've got the other man.'

'I'm the secret lover of Alexandros, but the more I sleep with Alexandros the more I can sleep with another man. I love Alexandros so much. He gives me the idea of love.'

'Have you ever defrosted an old refrigerator?' Barbara said.

'Yes, we have old refrigerators.'

'Well, you know how it goes drip, drip, drip, very slowly. I'm like that; only just beginning to defrost, drip, drip, drip.'

'Have you ever opened someone else's combination safe?'

'No.'

'Me neither, but I know how it's done. Sleeping with Freddy would be like that. One must find the right combination and one has to play around, try this way, try that way, gentle, and listen with the careful ear.'

Barbara smiled. She took a small mirror from her handbag and looked at herself in it. 'I'm the scarlet woman,' she said. She giggled feebly and settled down to sleep.

'It's God's blame. Ring the little bell by your side if you feel ill at all, but don't go out of your room, as the servants are inquisitive about you.'

Suzi next visited the girls' quarters in the north-east wing of the house; this was joined by a corridor to the south-west wing which Latifa occupied so that it should be easy for her to supervise the girls.

The girls had been brought in to train for night-club life and its lenient ramifications; they were one of Joe Ramdez's business enterprises; they came from Morocco, Marseilles, Lebanon, Syria, and other surrounding countries, although once a girl was brought in who had somehow originated in Vladivostok and two others who had been from Liverpool. There were usually four or five girls in the house at any one time. Joe Ramdez found them useful for his special tourists. Foreign civil servants and diplomats who had become more than usually involved with one of Joe's pretty prostitutes instead of taking a more sensible interest in his stable of Arab horses at Amman were usually persuaded, after a while, to join his Middle East Visitors' Union Life Trust, from which, one way or another, Joe had derived a good annual income for many years.

No sounds came from the girls' wing except heavy breathing from behind the doors; Suzi despised females who breathed noisily in sleep, she felt it was indelicate and a sign of carelessness, for women should blow their noses and sleep in seemly tranquillity. In general Suzi loathed the girls, not troubling to separate them fairly from the deeper object of her antipathy, the whole business operation in which they were involved. She had tried to persuade her father to give them up for a more profitable and more taste-ful, possibly more subtle, form of corruption. There were many ways of tempting foreigners into a vulnerable situation, besides these insufferable girls. Joe had replied that he was well aware of the alternatives to girls; one of them was boys, and as far as he was concerned he was not going to encourage the vile foreigner in his despicable habit of coming to the Arab countries for boys. It was his duty to the honour of his country to provide girls. Suzi said, very often, that the girls were not even good performers in the night-clubs. But Joe barked back at her, louder than his bite, that they were too good for the foreigners. Suzi had realised she was up against the amorphous mixture of honour and revenge that brewed within her father's heart, and continued to exhale vapours of resentment towards the girls from her own obscure heart's brew. Her aim at the moment was to prevent the girls from contact with Freddy and to preserve him from any hint of contact with them. She went to find her stepmother, Latifa.

She found her playing gin rummy with Ruth Gardnor, who lit up at the sight of Suzi. She was evidently bored, for Latifa was slow. Latifa said, 'Yusif is coming.' Her eyes remained on the cards. Latifa always called Joe by his Arab name, Yusif. Suzi was uncertain whether Latifa was making one of her mysterious prophecies or whether she had received definite word from her father that he was coming to the house.

She said, 'When? How soon?'

Latifa did not reply. Suzi concluded that Latifa was indulging her gift for second sight. At some time in her middle age this first wife of Joe Ramdez had been struck by an illness which left her with a facial twitch, a diminished pace of thought, and some extra intuition. Latifa's prophecies were not infallible, but they often came alarmingly true.

Suzi did not want her father in the house at this moment; not by any means.

She said to Ruth, 'Listen, I don't want my father to have anything to do with the sick girl.'

'That's all right. Leave it to me,' Ruth said, warmly. Suzi was very attached to Ruth Gardnor. She had found her to have a good heart, and to be particularly understanding and helpful in her affair with Alexandros. She admired Ruth's elegant figure, and felt she brought tone to the house.

Ruth said, 'I doubt if your father will be coming here if you're not expecting him. Latifa said earlier that she felt he was on his way to the house; he hasn't come yet.'

Latifa waited for the game to proceed. She never intruded on Suzi's affairs, but did merely what was required by her husband, and obliged Suzi if paid to do it.

Suzi said, 'Ruth, there is my other guest. I think you shouldn't let him see you, as you are maybe known to him.'

'Who? Alexandros?'

'No, it is not Alexandros. It's an Englishman.'

'Oh!'

'Just keep yourself concealed. He'll be leaving tomorrow.'

Ruth looked very worried. She said, 'Well, I'm going to bed. Goodnight, Latifa. Goodnight.'

Latifa, a large woman, sat in her fine draperies staring at the cards. Suzi kissed her, and followed Ruth to her room.

'What's his name?' Ruth said. 'Anyone I know?'

'Mr Hamilton of the British Government office in Israel.'

'Freddy Hamilton!'

'Yes. You know him?'

'My God! Why did you bring him here?'

'It's all right,' said Suzi. 'It's all right, my dear.' She was sure it was all right. She said, 'He's not here on any business.'

'I'll have to leave right away.' Ruth walked round the room, looking carefully. 'Has he seen me? Does he know where my room is?'

'No, no, of course not. Anyway, I tell you, Ruth, he has no brains for this job. He's not much in your government.'

'They don't need too much. They only need to be in the office.' She went to the wardrobe and looked inside. She said, 'Has he had any opportunity to snoop?'

Suzi laughed, and Ruth tried to laugh with her. Presently it emerged that Suzi thought 'snoop' was a sex term and that Ruth had been referring to the possibility of Freddy's meeting the girls. Ruth continued to laugh harshly at this mistake, and explained in a strange tone of voice that she had meant 'pry'. She displayed a special anxiety to be patient and calm with Suzi, and was obviously concealing a deeper anxiety about her business. This made Suzi feel like a stupid little Arab girl in the other's estimation, and she wanted to explain her personal view, unorthodox as it was to the Arab spy-trade, that the best way to avoid suspicion was to go about everything as naturally as possible. She had already tried to convince Ruth Gardnor that her business, whatever it was, could best be conducted by hand, by word-of-mouth, and by bribery. 'Let a man come to the door,' Suzi had said. 'Let him repeat his message, or let him hand a letter. Let him take his money and go.' But no, Ruth had devised, among other methods, one by which she collected code-messages from the bark of the palm-tree and deposited messages in the same place. Ruth had argued that the messenger, if he could be bribed to contact her, could be further bribed to describe her appearance. By no means, Ruth said, must she be seen; and anyway, those were her instructions. She would not be brought to understand that Suzi's father had influence with the Arab contacts; it was unthinkable that they could be bribed against Joe's honour and survive. But Ruth showed no confidence in the unspoken laws that had so far kept the Ramdez house inviolable. Suzi had wondered for a moment if her father's enemies were perhaps more powerful than she believed, but she put the tepid thought aside and insisted that Ruth was crazy in making all those intricate arrangements, and in bringing a radio transmitter into the house, when the Arab rumour-system was so much safer.

'I've hardly used it,' Ruth said. She was lifting the transmitter out of her wardrobe. 'Where can I hide this?' She got out a suitcase and started to put things away in it.

Ruth had panicked. Suzi was amazed; she had never seen the kindly woman in this mood before. Presently, Ruth seemed to become aware of Suzi's bewilderment. She said, 'Suzi, if you knew how serious it would be for me if Hamilton got on to anything . . .'

'You take a cigarette and sit down,' Suzi said. 'There's no need for him to see you if you keep in this end of the house. Why should he suspect? A matter of fact, the last place he would suspect espionage would be this place, since I have brought him here. This throws them off-scent. Now I tell you that Alexandros is a friend of Freddy, and I do all this for Alexandros. Freddy is not looking for spies, he's looking for fun, this trip.'

Ruth said, 'You don't know that type of Englishman as I do.' She went to the door, opened it, peered out and closed it again. Then she sat down and lit a cigarette. She looked at her watch. She said, 'The messenger should be here between half past one and two. It's one now. I wonder if my note's safe till he comes.'

'In the tree?'

'Yes, I'd better go and have a look.'

'That is crazy. You lose your nerve.'

'I'm going to have a look. I wish we'd never got mixed up in this business. But once you're in it, you're in it. I must send word to my husband that Hamilton's here. I'm going to –'

'Freddy might see you. Don't go out.'

'He can't see in the dark. At least, he can't do that.'

'Better you remain indoors,' Suzi said, 'as he might bump into you at the door or something. I'll go and look. How far up the tree is it?'

'About five feet.' Ruth stopped packing. She said, 'I can't leave the house. I've got to wait and meet a contact this week or next at the latest. It's very important. What shall I do? That message in the tree – go and see if it's all right. It's not important in itself, but I can't be too careful. Come back at once and tell me if it's still there.'

Suzi started to go. 'In fact, bring it back to me – Suzi dear – do you mind?'

Suzi left, but Ruth was at the door, whispering her back.

'No – leave it. Don't bring it. The man will get it between one-thirty and two. Just make sure it's still . . . Come back and –'

Suzi was on her way. Outside she walked softly round the house. The light was still on in Freddy's room. She crossed to the tree and began feeling up the bark. Five feet . . . no. Up the bark, and all round it, tuft after tuft, feeling sure she was missing the one small pocket where the folded paper would be. Up the tree and round it again, as far as she could reach. It must be higher, too high for her. Ruth was taller than she was, and probably . . . No, she couldn't reach, couldn't find the thing. The man had probably been to fetch it.

She returned to Ruth, earnest about keeping her friendship. 'It's there,' she said. 'Don't worry.'

Ruth produced a new anxiety. 'What has this sick girl to do with Freddy Hamilton?'

'Oh, nothing. She stayed in the same hotel as him in Israel, and she's on a pilgrimage. I brought them together in the car. Just tourists. You don't ask questions about this woman, Ruth, and we don't ask questions from you, like I told you.'

'Yes, I know. I understand.' Ruth looked strained and shaken. 'I'll keep my side of the bargain.'

'You have a drink. You go to bed.' Suzi wanted to see Freddy again before he went to sleep. She felt jittery, too, and said, 'I'll go to keep Freddy company. You don't think of him any more. He won't go near your tree or nothing.'

Ruth relaxed a little, and said, 'Goodness, are you having an affair with Freddy Hamilton?'

'Of course,' said Suzi.

'Well, I only wish you'd gone somewhere else to have it.'

'It's my father's house,' Suzi said. But she added, like a saleswoman, 'And it's the most discreet house in the kingdom of Jordan.'

'Goodnight,' Ruth said. 'And keep your eye on Hamilton, for my sake.'

Suzi started to make her way back along the dark corridor to her own part of the house, but turning towards the door that enclosed it, she decided instead to take another puzzled look at the tree.

This time she found the note easily. It was tucked firmly into a tuft of bark well within her reach. She wondered if Freddy was in his room, and if she could be seen in the moonlight.

He was in his room. He was scribbling with his pocket pen on a piece of paper. He had in fact just finished decoding the message which he had copied from the note he had replaced in the tree-bark; the code had been fairly simple, but he was pleased with himself, brisk and expert at cracking a code as he had been on H.M.S. *Achilles* in the war, when he had cracked many a tough code-signal. He was making a final, brief note of the formula, now, committing it to memory with the message it revealed, before destroying the record according to the old routine.

Suzi had entered without knocking. She said, 'What are you writing?'

'A poem,' Freddy said.

'Let me see.' She reached for it and tried hard to snatch it from his hand. He caught her arm playfully, and her gold bracelet became unclasped and fell to the floor. Freddy got it first, and made game with it, holding it out to her, then snatching it away and holding it behind his back, in an effort to distract her attention from the piece of paper in his left hand.

Suzi sat on the bed. 'Let me see the poem and you can keep the bracelet,' she said, holding out her hand for it.

'I'll read you the poem,' he said. He sat down some distance away from her, near a table-lamp which he adjusted to gain the small moment for thought under a good reading light; the necessity of the occasion forced him to act neatly. 'The poem is for you,' he said, 'naturally.' He peered at the paper. He said, 'It's crumpled and —' Then smoothing the crumpled sheet, he read:

> Now is the time for secret pleasantries
> With a girl-friend lurking in her corner ambush,
> The time to steal a token from
> Her arm or unprotesting finger.

'Go on,' Suzi said. Freddy was aware that she had an impression of the quantity of writing on the page he held. He said, 'Well, that's the last verse, in fact. I haven't really worked over the others. I usually finish the last first. Do you like it?'

'I've read something like it before, I seem to think,' said Suzi. 'But not so good, and not quite like written for me. But I remember a poem I read like it.'

Freddy laughed with quite genuine amusement. 'You cunning little thing,' he said. 'Of course you know it's a translation from Horace. I have the Latin here, too. Listen –'

> *nunc et latentis proditor intimo*
> *gratus puella rasus ab angulo*
> *pignusque dereptum lacertis*
> *aut digito male pertinaci.*

She came towards him for the paper. 'Let me see.' But he raised it high, and getting out his lighter, made a flame, as he had done when burning the Harrogate letters in order to send them easier down the lavatory drain. He said, as she caught his right arm, 'I'm going to follow a custom that we practised at Cambridge University, my dear, when I was young at Cambridge. When we wrote a poem to a beautiful lady we read it to her and burned it.' He set the paper alight and Suzi drew her hand away from the quick flame. As it consumed the page, Freddy moved only enough to drop it on the tiled floor between the rugs where it lay in black, furled ash. 'We burned the poem,' said Freddy, treading the charred flimsy furl to powder, 'as a symbol of consummation of our love for the lady. Even a translation – I offer it to you – it's something better than I could compose myself.' She was looking at the black powder on the floor mingled with tiny remaining shreds of white, unconsumed paper which could reveal nothing of that message, insignificant in itself, but really very important for Freddy's purpose; a mere report of some pipe-lines on the side of the road in Israel, measuring 185 inches. Quite a size; they had probably been planted there. However, that wasn't his business, the point was that this house was undoubtedly, undoubtedly, that one place in the whole vast area of possibility through which far more serious stuff from the office had been leaking to Cairo and beyond. It was Nasser's Post Office and Gardnor was the man.

It was only within a few days that Freddy would be sitting in his hotel, forgetful of this moment, wearily listening to Rupert Gardnor's long, insufferable story about the Israeli pipe-line. 'Those fake pipe-lines, you see . . . I think they were something like 195 inches in diameter, at least –'

'The size of those fake water-pipes is 185 inches, not 195.'

'How do you know?' Yes, how did he know? Gardnor made much of the need for an Intelligence investigation of Freddy during the two weeks that followed this conversation, and as it came out later, used that time to cover up or destroy most of the evidence against himself. But not all. Ruth Gardnor got away to Cairo. Gardnor alone stood trial in the winter to come.

'Are you sure you've got Gardnor?' Freddy said on that day when his memory returned like a high tide, with an undercurrent ebb and flow of details.

'Yes, we've got Gardnor.'

'Got a statement?'

'He's giving it now. Another day or two, and he'd have got away to Cairo.'

'Did they find the house at Jericho all right?'

'Of course. You're not to worry, Freddy. Take a rest and give us any more details when you're O.K. Just as and when. We've got all we need. The Jordan authorities have cooperated.'

'Did you find anything at Jericho?'

'Oh, a transmitter, you know, and cameras, the usual stuff in the usual places – the cellar, the wardrobe. We haven't got his wife, she's hiding somewhere. The Jordan authorities are having a good search. They've been very helpful. Very efficient.'

'I wouldn't count on them getting her,' said Freddy. 'They didn't get Barbara Vaughan.'

'Well, we've got Gardnor. That's the –'

'That's the main thing,' said Freddy, looking at the unbelievable telegrams and memoranda of telephone calls between the office in Israel and Harrogate. He clung to what was believable in those first hours of remembrance. Gardnor was under arrest.

'So you see,' he said to Suzi when he had burned the paper to fragments, 'the love poem is yours for ever.' He genuinely felt it to be so at that moment, as she looked at his triumph in black ash on the floor, with a half-smile and a half-frown, as if puzzled, hesitating to take his word, and yet pleased with his gesture, and in any case, respecting his victory. Freddy thought she was adorable in her sudden loss of confidence after being so sure of herself all day, and he was delighted with his own accomplishment. He decided that the next urgent move was to get her to bed, then tomorrow he might compose for her some verses of his own, in chant royal perhaps, or *haiku*, why not?

He said, 'It's bed-time, isn't it?'

She sifted the powdered ruins of the paper with the toe of her shoe and looked at him with becoming admiration. 'You telling me,' she said. 'It's been a busy day, Freddy, more or less. Where is that bracelet that you laid plots with your poem to steal? Did you have busy days at Cambridge University?' They found the bracelet.

As it turned out, it was she, not Freddy, who was uneasy in love-making, for she had the distracting suspicion that his very confidence in bed with her might derive from some secret success in counter-espionage. She wanted very much to believe in the poem that had been deftly and symbolically burnt for her, but an accurate translation of her Arabic thoughts in reserve would have been that it was damned unlikely. So she missed half the fun of sleeping with Freddy in his access of goodwill and ardour, and enjoyed only the other half.

At about three o'clock, when they had just fallen asleep, Suzi woke quickly from a sound in the stillness beyond the house and started up, waking Freddy. The sound became more specific, a car approaching.

'Listen,' she said.

Freddy was less sensitive to the approach of motor-cars outside his accustomed places of sleep. He said, 'What is it?'

Then, from the direction of Jericho the first of the three-o'clock cries arose, followed by another high call from another mosque. Freddy said, 'It sounds very beautiful,' and moved closer to her.

She said, 'It's a car coming to the house.' It was now an unmistakable sound. The car pulled up outside, near the front of the house. Suzi was out of bed, listening at the window. The night air was flooded with the distant chanting from many mosques, and presently overflowed with a louder voice from the courtyard, then the sound of a woman's grateful tones, a shuffle and arrangement of footsteps outside and the banging of the car door. 'Latifa!' shouted the man's voice. 'Latifa!'

'My father,' Suzi said. 'He's brought someone and he's shouting to be let in.'

'Do you mean that I am to share this room with you?' said Miss Rickward.

'Of course,' said Joe Ramdez. 'Or it is better to say I share it with you, since you are my honoured guest and I have made you this room at your disposal. It is yours, I share with you.'

'But where will you sleep?'

'With you, in the bed, my fruitful vine.'

It seemed to her that she had always known that this was how it was done. Ricky felt rescued, she felt vindicated, and she longed more than ever to crush Barbara Vaughan.

When Barbara first came to the fact, beyond all reckoning, the amazing fact, that Ricky was having a romantic love-affair with Joe Ramdez, a serious relationship and no mere spinster's holiday fling, she began to work backwards from that point to see where she had begun to miscalculate Ricky. Even doctors, she thought, sometimes do not know why a person does not die. But there was no telling at what point, over the six years she had known Ricky, she had failed to discover a dormant capacity for going to bed with a latent Joe Ramdez. It then occurred to Barbara, and recurred more strongly after she had learned of Ricky's marriage and her sale of the school in England, her eager embrace of Islam, and the total handing over of her lot to Joe Ramdez, that there had been no secret state of mind in Ricky. What had been overlooked was perfectly obvious, and it was, after all, precisely a woman of virile ways and blunt intellect, and yet of unfathomable emotions, who would respond and ramify most sensuously towards a muscular ageing Arab of lordly disposition, should that one chance occur, as it had done. Joe Ramdez was in fact the only type of man that Ricky could understand, and Barbara reflected that, most probably, Ricky imagined all love-affairs started and proceeded as directly as hers did, and that all women who go to bed with a man go to bed with a type of Joe Ramdez.

It was the only way she could explain the fact that Ricky, even after her meeting with Joe Ramdez, pursued the purpose for which she had followed Barbara to the Holy Land, which was to prevent her marriage to Harry Clegg. She had brought with her, of all things, a copy of the records of Harry's birth and baptism, which in desperate zeal she had managed to dig up, where Harry and his lawyers in their methodical defeatism had failed. Ricky's wild intention in doing so had been to prove to Barbara that the man she wanted to marry was illegitimate, a fact that Barbara knew already. And it turned out that the document Ricky produced for Barbara's inspection made it perfectly easy for Harry's previous marriage to be annulled by the Church, and for her to marry him within its communion. This business of the birth record was the joke of their lives.

But what neither Barbara, Harry, nor the Church knew, and were mercifully never to know, was that Ricky, shortly after her meeting with Joe, destroyed the first paper she had brought so carefully with her, substituting a second one, misguidedly devised, though brilliantly forged. This was done at the instigation of Ramdez in his eagerness to avenge Ricky against Barbara Vaughan, her treacherous friend who had grieved her, and his own enemy, the Jewess who passed as it were through his fingers and escaped the country.

'We were told,' said Ricky at that future date when she discovered that something had gone wrong with the scheme, '. . . we were assured, that a certificate which proves Clegg to be a baptised Catholic would prevent him from ever getting an annulment of his previous marriage, since Catholics do not recognise divorce. I simply cannot understand it.'

She was then talking to a Catholic priest. He seemed aware of vexation in her tone, and looked at her, puzzled. 'Well, it's better this way, isn't it?' he said. 'What a good thing for the couple that you found this certificate.'

Ricky, terrified of having aroused suspicion, agreed that it was.

The priest said that it was a common mistake, of course, to assume that a Catholic could not obtain an annulment of a previous marriage, since in fact if the Catholic had been first married outside the Church, as in the case of Harry Clegg, the Church did not recognise the marriage. But where a non-Catholic applied for annulment in such a case, difficulties arose, since this was outside the province of the Church. It was all perfectly logical, really . . .

If only, Ricky thought, I had given them the paper I brought over, that first paper . . . Born to Amelia Clegg . . . Father unknown . . . Christened at Tate Street Methodist Chapel . . .

Ramdez laid yet another curse upon his son Abdul for providing the false information about Catholic divorces. Abdul had claimed, when he was in hospital in Beirut, to have gone over to the Catholic Church. Ramdez did not know whether to believe him, but he cursed him then, even although Abdul explained that he was still a Moslem as well. Abdul had done that, if he had done it at all, to offend and shame his father. And now, when appealed to for the information that surely he, having received the Catholic teaching, was in a position to know, Abdul had answered falsely to spite his father's new, fine, substantial wife, who had come freely to him with all her confidence, her trouble, and her riches. Joe Ramdez laid a father's curse on Abdul again and yet again.

Barbara, in her relief, kept saying to Harry, 'I was going to marry you anyway.'

He said, 'I know. I'm not forgetting it.' The Congregation of the Rota had turned down his application for an annulment only a week before the new evidence, Ricky's bright information, turned up to make everything easy. He said, 'My aunts never told me my mother was a Catholic. Anyway, they were not really my aunts. Perhaps my father was a Catholic, too. An Irish couple, I expect, whoever they were. I know more about the Etruscans than I do about my own parents, and in fact I've got no curiosity about them at all, whereas the Etruscans –'

'It's so funny, Ricky thinking this was going to mess us up.'

'Yes, I know, silly old bitch.'

She said, 'I would have married you, anyway. But it would have taken courage to continue being out of the Church. It's the keeping it up I was afraid of.'

'From the way those clerics spoke,' he said, 'I was sure it would be impossible. Well, now it's possible.'

'With God, everything is possible,' said Barbara.

From time to time for years afterwards, and far into her long widowhood, Ricky would inquire of Catholic priests, as a matter of theoretical interest, what was the position of a Catholic marriage based on evidence which both parties believed to be true, but which, in reality, was faked.

They would all look puzzled, at first, and ask Ricky if she had ever heard of such a case. 'No, no,' Ricky always said. 'Only I read of it in a novel.' The priests all said in effect, 'Well, if both parties remain in ignorance and the Church is satisfied, then it's a valid marriage.'

'According to the logic of the Catholics, that seems impossible.'

No, they mostly said, it was quite logical if one started from the right premise. Others said, well, logic or no logic, that was the case. One of them replied, 'With God, everything is possible.' Another went into the question of the validity of the blessing Jacob received in place of Esau, even under conscious falsity.

If Ricky had been anywhere close to Barbara during those years after Joe Ramdez's death in 1963, she might, sooner or later, have been unable to prevent herself confessing to the forgery, at whatever risk. But she was nowhere near Barbara. She had started a private school for the children of English and American residents and wealthy Jordanians. She was not tempted to commit herself in any letter to Barbara.

All this was yet to be. The first night in the house at Jericho, Barbara on her drowsy bed heard a man's voice in the darkness. She felt cooler, and touched her forehead to make sure she actually was cooler, and the fever had gone. She did not care about the man's voice but let fate blow over her and presently fell asleep.

Suzi had said to Freddy before she rushed from his room, 'You are my tourist. Tomorrow we go to Jerash and see the ruins. My father must see I take this trouble over you as you are a British Government man.' She had gone to her own room, where she opened the window and called out in a sleepy voice, inquiring what was the matter. She could not see her father from the window, but her voice was answered by her father's from the front of the house. She had gone to the door and let him in. Latifa was just coming out of her room, and Suzi could hear her slopping along from the wing she occupied.

Her father had brought a visitor, a woman whom Suzi recognised as the tourist who had approached her that morning when she was with Barbara in the Holy Sepulchre. As they entered, Suzi stood well in the light so that the woman, Barbara's pursuer, could see her; and so she satisfied herself, then and there, that Miss Rickward did not recognise her. Suzi thought, she is a real enemy; and was partly resentful at not being recognised from their short encounter.

Miss Rickward showed herself eager to please Joe Ramdez's daughter. Latifa was not introduced to her but stood by as part of the reception machinery. In Arabic, Suzi explained to her father that a new girl had been sent that day and had immediately gone down with scarlet fever. She had the girl in isolation in the western section of the house, and warned her father not to go near it. The girl was not gravely ill, but highly infectious.

'See that the authorities don't get to hear of it,' Joe said, 'and start pushing their noses into our affairs here. Why have these thieves and whoremongers sent me a girl with disease?'

'It's Allah's blame,' Suzi said.

'Quiet, blasphemous slut!'

He then returned to the English tongue and Miss Rickward, enchanted as she was with everything.

And before long she was in the large dark-tapestried room with Ramdez.

'I share with you.'

'But where will you sleep?'

'With you, in the bed, my fruitful vine, my pillar of cedar, golden minaret.'

She said, 'I have always had a leaning towards Islam.' She looked round for her suitcase. Ramdez had placed it in a corner behind a dark screen that must have been bright at one time. Ricky went behind the screen to undress. She said, 'If these lovely tapestries were cleaned, they would come up exquisitely.'

One way and another the spirit of the Crusaders in their everyday aspect brooded over the house that night. Ricky, when she had got into bed, sat up in it and recited, in her buxom, bough-laden poetry voice, the famous Islamic Throne Verse in the English Translation:

God – there is no god but He, the Living, and Self-subsistent:
Slumber seizeth him not, neither sleep. To Him belongeth

whatsoever is in the Heavens and whatsoever is in the Earth. Who is there that shall intercede with Him save by His Will. He knoweth what is present with men and what shall befall them, and nought of His knowledge do they comprehend save what He willeth. His Throne is wide as the Heavens and the Earth, and the keeping of them wearieth Him not. And He is the High, the Mighty one.

'My rose of Islam!' said Joe in admiration, heaving himself into bed beside her. 'Well of sweet waters!'

Ricky said, 'I am a virgin. Does it signify?'

'It is highly satisfactory,' Joe said, as he used to say, long ago, when he was a young schoolteacher, and was giving a lesson in Arabic to one of the British administrators in his spare time.

Freddy contemplated a meeting with Joe Ramdez without panic, not even that panic he had always felt in his previous encounters, at the Cartwrights', with Joe, when it had been merely a matter of mental association. Normally, of course, he was terrified of blatant liars like Joe and always felt a ruinous urge to conspire with them, as he did with his mother, to the effect that they were honest people. In his youth at Cambridge Freddy had known a liar whom he hated so much that he had given him a solid-gold hunter watch – not his good one, but a very good one.

This Monday morning, however, Freddy felt quite equal to Joe Ramdez, whose daughter was so sweet. He sat and had breakfast with Suzi while the rest of the house was still asleep from its busy night's doings. He said, 'I'm going to miss a day at the office. Oh, well –' The day's newspapers arrived and he sat screened by the local English-language one, while Suzi waited with wifely patience to talk to him seriously. 'Australia Urges Britain Not to Join Common Market,' Freddy read aloud. 'What utter nonsense,' he said. 'Australia should keep her nose out of it. We must have our markets abroad and trade with the foreigners. We always have done and we always will. What's the point of having foreigners on your doorstep if you're going to let them put you out of business?'

'Very wise and true,' Suzi said.

'We simply must decide to join the Common Market.'

'My father has brought the woman called Miss Rickward. They both hunt for Barbara. I want you to know,' Suzi said.

'We'd better get her out of here, then,' Freddy said.

'She should rest in bed.'

'I wonder if her ex-fiancé could help? He's working at Qumran.'

'What ex-fiancé?'

'She was engaged to an archaeologist there, but she broke it off. Went right off him. So she said.'

'Well, she must have gone on him again. She says he's in Rome just now. She's going to marry him, definite.'

'Really? She might have told *me*.'

'She had the scarlet fever too bad to tell you yesterday, Freddy. Were you hoping to be the next fiancé?'

'No,' Freddy said. 'I had no such aspirations.'

'Well, we can't move her anywhere. So it means we stick around till my father goes back to Jerusalem with his woman, in case he finds Barbara. I have told him she is somebody else with scarlet fever, so I think he will keep away from my section of this house.'

'What about the other Englishwoman who's here?'

'She will take care of Barbara when we leave her. But I prefer to wait for my father to leave first. No risks.'

'I ought to be back in Israel tonight,' Freddy said.

'No, you wait tonight,' she said.

He said, 'It's a tempting thought.'

She said, 'If you mean what I think you mean, it's not so easy with my father in the house. He is the only one that's permitted to sleep with anyone he likes.'

'Well, he wouldn't be sleeping with Miss Rickward, if she's the woman Barbara's trying to avoid. Miss Rickward is the head of an English girls' school, if you know what that means.'

'Miss Rickward is in the bed with my father this moment, if you know what that means,' Suzi said.

'How remarkable!' Freddy said, his coffee-cup so moving in his hand, without a pause from the saucer to his lips, that he did not seem to think it very remarkable.

He was listening to the bang of a car door outside, the engine starting up and the sound of its being driven away from the house.

He finished his coffee. He examined the tips of his right index finger and thumb and rubbed them together.

'That was our other English guest that I told you of,' Suzi said. 'She has gone to visit some friends in Amman, but she'll be back tomorrow to look after Barbara. She will be good to her all right, but to tell you the truth this lady is a little bit mad.'

'Oh, really? What lady is that?'

'Remember I told you we have a woman staying here for a rest?'

'Oh yes, of course. Who is she, anyway?'

Suzi said, 'I shouldn't tell you this. It is our secret, poor woman. I shouldn't tell you as it is a lady married to a government officer of the British. Her name is Mrs Gardnor. She –'

'Gardnor!' Freddy said. 'Why I know the Gardnors, of course. He's stationed with me in Israel. Awfully nice chap. I know Ruth too, of course. What's wrong with her?'

He thought Suzi looked relieved. He was sure she had been testing him to find his response; but now she looked relieved, and he hoped he had passed the test. But, he thought, this darling girl knows damn well – must know, ought to know, maybe, though, isn't quite sure – that the paper I burned last night was no damn poem at all. He stopped himself fidgeting with the tips of his fingers and thumb where they had been nipped by the little flame.

She said, 'Yes, you must,' and then his ears caught up with the words she had spoken a split second before: 'You must promise to tell no one what I am going to tell you.' And now she said, 'Yes, you must.'

'Of course,' Freddy said. 'What is it?'

'Why are you looking so much at me?'

'Because you're so charming to look at with your fawn skin and those blue eyes.'

'My skin is not fawn, it is green this morning from never sleeping all the night.'

'It isn't green, it's lovely.'

'No, it's like an ancient scroll is my skin.'

'Nonsense.'

'You don't say "it's lovely" and "nonsense" when you make love talk to a lady in Jericho. This is a place of the true Arabian civilisation and if I say I look like old hell, then it's your place to say a speech about me, that I resemble the winding River Jordan, when I turn from the shoulders to the hips, and that my voice is the bleating of a thousand flocks, and my skin is smooth and perfecter than the udder of the camel.'

'Oh, I can think of more suitable things to say than that. Much more romantic. I'll write another poem for you. In chant royal, which is a romantic verse form, or *haiku* might be more right for you, as it's Oriental.'

'You know *Omar?*'

'Why yes, of course. The translation, I mean. It's –'

'All the English are crazy for *Omar*. Abdul learned it at school, he could say it all in English, not Persian, which we don't speak. Then Abdul got sick with T.B. and was in hospital, and there he said to me, *Omar Khayyám* is all olive oil poured over the troubled waters. Too much oil, and you don't see the truth. So don't copy *Omar* for a poem for me, I would make you put it on fire and burn your fingers. You have a lovely smile.'

'I would say you were a pomegranate,' Freddy said, 'only you taste sharper and sweeter. Pomegranates look good but they taste insipid.' And all this conversation was soon to be gone from his memory for many months, suddenly returning on a day when the sun was a crimson disc between the bare branches of Kensington Gardens, and the skaters on the Round Pond were all splashed over the heads and arms with red light, as they beat their mittens together and skimmed the dark white ice under the sky. So it was to be throughout the years; it was always unexpectedly, like a thief in the night, that the sweetest experiences of his madness returned; he was amazed at his irresponsibility for a space, then he marvelled that he could have been so light-hearted, and sooner or later he was overwhelmed with an image, here and there, of beauty and delight, as in occasional memories of childhood.

But he did remember almost immediately, when, three weeks later he remembered anything at all, the promise he had made to Suzi Ramdez that Monday morning at breakfast.

'Promise me that you won't speak of Mrs Gardnor's breakdown in your office. We have taken her as our guest, and there would be great distress for us to betray this poor woman's sickness, so that they laugh at her in her husband's office in Israel.'

'We wouldn't dream of laughing at –'

'Promise. Never speak of her. Promise, and I shall explain how she is mad.'

'Yes, of course, I promise. I won't say a word.'

'She imagines that she is being spied upon and is mixed up in political things to spy upon the Arabs, maybe. I don't know. She writes stupid letters in code and hides them places, to find them again and say, "Look what I find!" So we make her well again soon and let her rest as we have promised her husband who brought her to us.'

'Doesn't she see a doctor?'

'Oh yes, many doctors. Two times a week she goes to visit a psychiatrist, very clever, in Amman.'

'Poor woman.'

'She will take great care of Barbara. It will do good for herself to have this job, and she is so kind. Never will she betray Barbara if we tell her so. You say nothing of this to your government friends, please, as you promised. Then we count on her to be good to Barbara and keep her secret.'

Freddy said, 'I see.' At that time he was not sure how much Suzi expected him to believe. He said, 'I see. Oh, well, if she'll keep an eye on Barbara, that's all right.'

'I shall come myself many times while she is sick. Maybe she gets up in ten days. This morning she's O.K. already. No temperature or nothing. And the infection is past, so you could sleep with her, even.'

'I don't want to,' Freddy said. 'I want to sleep with you. But I'll go and see her now, I think. Does she know your father and Miss Rickward are in the house?'

'Oh no. It would only make her a fever perhaps. She knows only that some people are here and she must keep quiet in the room.'

On that day when the two young consuls brought and broke the news to Freddy that his mother was dead, murdered by Benny, knifed by Benny insane, killed in violent blood, and the memory of his absent days in Jordan first flooded upon him and was half-lost again, it was then some hours before detailed scenes, one by one, began to seep back. There was Benny's letter – Bloodshed, Mr Freddy . . . She . . . I hear those voices again . . . There will be Blood come from it . . .

'I thought it would be here,' Freddy said. 'Somewhere in my mind I knew there was to be bloodshed, but I thought the danger was here, I didn't think it was in Harrogate.'

And he recalled his answers to the letters. There was something urgent he had to remember. He had answered the letters, but hadn't posted them, hadn't posted them. Where had he left them? Yes, but he had set them on fire. That was so. He had burnt his finger and thumb. And presently, the image came to him of that moonlit wait outside Barbara's convent, while Alexandros went to bribe the janitor, and he heard again the chanting voices from minaret to minaret calling the faithful to prayer under the stars.

'Where is Barbara Vaughan?' Freddy said.

'Oh, her? Well, apparently she got back to Israel yesterday. We only heard this morning. We'd assumed, you know, that she'd gone to Rome, but it seems she's been hiding in Jordan. Her family are awfully relieved to know definitely that she's safe and so are we, of course. Silly woman.'

'Did she ask for me?' Freddy said.

'No, she didn't mention you. Look, Freddy, you should lie down, you know.'

'I must get back to London,' Freddy said. There was something urgent to remember. His head was in his hands, and it was then he saw, once more, that walk of Ruth Gardnor's across the forecourt to the palm-tree in Jericho.

The consuls did not leave after that. They stayed on for lunch, which Joanna herself served to them in a room alone, in compliance with their request, withdrawing as silently as their Arab boys when she had done so. One of the young men then left abruptly, returning at half past five in the afternoon. He announced, 'We've got Gardnor.'

And meanwhile Freddy had given every other part of the story he could then heave to mind. 'There was the Arab woman, you see, a daughter of Ramdez. Now, I know for a fact that she suspected I'd got this message from the tree that night, so next morning she went into a long rigmarole about Ruth Gardnor having had a nervous breakdown – a great secret, and Gardnor didn't wish it to be known to us.'

'Understandably,' said Freddy's colleague, with a bit of a smile.

'Yes, according to Miss Ramdez, Gardnor didn't wish anything to be known to us. This Arab girl's yarn was that Ruth was mad as a hatter, and was sending herself messages, believing herself to be a spy. I listened to it all, of course . . . Well, I can only say I'm sorry I didn't get this news to you immediately. I could easily have dropped into our embassy at Amman, but to be quite honest I'm sure I would have been followed and then Gardnor would probably have been alerted. And of course the telephones are all tapped. Spies everywhere over there. I waited over till Tuesday, hoping to get some more evidence, you know, and then, don't you see, it all went. It all went out of my mind. I just lost my memory, that's all. God knows what else I did all that time.'

Then he worked over the story again.

'Freddy, take it easy. I'll get Joanna. She'll –'

'You're sure you've got Gardnor?'

'Oh yes, we've got him. He isn't giving much trouble.'

'He's talking?'

'Well, he's begun.'

'I must get back to London.'

'You must get to bed.'

'Gardnor, of course, has been anxious to implicate me,' Freddy said. He was not sure, but he felt fairly certain he had been under unofficial house arrest at the Cartwrights' during the past few days of his amnesia.

'Oh goodness, Freddy. Gardnor's report would never have stood up. One needs evidence, you know.'

Yes, one needed evidence. And while investigating the sources of evidence, suspicion must have lingered. How long had his mother lain dead in a mess of blood? Freddy wanted to know the details. He said, 'Are you sure you've got Gardnor? Really got him? Was there any difficulty getting into the house at Jericho?'

'No, they say from Amman that the Jordan police were quite helpful. There were a few things there – cameras and a transmitter – the usual. Ruth Gardnor had gone, of course. She must have got wind of something from the police or someone.'

'Well, if you've got Gardnor, that's the main thing.'

After breakfast with Suzi he had gone to see how Barbara was. He said to her, 'You know, if we put you in the Embassy at Amman – send for them to fetch you – they'll look after you and you'll be quite safe. Don't you think you should do that, and cut out all this pilgrimage lark?'

She said, 'What would you do in my place?'

To his later horror, he said, 'I'd be inclined to stick it out, personally. I'd hate the idea of these fellows getting the better of me.'

'That's exactly how I feel,' she said. 'Now I'm in it, I'm going to stay in it.'

'Of course,' he said, 'I'm not a half-Jew and I haven't got scarlet fever. So I don't want to encourage you to take these risks. On the other hand, if you do manage to lie low for a couple of weeks, and then get up and put on those widow's weeds again, and get around the country, it would be rather a triumph for *us*.'

'That's what I'll do. The only thing I dread is the boredom. Is there anything to read in this house? Is there a wireless or something?'

'I wouldn't have a wireless on if I were you,' Freddy said. 'You might attract attention. I'll see if I can find you some books, or Suzi will get you something to read. But don't move from this room and don't make a noise. By the way, Joe Ramdez is in the house. He's supposed to be leaving tomorrow, but I'll wait till he leaves, so don't –'

'My God, he may be looking for me! Everyone must be looking for me after that piece in the Israeli paper.'

'Suzi has warned him to keep away from this part of the house. He thinks you're a Moroccan dancer, just arrived from Tangier with scarlet fever. Are you frightened, though? Because –'

'No, I'm not frightened. The danger doesn't seem so very real to me, somehow. It'll make a lovely story to tell afterwards.'

'Yes, that's what I was thinking, too,' Freddy said. He thought Barbara Vaughan was a jolly good sport, and it was the one solid opinion he formed during his lost days in Jordan that he retained ever afterwards.

She said to Harry later, when she was safe, 'I honestly

couldn't swear that I went through all that from a determination to pray at the Christian shrines. It's true I'd set my heart on the pilgrimage. But, to be perfectly honest, I might have taken refuge at the Embassy – Freddy did suggest it – only in fact, I could see he really wanted me to be a *good sport*. And Freddy was so very nice, I sort of couldn't let him down.'

'To hell with Freddy,' said Harry.

'Oh no, Freddy's nice. He got me out of the convent. I thought highly of him for that.'

'You thought he was a good sport.'

'Well, yes, that's about it. A jolly good one.'

'He was off his nut, though.'

'Well, I wasn't to know that. And really, he wasn't all that mad. You would like Freddy if you knew him.'

'I know. He sounds all right. Tell me – suppose you'd been killed – what's the technical Catholic difference between a martyr and a jolly good sport?'

Joe Ramdez was standing patriarchally by the well in the forecourt talking to Suzi in Arabic when Freddy came out into the sunny morning air.

He turned to Freddy with affable arms. 'Welcome to my home. Have you slept well?'

'Delightfully, thank you.'

Suzi had a haunted look. She said, 'I drive Mr Hamilton out for a day to see the general view of Jericho, Elisha's Fountain, the Mount of the Temptation in the Wilderness and the beautiful Greek convent there, also the River Jordan, the Allemby Bridge, and –'

'Alle-n-by,' said Ramdez. 'You always say "Allemby" like a Cockney corporal of the General's army. It is Allenby, may he rest in the Bosom of God.'

'The Allenby Bridge and through the hills of Judaea to the Dead Sea. We go also to Bethany, the Tomb of Lazarus that was raised from the dead, and the Inn of the Good Samaritan. Then we –'

'She does not stop talking once she has started. Suzi is the worst of all my women in my household for talking,' Ramdez said to Freddy. 'Only on the first times of meeting a new person she keeps quiet, but that is her trick, she's a clever one. When she meets a nice gentleman, he thinks she's a quiet good woman, but soon she is talking.'

'Your daughter's a splendid guide,' Freddy said.

Ramdez said, 'She is splendid also, for an insurance agent. Suzi – did you explain Mr Hamilton the proposal forms and the opportunities?'

'Yes, Father, and Mr Hamilton will get the medical test all right.'

Freddy said, 'As I told Abdul, I must wait till I have a reply from my lawyers in London. They look after all that side of things.'

'Lawyers are no good,' Ramdez said. 'Listen to me, lawyers are robbers.'

'Oh, I know that. I quite agree.'

'We have in this insurance scheme many diplomats from Britain and also from America. Mr Scriven is one, Mr Pole is two, Mr Carson is three, Mr Macintyre, who is gone from here and now in West Indies, is four, Mr Gardnor is five, Mr Redding, six – naturally, I do not remember all the names on the record, but these diplomats are all investors in Middle East Visitors' with great benefits.'

'Really? A very impressive list,' Freddy said. Scriven was a filing-clerk in the office at Tel Aviv; Pole was secretary in the Post Office in Amman; Carson he didn't know – probably someone in the American Embassy; Macintyre he remembered as the name of a chap who had been recalled from Israel two years ago for some misdemeanour with a girl; Gardnor, yes, Gardnor; Redding, he couldn't place. So much for the diplomats.

'You've got Gardnor?'

'Yes, Freddy, it's all right. He's coming across with it nicely today. Not that he was much trouble yesterday, but he probably thought it over during the night and today we're getting the lot. He says he feels liberated, in a way, now that it's all out.'

'Well, you might take a look into Scriven at Tel Aviv and a chap called Pole in Amman.'

'Yes, I believe we're working on Scriven and Pole, and a few others on Ramdez's list.'

'You've got hold of his list?'

'Yes, it cost us an absolute fortune. And I don't believe it's worth a penny to us. No big security risks except Gardnor; only chaps who've made fools of themselves with girls and so on.'

Scriven . . . Pole . . . Macintyre . . . In the forecourt at Jericho Freddy looked out at the Judaean wilderness and said to Ramdez, 'An impressive list.'

'So you must join also.'

'One's salary doesn't amount to much in the Foreign Service,' Freddy said. 'One has to make ends meet, you know. I'm afraid we'd better be on our way if we're to see all those delightful scenes that your daughter described.'

The cars were parked across the forecourt and Suzi started to move. Ramdez said, 'Wait, I have a favour to ask of Mr Hamilton.'

Suzi looked miserable and embarrassed, as she had on that first day that Freddy had seen her, in the Cartwrights' garden.

'You ask so many favours, Father, and Mr Hamilton has paid in advance for the pilgrimage-tour inclusive,' she said.

He had not in fact paid anything in advance, but was to settle the bill with Alexandros. Three weeks later, when the events came back to him, he did so, and meantime Alexandros had held his peace, not believing for one moment the rumour that Freddy was suffering from a lapse of memory, but rather assuming that Freddy had some good private reason, perhaps connected with his career or his social reputation, for choosing to regard the episode as non-existent.

'This is one small favour,' said Ramdez, 'which I am sure you will oblige with, Mr Hamilton, since it concerns a lady of your country. I have brought with me a very nice tourist who is on a pilgrimage and also has paid in advance. But I have now business to attend to in Amman today. So you take this nice woman along with you in the car today, returning with you this evening, and Suzi will adjust the small difference for one day's private tour for one, and one day's private tour for two; it makes a bit cheaper. But this would be a favour as this lady is so greatly distressed. She has followed from England to look for a lady-friend and maybe you will find the friend on your route.'

'Well, that should be all right,' Freddy said. 'Quite all right. Is she ready to come?'

'I'll go and summon her now from her room. By the way, do you know Miss Barbara Vaughan?'

'Oh yes, she's staying at my hotel in Israel. But surely she isn't the lady who's going to accompany us? She –'

'Oh no, she is the lady that my client, Miss Rickward, is looking for. Do you know where she might be?'

'So far as I know she's still in Israel –' Joe Ramdez clapped his hands over his ears at the repeated word 'Israel'; he smiled, but not very sweetly.

'– Occupied Palestine,' Freddy said with deference '. . . I know she was thinking of coming here but I believe she changed her mind. Anyway, she's either still in Occupied Palestine or on her way to Rome to join her fiancé, who is there at the moment. A very nice person, Miss Vaughan.'

'Ah, thank you. I will tell Miss Rickward what you say. Wait, excuse me, half a moment.'

Freddy said, then, to Suzi, 'That settles that. And I'll see that a notice goes into the Israeli paper tomorrow morning.'

'In Amman,' she said, 'it is possible they have a list of every name that has passed through the Mandelbaum Gate from Israel. And my father will find it.'

'Then we must make sure they understand she's left the country – gone to Rome. Let's wait and see how much your father discovers.'

Ricky bustled out with him, very voluble on the subject of Freddy's niece, who was a pupil at her school, and through whose mother Ricky had met Freddy's mother at Harrogate one day. 'It was only when your mother told me of the bits in your letter concerning Barbara Vaughan that I knew she was engaged to the man. Then she –'

'Let us go,' said Suzi, 'and you talk about the friend in the car. But I tell you this, that if you look for an English visitor in our country, you have to look well, since they are under every olive-tree and in every cave of the hills, and there is no stopping their curiosity for adventure everywhere.'

'My friend is on a pilgrimage. A Roman Catholic pilgrimage. That narrows it down, my dear,' Ricky said. She looked yearningly at Joe, who kissed her hand and placed her carefully in the back of the car. He evidently expected Freddy to go in beside her, but Freddy got in the front at the wheel, leaning to open the door beside him for Suzi.

'My daughter should drive,' said Joe, as Suzi got in beside Freddy. 'It is her job, and you should come back here to be comfortable with Miss Rickward.'

Freddy beamed at him. 'Mr Ramdez,' he said, 'a businessman like you should know that when one pays in advance one never gets full value.' He started up the car while Joe Ramdez leaned over the back window to say softly to Miss Rickward that he would be back from Amman, promptly, that evening. As Freddy drove off, Joe went over to his own car, then seemed to change his mind and returned to the house.

Freddy drew up a few yards from the house. 'I'm so very sorry,' he said. 'I'll have to go back for my sun-glasses.' He manoeuvred the car to a turn. His sun-glasses, which he wore only when absolutely necessary, were actually in his pocket, but he wanted to see what Ramdez was up to. He was uneasy about Barbara's being left without friends with that man on the premises. 'Stupid of me,' Freddy said.

Ricky had moved from her position behind Freddy to the position behind Suzi. Now, when they had turned round, she moved to the middle of the seat. 'While you are indoors,' she said, 'I would be so very grateful if you find me a cushion.'

'Are you not comfortable, Miss Rickward?' Suzi said. 'Would you like to change with me?' The car was a well-sprung, fairly new Chevrolet. 'The back seat,' Suzi said, 'is usually the more comfortable place.'

'No, no, a cushion will do. Yes, it is more comfortable at the back, I'm sure. It's only that I have a slight touch of cramp. It's probably due to the strain of travel. A cushion would be very satisfactory.'

The phrase 'very satisfactory' gave Suzi immediately to think of her father, who used it a lot when speaking to the British. And the live wires of her mind gave instantaneous connection from her father to Ricky's fidgeting in her seat. As Freddy drove up to the door, Suzi, attacked by the complete answer, put her hand to her mouth to suppress the burst of laughter which more or less spluttered forth. She jumped from the car and said, 'I get a cushion. Excuse me that I laugh at Freddy for forgetting his sun-glasses, he is so like all the Englishmen, they never get away from a place but have to return.'

'Stay here, I'll get the cushion,' said Freddy, as he got out. 'Just tell me where –'

'No, I must find a soft one.'

Joe appeared at the door just as they were entering. He looked extremely fierce-eyed at this return, although he smiled and nodded at Freddy's self-deprecating explanation.

'I was just about to depart,' said Ramdez in the tone of a man very distracted by other business. He raised his arm in salute to Miss Rickward, called that he would see her later, went straight to his car and drove off at speed. From this busy display, even before Freddy got to his room and found that his zipper-bag had been left unzipped, although not by himself, he had the sense of their having interrupted Ramdez at some leisurely snooping. There was nothing for Ramdez to find, anyway. He took his sun-glasses from his pocket and put them on. Suzi then appeared, carrying two large cushions, and collapsed into his arms, cushions and all, while she told him of her absolute conviction that her father had 'unflowered and nearly killed' poor Miss Rickward in the course of the previous night. 'A matter of fact,' Suzi said, 'I heard a noise. I thought it was cats. But it wasn't cats, it was Miss Ricky.'

They came soberly to the car and Suzi arranged the cushions for Ricky. 'You must have had a hard time on your travels,' said Suzi.

'I don't usually complain,' Ricky said, 'it's only –'

'Then you must have been tough, all your travels,' said Suzi, 'but you'll be O.K. now.'

'Ready?' said Freddy. 'Right. We're off! Let's try to get back early, and not give Miss Rickward too much travelling.'

It was late on Tuesday morning that Freddy and Suzi finally departed for Jerusalem. Barbara was very conscious now of being left in the house without anyone she knew, although, when she had said goodbye to Freddy and Suzi, she had been almost relieved at their departure, for their continual anxious popping in and out of her room with warnings about this and that had exhausted her. They had given instructions about what she might say or not say to Latifa and the woman who was coming to nurse her; while all Barbara really wanted to do was sleep and, on waking, drink water. Thirst and exhaustion were now the only lingering discomforts of the disease.

Freddy had said, 'I'll be back at the weekend. As soon as I get back to Israel this afternoon I'll see about getting that notice in the paper to put the people here off the scent. And I'll get hold of Dr Clegg in Rome and tell him what's happened. You've nothing to worry about. Only, Barbara, this woman who's going to look after you – be very careful what you say to her, won't you?'

'Yes, Suzi has told me. I'm not to talk and not to ask any questions of Miss White.'

'Miss White isn't her real name, of course. But –'

'Isn't it? What a bloody peculiar set-up this all is.'

'Yes, but you're in a bloody peculiar position. Of course, it's my fault, in a way, for not insisting on your going to the Embassy. If you want –'

'No – oh no. I'm going through with it.'

'You're a good sport, you know.'

'Well, one wants to do what one wants to do, that's all.' She hadn't the slightest notion what she meant by this, but she meant it and it sounded all right. She was sure that Freddy was relieved by her refusal; for some reason he was reluctant to contact the Embassy himself.

'Really a sport,' Freddy was saying. 'Now, I want to tell you about so-called Miss White. If there's anything, Barbara, you can get out of her in the meantime – I mean, what she's actually up to here – without, of course, appearing to be inquisitive, I'd be awfully grateful. I can't really explain, but maybe you realise there are a few people roaming round this part of the world whom the F.O. likes to know a little about. Don't take this too seriously, of course, but –'

'My God!' said Barbara. 'Don't tell me there's a British Gestapo keeping track of us all when we go abroad.' She sat up in bed.

'Barbara *dear*!'

She lay down again. 'Well, Freddy, it's bad enough for me to have to hide here in Jordan, and go about in disguise. But one doesn't expect that sort of thing amongst ourselves. Why should I be a government snooper? I detest government snooping.'

'Don't think any more of it,' Freddy said. 'I apologise. I withdraw my request. I beg your pardon. But I trust you to keep your discretion about my request.'

'Oh, Freddy, now you're taking up an attitude. Don't take up attitudes, I can't bear them. What have you got against Miss White, or whoever she is?'

'I couldn't tell you even if I knew. My dear, you're quite right in all you say. I shouldn't have mentioned this matter at all. It was only that, when there's a possibility of the country being damaged in some way –'

'Which country? This country?'

'Of course not. Ours. What do you think I've been talking about?'

'I smell an ideology, that's all.'

Barbara recalled he had become very amused, he had just about hugged her with joy, and at least he had taken both her hands and looked at her with the affection of one who detested ideologies, too. He said, 'Yes, that's the point . . .'

They were gone, they were gone, now. Yesterday she had slept most of the five hours when Freddy and Suzi had taken their drive to keep up the appearance of touring. But now Freddy was gone for almost a week and Suzi for some days.

Much earlier that morning, a car had left the house and Suzi had come to Barbara's room to announce the departure of her father with his tourist for Jerusalem. A little later she heard an arrival. Suzi came, with a tray of coffee and biscuits for two, to sit with Barbara and inform her that Miss White had returned and was resting.

Now they were gone. Resting, thought Barbara, and what am I supposed to be doing? She began to think of Freddy and to speculate upon his sex life, whatever it should be. For, plainly, Suzi had greatly taken to him.

But it's none of my business, she thought. Sex is child's play. Jesus Christ was very sophisticated on the subject of sex. And didn't harp on it. Why is it so predominant and serious for us? There are more serious things in the world. And if sex is not child's play, in any case it is worthless. For she was thinking of her own recent experiences of sex, which were the only experiences she knew that were worth thinking about. It was child's play, unselfconscious and so full of fun and therefore of peace, that she had not bothered to analyse or define it. And, she thought, we have invented sex guilt to take our minds off the real thing. She thought finally of

Freddy, and quite saw, partly through Suzi's eyes, that he had his attractions, especially here in Jordan.

Suzi, when she had come to say goodbye, promising to be back before the end of the week, was very buoyant. 'You know,' she said, 'I'm a little bit in love with Freddy.'

Jolly good for Freddy.

From being confined with the fever like this, Barbara Vaughan had taken one of her religious turns and was truly given to the love of God, and all things were possible. And, she thought, we must all think in these vague terms: with God, all things are possible; because the only possibilities we ever seem able to envisage in a precise manner are disastrous events; and we fear both vaguely and specifically, and I have myself too long laid plans against eventualities. Against good ones? No, bad ones. It would be interesting, for a change, to prepare and be ready for possibilities of, I don't know what, since all things are possible with God and nothing is inevitable. And then, it is said in the Scriptures: The race is not to the swift nor the battle to the strong . . . She was trying to remember how it went on when into the room walked Ruth Gardnor. Barbara was sure it was Ruth Gardnor. Then Ruth said, 'Barbara, goodness, it's you!'

'What are you doing here?' Barbara said.

'Now, now!' said Ruth.

Barbara thought this strange. She said, 'What's wrong?'

'You don't ask questions,' Ruth said. 'You're not really ill, are you?'

'Well, yes, I'm down with scarlet fever. But I'm past the infectious stage.'

Only then it occurred to Barbara that Ruth Gardnor was the Miss White she had been told to expect. Suzi had certainly warned her not to ask questions of Miss White. 'Are you the Miss White?' Barbara said.

Ruth crossed her legs and puffed her cigarette, leaning back in the soft chair. She said, 'Yes, of course. And you're not the Barbara I expected to find. But I expect you're used to that. You're not really ill, are you?'

'I've had scarlet fever. To tell you the truth, I'm on the run.'

'Yes, I know. I heard in Amman today that you're being looked for by the local boys.' She laughed then, and said, 'I actually told some people connected with the Jordan Intelligence that I knew you slightly and would look out for you.' She was still laughing. 'How was I to know that the Barbara Vaughan I already knew was the Barbara I've got to look after, here?'

Barbara felt safe in saying little. It was the most plausible course, until she should find out what Ruth was up to. Which was exactly what Freddy had been suggesting. It appeared that Ruth assumed Barbara to be someone importantly on her side, secretly connected with whatever activity she herself was here for, and to be faking illness while lying low.

The fact that Ruth was extremely kind to Barbara throughout the next two weeks was something that Barbara kept repeating when the Foreign Office man came to question her shortly after her escape back to Israel through the narrow Mandelbaum Gate.

'But you know,' said Barbara, 'as soon as she was convinced I really was feeling rather weak she couldn't do enough for me. On the personal level she was terribly sweet.'

The nice young man was amused, because Barbara had just been telling him about her fight with Ruth Gardnor. 'Yes, I do mean a fight,' she said. 'Hands, fists, nails, and feet.' And she said one of the tendons of her neck still hurt from the force of the wrench Ruth gave it, holding Barbara's head in her hands to try to subdue her, while Barbara scratched and bit some part of Ruth. To the Foreign Office man, fascinated beyond the call of duty by the details, Barbara had said, 'I just couldn't stand it any longer. She assumed, of course, that I was part of her organisation. I'm sure of that, because after a day or two she said to me, "Oh, come off it. Suzi's told me you're one of us" – or something to that effect. Then, day after day, I had to pretend to be in sympathy or at least refrain from speaking my mind. So it came to a fight . . .'

In the retrospect of a few weeks it was curiously more vivid than the reality had been. In her low physical condition at the time Barbara could hardly believe what was going on, and the two weeks passed like an amorphous cloud of cosmic matter interrupted at intervals by specific points of occurrence, small explosions in the spacious night-sky of her boredom. She had no books to read. No one in the house had a book. Freddy had gone away without producing any papers or magazines. Yes, someone in the house had a book. It was in Arabic. Ruth Gardnor told her it was a book of mystical poetry by a Sufi woman mystic of the eighth century. Ruth could read Arabic and translated, 'O Lord, if I worship thee from fear of hell, burn me in hell, and if I worship you in the hope of heaven, reject me from heaven, but if I worship thee for thine own sake then do not withhold thyself from me in thine eternal beauty.'

This was about Thursday, two days after Freddy and Suzi had left. Barbara listened out for Suzi's return. 'Shall I read you some more?' Ruth said.

'No thanks.'

'She's as good as any of the Christian mystics.'

'I know. There's no need to be defensive. All the mystics are much alike to me.'

'*So* many Catholics won't listen to any other religious writings. It's killing. And the things they swallow themselves . . .'

This was nothing new to Barbara; ever since her conversion she had met sophisticated women who, on the subject of Catholicism, sneered like French village atheists, and expected to be excused from normal good manners, let alone intelligence, on this one subject. But she thought it worthy of note that Ruth did not doubt she was a Catholic. That Barbara was a half-Jew on a clandestine Christian pilgrimage, Ruth did not for one moment believe. She knew for certain that she had roused the Jordanian authorities' suspicions, and by now she had come to accept that Barbara was genuinely feeling rather weak and by no means feigning her illness.

Ruth was fully convinced that Barbara was part of her spy organisation. It was difficult for Barbara, at the time, to piece together exactly what or whom it served, although later, when the episode became a vivid whole in her mind, it was plain that the organisation was an Arab nationalist one, communist-affiliated, with headquarters in Cairo.

Now Ruth would say puzzling things as she sat and talked to Barbara. Ruth sat always languidly, with crossed legs and her head leaning back. She had a good, rather raddled, tanned face, long streaked blonde hair and an effortless look of glamour. Somewhere in London Barbara had first met her, years ago, at someone's house, at someone's dinner party – when? where? – just after the war, during the war – no, not during the war or just after, since Barbara did not recall any uniforms at that party. Maybe, though, it just happened there was no one in uniform at that party.

While she listened to Ruth she drank endless grape juice, orange juice, all prepared carefully by hand; by Ruth's kindly hand. 'Rupert and I are fed up with Britain. It's finished. It's become a bloody debating society. Europe is finished. The Jews have finished us off. There's a Jews' world-network, my dear. The American Jews are just plotting to demolish the rest of the world. Even the Kremlin knows that. I met a chap at the Russian Economic Mission the other day, he'd just arrived in Israel. He said he'd yet to find a Jew who was a docker in the Soviet Union. I said, "By God, you'd have to look hard for one who was a docker in the West."'

'What about in Israel?' Suddenly Barbara remembered the party where she had first met Ruth Gardnor with her husband. The night of the dinner party. And the cello: it had been an indifferent performance. Ruth had sat listening. 'The cello,' Ruth had said afterwards, 'is my favourite instrument. It *speaks* to me.' She said to Barbara, 'You know what I mean?' Barbara had said, 'No, I don't.' Now Ruth was speaking again: 'Israel? In Israel they'd have the whole Arab world doing manual labour for them if they could get them. Israel will burn itself out and just become another Levantine state.'

At the time this talk confused Barbara on the point of Ruth's political allegiance. She was accustomed to regard anti-Semitism as a note of fascism, not communism. Anyway, it went on day after day, and Ruth assumed that Barbara was like-minded, as apparently was everyone else connected with the headquarters in Cairo.

In her absence, Barbara fumed and imagined a fight with Ruth, how she would hit and kick her. She jumped from her bed frequently and went into the adjoining wash-room, a small closet with only a shower, no bath. There she would take cold showers and hot showers, many and many times a day, regardless of her weakness.

On no account was she to leave the room. On no account. Freddy had said so. Suzi had said, on no account. Ruth kept saying so. Ruth prepared food of an extremely rare and elaborate order to tempt Barbara. She must have spent all the hours that she did not spend with Barbara on planning, preparing and cooking these meals – chilled exotic soups, veal, chicken or lamb with herb-laden sauces. All for Barbara. They were served on a tray with lace-edged white cloths, for brave Barbara, who, like Ruth, thought Nasser was so marvellous and the nationalist cause so good and so essentially exploitable. 'The Party in Latin America is well aware that the big struggle to come, the final world-struggle, is with the Jews,' said Ruth. Barbara could not eat, her cheeks were sunk when she saw herself in the glass. She wondered if she was going mad, and at times this long thought was indistinguishable from madness.

'How long have you known Freddy Hamilton?' said Ruth.

'Well, I don't really know him at all.'

'He was *here*, you know.'

'Yes. I got a lift from Suzi with him.'

'What was he doing here?'

'Only touring.'

'Are you sure?'

'Yes, quite sure. He's harmless.'

'Don't you think,' said Ruth, 'that Suzi's a bit irresponsible? I mean, bringing him here. It's awfully dangerous.'

'No, I think it's the sort of thing that would put them off the scent if they were at all on the scent.'

'Of course, you realise, we pay those Ramdez people for the use of this house. They're well paid. They ought to protect us.'

Suzi at last returned. Barbara later placed this day as the Saturday of that first week.

'I can't go on like this,' she said to Suzi.

'Only one more week. I'm here for the weekend and Alexandros is here also with me. Sunday night, we return to

Jerusalem. But next Saturday, Sunday, I come back to fetch you. Better you should get well and stay in bed the full period that the doctor said. Then the police forget to find you. They already have said you must have left the country.'

Suzi had brought a pile of travel pamphlets, so that Barbara could choose the places she wanted to visit when, a week hence, she would start off with Suzi on the pilgrimage. 'Because,' said Suzi, 'we must have the pilgrimage. This time there is no trouble to anticipate, except you must be dressed still like an Arab woman to prevent trouble.'

'Where are my own clothes?' Barbara said.

'I have them in Jerusalem.'

Barbara was eating quite a lot of cucumber sandwiches. She said, 'I can't eat anything that Ruth Gardnor brings me. I try, but I can't.'

'That woman is crazy. She is now all at once my enemy because I don't join with the nationalist party or this, that, party. We give her the house where she operates, and if they catch her we take the risk for this crime of plot, so what more does she ask of us? She is like a fierce animal to me since I brought here Freddy. Before, she was my friend of the very best. Now she says it's wrong that I bring Alexandros here, and she dislikes that we keep here the girls for the night-clubs. All these things she's afraid of for her secrets which are nothing so very much, according to my father.'

Alexandros paid Barbara a visit, so noisy with greetings and celebration of the long-lost, that various whispers, titters and tripping footsteps at the end of the corridor occurred, whereupon Suzi could be heard chiding in Arabic and French. These were the night-club girls, who were habitually kept out of this side of the house.

Alexandros closed Barbara's door and at Suzi's request kept quieter. He said, 'Mr Hamilton is not so very well.'

'What's the matter?'

'This I can't tell you. But I have heard he is not very well, and perhaps it is sunstroke.'

'Isn't he coming here to Jericho this weekend? He promised to come and see me.'

'No, but I am here with Suzi instead.'

Barbara let herself float on the waves of what was to be. She began to feel stronger on that second Sunday of her illness. She wanted to walk in the cool evening, but Suzi and Alexandros insisted this was dangerous.

'Oh, I don't care about the danger any longer. What have I done? I'm not an Israeli spy.'

'It's dangerous for your health,' said Alexandros. 'For anyone to rise from a bed to walk in the evening is dangerous.'

He seemed to have turned melancholy after talking about Freddy. Later, Suzi came and said to Barbara, 'Freddy is now with his friends the Cartwrights, but he has not sent me a message or nothing. I'm too proud to go there to ask for him. How could I make excuse to call there unless he asks for me?'

'Did he get that piece put in the Israeli newspaper as he promised?'

'Piece?'

'To say I'd changed my mind about coming to Jordan.'

'I haven't heard of it. No, I don't think so.'

'It doesn't matter, of course.' Barbara discerned that Suzi was personally troubled about Freddy's ignoring her since his return to Jordan.

Suzi said, 'I left him at the Via Dolorosa last Tuesday and he walked the rest of the way. He was O.K. then, you know. Alexandros says he's sick, also occupied with affairs; but he could remember to write a note. He can get a letter through the diplomatic courier, easy. He hasn't got the scarlet fever,

Alexandros says. Now I don't want Alexandros to see so much why I'm sad about Freddy. Maybe Freddy will leave a message for me at my home in Jerusalem when I return tonight.'

Barbara thought, he's taken fright. Freddy must have decided to withdraw from the tangle. But, she thought, he wouldn't do it this way. He wouldn't do just nothing. Something must be wrong, that's all.

But Suzi, to cheer up the atmosphere, was already recommending the route of their pilgrimage the following week.

They did get away the following week, but not before Barbara amazed herself by throwing at Ruth Gardnor a clock and a vase. Ruth was even more amazed. She was carrying a wireless set with large ear-phones of the early vintage, which she had managed very cleverly to piece together from two separate sets, one old and one new; this was for Barbara's benefit, for Suzi had not wanted her to draw undue attention to her presence by the sound of a wireless in her room. Barbara threw these objects at Ruth, then in a frenzy leapt upon the woman and battered her head with the disconnected ear-phones of the wireless. Ruth kept saying, 'My God, please, Barbara, quiet! Quiet, Barbara, please – quiet!' Barbara scratched. Every obscene word that she had ever heard and (what was so strange) never heard, Barbara pelted forth at Ruth Gardnor. Ruth took Barbara's head in her hands and wrenched it. It took them seven minutes to wear themselves out. Ruth was wounded with a cut on the forehead and a deep scratch on her chin. Barbara had some bruises that came up later, and her neck ached for weeks. It was something like the rehearsal that had been going on in her mind for ten days. Over and over again, when Ruth in her kindness had brought her some tempting thing and tried to wheedle and coax, very sweetly – over and over again – tried to coax, then sat to talk confidentially about the ideals that she served and those that she felt by instinct only, then Barbara had listened and not argued. Over and over again Barbara had rehearsed the fight, and it had amazingly taken place. Ruth was frightened. She sobbed softly and said, 'How ill you are! Oh, God, and I've no one here to help me.'

Barbara got back to bed, spent out. She said nothing, only listening still in memory to the pounding waves of Ruth's chatter, day after day. Nasser is marvellous. Really, let's face it, Hitler had the right idea. Ten days of Ruth's chatter. It's a network on a world scale. The Jews. They've got us in a net. If you knew how the banking system worked, you'd realise . . . Would you like to sleep now? Would you like to sit up? I've got to go out for a while, do you mind? But now Ruth was only sobbing in the chair, with blood on her face. Barbara lay and watched her through slit eyes and heard her murmur. 'Oh, I wish I'd someone to help me!' Then Ruth said, 'Have you been told to do this to me?' Barbara said nothing. Ruth said, 'Oh God! Don't they trust me? What have I done? Rupert will have to come over – I can't wait on and on.'

Barbara said, 'Yes, you'll let them down, all right.' She said this out of the dark, but meant it decidedly for a thrust, which it turned out to be. Ruth looked cornered. She said, 'I see.'

Barbara had no idea how they would go on for the rest of the week. This was eight o'clock on Thursday morning. Ruth picked up all the fragments of clock, wireless sets, and vase. Suzi was to come on Saturday or Sunday. Ruth went away after a while, and Barbara fell into a moaning exhaustion, and finally a deep sleep such as she had not enjoyed since her arrival.

She woke in the afternoon when she heard a whistling scrape on the front door of the house, and a car drew up. Shortly afterwards, Ruth came in with tea. Barbara was horrified: Ruth was haggard and patched with small pieces of plaster; she was frantic with worry.

She said to Barbara, 'Listen – don't please, please, make any more fuss, more noise. Joe Ramdez has come again with his tourist woman. If you're caught, I'll be in trouble. H.Q. will blame me. How do you feel?'

Barbara felt like an animal. She wanted to ask, honestly, 'Who are H.Q.?' But she kept silent. Suzi had said on her last visit, 'It's lucky you have none of your own clothes, she has noticed only the garment of Kyra hung up in the press, and this makes her sure that you are a spy with her organsation . . . She was foolish to let you know of her activities for this organisation. But she has told, not I.'

'Which organisation?'

'I don't know, I don't ask. To tell every Arab organisation would take a day, if I should tell you the list. But you must keep quiet about this to your friends, or you make trouble for me. She is only a mad woman.'

'You make trouble for me,' said every face in Barbara's crowded dreams. Later, when the Foreign Office man came to visit her in Israel, there was no point in keeping quiet. Not only had they seen Freddy the day before, but she had seen Abdul that morning. He had come straight up to her room, and she found him at the door, beaming with some extra pleasure.

He took a telegram from his pocket. 'Suzi's safe,' he said. 'Suzi is in Athens.'

'In Athens? I didn't know she was in danger.'

'The police put her under arrest when they broke into the house at Jericho to find Mrs Gardnor. They had to take someone in custody, so they took Suzi.'

'How did she get away? Did they let her go?'

'Suzi is a rich woman.'

'Of course, Miss Vaughan,' said the young man from the Foreign Office, who was her next caller that day, 'we've got Gardnor. But his wife has got away. She's probably in Cairo. Have you any idea –?'

'I'm afraid I can't help you much,' Barbara said in a weak-minded way. 'It was rather a nightmare until, of course, we got off on our pilgrimage at last. The pilgrimage was all right.'

'All these spy renegades lead nightmare lives,' he said. 'Odd people.'

'I'm a bit tired,' Barbara said. 'Do you mind if we leave off now?' She passed her hand up and down the side of her neck. He was a nice young man but he made her feel neurotic.

'Of course, of course. I'm sorry. It must have been an ordeal, that return to Israel. Quite a risk. You might have caused us some trouble, you know.'

'You make trouble for me,' said all the voices still, in her dreams.

'I'm expecting a telephone call from Rome,' Barbara said. To hell with their questions. One had a private life to lead.

The young man was leaving. He said, 'Will you spare me about twenty minutes tomorrow? – a few more things.'

'Well, yes. But I'm afraid I won't be able to help you much on your side. Maybe one of your men in Jordan could talk nicely to Suzi Ramdez, the travel agent. She could tell you more than I could.'

'They've got Suzi Ramdez, I'm afraid.'

'Who have got Suzi?'

'The Jordan police have picked her up. They're very zealous when they get moving, but they usually move too late. Anyway, I'm glad they didn't get you.'

She did not give him Abdul's news. She said, 'Have they really got Suzi? Are you sure?'

'Of course. Certainly. We're pretty alert, you know, although we don't look it.' Yes, and Suzi was in Athens.

'Will she go on trial? She wasn't really involved.'

'One never knows what will happen in these political cases. But I'm sure she was involved with everything. Everyone out here's involved with everything.'

Oh, go away, she thought. Keep nice and safe. Take no risks. Look both ways and always brush your teeth.

He said, 'I'll look in tomorrow, then. It's only to check a few things. We want to be on the safe side.'

'One more day shut up in that room,' said Barbara, 'and I would have died of claustrophobia and frustration.' – She was sitting beside Suzi in the car, dressed in her Arab clothes.

'Or perhaps murdered Ruth Gardnor.' And slowly, under her veil, she was rubbing ointment into the strained tendon of her neck. They were driving through the bare Judaean hills, that wilderness of John the Baptist, who was a voice crying there, 'Prepare the way of the Lord.' She thought, it was a voice crying from the hill-top that is meant by a voice crying in the wilderness, for she had previously always thought of that phrase as a piece of delicate rhetoric, signifying a lonely, unprevailing plaint of a wandering prophet. But it looked to Barbara that this voice in the wilderness must have been a high crag-top proclamation, good, loud and frightening, for everyone in the valleys to hear, echoing from peak to peak.

They had left the house at Jericho the day before, Sunday, at nightfall. She had followed Suzi out into the sweet air and walked to the car, two weeks after she had arrived. Their departure had been perfectly simple, for Ruth had again

338

gone to Amman for the weekend and Joe Ramdez had left with Ricky on Friday, that day when Barbara had wandered into his room and found him in bed with Ricky. She had been all that night pacing herself to exhaustion, up and down and round her room. At two in the morning she had taken a warm shower in the small cubicle adjoining her bedroom. If only, she thought, I could lie for a long time in a warm bath, it would soothe away the irritation of Ruth Gardnor. But she turned on the shower which creaked as it sprayed. She had gone back to bed, and tried, as a spiritual exercise, to be grateful for her safety in this room and her recovery to the extent that her energy now seemed nearly to burst her skin open. But she could only tremble with anger; Ruth would come in at seven in the morning with a tray of coffee, meekly terrified of Barbara after the fight, and very anxious to propitiate her against some power she obviously suspected Barbara to hold over her, and against the eventuality of trouble. This was quite clear, although Barbara was in no way informed what sort of power Ruth feared, except that it was to do with the spy business. And Barbara fumed against Ruth's totally womanly solicitude combined with her totally repugnant human theories, and against the total misunderstanding. She lay and tried to feel grateful, but even her capacity for gratitude felt gagged; she was the half-witted mute she had undertaken to be when she first set out with Suzi in disguise.

And so she had leapt from her bed again, convulsively, and taken another shower, a cold one. Her neck was painful. Then she had walked up and down the room till dawn.

Light footsteps outside her window: this was not unusual. Several times during the two weeks Barbara had heard these morning footsteps and, peering out, had seen a tall girl sidling along the wall of the house, pausing at every few steps as if to make sure she had not been heard. The girl had passed Barbara's window and turned the corner of the house. The first time, she had been wearing a shirt with blue jeans. She had Asiatic features with dark, lank hair. On the next occasion that Barbara had seen her, she had at first thought this was a different girl, for she was wearing a short, pink organdie dance-dress and was barefooted, carrying high-heeled gold sandals, but Barbara recognised the girl's features as she looked round her before turning the corner. On subsequent mornings the girl was always dressed in her pink frills, but once Barbara was puzzled by a matted pile of blonde hair until the girl turned her face enough to show that she was the same girl wearing a theatrical wig. Obviously, she was returning from a secret rendezvous.

Barbara had asked no questions about the occupants of the house, either of Ruth Gardnor or Suzi. The girl did not look like a political prisoner. But occasional ripples of talk or a shrill quarrel-burst came through an open window from the opposite end of the large house, perhaps when the breeze happened to blow in a certain direction; and once Suzi had referred to 'the girls' without explanation; and so Barbara was certain there were a number of girls in the house, and suspected they were enclosed under some sort of supervision for some purpose.

All through those weeks at the house in Jericho Barbara had been weaving plots to run away and take refuge at the British Embassy in Amman, or with Harry's friend at the American Embassy. But with only the Arab woman's clothes to wear there was scarcely any chance of her being able to stop a car for a lift, or of getting near to the town of Jericho, or of reaching a telephone. It was almost certain that she would have been picked up by the police. A bicycle . . . she longed to steal a bicycle. She could hear bicycle wheels occasionally approaching the house. How did one ride a bicycle in long clothes? It could be done. Cars came and went. She could steal a car. Another week and perhaps this is what she would have done. Who could tell what would have happened if her imprisonment at Jericho had lasted another week, or another day? There would have been no pilgrimage. She would not have been a jolly good sport, but merely someone who made trouble for everybody. Afterwards, she had reason to feel fairly certain that if she had tried to get away she would have fallen into danger or been caused to disappear.

But on that last Friday in the house after the troubled night of creaking shower-baths and frantic thoughts, on that early morning when she once more saw the fly-by-night girl creeping back from her enterprise, the urge pressed on her at least to leave the house and stand for a few moments breathing under the sky. She put on the cotton kimono that Suzi had lent her and left her room. She went on tip-toe along the corridor where she knew a door led to the central area of the house, which in turn led up to the courtyard. There she breathed under the sky and watched the misty pink of dawn on the cliff-tops of the Judaean desert in the distance. Only a well and a palm-tree kept her company in the courtyard. She walked once round the large, spreading house, turning corner after corner, keeping near to the wall, and felt weak from the walk. She heard a sound as she turned into the courtyard and saw an old Arab man with a sack over his shoulder approaching the main door to deliver provisions. He had not seen Barbara. She turned back and tried another door, which was locked. She tried another, which was open and which led to a long corridor similar to that where her room was. She walked to the end, hearing from the various rooms on either side the sound of sleepers and of people stirring themselves to rise from bed. She found a door at the end of the corridor, and in the hope that it would lead to Suzi's part of the house, opened it. The window curtains were drawn and streaks of pink dawn that came through the window at the sides of the curtains and at their points of meeting enlightened a huge bed. A man and a woman lay sleeping. The woman was Ricky. The man was a dark-skinned, large-faced Semite, an Arab with a mane of grey hair. Barbara peered in the half-light of the room and definitely saw Ricky. It was Ricky with her head thrown back in sleep, a profile on the pillow, her arms outspread so that one of them lay limply across the man's body. Barbara had not yet made another movement since opening the door, but now the man sprang up, wide awake. He seemed enormous, his legs beneath a long white shirt leaping from the bed. Barbara fled back along the corridor and out to the courtyard, pursued by the man, who shouted furiously at her in Arabic, French, English, and some other language. She was not listening. She ran to the front door where Latifa, smelling strongly from her night's sleep, was hauling into the house the sack which the old man had brought. Barbara pushed past her, and as she sped through the entrance chamber and along the passage to her room, she heard behind her a roar and rush of abusive vowels from the doorway against Latifa. Barbara then lay on her bed, worn out. She had lost one of her sandals and her foot had been cut somewhere on the wild run. In about twenty minutes, after she had heard many unusual noises, Ruth Gardnor came in, wearing her dressing-gown. Ruth said, 'Oh, you shouldn't have done that, Barbara. You know I'm responsible for you, I'll be held responsible if anything happens to you. They'll never trust me again.'

'I must be a hell of an important agent,' said Barbara, not caring, at that moment, what happened to her.

'Suzi's told me,' said Ruth. 'So there's no use pretending.'

'Told you what? Told you what? Suzi tells everyone something different.'

'Keep quiet, oh, please do.'

I must be even more of a hell of an important Cairo agent, thought Barbara, than I guessed I was. She was feeling easier, though. The storm was over. She said, 'I've hurt my foot,' and let Ruth Gardnor bathe it and fuss over it with bits of plaster.

Barbara said, 'Who is that man?'

'Joe Ramdez. Fortunately, he thinks you are a whore with scarlet fever.'

Barbara said, 'I'm hungry.'

Ruth disappeared to fetch her some breakfast, and when she returned with a large loaded tray, Barbara said, 'I don't want anything. I want to sleep.'

Ruth started to cry and wept for a long time. She said, 'It isn't only that I've got to look after you. I've become so fond of you. I'm genuinely fond of you, I really am. I admire your courage tremendously and what you're doing for us . . . And you won't even give me a kind look.'

'I need eyebrow tweezers,' said Barbara. 'Find a pair, please.'

'What for? What for?'

'For my eyebrows.'

Suzi had arrived early on Sunday and they were off at last. Suzi's plans for the week to come were well-made in so far as they did not go wrong, although, in the theory of the layout, nothing should have gone right.

'First,' said Suzi, 'you do not pay me for all this touring and all this schemes and trouble to me that you've been. You pay my brother Abdul on the Israeli territory, when you return by means that we have planned for you. Poor Abdul, he needs this money. But one time we have lost big money in sending it across to him. Money is a temptation to kill. Never will I give Abdul money to take over with him. An Arab soldier even might kill and take, and report afterwards.'

'Does he come over here then?'

'Oh, yes, sometimes Abdul comes. He will come next Sunday and return you to Israel with him. He knows you're with me, because I've sent a message by a friend of his, Mendel, a Jew who I spoke to at the Mass in the Holy Sepulchre when you were taken sick. You were by my side that time.'

It was all one to Barbara how a Jew called Mendel had been at Mass in the Holy Sepulchre. She did not think, now, of unpicking knots, for there was some definite purpose in the air about her, liberated as she was under the black clothes with the landscape flying past the car. Knots were not necessarily created to be untied. Questions were things that sufficed in their still beauty, answering themselves. What am I doing here on a pilgrimage, after so much involvement? Because I am what I am. Suzi said, 'You would not have come to Jordan, perhaps, if you knew first what would happen and how it would bring you the fever. Now your relatives are anxious for you, but Abdul very soon tells them news by secret messages that you are safe.'

'If one knew everything that was going to happen one would never do a thing,' Barbara said.

'Abdul will give you a great bill for the pilgrimage. Freddy does not pay nothing so far, and he keeps far from me.'

Suzi was melancholy about Freddy's desertion. Barbara tried not to mention him very much, so greatly had Suzi taken to him, and so unhappy was she about his silence.

They entertained each other with stories from their lives. Barbara described bits of her love-affair with Harry Clegg, and her life before that, how it now seemed that she had been living like a nun without the intensity and reality of a nun's life. 'It was like going about in disguise,' she said. 'Although I didn't know it at the time, I was no more a celibate type of woman than at the moment, under these clothes, I am your servant Kyra.'

'If you didn't fall in love with Harry that time, you would remain a spinster like me,' Suzi said.

'It's better to be a spinster like you and have lovers that you can give some actual love to, than have shadows in your heart of men that you don't know, and hate them.'

'Many women, not spinsters, do like this.'

'Yes, and men too.'

Still, now and then, Suzi fell gloomy about Freddy's desertion. She said, 'Alexandros has guessed that I had love with Freddy, but he's too delicate to judge me for it. He's a Catholic Arab and can have one wife only; he does not possess me. Freddy did not pay me for his lodging, nor nothing.' Whenever Suzi came to the depth of her disappointment with Freddy she always fell back on the question of his failure to pay the bill. It was a way of kicking the piece of furniture into which one had bumped in the dark and hurt one's leg; and it was easier for her to accuse him about money than say nothing. Barbara said, 'I'll pay Freddy's share to Abdul.' 'That's not the point,' said Suzi. Barbara knew it was not the point. Love, love-affairs, men and women and true-life stories formed the daily entertainment and talk of their week's travelling. Barbara said, 'I'm quite sure Freddy isn't well.' And a few days later, when they had chewed it all over again, Barbara said, 'It may be that he wasn't really well that weekend, for he was rather different from his normal self. But I never noticed him so happy before.'

All the nights of the pilgrimage were spent under strange roofs, off the main tracks, in the desert villages of the Transjordan. The first night, Suzi drove straight to Madaba and, leaving the car outside the Orthodox church there, led Barbara in the moonlight among the poor, low-built houses that formed themselves into streets, part-streets, and no streets. Three small boys joined them silently. The paths were stony and steep. The children stared at Barbara from time to time, as if discerning, without being able to place the cause, that she was no Arab woman. They came to a house and Suzi stopped. She spoke to the boys, who disappeared together in another direction. Suzi murmured, 'They are gone to bring a doctor for you. I know these people and arrange this last week with them, so you need not fear. This is Transjordan country, not Palestine, and here they are more real Arabs that understand arrangements. Here is the house where Abdul was born. You don't speak, just follow.'

'I feel all right, Suzi. Only tired. I don't really need a doctor.'

'I like a doctor to see you, now, to be O.K. for the pilgrimage.'

'You're kind.'

'Don't speak.'

It was difficult, anyway, to express gratitude to Suzi. She said, 'You pay to Abdul the expenses. All arrangements with everyone is costing me money.'

'Yes, but I mean –'

'I do it for Alexandros, not Freddy.' She had opened the door to a long room lit by an oil lamp at the far end. She stood on the threshold and listened for a moment. 'Also,' she whispered, 'I do these things for you as you are more worth than fifty of Miss Rickward.' And she led the way along the room, which now produced three arches on either side and was paved with dusty, broken mosaic designs. It was obviously an ancient and priceless hovel, one of many that stood unselfconsciously haphazard among the dilapidated buildings of the present century in the towns and villages where Barbara spent the nights of the pilgrimage. And as she followed, she saw, within alcoves leading off these arches on either side, many sleeping or merely reclining women, their clothes hung on pegs all round the walls. No one stirred or spoke. Barbara followed Suzi. At the blank end of the room a passage now appeared, turning off to the right. They went along it, descended some of the winding stone stairs, and were in a lamp-lit cellar furnished with a large bare mattress on a wooden base, a tall water-jug on a table with a small water-jug. A thin film of dark sand covered the floor. Suzi said, 'Here we sleep with our clothes on in case of damp. This was a better house when Abdul was born. He doesn't remember it, but he remembers often the other house where they took him the next year, where I was born. It is in Palestine. My father was only a teacher then.' She took Barbara's arm and showed her a small door which might lead to a cupboard, but when opened, it gave off a strong smell of disinfectant. Suzi brought close the oil lamp and laughed. 'This is lady's toilet.' There was a hole in the earthy floor. 'You pour water down from the big jug when you use. This is Arabian Nights' Entertainment,' said Suzi.

It was unforgettable. The whole week was unforgettable, and Suzi most of all. She wondered, later, how it was that Freddy had forgotten Suzi Ramdez. And, of course, the question answered itself: she had been too memorable to remember.

'That Suzi Ramdez woman,' said the Foreign Office man, when he spoke again to Barbara, '. . . I wish we'd had a chance to talk to her. But of course the Jordan police have got her. There's no news. She's probably been shot.'

'I doubt it,' was all Barbara said.

'Why?'

'Well, she isn't the type to be shot easily.'

'Oh, you don't know what they're like, Miss Vaughan. This is the East, you know.'

Well, let him find out that Suzi was in Athens. Let them find out themselves, if they wanted to track her down for questioning and make trouble for her in Athens . . . You make trouble for me.

'Does Freddy Hamilton know she was arrested?'

'Oh, yes. At least, we've told him everything that's happened. He doesn't recall much about her. Of course, she was only a guide. They usually don't have women guides, but as you got into these absurd difficulties, you know, of course, well . . . You were lucky to find a travel agent who'd take care of you, don't you think?'

'It led to your getting your information.'

'Oh, yes, we're thankful for that. I don't mean . . . but there might have been trouble.'

He was a young tall doctor carrying a smart leather case, newly qualified in Cairo. He was dressed in a black suit with his shirt collar and cuffs gleaming white as they caught the light from the smoky lamp. His shoes, shuffling on the sandy floor, were the only parts of his appearance that caught the dust of the place. His brown face and glossy dark hair shone with newly qualified immaculateness. He told her, in good English, that he was newly graduated from the University of Cairo. He asked no questions but those pertaining to her fever and the treatment she had received, her past illnesses, and how she felt now. He told her this was his first job and he

348

was employed by the Jordanian Government at a clinic. Barbara lay on the mattress and did not respond to this information, as she had done at first, with so much as an 'Oh, really?' or a 'That must be very interesting.' Suzi, squatting in the gloom with a cigarette in her hand, said immediately, 'He isn't a government officer now with you, Barbara.'

Barbara smiled, whereupon the doctor, neatly holding up in one hand a hypodermic needle to gauge some stuff he was going to inject into her, and, with a white cloth held in the other, at the same time stood back, and carefully, in the brightest patch of light that fell on the floor, made a movement with a toe of his new shoes. It was a slow movement, with a practised quality. The movement was plainly intended to draw Barbara's attention to its significance. Barbara did not know what it signified. The doctor watched her face. Then he stood further back. She looked at him, then at the floor, and saw that it was not the movement of his foot but the mark he had traced in the dust that he wanted her to notice. It was the simple shape of a fish. When he saw her recognition, he went on with his business, gave her the injection, wiped the needle, packed it away carefully in his new case, gave her some pills, and directed her when to take them. He then told Suzi that Barbara should not travel more than four hours a day for the next week, but should lie down and sleep as much as possible, shook hands with Barbara, wished her a pleasant journey, said in reply to her thanks that it had been a pleasure, and departed.

'What is this dance he does on the floor for you?' said Suzi, who had not seen the mark he had traced.

Barbara pointed it out. 'It's a Christian symbol. The very early Christians under the first persecution used to trace the shape of a fish in the sand as a sign of recognition to each other. Then they would quickly obliterate it.'

'Why couldn't he say? The Arab makes ceremony of every little thing. We must obliterate this mark.'

'No, leave it, it's beautiful.'

'Then, in the morning, we obliterate. For the poor people of this house might be frightened to see it. The poor always remember signs for thousands of years, and they mix all things in their minds with magic and great fear and horrible trouble. It's God's blame.'

'Wipe it out now, then. It was meant to be seen and remembered.'

Suzi shuffled the sand into shapelessness and said, 'I can eat a camel now as I'm feeling empty. How are you?'

'Very hungry.'

'There is chicken, nothing special, but I bring it anyway. There is a little bit whisky also that I ordered for me here; it's hidden in a secret place as these poor people don't understand whisky, and anyway it's against my religion, too.'

The actual sites that they visited could have been covered in three days had they been able to go by direct routes. But each journey was a brief, cross-country run between the places of pilgrimage and Suzi's houses of refuge. The hours of their travels were mostly marked off by the calls to prayer from all corners of the world, so that the noon call corresponded with their return journey, for they set off early to merge, as far as possible, with the morning crowds at the shrines and churches.

It was a new experience to Suzi, so she said, to go with a pilgrim from England or America who was not in a state of religion all the way and who did not talk all the time of 'prayers and self-sacrifices and charity. Or else, when you have two Catholics, they are talking of Our Lady and the Rosary and Mass for St Peter, and the Novena for St Holy Ghost and St Anthony.'

'I think they are probably sincere,' Barbara said. 'But they do seem to make a career of it.'

'Are you sincere in these devotions, when you go to them talking and laughing with me so much about love-affairs and men and sex? Oh, Barbara, I don't mean that you're not sincere, as I like it so much when everything can be said.'

'Well, either religious faith penetrates everything in life or it doesn't. There are some experiences that seem to make nonsense of all separations of sacred from profane – they seem childish. Either the whole of life is unified under God or everything falls apart. Sex is child's play in the argument.' She was thinking of the Eichmann trial, and was aware that there were other events too, which had rolled away the stone that revealed an empty hole in the earth, that led to a bottomless pit. So that people drew back quickly and looked elsewhere for reality, and found it, and made decisions, in the way that she had decided to get married, anyway.

'What is profane?' Suzi said.

'Your sexy conversation.'

'No, yours. I never had such a sexy pilgrim. But I see what you say of the child's play is true. I hate the man in bed who plays at it like he conducts the military band for King Hussein to review the soldiers.'

At Bethlehem, at the Garden of Gethsemane, at the Basilica of the Agony, Barbara knelt for only a few moments and very quickly left, following Suzi up the hewn stairways of caves and crypts.

'What a lot of trouble for such a small moment, here and there,' Suzi said.

'It's an act of presence,' Barbara said, 'as when you visit a bereaved friend and there's nothing to say. The whole point is, that a meeting has materialised.' They stood on the cliff-edge outside the Church of St Peter in Gallicantu and looked across the valley into Israel, where men were working in the fields.

Suzi said, 'We're not being followed, so I know we're safe. Abdul is to take you by the Potter's Field. We should be there by noon on Sunday. You leave with him on Sunday night or Monday before the dawn.'

Barbara was feeling healthier and fuller. She said, 'The fatter I get, the more the thought of crossing the border frightens me. Probably because there's more life to lose in a fat body than a thin one.'

'You talk so silly. Abdul doesn't get caught never.'

That day on the return to the small room in the village near Bethany where they had spent the previous night, and were again to stay, they passed the steep turning off the high road where the Tomb of Lazarus stood open-mouthed by the roadside. They had already visited the place, but Barbara said, 'Let's stop again for a moment.'

She followed Suzi down the rocky path, towards the entrance to the tomb, where two or three Europeans were gathered, and was meanwhile watching a laughing young Arab boy; he was trying to sell something to an American couple who were taking an interest in him. He was offering a simple net sling, and kept repeating, 'The same that David killed Goli-att. Made like the same.' He put a stone in the sling and whizzed it beautifully, far into the air and out across the roof-tops. At the passing sound of this rapid-flung object, another woman turned to see what it was. The woman was Ricky. Barbara was less surprised than she might have been, and now realised that she had been expecting, at the back of her mind, to see her, and had been looking out for her across the country as she rode with Suzi; she had even been watching for Ricky on the scrub plains, amongst the shaggy Bedouin and the lean, quivering camels, so obscure had been her watchfulness.

Barbara had been following Suzi to the tomb with automatic steps and now found that she had disappeared. Ricky glanced towards Barbara only as part of the passing scene. Barbara, behind her veil, her lips shut tight against conversation, looked about her and, a short way behind, saw Suzi's head protrude and her eyes beckon from a low house doorway. Barbara went fairly slowly towards the door, stooped, and entered. There, Suzi was handing out money to a large dark woman and a child of tough honey-coloured skin and flaxen hair, one of those chance relics of the late Occupation. Suzi whispered, 'I saw her in time. She must be in the car with those Americans. I think she still looks for you.'

Eventually, the small party left and drove away. Barbara, feeling sick, went and peered down to the musty tomb, descended a few of the steps, breathed the emptiness of earth, but did not follow Suzi, who always thought this particular tomb was fun to go right down into. She liked to frighten herself, she said.

This was the last time Barbara ever saw Ricky. It was the only danger-point of their journey. The police did not trouble them. Tourists and the population passed them on the road, in cars, and occasionally a handsome farming Arab, tall with billowing robes, paced along at the side of the road, his eyes fixed, even by daylight, on the stars.

'They've stopped looking for you here,' Suzi said, 'as I have told so many people you go away to Rome by Saudi Arabia.'

Barbara already knew that Harry had been told she was no longer in Jordan. Barbara had at first objected to this. She had hoped Suzi would get a cable or a telephone call to him through Abdul in Israel, to tell him where she was. But Suzi had said, 'No, he naturally would then come and find you. He might then get in touch with his friend at the American

Embassy or with the British Embassy, and it would be an official business to deport you and so forth. Once you have started this you better go on and be that jolly good sport for Freddy. And you have to be a jolly good sport to pay his money for his trip that he owes the firm Ramdez.'

On the way to some Graeco-Roman ruins Suzi told Barbara that the first true love of her life was Abdul, whose story she told, and whose orange groves she explained.

Another time, on the way to see some lovely Arab palaces and Crusader forts far inside the Transjordan, Barbara told Suzi how she recalled her first meeting with Ruth Gardnor and her husband seven years ago in London. There had been nothing special to remember them by, they were guests at a private dinner party in London, and so had Barbara been. She had not spoken much to them. But she remembered the party, indeed she remembered every guest there, because it was at that party she had played the cello for the last time. That was how she remembered having first met Ruth Gardnor. Once or twice after that she had come across her, but that dinner party, a good-looking affair, was the meeting she distinctly remembered.

'You play the cello?' said Suzi.

'No, not now. Not any more.'

'You should continue. Music is beautiful. I learned piano but gave up at thirteen. You play good?'

'I was thought to be a promising cellist,' Barbara said.

'Not everyone can be the best. You should continue.'

'No, I went to teach English about that time, at Ricky's school. I had already decided to give up the cello when I played at that party where I first met Ruth Gardnor.'

'That woman is not good in her head,' Suzi said. 'She gets the sack from Cairo, I think. I'm sorry for that. I told her you were their top agent, and I made her messenger swear also to it. She believed it.'

'I know she did. And how did you make her messenger swear?'

'Nothing. His child is needing treatment in hospital, so I sign a document that he's a refugee from Palestine, then his child gets hospital treatment through U.N.R.W.A. I do this for many poor Arabs. Only refugees get big treatments free. So I sign, and he swears.'

On the way into Jerusalem, to the Holy Sepulchre, and at last to the Potter's Field, they talked in the car and were silent outside, and talked when they drove on again.

She said, 'I'm afraid. Really frightened.'

Abdul said, 'Why? There is no fear in me, why should you fear? I harness myself to the cart and I take it down a hill and up a hill, and already you are in Israel. Ten, fifteen minutes you are in the cart among the sandals. Then I stamp these sandals with a marker that reads "Made in Israel" and you also I stamp with this, and sell you back to your family for great profit.'

They were to move off in the early morning mist, for there was a dangerous full moon that night. Abdul looked out over the hills and fields of Palestine under the moon. He said, 'It's beautiful but I'm sick of this beauty, as it gives me no admiration in return and no nourishment for my soul in recognition of the worship I give to the land. Very soon I'm going to take a certain one of my friends who is in business with me, and we go together to Tangier and start a café. We have the plan. He is sick, too, of the beauty, although he is a Jew and has some chances in Israel.'

She was too sick with fear to reply. She was wearing her own clothes again and felt vulnerable. She had slept most of the afternoon, since Suzi's departure, in the same upper room near the Potter's Field from which she had set out. Her suitcase was there. Abdul had come to her room at six, smiling, and she thought for a moment she was already back in Israel since she had only seen him there.

Abdul said, 'Take everything small that you value from the suitcase, for you won't see it again. We give your clothes to the poor.'

He said they had better leave the house in a few hours' time and start preparing for the move at dawn, when the mists would fall. He said they could not sleep in the house that night, but must wait in a field.

She said then that she was frightened. He said there would soon be no time for her to feel frightened. They must go and prepare. Meanwhile they ate bread and cheese and drank mint-flavoured tea in the empty kitchen below, where Freddy had once been to breakfast. Abdul made up some marijuana cigarettes and gave one to Barbara. 'It will make you feel good and take away fear. Have you smoked this before?'

'No.'

'It's nothing so much.' He showed her how to smoke it.

She said, after a while, 'I don't feel the slightest effect.'

'First time is never an effect. Two has the effect.'

She smoked another while Abdul talked. He said he would like to play the guitar and sing, but there was no guitar, and singing or sound was not wise on this night.

She said she felt sick, either from fear or the marijuana or the tea.

'Smoke to the end and the sickness will go. The reason I would like to play the guitar and sing a great song is that I have just seen my father. I see him once, twice a year. The reason I like to sing when I have just seen him, Miss Vaughan, is that I no longer have to see him soon. I have seen him and it's in the past tense. You shouldn't think I hate my father. I say only that I sing when I leave him.'

She said, 'It's having no effect whatsoever.'

'Oh yes. You are red around the eyes. That is the first sign of an effect. Your friend, Mr Hamilton, is not well. I like Mr Hamilton, he's my friend, too.'

'What's wrong with him?'

'He has lost a piece of his memory. Some believe this, some don't. I believe it.'

'Is he at the hotel?'

'No, he's now here in Jordan with his friends, Mr and Mrs Cartwright. The doctor has made him stay there. Also, his friends of the British Legation are asking themselves what he has done with his memory. They are friends to him when he is all right to go punctual to the job, but when he has lost his way for a time they suspect and inquire. I hear all these things, Miss Vaughan. And he is also asking for you. Soon we will tell him all is well. Tomorrow we send by signal a message that you are found in Israel.'

They were among the cool grass under the moon. Barbara dozed and woke. Abdul spoke to her when she moved, in case she should cry out in waking. He said, 'It's all ready. You climb in when I tell you.'

'When?'

'Two more hours. Try to speak to me in case I catch your fear.' He was looking across the field as he spoke, and she now saw, where he was looking, the armed border patrol, two men moving in their direction; they halted at a certain point, and returned along the border-line.

She said, 'Are there any letters at the hotel for me, do you know?'

'I haven't asked this. Soon you will be there. A great comfortable car is waiting for us and soon you will be in your hotel. But now I remember – you know Dr Ephraim the archaeologist?'

'Saul Ephraim? – Yes.'

'He knows of your return and said he would not wire or phone to your husband until you arrive safe, in case of interception by the Arabs.'

'I'm not married yet.'

'Your husband that is to become.' Abdul started to ask many questions about her marriage, and how she could get this marriage that her lover had been to Rome to arrange. She thought, in passing, that he was unusually interested in the affair, but he was not objectionably so; and he explained that as he had once become a Roman Catholic, while a student in Cairo, he was concerned about these things. He said, 'I am not now a believer. I have no faith. I try to do good a little bit, that's all.'

She said, 'I've got a lot of faith. It's all I've got. I don't do good, very much, somehow. I'm not cut out for it.'

He asked again the details of the marriage. She said, 'I doubt if he'll get an annulment. It's very unlikely. I'll marry him outside the Church.'

'That's all right, anyhow.'

'Maybe. It remains to be seen.'

'We go to the cart now. The dawn is coming soon, Monday morning blues. You will climb into the cart and lie still. Keep your head low, low, and never look up till I tell you. Come now.'

The day before the news from Harrogate was brought to the Cartwrights' house that Freddy's mother had been stabbed to death by a mad old servant, Miss Bennett, Joanna was up very early and was out looking at her wild-flower garden. It was a warm, misty morning. The Cartwrights were usually up early on week-days so that they could get in a few busy hours at their hobbies and favourite occupations before going off to their busy clinic. Like most childless couples they were happiest when organised and at it all day. Monday mornings, without their quite realising it, were specially early-risen and active, as if to atone for their comparatively lazy Sunday.

It was Monday morning, the day before the men from the Consulate came with the news for Freddy. Freddy was very much on their hands now, and both Joanna and Matt Cartwright had decided to carry on as far as possible as if nothing had gone wrong with him. However, at five in the morning, Joanna found him already out in the garden, walking up and down with a hand to his head, and his head bent.

'Freddy, darling, aren't you feeling well?'

'Oh, it's you, Joanna.'

'You needn't have got up so early, Freddy. I wish you'd take breakfast in bed.'

'I couldn't sleep, really. I'm afraid that puppet show set me thinking again. Joanna, you know I keep thinking of –'

Joanna knew he would say 'bloodshed', which he did. The previous night she had shown her latest puppet acquisition, newly arrived from England; it was a plain old-fashioned Punch and Judy show, but it was electrically operated. They had turned out the big lights and sat in the dim room watching Punch batter Judy and Judy quarrel and squeak, and Punch with his stick batter Judy again. 'Doesn't it take one back to one's childhood?' Joanna said. 'Remember, at the seaside, the Punch and Judy boxes – don't you remember, Freddy?'

'Oh, my God!' Freddy called out. 'Stop it. I can't stand it. I can't watch this. Excuse me . . . just let me, please . . . I'm going to bed.'

When he had gone, Joanna and Matt turned on the big lights for a few minutes and wondered whether to call the doctor. Then they decided to leave well alone. They turned off the big lights and watched the show again, with less delight, but now with the more rational eyes and comments of puppet connoisseurs.

'I'm sorry it upset you, Freddy,' Joanna said when she found him in the garden next morning.

He said, 'You look very sweet and fresh, Joanna.' She was wearing her red linen dress, with a white cardigan thrown over her shoulders.

She was afraid he was going to say more about blood and bloodshed; this was so often his fear since his lapse of memory – 'I feel there's going to be bloodshed. I wonder if Miss Vaughan . . .' Joanna had earlier recalled that once, when he was in his former good health, Freddy had quietly confided in her his irritation with his mother who, apparently, continually provoked her old companion, Benny. Freddy had not been unduly concerned, but he had said, 'Of course, Benny also takes an odd turn now and then. Religious melancholia. She writes to me that she dreams of murder, bloodshed, and so forth. Oh, these old women.' And she had debated recently with Matt whether Freddy had not meant that his mother, not Benny, was given to this melancholy bloodshed notion, and had inherited the morbidity from her. But Matt had thought this far-fetched. 'If he can be got to a psychiatrist, good and well. But I wouldn't take it upon myself, personally, to diagnose anything off-hand. It will come to a crisis soon, that's certain. Then we'll see.'

'He isn't really morbid,' Joanna had said. 'Not all the time. He's really adorable, is Freddy.'

There was no question of anyone ever disliking Freddy. In most ways he was pleasant for them to have round the house.

And as they had become his closest friends in this part of the world it was natural that they should have him round the house when he needed them. Visits from the Consulate seemed to upset Freddy. Joanna wanted Matt to discourage them, but Matt was anxious not to interfere with these men, who were only trying to get Freddy's memory back.

But Joanna's mental nerves, which she did not admit to possessing, were being attacked every time Freddy spoke of his premonitions of bloodshed, and he spoke of them on the average of twice a day.

'I can't help feeling it,' he said, that morning. 'It's as if I've already been told. It's as if someone had sent me a letter or a message by word of mouth, warning me to prevent this bloodshed that's impending. I wish I could place –'

'Freddy dear, I'm going for one of my flower-hunts. It's just the morning for a find. Matt's gone riding, so go and make yourself comfortable in the study and we'll all have breakfast together. Six-thirty sharp.'

She was away across the misty lawn, with her black hair shining and her white cardigan flashing above the skirt of her red dress. Freddy felt untold guilt. There was something forgotten, many things forgotten, but one thing overlooked, cast aside. Sometimes he felt he was drawing near to recalling what it was. Hotter and hotter – as in a game of blind-man's-buff or . . . Joe Ramdez had called at the house last Friday while Matt and Joanna were out. He had specifically wanted to speak to Freddy about joining his wretched insurance scheme. 'I'm under medical attention at the moment,' Freddy said. 'I couldn't think of it.' They had sat in Matt's study. The man Ramdez had been shown in deferentially by the Cartwrights' servant, and Freddy did not feel in a position to excuse himself from the interview. Ramdez had said some disturbing things. 'Mr Hamilton,' he had said, 'you enjoyed your trip very much, I believe?'

'Oh, very,' said Freddy, hoping for enlightenment.

'And the young lady? She was satisfactory?'

'What young lady?' Freddy said.

'Mr Hamilton!'

'I honestly don't know who or what you are talking about, Mr Ramdez.'

'The young lady, Mr Hamilton, from Morocco. Or was it the better qualified lady who is best liked of all, and yet she is a local product of the town of Jericho itself? Whichever, Mr Hamilton, is not important. My house is welcome to all.' He got up and bent over Freddy to whisper, 'And to many of your colleagues. They, too, have poor memories on this point, as it should be with any gentleman. But they sign my proposal form and join my Trust.'

'I'm afraid,' Freddy said, 'there must be a mistake, Ramdez. I have no recollection of meeting ladies or of visiting you. I'm sorry, but that's that.'

'I leave you the proposal form,' Ramdez said. 'In the view of your present ill health it may be that the annual premium comes a fraction steeper. But our doctor, Russeifa, examines clients with leniency always towards the client for insurance, not the company.'

'I don't want a form, thank you.'

'So now I go to see my old friend Mr Hedges at the British Consulate, I am invited to lunch with him. But I keep discretion of your private affairs, naturally, when I converse with him.'

Hedges had been posted elsewhere a few weeks ago. Freddy's heart smiled again. He had known it was a bluff. And yet . . . 'Say what you like to Hedges,' he said. 'Anything you care.'

It had been a bluff. And yet there had been moments while Ramdez was talking when Freddy felt himself coming close to forgotten things. He mentioned the visit to Matt and Joanna, casually. 'He was after that ridiculous insurance policy.' Warmer and warmer . . . Joanna said, 'I hope you got rid of him.'

He held his hand to his head and walked with head bent. He saw the stones beneath his feet and realised he had been following Joanna from the garden, and was climbing the hill with Joanna's red dress visible here and there through the misty greenery, as she took the winding path upwards. 'Joanna!' he called. 'Joanna! Come back, my dear.' She had turned. 'Oh, Freddy, do, please –'

He caught up with her. 'Joanna,' he said. 'You know it's dangerous up there.' They were already on the hill-path that bordered so dangerously on Israeli territory that it was often said by sensible local people that there would one day be a shooting incident on that spot. And this was the time of year, in the heat, when border tempers flared.

She said, very patiently, 'I've been here before at this hour. One gets marvellous wild flowers coming from the dew. An hour later, they're withered. But you see, Freddy, if I get them by the root and replant them at once in the shade, and keep them well-watered –'

'I'm thinking of the danger,' Freddy said.

She said, quickly, 'There's going to be no bloodshed. Now do leave me, I like to have a time to myself before breakfast, you know.'

He returned down the path while she continued to climb. He had almost reached the house when he heard a shot resounding on the hillside above him. He turned, and heard another shot. Then he ran back up the path calling Joanna, and gouging up the sand and stones with his shoes as he ran.

She didn't reply to his call. He couldn't see her, and he was approaching the flat summit of the hill. She was nowhere. He looked all round. Then he saw by the side of the path a few yards below, a red movement, a crawling. He had run past her and missed her. 'Freddy get down, lie down,' she screamed at him as he came towards her. 'There's something going on.' He bent and walked back from the path, and crouched down. 'Are you all right?' he said. 'Yes, but I damn near got hit. There's something going on down there. I saw something.'

'That dress of yours is an easy target,' Freddy said.

'Shut up.'

'Joanna dear!'

'We'll wait a few more minutes, then if it's quiet we'll beat it,' she said.

'I saw your dress. I thought it was blood.'

'I've got a bloody cut knee. Does that satisfy you, Freddy?'

He raised himself sufficiently to see part of the valley below. Then he moved closer to the path.

'Take care,' Joanna said. 'I saw some men moving down there just as the first shot whizzed up at me.'

'I can see three of the border guard down there. They're looking at a plough or a cart or something,' Freddy said.

'Are they Jordanian or Israelis?'

'I've no idea. Does it matter?'

'Not in the least. Anyway, they were firing up at me, and I was looking down the valley. I heard a sort of noise and then I saw two men coming out of the mist, then it looked as if one of them was dragging the other. Why did they fire at me?'

'I suppose they heard a suspicious noise, saw your dress and fired.'

'The second bullet went right over my head, quite close. I *felt* it.'

*

The two men, one dragging the other, were not two men, but Abdul and Barbara. They had reached the bottom of their hill and were about to cross the field that led straight to the hill they were to climb, into Israel, when Abdul saw distant shadows moving among some trees bordering the farthest side of the field. He stopped immediately. The stopping of the wheel-creaks must itself have sent suspicion to the alert ears of the guard. Abdul unharnessed himself from the cart and said to Barbara, 'Climb out.' She did so immediately. He took her hand and said, 'Run.' She ran, but not fast enough for him. Presently, he was half-dragging her. A shot was fired, resounding on another side of the hill to their left. Another shot, far away from them, followed it. Abdul stopped. They had got half-way up the hill they had descended. He pushed Barbara off the path, and told her to lie flat. Nothing else occurred, but below them they could hear voices. 'My sandals,' Abdul said. 'They've got my stock of sandals.'

'My legs have got scraped,' Barbara said, still in a daze. 'They feel awful.' She had felt no fear. There had been no time to feel anything.

She limped with him back to the house near the Potter's Field, passing on their way the monk at his door, feeding his chickens as if no shots had been fired.

When they had cleaned up Barbara's legs, which were less damaged than were the shredded toes of her shoes where they had been scraped from the dragging, and when Abdul had thrown cold well-water over his head, and they were able to sit down and speak in small gusts to each other or to themselves, it was plain that Abdul's pride, as well as his sandals, was lost.

Barbara said, 'I'm going to the British Consulate to give

myself up. After all, what crime have I committed? I'm entitled to protection.'

Abdul said only, 'Quiet! I make a plan in my head.'

'No,' she said. 'The sensible thing for me to do is to go to the Consulate. I've had the pilgrimage, and that's what I came for, after all.'

'Yes, you had the pilgrimage, Miss. And what about me? What of us?'

'Must you go back? Can't you stay here?'

'Yes, and be a Palestine refugee in a camp, thank you so much, Miss. They look for me here, besides. I am known, and hated also. When the Arab hates he hates well. They say I'm an Israeli spy, as they say of you, Miss.'

'Oh, Abdul, don't call me Miss.'

He said, 'Look, Barbara, if you want to go to the British Consulate, O.K. But they ask you to talk, where have you been, and with whom.'

'I need not answer. They'll probably ask me the same in Israel.'

'In Israel they don't need answers from you to satisfy the police. In Jordan your embassy needs these answers, or they will be unwilling to help you. The Jordanians make difficulties unless they know where exactly you have been, and who it was with. They will never believe a pilgrimage, a fever. Who goes on a pilgrimage like this? You went like a spy, and they'll arrest Suzi and take my father's house at Jericho, and his wives, if you tell the facts. And if you don't tell the facts there is trouble for you from your own government. Who believes all this hiding for a pilgrimage?'

She said, 'Yes, I understand. You make trouble for me, I make trouble –'

'Who believes?'

'I understand. Abdul, let's eat something.'

'You have seen the mice?'

'What mice?'

'When we came in there was mice on the table eating this bread. You didn't see, but I did.' They had left their bread and cheese from the night before exposed on the table.

Barbara said, 'Where shall I put it? I'll throw it all out.'

'It goes for the chickens.'

She investigated for herself and found a covered tin box in the yard with a few crusts at the bottom. She tipped all the mouse-eaten food into it.

She came back to the kitchen and said, 'It's all gone, Abdul. Just in case we should reach the point of starvation and be tempted to eat it.' He was fully smiling again. He said, 'I'm going for food. I have good friends. Now I need to use your money also for another plan if I find one. So good-bye also to your travellers' cheques. Maybe I give you back a few in Israel.'

He already had her bank-notes in his pocket, where he had put them for safety before starting off with the cart. He had said at the time, 'We are safe. But in case we have to run we have to throw away all money and cheques, for always a captive with money is killed on the spot to shut him up.'

He said now, counting the cheque money, 'This is a great lot, many pounds, but Suzi will cash some as I do not deal in cheques with my friends. Suzi will have to cash, as these cheques may be traced. She'll keep them till we're out of it safely. Maybe I give you a little bit back, Barbara, if you marry me instead of your husband.'

Oh now I go and sing the plainchant
And bring to prayer the people of Abdul
Who are stealing now his sandals and leather goods in the
    field

We dance and sing although our servant has gone away
All the time past there was a servant in this house
But he died and the old monk has no man left
But I get from him a chicken to cook
And I will bring those grapes and lovely cheeses
And the coffee from Abdul's orange groves.

He said, 'It sounds better in the original language, but it's not too bad in English. With a guitar it's very excellent.'

She went upstairs to the camp-bed to sleep it off, and was still sleeping when he returned. And he woke her up, coming into the room with a bundle of clothes over his arm. He sat down in the horse-hair arm-chair and spread out his legs. He said, 'I got a lift in a very grand car, but I had to crouch not to be seen. I will one day be seen grand.'

She said, 'What are these clothes? They look like disguises.' She said, 'I don't think I want another disguise, Abdul.'

'It's all planned for four o'clock this afternoon. Come and eat a lot of food, and I tell you. This time is safe, because I smell this fact.'

This time the plan worked and they got into Israel safely. It was simpler and yet more terrifying than the attempted trek with the cart.

At half past three a car, driven by an Arab, arrived at the house. Barbara, drugged into a euphoristic near-trance by a very effective tablet that Abdul had given her, was dressed in a black nun's habit with a starchy white coif, the skirt slightly too short; she carried a black shopping-bag. She entered the car. Abdul followed, an Arab Franciscan friar in a brown habit, very handsome. They sat boldly in the back. Barbara examined once more the contents of the shopping-bag. A bottle of eau-de-cologne. A passport bearing a nun's photograph with an anonymous nun-like face slightly fatter and older than Barbara's – the name Sister Marie-Joseph Minton of the Holy Ghost Sisters, Paxton, Huntingdonshire, England, the date of birth, 1920, and a pilgrim's visa. She had the passport by heart, and hoped she wouldn't need to put it to the test. Also in the bag were a rosary, four white linen handkerchiefs, a purse containing some English and some Jordanian coins, a missal, a book of religious offices, a small roll of cotton wool, a black cotton reel with a needle stuck through it, a yellow plastic thimble, a small tin box of blackcurrant throat pastilles, a pair of black woollen stockings, a small paper bag containing pictures of the Christian shrines in Jordan, an empty spectacles-case, a ball-point pen, and, for some reason, an empty soda-water bottle. In the cheerfulness of Abdul's drug Barbara examined these objects with great joy, marvelling at the genius of the collection. 'The only things that are wrong,' she said, 'are the absence of glasses to put in the case, and the absence of a sponge-bag and toothbrush. Otherwise it's a perfect nun's outfit, and who-ever did it is absolutely brilliant.'

'We had no time to look inside,' Abdul said. 'My friend that helped me took this bag exactly as it stood.'

Barbara decided to leave the spectacles-case behind in the car. She felt very happy. Alexandros, at his shop door, did not recognise them. Abdul stared directly at the shop and she did too, but Alexandros observed nothing. Meantime, Barbara had noticed Abdul's head as he turned towards the car window. She said, 'What have you done to your head, Abdul?'

'It is shaved for tonsure of Franciscan friar,' he said hero-ically.

'I think you're a hero,' she said.

He said, 'It looks quite good, matter of fact. A few weeks, if I wear this tonsure around the place, many youths wear it also.'

They came to the Mandelbaum Gate, where a large crowd was gathered.

There she was very much afraid. Abdul was quiet, she was not sure whether from circumspection or anxiety. She remembered she was a nun, and must not show excitement. She rather regretted taking the drug, although she quite saw, later, that it had helped her through. The large crowd was not so large as it had seemed at first. As she pulled herself together she saw it was a pilgrim-group of about forty, attended by two priests. A separate group of five women seemed to be in a sensational buzz. Barbara looked hard at every head in the vicinity in case it should be Ricky's, and, nodding courteously to Abdul, moved aside to hear what the five women were discussing in such exclamatory tones. She perceived that they came from the north of England.

'Perhaps I should wait for her.' . . . 'Poor soul, the poor soul!' . . . 'No, she said, no, definitely to go on without her; it's the Lord's will, she said, it's the Lord's good will.' . . . 'Margaret, would you and I wait with her till she gets her things back?' . . . 'Poor woman, she was only two minutes having a shower-bath, and then she comes out of the cubicle and all her things gone.' . . . 'Not a mortal stitch to put on.' . . . 'The passport too.' . . . 'The police surely will get them back. Who'd want a nun's clothing, for the Lord's sake?'

Barbara moved back to Abdul, who stood politely behind the hubbub of the large group. 'What time is it now?'

'Five minutes to four.'

'And the pilgrimage doesn't go through till four.'

'Don't get excited.'

'But the police will be checking the passports. I've heard some women talking over there, about the nun whose clothing was stolen. Where did you get the stuff?'

'From a room in a convent where some Englishwomen were staying. My friend is the porter, which is a very fine post to hold. These clothes cost a great price.'

The crowd began to move forward. Barbara was in a hurry, Abdul touched her arm and shook his head. She held back humbly. 'It's two minutes to four,' Abdul said, 'so we are well ahead of time.'

'What time?' She thought he meant the time when the police could be expected to arrive.

'We are well ahead of four o'clock.' He was an admirable Franciscan. This gave her courage.

She saw one of the priests who attended the large group of pilgrims walk back from the front of the moving crowd, to help it to get in order. 'Have the bags gone through, Father Colin?' said a woman's voice.

'Yes, they've all gone ahead, don't worry.'

He looked for a moment at Abdul and Barbara, newcomers to him. Barbara now recognised him as the priest who had said Mass at the Holy Sepulchre while she endured the agonising onslaught of her sickness. Barbara smiled cheerily at him and he gave her an unquestioning smile in return, including Abdul in it. Abdul nodded once or twice, severely, as befitted a Franciscan of the Holy Land. Then the priest was busy with his people again. As they came near to the Gate, Barbara, waiting her turn, was aware that some of the faithful were making way for her and for Abdul, and she remembered that they were objects of reverence and accepted the courtesies.

The Jordanian official said he hoped she had enjoyed her visit to Jordan 'where is many Christian faith'. Barbara said softly that it had been a great experience, and in the meantime the official looked at her visa, closed the passport and handed it back. She walked on with the crowd, not looking round for Abdul until she had to halt with the rest at the Israeli immigration hut. She saw him talking to the Jordanian official, explaining something. She looked away.

The Israeli official looked at her passport photograph and said, as he stamped her visa, 'The photographer might have done you better justice than that, Sister.'

'It's a matter of luck,' she said. She opened her shopping-bag for the customs clerk and he peered into it, jokingly. Through the door she saw Abdul joining the crowd, and as she left the hut he said, 'Wait for me.'

She waited, and again it seemed he was explaining something. At last he got through.

They followed the crowd, most of whom were now climbing into a waiting motor-coach. Abdul said, 'My visa wasn't quite right for the date, but I explained in Arabic to the Jordanian and in Hebrew to the Jew, that I am here for one day only and have now no time to get the correct visa. They are always impressed when a monk speaks their language.'

'Where are we now?' said Barbara.

'In Jerusalem. In Israel.'

'Already?' The drug carried her off. She started to run for it, all along the narrow streets of the Orthodox Jews. Abdul ran after her, and caught her. 'Wait, we'll get a taxi. Wait, please, we'll be arrested.' She wanted to run along the pavements of the sweet, rational streets. All the people in the shops had come to the doorways and the passers-by had stopped to stare at the astonishing thing, a running nun with a monk in pursuit. A small shrivelled man shouted up the street to a taxi which was passing diagonally. It turned towards them and they entered it with all their skirts bundling with them. 'I get you clothes to put on very soon,' said Abdul, cool and proud.

Three days after her return, when she had come back to the hotel after a long afternoon's shopping for some clothes in which to travel back to London, she found an envelope had been slipped under the door of her room. She had not been expecting any letter by this means, for Harry was already here with her, in the hotel.

It was a letter from Ricky, enclosing a photographed copy of Harry's birth certificate. The letter was headed 'Ramdez Travel Agency, Jerusalem, Jordan'. It read:

DEAR BARBARA,

I have tried to locate you, but evidently you purposely eluded me. I now find you are returned to Occupied Palestine and the people of your origin.

Your defection from your school commitments has forced me to sell the establishment as a going concern. I cannot carry on without reliable assistance.

I wished to see you for a reason. This was to hand to you the enclosed photographic copy of a document which I located in Coventry after much search in parish registers, etc. It is a copy of the baptismal certificate of Mr Clegg, whom you say you had decided to marry. You will see from this that not only is he illegitimate (bearing the 'mother's name' without entry under 'father's name' is the significant point here), but he is also R.C. by birth, as you will see from an examination of the enclosed. Therefore, as the Romans do not allow divorce, I am sure you would wish to know in time that a marriage with Clegg would not be consonant with your Church, which, I am bound to say, compares unfavourably with other religions (e.g. Moslem) in this respect.

373

As you would not wish to act out of consonance with your principles, as you have frequently indicated, I am convinced you would wish to have this document, for Clegg's information as well as your own.

I trust I have done my duty and that you will find a man, as you appear to wish this after all these years. I trust a fuller and more grateful life awaits me after I have wound up the school.

Yours in anticipation of acknowledgement,

E. RICKWARD

Barbara saw immediately what Harry's birth certificate signified. She went along to Harry's room with it. He, educated in these matters by his recent experience in Rome, saw it too. 'But I never knew my mother was a Catholic,' he said. 'My aunts didn't tell me that. Of course, they weren't actually aunts at all. Perhaps they didn't know.' Manuscriptman that he was, he held the paper up to the light to see the water-mark. There was none. It was just a photographed copy.

She said, 'It's marvellous.'

He smiled. But he smiled more at Ricky's letter.

That evening they cornered a priest who was staying at the hotel, to confirm their assumption that Harry's previous marriage was now invalid. This was easy enough.

'Do they accept photographed copies in Rome?' said Barbara, 'or do we send for the original?' The priest had to corner another priest for the answer. The other priest was that Father Colin Ballantyne who had preached at the Holy Sepulchre and brought his pilgrimage through the Gate with Barbara. 'Yes, a copy is all right, of course,' he said. 'One can never get parishes to part with the originals.' He looked at Barbara again. 'Haven't we met somewhere before?'

374

She said. 'I came through the Mandelbaum Gate with your party on Monday.'

'Oh, is that where it was . . .' He still seemed puzzled, and they left him with the mystery.

Abdul Ramdez and Mendel Ephraim left Israel by way of Syria a few months later and managed to reach Tangier, where they opened a café.

Suzi married a lawyer in Athens.

Freddy remembered Suzi gradually, and especially on that day in Kensington Gardens when the red sun touched the skaters under the winter sky. He wondered, then, whether she was alive.

'You've got Gardnor's statement?'

'Yes. His wife's got away to Cairo, we hear. The Ramdez girl was arrested, probably shot. The police were keen to show willing.'

'Oh, well. At least you've got Gardnor.'

'Old Ramdez seems to have wriggled out of it. He's still going about.'

'Destestable fellow,' Freddy said.

And when it came at last to his wondering whether Suzi was alive, he didn't take steps to inquire, and was reminded again of that story of the man who went away for a holiday and left his dog chained up, and feared to return in case of what he should find.

Barbara and Harry were married and got along fairly well together ever after. They had one child, a girl, whom they fussed over continually. They saw Suzi many times in Athens and London. Her husband was not unlike Alexandros, but leaner and less large in manner.

Before he left Jordan Freddy bought the icon from Alexandros, who condoled with him formally, in Lebanese

French, over the death of his mother, and, in Arab English, assured Freddy that there was no obligation for him to buy the icon.

'I'm afraid,' said Freddy, 'that I'm a little better off now.'

'Yes, the mother leaves to the son. The old must die. But she has had a life.'

Joanna said, 'Freddy, you simply aren't fit to travel, let alone face all those tragic details. There's nothing you can do now. Let your sisters cope.'

'I must see about Benny,' Freddy said. 'I must go home and see to poor Benny. My sisters will do nothing for Benny.'

'There's the Welfare State, you know.'

'I must see about her. I can't have her locked up in some lunatic asylum without seeing the actual place, at least.'

Before he left for Israel to collect his belongings and return home, Freddy walked round Old Jerusalem, up the Via Dolorosa, past the Temple site and the Dome of the Rock, locating the places of history that had become familiar to him, as well as those he had neglected to look into. He followed the ancient walls of the city and Temple, past the gates of historic meaning, sealed and barred against Israel – the Zion Gate, Dung Gate, Jaffa Gate, New Gate. Then St Stephen's Gate opened within the Old City to another medieval maze of streets – Damascus Gate, that gate of the Lord's triumphal entry into Jerusalem on Palm Sunday, and Herod's Gate. He walked round the city until at last, fumbling in his pocket for his diplomatic pass, he came to the Mandelbaum Gate, hardly a gate at all, but a piece of street between Jerusalem and Jerusalem, flanked by two huts, and called by that name because a house at the other end once belonged to a Mr Mandelbaum.